Private
Lies

Muna Shehadi's lifelong love of reading inspired her to become a writer. She got her start in romance but is excited to be making her debut now in women's fiction.

Muna grew up in Princeton, New Jersey, lives in Wisconsin, and has a much-loved summer place on the beautiful coast of Maine, all of which she couldn't resist featuring in her Fortune's Daughters trilogy.

For more information, visit her website: **munashehadi.com**

In the Fortune's Daughters trilogy:

Private Lies
Hidden Truths
Honest Secrets

Private
Lies

Muna Shehadi

REVIEW

First published in Great Britain in 2019
by HEADLINE REVIEW
An imprint of HEADLINE PUBLISHING GROUP

1

Cataloguing in Publication Data is available from the British Library

ISBN 978 1 4722 5870 0

Typeset in Sabon by Avon DataSet Ltd, Bidford-on-Avon, Warwickshire

Printed and bound in Great Britain by Clays Ltd, Elcograf S.p.A.

HEADLINE PUBLISHING GROUP
An Hachette UK Company
Carmelite House
50 Victoria Embankment
London EC4Y 0DZ

www.headline.co.uk
www.hachette.co.uk

In memory of my wonderful parents,
Fadlou and Alison Shehadi,
who would have been so proud.

Warmest thanks to my dream editor Kate Byrne, for giving this story a chance, then letting me tell it the way I saw fit. Thanks also to the brilliant artist Tracy Miller, who patiently fielded my questions about her profession and training. Last but not least, deep gratitude to my husband Mark Stodder, for his solid faith in me, especially during those times mine showed cracks.

Private Lies

Chapter 1

January 20, 1967 (Friday)

Today I got the absolute best news in the world and the absolute worst. The best was that I got the part of Sarah Brown in the spring musical, Guys and Dolls! *The lead role and I'm only a sophomore! Deedee Cutler was all snotty and said it's because I'm Mr McGregor's pet. I told her green is an ugly color and she looks terrible in it. That made her furious, but I don't care, it's true.*

I would have been so happy today, like up-in-the-clouds happy all day long, but then the worst thing also happened and ruined my celebration. Nan got her period. She was the only one left in our whole grade, besides me. When she told me, I lied and said I got mine a long time ago but didn't want to hurt her feelings. I can't stand being the last one. The last one in the whole school. The last one in the whole state probably. I'm crying writing this. Mom acts like it's no big deal, but she acts that way about everything. Christina makes me feel freakish and scared by telling me I have to go to the doctor, that sixteen is way too late. I might have to start lying to her, too, so she'll shut up. But we share a bathroom, I'd have to really do a good job faking it.

I'm crying harder now. I hope I read this someday and laugh

1

at how worried I was, when I was young and silly enough to think there was something wrong with me.

I think there is something wrong with me.

Rosalind ripped the tape off the next cardboard box out of what seemed to be a hundred brought down from her father and stepmother's attic. She was hoping for something special this time, one of her mother's fabulous outfits from a Hollywood premiere or awards ceremony, new family pictures, letters or diaries – forgotten jewels? Anything but having to go through more papers: academic papers, financial papers, legal papers.

Rosalind and her sisters, Olivia and Eve, were searching every item, every file, every envelope in every box that had been shipped here to Maine from the California house they grew up in. In the years before her death, the worst years, Mom had been notorious for hiding things she cherished, convinced someone would try to steal from her. Silver hairbrush in a stack of cooking pots. Diamond necklace at the bottom of a Kleenex box. Autographed picture of a famous co-star in the pages of a travel book. When Dad had retired from teaching and moved diagonally across the country to this modest Cape house on the coast of Maine – the family's former summer home – everything to be sold or thrown away from the enormous Mediterranean in Beverly Hills had to be practically torn apart. Now, with Dad and Lauren abruptly relocated to the retirement community in Blue Hill after Dad's stroke, the three sisters were at it again, examining every millimeter of every box that hadn't been gone through ten years earlier.

Lifting the cardboard flaps, peeking cautiously, Rosalind grimaced. Files, all neatly labeled in their father's precise handwriting. Her fingers made a clicking sound drifting across the tabs; a familiar sadness kicked in as she realized what they contained. Jillian Croft's movie and commercial contracts, dozens of them, filed chronologically from 1970, when she was first cast in a Steve McQueen movie as the waitress who took his order, to 2001, the year she died, a small part in a B movie and a commercial for L'Oréal.

Resigned, Rosalind went through every folder, flipping through single sheets, shaking stapled pages, willing something forgotten and fabulous to fall out and cheer her up.

Nothing.

'What do we do with Mom's contracts?' She waited for her sisters' answers, betting they'd be totally opposite.

'Toss them.'

'Save them.'

After a week with Olivia and Eve, she was getting good.

'If you two don't want them, save them for me,' Olivia said. 'I'd like to read them, see how showbiz contracts have changed.'

'Done.' Rosalind got up and lugged the box over to Olivia, avoiding Eve's eyes, knowing her younger sister wanted to point out that the contracts for Olivia's cable cooking show probably didn't have much in common with those for Mom's starring roles in international blockbusters.

She grabbed the next box from the still impressive pile. Slice, rip, open. A quick paw through the tissue-paper-wrapped contents. Ha! She smiled as a plastic shoulder emerged from its white cocoon. This was more like it. Her Heart Family dolls, long-cherished playthings and companions.

She unwrapped them eagerly. First Mom, in her starchy pink dress, blond poufy hair frizzed from years of stress, skin still flawless except for a red line on her right calf. Surgery? Or a run-in with a pen? Next Dad, natty in a white-collared

3

blue business shirt, red tie and awesome white suspenders. Cool and unruffled, not a mark on him. Men had life so much easier.

'Look.' She held up the happy couple. While Eve and Olivia had surfed and sailed with Ken, Barbie and their groovin' friends, Rosalind had stuck with the solid tradition of the Hearts. Dad off to work every morning in his boxy Volkswagen Cabriolet. Mom at home caring for the adorable baby twins, a boy and a girl. 'Hot housewife and her handsome husband, still married after all these years.'

Eve looked up, blond ponytail cascading over a shoulder nearly bared by her ripped T-shirt. 'Oh my God. I remember those things. *So* corny. You played with them constantly.'

'Obsessively, more like it.' Olivia yawned, stretching impressively toned arms over her head. 'I always figured by now you'd be married with ten kids.'

'Yeah, what about that?' Eve asked.

'Are you kidding me? What guy could come close to *this*?' Rosalind shook Daddy Heart emphatically. 'White suspenders! When was the last time you saw a pair of those? He ruined me for other men.'

'Don was perfect for you.' Olivia shook her head ruefully. 'You could have bought him a pair.'

'Don needed to grow a pair on his own.'

Eve cracked up. Olivia opened her mouth to speak, then lost whatever she was going to say in a burst of laughter. 'You are terrible.'

'Thanks.' Rosalind grinned, hoping the subject would drop. Her sisters meant well, but 'meaning well' usually involved being royal pains in her ass. She went back to work and uncovered the Heart twins, still resting comfortably in their double stroller, white and blue with pink wheels. They too had aged very well, for not aging at all.

'Look what I found!' Olivia held up a clipping. 'An article from *People*, April 1981, called "Our Prayers Were Answered". Listen to this. "After seven years of heartbreaking disappointment, the ever-glamorous Jillian Croft and her hunky acting-teacher hubby, Daniel Braddock, finally welcomed their first child, Olivia Claudette Braddock, on March thirtieth."' She clutched the paper to her chest, glowing with pride. 'I can't believe I never saw this.'

'You didn't? Mom showed me mine.' Rosalind hit a dead end in her box, unable to find the remainder of the Hearts' fabulous estate.

'Mine's in my baby book.' Eve glanced at her oldest sister. 'I didn't know it took seven years to conceive you, Olivia. Rosalind and I came along relatively quickly after. Four years and then five. I guess you jump-started the equipment.'

Olivia pouted her perfectly outlined lips. 'Why didn't they ever show me this?'

'Who knows? Look here.' Eve held up a bag full of name tags encased in plastic holders. '"Hello I'm Daniel Braddock" about two dozen times, probably from every conference he ever attended. Why would he keep all these?'

Rosalind blinked innocently. 'In case he forgot who he was?'

Eve snorted. 'As if the great Daniel Braddock could *possibly* forget who he was. Or let anyone else forget.'

'Jesus, Eve.' Olivia plunked her hands on to her designer-jeans-clad hips. 'Dad's in the hospital in terrible shape, and you think this is a good time to insult him?'

Rosalind sighed. If Eve turned right, Olivia went left.

'His health doesn't change who he was, Olivia.'

'Who he *is*, not was.'

'Hey, kids!' Rosalind bounced Mrs Heart up and down in excitement. 'Who wants to make a Spam Jello mold with Mommy?!'

Eve ignored her. 'Who knows *who* he'll be now? It was a bad stroke.'

'The staff at Pine Ridge says he's likely to come back to normal, or at least close. He was healthy.'

'He's seventy-nine, Olivia.'

'I *know* how old he is.'

Mommy Heart was getting so sick of the bickering! 'If you two stop fighting, you can make Shake-a-Pudding for dessert.'

'Wow, Shake-a-Pudding.' Eve broke from the stand-off. 'I haven't heard that name in decades. What was it again?'

'Brilliantly marketed instant pudding.'

'Anyway, Daddy lived through the Great Depression. Therefore the name tags.' Olivia went back to her box, never one to let an argument die without stomping on its corpse. 'He was not part of the disposable generation.'

'Well, I am.' Eve smiled coolly and dumped the name tags into the latest bulging lawn and leaf bag. The living room was strewn with them.

'Let's take a timeout.' Rosalind put the doll down. 'I need some Maine air.'

'If we keep taking breaks, we'll never get this done.'

'Then since this is the only week you'll be out here, Olivia, unlike Rosalind and me, why don't you stay and keep working?' Eve suggested sweetly.

Olivia gave her the stink eye, one of her greatest talents. 'I have a cooking spot scheduled on Tuesday's morning news, plus I'm ovulating this week so I have to get nookie from Derek. If I can find time to get back here and help again, I will.

But it's a lot harder for me coming from LA than for you two easterners.'

'Let's go out on to the porch.' Rosalind stood up. 'It's been foggy all weekend, we're worried about Dad, and this job sucks. A quick break will do us good.'

Silence.

She put on an authoritative scowl. 'Don't make me get Mommy Heart out again.'

'Okay, okay.' Eve reached into her box. 'One more folder and I'll go. Last one in this box.'

'I'll come now.' Olivia peeled off the cotton gloves she'd been wearing to protect her manicure and tucked a stray lock of hair back under a silk scarf wrapped around her head. Olivia could fling rags up in the air, be under them when they landed, and still look stylish and voluptuous. Eve dressed like she didn't care how she looked, but her height and flawless features made her a knockout anyway.

Rosalind was 'cute', had always been 'cute' and would probably be 'cute' until she died. Sometimes she thought she'd been dropped into her freaky-beautiful family by a drunk stork.

Stepping and hopping over piles, boxes and bags, she preceded Olivia out on to the house's screened-in porch, which on clear days provided a gorgeous view of Mount Desert Island – pronounced 'dessert' instead of 'desert' – and its most famous denizen, Mount Cadillac. Not much of a mountain compared to, say, the Matterhorn, but a source of local pride, with a stunning view up the jagged, wrinkled coast from its top.

This afternoon, however, fog clung stubbornly to the shore as it had been clinging for the past three days, not even the suggestion of a breeze that might blow it away, or a thinning of clouds that might let sun through to burn it off. Even Rosalind was struggling to find something positive in the monochrome.

At least the smell outside was still addictive, salty from the sea, fresh from the pines growing thickly around the house – a smell of late August and the aging season. The Braddock family had always spent whatever summertime they could out on Candlewood Point, a bumpy eight-mile dirt-road trip from the closest tiny town of Stirling. Up here, away from the increasingly crowded southern part of the state, there was still wildness and space, places where you could sit on the shore and imagine yourself centuries earlier.

The girls hadn't visited the Maine house often after Mom died. Even less after Dad married Lauren, a woman twenty years his junior. Busy lives, they'd said, so hard to get away.

Did they fool anyone? Maybe themselves. It was good to be back.

Rosalind inhaled deeply, remembering Mom out here doing the same, exulting in the freshness and clarity, so unlike LA. Jillian Croft had loved her home state, its smells, its topography, its coast and its freedom. She and Dad had found this property in the late 1970s at the peak of her movie career – a place to hide from her adoring public. Rosalind's fondest maternal memories were all born here. Lobster boils and annual clambakes, sailing and kayaking, hikes and beach parties, charades and sing-alongs. Most of all, precious memories of a mother who was relatively calm and relatively stable and who had time for her girls. A mom who made dinners and read books and played games. Who fished and dug for clams and sat in the Laundromat in old clothes wearing a Red Sox baseball cap and dark glasses even though everyone in town knew who she was, and who laughed with Dad at night when the girls were in bed, instead of fighting.

Mom always took her meds up here. The rest of the year it was hit or miss. At the height of Rosalind's judgmental preteens, as infatuated with the summertime peace as she'd been bewildered and exhausted the rest of the year by her mother's shifting moods and tempers, she had asked why. Jillian had hugged her middle daughter, apron smelling of the herbed chicken she was roasting for dinner in the house's quirky oven, and said, 'Because out here I'm Sylvia Moore, and Sylvia Moore isn't bipolar.'

Like so much her mother said, that had made no sense to young Rosalind. Sylvia Moore and Jillian Croft were the same person; they must have the same illness. Now she thought she understood. Mom had left Maine when she was seventeen and changed her name not long after, when she'd begun seriously pursuing an acting career. The bipolar disorder had surfaced in her early twenties.

Olivia stepped down on to the porch, pulled off her scarf and shook out her long, enviably thick auburn hair, the same shade their mother had used.

'Nice non-view.' She grimaced out at the-bay-that-currently-wasn't.

'You're missing the subtleties. Over there, gray.' Rosalind pointed. 'Over *there*, between the gray and the gray, there's more gray. See?'

'Remember the year Mom was up with Dad and said it was foggy three weeks straight? Even she was ready to get out of here by the time the sun came out.' Olivia sighed. 'God, I miss her.'

'I was just thinking how she was so much more herself here.'

'Yeah.' Olivia put a hand to the screen, gazing wistfully out at the nothing. 'It was great, wasn't it? When she was so happy and doing so well? And then everything got so horrible toward the end.'

'Right.' Rosalind hated thinking about that part. And she

hated when Olivia got all actressy sad about it. 'What's going on with Derek? Things okay?'

'Who knows?' Olivia blew a raspberry that startled a mosquito from the screen. 'He's busy. Working hard. A lot of travel. The baby thing is a big strain, at least on me. He seems to take it in stride, but I'll be forty in two years. I'm ready to go to in vitro, but he keeps putting it off.'

'I had a friend who tried IVF. Worked the first time for her.' That was a lie, but the white ones could be important. Rosalind worried Olivia was becoming convinced she wouldn't ever get pregnant, which could help make it true.

'Mom had trouble, also. Seven years before I came along, the article said. I thought they just waited to have me until pregnancy worked with her career. I guess it figures I'd have trouble, since of the three of us I'm the most like her.'

Rosalind gave her sister a hug, though she was getting a little sick of Olivia claiming that title, even if it was true. Olivia had inherited not only Mom's hair and lush figure, but also her overt sensuality. Men were just as attracted to Eve, but, intimidated by her coolness, they kept their distance. Over Olivia, they slobbered in packs.

'Are you seeing anyone, Rozzy? I still think it was a mistake to leave Don. At least he was better than that tree-hugger in Denver, and *much* better than the animal you dated before you left LA . . . what was his name?'

'Wolf.'

'*Wolf!* That's right.'

'Not seeing anyone now.' She joined Olivia staring out into gray, wondering which she hated more, persistent fog, having her judgment questioned, or being called Rozzy. 'I have a good life. I'm enjoying New York. I like working at the coffee shop, I have my painting, and—'

'Painting? Walls or canvas?'

'Canvas. Oils.'

'Oils.' Olivia turned and looked at her curiously. 'I remember you drawing constantly, but since when painting?'

'I started in Colorado.' She could talk openly about every other part of her life, but the minute the subject turned to her art, she felt naked. Not gloriously naked, but haven't-shaved, retaining-water naked. Already she regretted mentioning it. 'I'm also still doing clothing design, I work out regularly, I've got book clubs, lot of friends. That's enough for me.'

'Give me a break. You're the most romantic of the three of us. You'd shrivel and die alone. Look at those dolls you loved so much.' She gestured at Rosalind, head to toe. 'Why don't you wear normal clothes and get a decent hairstyle? That bleached look is too severe, especially so short, and the loud mismatched outfit is . . . Well, you're probably scaring off all the normal good guys. You look like a kook.'

'I *am* a kook.' Rosalind rubbed her spiky head, smiling. All this week she'd worked to let her sisters' words roll off her, telling herself they were speaking from places of love, and that she only had to listen and be kind.

Which didn't stop her wanting to smack them.

'You are not a kook. You're just acting like one. From this to that to the next thing . . . you need to settle—'

'I've always been like this. A hummingbird, Dad called me, remember?' She'd loved the nickname, nearly as much as the shimmering, darting birds themselves, until she overheard a conversation between him and Mom that made it clear it wasn't a compliment.

Dad gaveth, and Dad invariably tooketh away.

'The hummingbird thing is an excuse. Nothing stays as exciting as the first rush. Not haircuts, not jobs, not cities, and certainly not relationships. You need to stay with a man long enough to discover something deeper.'

'So you keep saying.' If Olivia counted her relationship with Derek as deep, Rosalind preferred shallow.

'Hey, guys?' Eve came out on the porch holding an open folder, looking troubled. 'I found something really weird stuck in with the tax forms. It's a medical record for Mom.'

Olivia snorted. 'Why is *that* weird? She was seeing doctors her whole life.'

'It's not from Dr Townsend or her psychiatrist or the rehab doctors. It's from a gynecologist in New York in January 1969, the year before she married Dad. It says, "Patient complains of difficulty having intercourse."'

'Ugh.' Olivia put her hands over her ears. 'Do *not* want to know.'

Rosalind grimaced. 'Poor Mom.'

'She was eighteen and "amenorrheic".'

'Ameno-what?'

'I know that one.' Olivia raised her hand like a school kid. 'No periods.'

'So was she pregnant?' Rosalind asked. 'What happened to the baby?'

'No. Listen.' Eve went back to the paper, which was trembling in her hand. '"Shows pelvic scars consistent with testicular removal. Appears ignorant of her condition."'

'What condition?'

'*Testicular* removal? Did he not notice she was a *woman*?' Olivia rolled her eyes. 'I remember Mom's scars. I saw them once when she was getting dressed, one on each side, near her hip bones. She had benign tumors removed when she was a girl. Testicles! What a quack.'

Rosalind's skin started crawling, the way it always did

when bad news was imminent. 'Does it say what condition?'

'There's a diagnosis typed at the bottom. "Complete andro-gen insensitivity syndrome."'

'Huh?' Olivia crossed the porch and peered at the paper over her sister's shoulder. 'Complete androgen insensitivity? What does that mean?'

Rosalind stepped closer too, digging her nails into her arms. 'She couldn't tolerate people with gender confusion?'

'Oh no, no.' Olivia shook her head drily. 'They didn't *have* gender confusion in the seventies.'

Eve didn't smile at either joke. 'I tried to look up the syndrome, but I can never get Google to load out here. We shouldn't have cancelled Dad's Internet so soon.'

'I'm sure it's nothing serious.' Rosalind wasn't sure at all, but it made her feel better to say so, and anyway, their mother had died of a drug overdose eighteen years earlier, so it wasn't like whatever this was could kill her retroactively. 'We can look it up next time we're in town.'

'I'm not waiting that long.' Olivia dug out her phone, poked at it, then put it to her left ear, right hand to her hip. 'Donna, hey.'

Rosalind exchanged a look with Eve, who made a sound of impatience. 'Tell me you're not asking your assistant to—'

'Fine. Busy. Hey, can you look something up for me? Phone works up here, but the nearest Internet is half an hour away.' Olivia turned from Eve's eye-rolling. 'Thanks. What is "complete androgen insensitivity syndrome"? Yes, I'll wait.'

'Jeez, Olivia.' Still looking through the file, Eve perched on a rather clunky chair Dad had nailed together from driftwood. Ugly but functional, and he'd been so proud. Mom had sat in it while he was around, then moved off as soon as he left the room. 'There might be something else in here that will tell us. You didn't need to bother her.'

'No problem.' Olivia tossed her hair and resettled the phone at her ear. 'It's her job.'

Rosalind seriously doubted that. Or that it had been Donna's job to search – in vain, as predicted – for a place that would deliver Chinese food to Candlewood Point.

'You found it? Good. What does it say?' Olivia listened intently. Her face fell. She gasped, eyes widening. 'But that's . . . absurd.'

Rosalind moved toward her. Underneath the drama, her sister was genuinely upset. 'What is it?'

'Are you sure?' Olivia held up her hand to ward Rosalind off. 'Are you *sure*? There's no other definition? Nothing anywhere? This is "complete androgen insensitivity syndrome"? That's what you said, right, Eve?'

'Yes.' Eve rose from the chair, still clutching the file. 'What is she saying? You're making me nervous.'

'Thanks, Donna.' Olivia disconnected the call and faced her sisters, looking shaky. 'The diagnosis must have been typed wrong. Or it was mixed up with someone else's record. Or it's fake. If our mother had that, she could not have given birth to any of us. She'd have had no uterus. No ovaries. No Fallopian tubes. No female reproductive ability at all. Period.'

Fog condensation dripped off the trees on to the porch roof in a spattering drumbeat.

Rosalind shivered. 'What the hell?'

'That's impossible,' Eve said.

'Of course it's impossible,' Olivia snapped. 'We're standing right here, all three of us.'

'Can I see that?' Rosalind took the document from Eve's folder and studied it carefully. It looked entirely legitimate, the doctor's name and address printed across the top – James R. Winston, MD – her mother's maiden name typed in Courier font in the appropriate spaces, 'Sylvia Moore'. 'I'm sure there's a mistake. Monday morning, tomorrow, we should call the office in New York and talk to this doctor or his assistant or something.'

'This was *fifty years* ago. The guy won't still be practicing. He probably won't even be *alive*.' Olivia started pacing, still clutching her phone. 'And the office wouldn't keep records that long.'

'We could ask Lauren.' Rosalind dropped the paper back into the file. She didn't want to look at it anymore. 'She might know.'

'No.' Olivia spoke sharply. 'We are not asking Lauren about Mom's health issues.'

Rosalind barely suppressed an impatient retort. Dad had married Lauren fifteen years earlier, three years after their mother died. Olivia still acted as if he'd committed a crime. 'We can't ask Dad, at least not until he's recovered enough for full sentences. Yesterday he called me "Roland".'

'No Lauren.' Olivia crossed her arms over her chest. 'None of her business.'

'I understand how you feel.' Rosalind gentled her voice. 'But if Lauren knows something, she can save us a lot of—'

'If she doesn't, you'd effectively be telling her something I am only about four thousand percent sure Mom wouldn't *ever* want her to know.'

'Okay, but—'

'Drop it, Rosalind.' Eve tossed the folder on to the big table the family had gathered around countless times for lobster feasts. 'No point.'

'I want to understand what's going on.'

'We all do, but that's not the way.'

'This is ludicrous. I can't believe we're giving this any

credence at all.' Olivia stomped into the house, leaving Eve to shrug at Rosalind, and Rosalind to shrug back. Moments later, Olivia stomped out again, holding a photo album. 'I was saving this to look at during dinner. We have picture proof right here, a whole book full.'

'God, that's right.' Rosalind wilted into relief. 'The pregnancy bible.'

'Hallelujah!' Eve got up and crowded around the album with Rosalind.

'Pregnant with me.' Olivia stabbed a finger on to a picture, flipped a few more pages and stabbed another. 'About to give birth to me, standing in front of the house in Beverly Hills. And there's Aunt Christina, who was midwife for all three of us. Here's Mom pregnant with you, Rosalind. At six months, then at eight.'

'So why the diagnosis?' Eve asked. 'If it's a mistake, why would she or Dad keep the paper?'

'Pregnant here with you, Eve, on a trip to Paris at the end of 1989. That's all three of us.' Olivia shut the book with a snap. 'Told you.'

'So what happened? They fixed her?' Eve took the album from Olivia. 'So she could have us?'

Rosalind shook her head, a little queasy again. 'No reproductive organs whatever, Donna said. It's not like they could have grown her new ones.'

'Could they transplant—'

'Not back then. Don't know about now.'

A bird rustled through the lower branches of infant pines, gave a tentative peep, then was quiet. The stillness was eerie. Even the little waves seemed to have gone silent against the rocky shore.

'She could have been preparing for a role. She really got into

16

that stuff.' Eve's face lit hopefully. 'Remember when she flew to Montana to learn how to ride and take care of horses for her first movie with Burt Reynolds? And for the *Pioneer Spirit* role, she stayed in a log cabin for a week without anything modern. She hated every second, but she did it.'

Rosalind really wanted Eve's solution to make sense, in spite of the fact that it didn't. 'I don't remember any role she played where she couldn't have kids.'

'Why would she bother creating a whole medical sheet about it?'

'To make it seem really real.' Eve's voice cracked. 'I could see her studying it, getting herself to feel all miserable.'

'Not buying it.' Olivia shook her head.

Eve sighed. 'Maybe we *should* talk to Lauren. If this is true, Dad must have told her *something*.'

'Not if there was nothing to tell,' Olivia shot back. 'If we tell Lauren, we'd be betraying our mother. And what if this got out? What would that do to Mom?'

Eve laughed bitterly. 'Mom's not really in a place where she can care.'

'Jesus, Eve. That is cold. I'm talking about the press. It would be a madhouse. They were even all over Dad after his stroke.'

'The thing is . . .' Rosalind wrapped her arms around herself, looking back and forth between her sisters, stomach positively roiling now. 'We do look really different from each other. Blonde, brunette, redhead, different eyes, noses, you're both tall, and I'm—'

'Stop. Stop right now.' Olivia picked up the pregnancy album and brandished it. 'Three pregnancies, three daughters. Enough already.'

'I get that you're upset, Olivia. We all are. But we have to look at all possibilities.'

'Okay.' Olivia tossed the album on to the table and folded her arms. 'Given what we know for sure to be true, that she was pregnant and delivered each of us, what *are* the possibilities?'

'That . . .' Rosalind shrugged. 'I don't know, that she faked the pregnancies?'

'*What?*' Olivia looked horrified. 'Why would she fake pregnancies?'

Eve lifted an eyebrow. 'Well, duh.'

'So no one would know she couldn't have children,' Rosalind said.

'Why would she care that much?'

'Because image was so important to her.' Eve's tone was bitter. 'You know that. It's vital to your biz.'

'Enough to make it worth *faking* three pregnancies? Three births?' Olivia shook her head. 'Not buying that either.'

Eve stayed silent, studying the diagnosis. Rosalind didn't want to admit out loud what her sister was probably thinking: that yes, as much as she adored her mother, to Jillian Croft the risk might well have been worth it.

'Okay, so then where did we come from?' Olivia flung out her arm and let it slap down on her hip 'Test tubes? Storks? Amazonbaby.com?'

'Adoption.' Rosalind had to whisper the word to get it out, but she might as well have screamed it. Olivia and Eve froze into shocked silence. A seal barked off in the distance. A bird rustled through leaves on the forest floor.

Eve closed her folder. 'That would mean Dad's not our biological father.'

'This is bullshit!' Olivia clutched the album to her chest. 'Mom's name is on all our birth certificates, and so is Dad's. Those are legal documents. What you're suggesting, Roz, that she somehow faked the pregnancies, faked our births, faked our certificates . . . it's a ridiculous farce involving so many people over such a long time that it would be unlikely to work *once*, let alone three times.'

'You're right.' Eve shook her head. 'You're right. It's crazy.'

'And what about all our birth stories?' Olivia was on a roll now. 'Each of us knows all the details of Mom's labor and our delivery.'

'Yes . . .' Rosalind was thinking of her mom's extraordinary talent as an actress and storyteller. Thinking of the excruciatingly awkward and vague talk Mom had had with her about menstruation, how inept she'd seemed at answering Rosalind's questions. The way she'd never let her daughters see her totally naked, yet posed topless in *Playboy*. 'Bottom line, there's no point arguing because we don't know enough yet.'

'That is absolutely true. Let's get back to work.' Olivia marched into the house. Eve glanced at Rosalind and followed.

Rosalind trudged after them, feeling as if she'd entered another dimension, in which everything was still totally familiar around her, but nothing was the same. Her mother had been publicly pregnant three times and had supposedly given birth to each of them with her sister as midwife. A sister who could have written any name she wanted on a birth certificate. Or on three.

But she wasn't going to add that final straw to the pile that poor camels Olivia and Eve already staggered under. Not now. There had to be a logical explanation for this medical diagnosis being so at odds with what they knew about their mother.

Because otherwise this worn, forgotten, misfiled piece of paper could totally upend their lives.

Chapter 2

Mom took me to the doctor today after school. Christina told her she had to after she found me crying and I was stupid and told her why. Because I'm sixteen and a sophomore in high school and I'm still not menstruating. *I'm not talking to her probably ever again. The appointment was awful. I don't like Dr Tibbet anyway, he smells bad and you have to laugh at jokes even a four year old wouldn't think were funny. I didn't want him even* looking *at me without my clothes on, but he started pushing and poking at me all over, even down* there. *And then it got worse, he was poking in* me *with this metal thing and muttering and looking confused. Mom did* nothing *to help me or tell him to stop, even though I kept looking at her and was obviously so miserable.*

He kept adjusting the light and doing it again, and it hurt like hell, but I didn't say anything. I wanted to act like it was normal, so he'd think I was normal and leave me alone.

Now I have to see some other doctor in Bangor. That's all they told me, and I was too scared to ask. I asked Mom later, and she said everything was fine, they just wanted to check something. I don't believe her. I knew there was something wrong.

I don't want to go to this other doctor. I want to have fun in the play and enjoy being the youngest star ever in my school. I want to live forever and be on Broadway and in the movies. Christina wanted to know what was wrong but I told her to shut up. I wish I had my own room. I hate that I can't lock her and everyone else out.

Rosalind opened her eyes and blinked at the pine walls of her bedroom, feeling hollow and dulled, aware that something big and unpleasant had happened, but not remembering.

And then remembering, with a surge of sickening adrenaline. Mom.

She turned to her side, curled up tightly, waiting for the spell to pass. No proof yet that her mother had the androgen insensitivity. No reason to get this upset. And yet, even last night, the diagnosis had clicked pieces into place in Rosalind's subconscious that made her accept it as true, even without the proof. She trusted that subconscious, if not absolutely, at least more than her sisters.

Soft gray light came in from under the shades. Morning, either very early or still very foggy, or both. Noise downstairs and a glance at the clock next to her bed gave her one answer: very early. Olivia was up and getting ready to catch her plane.

It was a relief to be able to ditch the farce of trying to sleep. The only positive of her insomniac night had been her decision to pursue proof of her mother's diagnosis and, if necessary, go further to find out how she and her sisters had come to be family.

Last night, after the unpleasant discovery, she, Olivia and Eve had decided to ditch unpacking in favor of the family's traditional Maine celebration. Not the biggest one, her mother's favorite, the annual clambake, but a wonderful secondary

21

tradition, the defining seafood of the Maine coast: boiled lobster, with fluffy white bakery rolls, tossed salad, and Betty Crocker gingerbread under drifts of whipped cream. The three of them might not be together again for a while, depending on whether Olivia returned to Maine. No doubt she meant to and wanted to, but for Olivia, that was far different than actually doing so.

Dinner had been delicious but subdued, in spite of champagne with locally smoked mussels before the meal, and a bottle of Chablis during. The sisters had been unable either to forget what had happened so they could enjoy themselves, or to process the discovery adequately enough to discuss it. Rosalind figured that would take more time and more information.

She pushed off the covers and grabbed a sweatshirt from the chair she'd tossed it on the night before, shoved her feet into a worn pair of pink slippers kept here in Maine for chilly mornings, and padded over to the window to open the shade, fingers crossed that the fog had lifted.

Sigh of relief. The sun was still low in the east, its rays blocked by trees behind the house, but the sky was pinking up, the bay wide again, and the opposite coast sharply defined. The still water, strewn with colorful lobster buoys, made a perfect mirror for pine-covered islands, their rocky undergarments bared by the dropping tide. Down at the shore in front of the house, barnacled stones were likewise exposed, covered with limp clumps of rockweed that would revive into a rippling golden-brown meadow when the waves returned.

Rosalind's dread at having to confront Olivia and Eve with her decision lessened. The good weather felt like a positive omen.

Downstairs, Olivia was standing in front of the sink, casual-chic in a white sleeveless shirt, fitted black capris and high-heeled black sandals, hair and makeup already perfect. 'Hey, Rosalind, what are you doing up so early?'

'I couldn't sleep.'

'Tell me about it. But then I never do before one of these ridiculously early flights. I keep waking up wondering if it's time to get out of bed yet, terrified I'll oversleep.'

Rosalind gaped. '*That's* why you didn't sleep well?'

'Want some coffee? I made plenty in that thing.' She pointed to the sleek stainless-steel machine that had replaced the old Krups Mom and Dad had used for decades. 'I really hate what Lauren did to this kitchen. She killed its soul.'

'It was in pretty bad shape.' Rosalind went to the refrigerator and pulled out the orange juice, needing its refreshing, sweet acidity. 'Mom wasn't a real cook, and nothing worked that well. It might have been fun for us to keep opening and closing the oven door to maintain temperature, but . . .'

'True.' Olivia drew her hand wistfully across the smooth surface of the granite counter. 'I really miss the big old iron sink.'

'It was rusting.'

'You're right, you're right, it was a mess. But this . . .' She gestured around her contemptuously. 'This could be any kitchen in any suburb in any town anywhere. Before, it was the kitchen to *this* house, you know?'

'Yes. I know.' Rosalind took a seat at the island. 'It is sorta generic. But for us, the house was a magical summer escape. The weirdness was just part of its charm. Lauren had to live here for real.'

'Yeah, but she could have made about a billion better choices. Black appliances instead of stainless, butcher-block countertops, natural wood cabinets with iron hardware . . .'

'I don't mind the white. It was so dark in here before.'

Rosalind downed her juice and poured herself half a cup of coffee. Olivia liked hers so weak it was hardly worth drinking. 'So what do you do when you get back to California? Pin Derek to the bed and demand servicing?'

'Practically.' Olivia refilled her own cup. 'I swear, this baby stuff is killing our sex life. We used to love being spontaneous and a little wild. Now it's scheduled every two days during ovulation, he has to be on top, and the whole time I'm dying for him to come already, so I can root for the little spermies to choose the right route and score. He can tell what I'm thinking, so he feels like his orgasm doesn't have anything to do with us anymore. I don't even care if I have one.'

'Good Lord, Olivia, I think I might feel sorry for Derek. First time ever.'

'I know. I'm awful. Even sexier? Afterward, I spend an hour with a pillow under my ass and my legs sticking up in the air like a dead bug.'

Rosalind burst into giggles. 'You're kidding.'

'Using gravity to help the little guys along.' Olivia shook her head ruefully. 'It's hell.'

'Is it still worth it?' Rosalind tried not to look distraught, knowing her sister hated pity. 'After all these years?'

'Of course it's worth it. The doctor says nothing is wrong with me, and Derek's doctor says the same about him. It's got to work eventually.'

'Is it still worth it to Derek?'

Olivia's face fell. 'Not so much. He still wants kids, I guess, he just isn't making it easy to try.'

Rosalind frowned, sipping her coffee. She'd said her piece when Olivia got engaged, and promised herself she'd be supportive after the marriage. Given that she thought Derek was an utter asshole, that was often difficult. 'Wouldn't you rather be married to a guy who wants kids as much as you do?'

'Of course I would. But what am I going to do, snap my fingers and poof, the perfect man will show up immediately?' Olivia laughed bitterly. 'I'm almost forty, I don't have time for that. Derek isn't perfect, but I'm not the easiest person to put up with either.'

'No, you are. Really.' Rosalind grinned at the black look her sister sent her. 'Have you talked about adopting?'

'We're not adopting.' Olivia got up and dumped the rest of her coffee into the sink. 'I want my own kids, not someone else's.'

'Why not?' Rosalind tried to keep her voice casual. 'If what we found out yesterday is true, it seems like Mom and Dad did fine adopting us.'

'Stop.' Olivia spun around, looking murderous. 'I don't want to talk about that bullshit, Rosalind. Ever. Got it?'

'Seriously?' Rosalind put down her mug and stared at her sister. She'd expected pushback, but not outright denial. 'You're going to ignore this?'

'That's exactly what I'm going to do.'

'Why? Olivia, this could be a huge deal.'

'It's nothing like a huge deal. In fact it's a tiny flea on my very fine ass. I am Jillian Croft and Daniel Braddock's daughter.' Olivia jabbed at her chest, than pointed first at Rosalind, then at the ceiling. 'You and Eve are my sisters. That is not going to change, no matter what the other details are, so I don't need them. Forget about it.'

'I can't. I need to know.'

'It's a mistake to pursue this, Rosalind.'

'Why do you say that?'

'Your past is part of you; you can't get rid of one you don't like by trying to jump into a new one, the way you do with every other part of your life.' Olivia counted on her fingers. 'Where you live, where you work, who you date, how you look . . . Mom and Dad might not have been ideal parents, but they were ours, and that's all we need to know.'

Rosalind took a deep breath. 'I understand how you feel. But—'

'But you're going to follow this anyway.'

She nodded slowly, watching her sister's chin set, her face go blank, Olivia's method for hiding unwelcome emotions. 'I want to know the truth. And if it turns out Mom couldn't have given birth to us, at least I want to know who did have me.'

Olivia turned back to the sink, rinsed her cup, put it into the dishwasher, shoulders hunched, and leaned against the counter for a long moment. Then she faced Rosalind again, folding her arms across her chest. 'Okay, fine. Nothing I can do about that, it's your decision. Just keep me out of it, okay? My life is complicated enough right now.'

'Okay.' Rosalind hid her relief. 'Thank you. I know that was hard for you, and I want you to know I—'

'Yeah, whatever.' Olivia grinned at her, grabbed her phone off the counter and poked at it to bring it to life. 'Argh. Nearly five. I have to go.'

Rosalind stood, still sick with tension, but grateful Olivia hadn't come at her with a cleaver – figuratively speaking. The talk with Eve would be easier. 'Need help carrying anything out to the car?'

'Sure, thanks.'

She followed her sister into the living room, then to the front hall, where Olivia's huge suitcase and smaller extra bag were sitting against the door. She hefted the case and staggered outside, down the shell-lined path to the driveway, wondering why she and Eve always treated Olivia as if she were fragile when she spent ridiculous amounts of money on a personal trainer and could probably whup both of them. 'Can you open the trunk?'

'Here. I'll put it in the back seat.' Olivia picked up the suitcase as if it weighed ten pounds and tossed it in the back with her other bag. 'Thanks for helping.'

'Sure.' Rosalind opened her arms to her sister. 'Fly safe, Olivia. I hope the boinking works this month.'

'God, me too.' Olivia hugged her, long and hard. As usual, she smelled fresh and subtly expensive. 'I want this little person so badly.'

'It'll happen. I know it will.'

Olivia released her, sniffed a couple of times. Blinked. 'I know I'm spoiled, I know I've been incredibly blessed, I know life has been easier for me than for so many others. I try very hard not to take anything for granted. But it's still impossible for me to believe that this child might not happen.'

Her voice broke; she tried to smile bravely and failed, making Rosalind's heart ache.

'Keep believing it, keep visualizing the baby. Keep cheering on those sperm.' She smiled encouragingly, then snapped her fingers. 'I know! You should buy Derek pom-poms and teach him a routine.'

'*What?*'

'He can perform it while you're doing your dead bug thing.' Rosalind struck a pose and shook pretend pom-poms. 'Hey, sperm, *hey*, get on your *way*, find that egg and merge D-N-A.'

Olivia cracked up. 'You're right, you are a kook.'

'Told you.'

'Take care of yourself, Rozzy.' Olivia hugged her again and scrubbed the top of her head. 'I worry about you with this new project. I don't want you getting hurt.'

27

'Nah. I won't get hurt. I'm tough.'

'Uh-huh.' She got into the car. 'And grow some hair.'

'Bye, Olivia.'

'In a real color.'

'*Bye*, Olivia!'

'I'll send you some clothes. Size eight? Ten? You'll be amazed what a difference it makes in how people treat you.'

'*By-y-ye, Olivia!*'

Olivia laughed and started the car. 'Okay, okay, I'm going. Kiss Eve for me!' She took off down the driveway, pebbles flung behind her wheels, blasted the horn twice as she turned on to the main road, then roared off.

Rosalind flinched, wondering how many people that horn had woken up. The closest neighbors were football-field lengths away through the woods, but sound traveled like crazy up here in the remarkable silence.

Back inside, she cleaned out the coffee maker and brewed up another batch, this one fit for human consumption. Since Mom's death, Rosalind had been the family's only late riser. Eve would be up fairly soon, even if the honking hadn't woken her. A good breakfast before her long drive back to Boston, where she worked for an architecture firm that designed hotels, would do her good, maybe put her in the right frame of mind to accept Rosalind's plans.

A quick look through cupboards turned up an unopened package of Bob's Red Mill wholegrain pancake mix, which looked decent. She followed the directions mixing the batter, and found a griddle pan in a cabinet that must have come with Lauren's fancy stove, because it fit the oval fifth burner perfectly. While it preheated, she dug out a frying pan and broke four eggs into another bowl, then added a splash of milk and some salt for making scrambled eggs when her sister came downstairs.

The pancake batter hit the griddle with a satisfying sizzle. As the first batch cooked, and the next, she sliced a fragrant peach into a dish and added Maine wild blueberries, whose small size and intense flavor spoiled the taste of any other variety. As each batch of pancakes was done, she put them on a metal platter kept warm in a low oven.

The last of the batter had just been poured when she heard Eve's footsteps upstairs. By the time her sister appeared, rumpled and sleepy, wearing a scruffy gray T-shirt and navy sweats, Rosalind had the eggs scrambling on the stove.

'Mm, that looks good. Fruit, too! Thank you.' Eve yawned and rubbed her hip. 'Is there toast?'

'Nope. Something better.' Rosalind opened the oven door. 'Les cakes du pan.'

'Ooh. You are a goddess, thank you.' Eve poured herself a cup of coffee. 'Olivia get off okay this morning?'

'Yup. She even left sort of on time.'

'Good.' She took a seat at the kitchen island, holding her cup in both hands. 'Hope the traffic to Bangor isn't bad.'

'Same here.' Rosalind glugged Maine maple syrup into a tiny pitcher and put it in the microwave to heat. 'You and Mike have any fun plans coming up this week?'

'Nope.' Eve sliced a big pat of butter and smeared it on to her pancake stack. If Rosalind used that much butter, she'd be five pounds heavier by the time she ate the last bite. Eve would probably lose weight from the exertion of spreading. 'No plans at all.'

'Well, that sounds exciting.'

'Yeah, it's not.'

Rosalind turned to look at her sister. She didn't like that dull tone of voice. 'Why don't you think of some? Try a new restaurant or something?'

'Mike probably won't want to.' She poured syrup, which pooled and slid off the edge of her stack.

'Why not?' Rosalind pulled out a chair and sat opposite. Mike was a nice enough guy, but not exactly a thrill a minute. 'What's going on?'

'He hardly wants to go out anymore. Or do much of anything.' Eve forked up a dripping bite. 'It's tough when he's not working over the summer.'

That did not sound good. 'Is he depressed? Tired of teaching?'

'Maybe both.'

Rosalind frowned and ate eggs, trying to figure out how she could help. 'Are *you* depressed?'

'Maybe.'

'Eve.' She put down her fork, horrified that she hadn't noticed anything unusual in her sister's behavior. 'You didn't say anything.'

'Didn't seem like it was necessary. The family has enough going on, to put it mildly.'

'What are you going to do? Therapy? Meds?'

'I don't know. I'm only really starting to realize. Depression is a creepy little devil, you know? First I told myself we've been together three years, passion doesn't last and all that. Then I told myself I was feeling contentment, not boredom. Peace, not stagnation. A million other reasons for the lethargy. And work is work. I thought I'd be promoted by now. I'll be thirty next year and I'm still designing bathrooms and elevator shafts. Necessary, important, but . . .'

'You need a big change.'

Eve rolled her eyes. 'You always think that.'

'I'm serious. New job, new boyfriend, new town, new something.'

'That's your solution to everything. Not happy? Run away!'

'It's not running away. It's keeping yourself from getting trapped in a spot that's bad for you, or that doesn't fit. And by the way, I get that you and Olivia don't approve of the way I live my life. You can stop pointing it out.'

Eve glanced up from her pancakes. 'Sorry.'

Rosalind had to look away. Confronting someone always felt worse than sucking it up like she usually did. She'd scored a point and now *she* wanted to apologize. 'I know you're trying to help. Just think about what I said. Maybe a kick in the pants would help. Take a new course, get a puppy to keep Marx company, paint your apartment purple. Something new.'

'Maybe you're right.'

'Of course I'm right!' Rosalind grinned and ate another pancake, sneaking glances at her sister, waiting for what felt like the right moment. 'So . . . I'm thinking of going after this thing with Mom.'

'I had a feeling you would.'

'I want to know for sure whether she had the disorder, and if so, I want to know how we were adopted and, at least for me, from whom.'

'Okay.' Eve put down her fork and picked up her coffee. 'Why?'

'If I didn't come out of Mom and Dad, who did I come from? Am I more like these other people? Do they know about me? Did they ever look for me?'

'Why just you? They could be all our parents.'

'No.' Rosalind shook her head. 'I don't think so.'

'Okay.' Eve took a sip. 'I'm listening.'

'Look at us. We're different physically, different temperamentally, different in the way we learn and process things.'

'Not proof, but true.'

'I want proof.' Rosalind took another bite of her eggs. 'Aren't you curious?'

'I was awake most of the night thinking about it. I assume we all were.'

'Olivia wouldn't admit it.'

'No, not yet. Give her time.' Eve put her coffee down and folded her arms on the table. 'I get why you want to know, Rosalind. But I worry this is going to hurt you.'

'*Et tu*, Eve?' She gestured to her own sturdy body. 'Do I look like I'm made of fluff and toothpicks?'

'You're not going to find the Hearts. Our family was messed up, but so is—'

'Are you *kidding* me?' Rosalind put down her fork before she stabbed it into her sister's hand. 'The Heart Family is a *toy*. Fantasy play. You think I don't know that?'

Eve shrugged. 'Just testing a theory.'

'I'm not looking for the Heart Family. I couldn't stand all that ordinariness. All that predictability.' Rosalind shuddered comically. 'All that pink, white and blue plastic.'

'Okay. So what's the first step?' Eve reached for the coffee pot and poured herself another cup. 'Are you going to talk to Lauren?'

'I don't know where else to start. I can't ask Dad. If he gets upset, it could kill him.'

'You *could* wait until he's better.'

'Uh . . .' Rosalind looked aimlessly around the kitchen, whistling, tapping the granite counter.

Eve laughed. 'You don't want to wait.'

'Of course not. I need to know *now*.'

'That's my calm, patient sister.'

Rosalind loaded her fork with more eggs, then jerked her head up to stare at Eve. 'Hey, you know what?'

'Uh-oh.' Eve narrowed her eyes. 'That look scares me.'

'Looking for your birth family might be just what you need to do, too.'

'Or just what I *don't* need to do. I might have come from a family of clinically depressed mass murderers.'

'At least they'd be tall, beautiful clinically depressed mass murderers. I probably came from a long line of trolls.'

'Seriously, Rosalind. Our family could have been a lot worse.'

'True. I mean I guess.' Rosalind took her plate to the sink, then turned back. 'Wait, really?'

'Ha!' Eve got up and stretched her lean body, grinning. 'I have to get going. Thanks for breakfast.'

'You're welcome. Leave the dishes. You did most of them last night.'

'You sure? Thanks for that, too. When are you going to talk to Lauren?' She immediately held up her hand. 'No, don't tell me. As soon as I leave.'

'Pretty much.'

She shook her head, still smiling. 'Just don't give her a stroke, too.'

'Nothing could kill her. She's the most even-tempered person I've ever met.'

'This is pretty big stuff, though. Be careful. Of yourself, I mean.' She hugged Rosalind and picked up her coffee.

'I promise.'

'Be down soon.'

Eve went upstairs and Rosalind got to work cleaning the kitchen. She adored her sisters, but sometimes felt as if she'd had four parents in her life. Five, if she included Lauren. Now she wanted to add two more?

When Eve reappeared, carrying her small overnight bag,

Rosalind walked her out to her sleek forest-green Mercedes, the car Eve had bought for herself when she went to college. Ten years old, it still looked practically brand new, which Eve said was because she refused to use it in Boston, home to notoriously crazy drivers.

'Safe travels.' She hugged Eve hard.

'Thanks.' Eve got into the car and rolled down the window. 'I'll try to come back in a couple of weeks to help out here again. Good luck with the research. Call if you find something that freaks you out. Or just to let me know what's going on.'

'I will, thanks.' Rosalind hadn't realized how tense she felt about tackling the issue alone until Eve's offer brought gratitude and relief.

'Bye!' Eve backed slowly out of the driveway and gave a graceful long-armed wave before she drove off nearly silently through the woods.

Rosalind hugged her arms around herself, standing looking after the car even long after it was out of sight. She'd been smart to approach her sisters in person, and even smarter to do it individually, so they weren't able to band together against her and each other. She had the permission she wanted. Now she was left with the monumental task of discovering whether her parents had lied, and if so, of putting together an entirely new vision of her family and where she'd come from.

Huh. That didn't sound too hard.

A brief laugh, then she turned reluctantly, and walked back into the too-silent house.

Chapter 3

February 15, 1967 (Wednesday)

I'm not thinking about that doctor stuff anymore. I refuse. I don't have cancer, and that's that. I feel too fine to be sick, full of energy, sleeping well. No symptoms. It's impossible.

Guys and Dolls *rehearsals are going so well! I was born for this, I know it. It feels like another person comes alive in me on stage, a person not so beaten down by my small-minded parents and this boring town and my caged life. A person with a deep need to shine out, somewhere far from here, somewhere big. That sounds conceited, but this diary is my private place, where I can be honest and not worry about how I sound. Though just in case someone reads this someday – maybe I became a star and you love me, and bought my diary at auction after my death? Hello, you person, I know I sound conceited, and I don't care! That's how happy, happy, happy I am to have something I can be this good at, this special at. Sarah Brown is a role I play, but she is so real to me. I feel her, all parts of her, the devout good girl and the free spirit inside longing to break free. She's very real, and very much part of me.*

Except I bet she got her period at exactly the right time.

* * *

Rosalind walked through the automatic glass doors at Pine Ridge into the lobby that smelled faintly of either what the residents had had for lunch or whatever was cooking for dinner.

The retirement community was situated southeast of Blue Hill on top of a small rise with a lovely view of the opposite side of Mount Desert Island from the one the girls could see on Candlewood Point. If you had to live in an institution, you couldn't find a much better setting.

On the way, she had stopped at the Blue Hill Public Library and used the second-floor computers to look up more about complete androgen insensitivity syndrome. The sinking, sick feeling that had crept into her chest and stomach while she sat peering at the monitor had followed her here.

Women with CAIS developed normal hourglass silhouettes and female features, like Mom had had. They overwhelmingly identified as female, and the hetero- to homosexual ratio was the same as the normal population. But these girls were born with no female plumbing, and with undescended testicles that had to be removed at the onset of puberty to avoid the risk of cancer. They generally had no pubic hair and less than fully formed vaginas, which, in order to accommodate penises, had to be gradually stretched with increasingly large dilators over a period of months.

Good God.

It was still hard to take in. Jillian Croft had been the virtual embodiment of female sexuality, one of those women who could reduce anyone, man or woman, gay or straight, to blush-and-stutter idiocy just by asking what time it was. Large hazel eyes she used like a weapon, an utterly contagious, luminescent smile, a rich, musical and slightly husky voice, and a way of tipping her head when she spoke that was both practiced and vulnerable. Even her normal stance broadcasted sensuality – one hip thrust out, back slightly arched, as if she were continuously posing on a red carpet.

This woman was born with testicles?

Except that when the diagnosis was made, the magnificent Jillian Croft was still Sylvia Moore, a teenager who'd hopped a bus from Maine to Manhattan against her parents' wishes and without their knowledge, and hung around the Stella Adler Studio of Acting until Daniel Braddock, nearing thirty at the time and a teacher at the school, took notice. 'Boy, did I,' her father always said, at which point Mom would smile, and Rosalind would try not to throw up.

According to the diagnosis paper, at eighteen Sylvia Moore had still been 'ignorant of her condition'. Mom had told Olivia her scars were from the removal of benign tumors, which could have been what she'd been told as a girl, instead of the truth. The surgery meant she'd been to a doctor previous to the January 1969 visit, a doctor who understood her disorder and took the appropriate medical action.

Unbelievably, neither that doctor nor her own mother had bothered to explain to Sylvia what was really going on with her body, and why she wasn't going through puberty like every other girl around her. It made Rosalind want to drive up to Grandma Betty's house and pummel her. Who would do that to her daughter?

Sadly, Mom wasn't the only girl who'd been lied to. On a support website for CAIS, Rosalind had found testimonials written by a heartbreaking number of women from her mother's generation and younger, who shared stories of alienation, fear, depression and self-loathing. They knew they weren't like other girls, but in doctors' offices too many of them were prodded, photographed and paraded as freaks, instead of being offered information, compassion, counseling, or support.

Rosalind could only hope post-diagnosis care was a lot better now.

At the reception desk, she signed herself in as a visitor, and under 'purpose for visit' drew a couple of hearts, just to be cute. Anything was better than admitting she was there to ask her stepmother what she knew about Jillian Croft being gender-messed-up.

'Hello.' The receptionist greeted her with a genuine smile. That smile, also on the faces of most staff and residents, had gone a long way toward making Pine Ridge seem like a place the Braddock sisters' fiercely independent father might tolerate. 'Nice to have the fog gone.'

'Yes. We'd had enough.' Rosalind released the pen and headed down the teal and mauve carpeted hallway toward the elevator to the skilled nursing floor, where people stayed who were either struggling toward death or struggling back from a major illness or injury. The staff and occupants did what they could to make the area as comfortable and homey as possible, but it was still a depressing place compared to the spacious apartments and charming cottages for those still able to live independently. The cottage Dad and Lauren originally had their hearts set on wasn't available at short notice after Dad's stroke, but Lauren had settled into a nearly identical one that had opened up.

'Opened up' being a euphemism for another family's grief.

Rosalind paused outside the door to her dad's room, shaky from nerves, reminding herself that even if Daniel Braddock turned out not to be her biological father, he would always be Dad, and Jillian Croft would always be Mom. That he and Mom might have had solid and unassailable reasons for not telling the girls the truth, and that someday they might understand.

If she repeated that enough times, it was entirely possible she'd eventually believe it.

So far no luck. Even after hours trying, she couldn't think of a single reason to keep the truth from her and her sisters except massive ego. Either her mother couldn't bear the general public thinking she was barren, or her father couldn't bear the general public thinking he couldn't impregnate his wife.

Or both.

Dad was sitting up today, looking small and gaunt in the hospital bed, staring intently at his wife as if she'd just said something he was struggling to interpret. He was not a large man, five-seven or -eight at most, shorter than her five-ten mother, especially in heels, but with a barrel chest and imposing personality that meant until Rosalind left for college and came back home with more objective eyes, she'd thought him a giant. A giant pain in the ass a lot of the time. Dad believed there was only one right way to do and think about everything, and of course counted himself as one of the very few who knew exactly what that was.

'Hi, Dad. Hi, Lauren.'

Her father turned his head, dark eyes oddly vacant. Rosalind still couldn't reconcile this invalid in a hospital bed with the handsome, vibrant tyrant of her youth. As often as she'd tangled with him throughout her life, she still felt protective, as if it was her job somehow to keep him happy and healthy.

'Hi,' he managed.

'How are you feeling today?'

'Guh.' By which he meant 'good'.

'He's better today. Sitting up.' Lauren nodded. She nodded a lot. She reminded Rosalind of those little figures with bobbing heads in the backs of people's cars, yes, yes, yes, yes.

Dad had first brought Lauren into contact with his daughters not long after Mom died. Not long *enough*, anyway, as far as the girls were concerned: a little over a year, barely enough time for them to begin surfacing from their shock and grief.

The introductions had been made much too heartily by their father; compensating for nerves, Rosalind got that now, but at the time his cheer had felt like rubbing in their faces that their remarkable mother was replaceable. The girls had stood side by side, Eve sullen, Olivia sneering, Rosalind doing her best to smile while wanting to scream and kick dirt on to Lauren's sensible shoes. Lauren had stood silent, blinking behind her glasses, nodding to acknowledge each of them. Her bland passivity had baffled them as much as her glamour-free embrace of approaching middle-age. Dad had produced a girl-friend as different from their larger-than-life mother as possible. He probably deserved peace and quiet after being married to the maelstrom that was Jillian Croft, but his daughters immediately equated Lauren with a rejection of the mother they'd adored. Olivia still hadn't forgiven her, or their father. Rosalind was getting there. Eve had stopped caring long ago, or so she claimed.

'Do they have any idea when you can get out of this unit and move into the cottage with Lauren?'

Her father looked blank. Rosalind sighed. She'd forgotten. Again.

'*Slowly,*' Lauren said. 'He can't keep up yet. You have to remember.'

'Right.' Rosalind sat on the edge of the bed, whose railings hung down like discarded suspenders. 'Do . . . you . . . have—'

'Another couple of weeks,' Lauren said primly. 'Then he can join me in the cottage, but with a nurse for round-the-clock care.'

Thank you, Lauren. First impression of her stepmother was

pale, plump submission, but she had a sneaky passive-aggressive streak.

'That's good, Dad. You'll be . . . more . . . comfortable . . . in the cottage.'

'Yes.' He grimaced. 'This . . . odors.'

'Odors?' Rosalind sniffed cautiously.

'Stinks, he means. Not literally.'

'Yeah, it does.' Rosalind chuckled, pleased Dad was talking more today. 'But you won't be here long.'

Her father narrowed his eyes. 'Or . . . else.'

She reached to squeeze his hand, a lump in her throat, the relative normalcy of their conversation reassuring. The morning's research seemed, temporarily at least, to belong to a distant movie plot. 'Or else' had been Dad's eternal disciplinary threat, never specified, never needed to be. Once the girls were too old for threats, the phrase became a family joke. 'Or else.'

'How's the house?' Lauren asked. 'Are you girls finished yet?'

'Getting there. It's a big job.' Rosalind looked down at the coarsely textured sheets on the bed. A huge job, but all she could think about was the one piece of paper that shouldn't have been there.

'Start with . . . upstairs. One Rome at time.'

She grinned at her father's need to be boss, even from a hospital bed. 'Room wasn't built in a day.'

'You're confusing him.' Lauren put a protective hand on the mattress near his leg. 'Daniel, don't listen . . .'

'Room, Rome.' He nodded approvingly, as usual making Rosalind feel like she'd won the lottery. Daddy's holy blessing. Would she ever outgrow the pleasure?

A knock at the door. A large woman with a hairstyle several decades old breezed in without waiting for an answer, bringing with her a pleasant floral scent. 'Hello, Mr Braddock. I see you have family around again today. Isn't that nice? It's time for your speech therapy.'

Dad's face darkened. 'Later.'

'I know, it's not your favorite class. Sorry about that. But we'll get you talking again much sooner if you work at it.'

Rosalind pounced on the opportunity. 'Lauren, why don't I buy you a coffee while Dad's at his appointment?'

'All right.' She leaned over to kiss her husband's forehead. 'Back soon. Don't give Clarissa a hard time. She's here to help you.'

'Bushy.'

Rosalind's eyebrows shot up. 'Bushy?'

Lauren pointed her out of the room and followed into the antiseptic hallway. 'He means bullshit.'

Rosalind stifled a snort of laughter. 'I guess you've had time to figure out his language.'

'Yes.' Lauren said nothing more until they were seated across from each other in a booth at the downstairs café, which allowed visitors to Pine Ridge as well as residents. Rosalind had gotten used to her silences. Sentences would end, then be taken up again minutes later, sometimes when Rosalind had forgotten what they were talking about. 'It's been difficult.'

'All of it must have been difficult.' Rosalind gestured with her coffee. 'His stroke, your quick move here, leaving the job of emptying the house to us. And now you have to interpret Dad's words as if he's a toddler.'

Lauren shrugged and turned away. Rosalind had gotten used to that habit too, and no longer followed her gaze across the room to see what had caught her attention. 'I suppose so.'

'I'm curious.' Rosalind reached across the table to lay her

hand on its surface, just shy of her stepmother's arm. 'Did you ever want children? Of your own, I mean?'

'No.' Lauren looked away again, faster that time. A flush started on the small triangle of skin exposed by her shirt's open top button; soon it would creep upward, a clear sign she was uncomfortable.

'It must have been hard taking on three of us at once.' Rosalind spoke evenly, guilty for dumping this emotional burden on Lauren in pursuit of her own ends. But it beat blurting out-of-the-blue questions about her mother's internal organs. 'Olivia, Eve and I were talking at the house, and it occurred to us Mom had never really mentioned the circumstances of our births.' That was a lie. Jillian had provided lurid details for all three deliveries over and over again, which, now that Rosalind had doubts, seemed like red-flag overkill. 'Did Dad ever tell you about—'

'Of course not. Why would he?' Lauren glanced again at Rosalind. The flush was halfway up her neck, heading determinedly for her chin, cheeks, and forehead, and the glimpse of scalp visible at the part through her salt-and-pepper hair. 'That had nothing to do with me.'

'True.' She'd taken the wrong tack. 'What I'm trying to ask is . . . did Dad ever say anything about our mother having fertility issues?'

'What do you mean? What do you mean by that?' Lauren fixed her with a pale blue stare magnified by the lenses in her silvery plastic frames. Her hand twitched several times on the table. 'Why are you asking me about this? Why all of a sudden? Why now?'

Rosalind's heart started pounding. She had to loosen her grip on the coffee. One of them needed to stay calm during this discussion. It looked as if she'd been elected. 'Because we found a reference to troubles in one of the boxes that was in the attic. Mom never mentioned—'

'You'll need to ask your dad. Not me. And don't ask him now. Or even soon. When he's better. No, not even then. Leave it. Just leave it alone. There's no point.' Lauren stood, gazing longingly at the exit.

Rosalind pressed her lips together, wanting to shriek at her stepmother, reminding herself that Lauren had been under terrible pressure for weeks already, that it had been selfish to confront her with this now. At the same time, she'd been desperately hoping Lauren would convincingly deny and/or explain the whole mystery away. 'It's kind of a big deal,' she said. 'It would mean all three of us were adopted, which is a hell of a concept to have to start wrapping your brain around at our ages. If you could just help me—'

'I should get back up there. Daniel gets upset at the speech teacher. He thinks it's stupid that he has to practice talking. I'll need to help her.'

'Lauren . . .' She was going to pretend deafness now?

'I'm sorry, Rosalind, I can't help you.' She thanked Rosalind for the coffee and left without it.

Crap. Rosalind's vision seemed altered; everything had taken on a shiny, sparkly aura. Her ears were ringing, breath coming in and out too quickly. Lauren's reaction all but clinched it. The paper must be real. Jillian Croft couldn't have children.

Ha! She thought she'd been prepared for this. She thought that she, among her sisters, had the only brain agile and sensible enough to process the information relatively calmly.

She was wrong.

A meaningless syllable exploded out of her, too loudly, garnering attention from the residents, some with forks halfway to their mouths.

She attempted a smile to show she was fine, just fine, only slightly out of her head.

And then, in a flash, she was furious. Shaking and furious, like another being had come in and taken over her body. Maybe Satan.

There was no shame in infertility, no shame in adopting if you were unable to have children and chose that path. But in Rosalind's view of the universe, there was enormous, world-altering shame in adopting not once, but *three* times, and not just glossing over that fact, but going out of your way to lie to your children and provide reams of phony proof that they were biologically yours when they weren't.

Goddammit, Mom.

This was more selfish, melodramatic and cruel than Rosalind could ever have imagined her selfish, melodramatic mother behaving. Worse than the temper tantrums and paranoia, the flung objects and accusations. Worse than the days she'd spent all but motionless in bed, foundering in depression, freaking out her daughters, when all she had to do was take her goddam meds to remain a decent parent and person. Even worse than the day Rosalind had crept into Mom's dark bedroom to read *Where the Wild Things Are*, since that was what Mom did to make Rosalind feel better, and Mom had told her she didn't want to hear *Where the Wild Things Are*. Just as Rosalind was going to ask what other book she wanted to hear, her mother had told her she wanted to die instead.

While Rosalind was raging, Dad deserved swearing at, too, because there was no way Mom could have pulled this off without his help. Actually, Rosalind wouldn't put it past him to have masterminded the whole plot. Mom didn't have half the organizational expertise necessary for an operation like this. Dad was always catering to her, as if her bipolar disorder was

his failure, always making excuses for her behavior and his in-
dulgences, and never mind the collateral damage to his daughters.

But he was the puppeteer, who'd built her from a naïve
country girl to an international commodity. It made perfect
sense that he'd be in charge of this baby-procuring operation,
again giving his beautiful wife everything she wanted, reinforcing
to the public that she was as supremely female inside as she was
out. And in the process, reinforcing that he, of all men, had
landed this bastion of female perfection, and put a bun in her
oven not once but three times.

Goddammit to you, too, Dad.

Half an hour passed before she could calm herself enough to
walk out of the café, another fifteen minutes before she stopped
shaking enough to drive back to the house, and another forty-
five before she'd stopped crying enough to pick up the phone
and call the doctor's office listed on her mother's diagnosis. Just
to make absolutely sure. Or because she was a masochist and
needed to be hit on the head over and over again.

'Hello, I'm trying to confirm that a record from your office
is legitimate. Dr James R. Winston, January fifth, 1969. The
patient was Sylvia Moore.'

'I'm sorry, ma'am, we don't keep records that long.'

'I guess I expected that. Does Dr Winston still work there?'

'No, ma'am. I've been here fifteen years and I've never heard
of him.'

'Are there any nurses there who might have worked with
him or who can put me in touch with him?'

A short silence that felt hostile. 'One moment.'

Hold music came on, bland, cheerful harmonies over a
pulsing beat that made listening for any length of time nearly
unbearable. Rosalind paced out on to the porch, then back into
the house. Then back out again. And in.

The line clicked on. 'Ma'am? We have a nurse here who worked with Dr Winston for one year before he retired. She said he passed away a few years after that. However, she was not here in 1969, so there is no way she could confirm your information.'

'May I speak to her?'

'She's with a patient. Who is this?'

Her immediate instinct was to use a fake name, but this type of information would be released only to a close relative if at all. It was a risk she'd have to take. 'Rosalind Braddock.'

'And what is the question, please?'

Rosalind opened her mouth, but nothing came out. What the hell *was* the question? 'I guess I want to find out if it's true.'

'If *what* is true?'

She closed her eyes and took a deep breath. 'Sorry, I didn't realize my mother had this . . . problem. And so I was wondering if there was any way your office would have put out a fake diagnosis.'

'A misdiagnosis?'

'No, deliberately wrong. If the patient asked you to. Or paid . . . or, I don't know, some extraordinary circumstance.'

Long pause. 'A *fake* diagnosis?'

Rosalind sighed. She did sound ridiculous. 'Never mind. Grasping at straws.'

'What did the record indicate?'

'Complete androgen insensitivity syndrome. Can you leave a message for the nurse who knew Dr Winston to call me, please?'

Another pause. Rosalind had a feeling she was taking up the nurse's daily quota of annoying people all by herself. 'Ma'am, it would have been a serious violation of ethics for Dr Winston to discuss a former patient with a nurse who did not treat her, who was not even working here when the patient was seen. We are extremely careful to protect patient privacy in this office. I am quite sure the nurse would have nothing to tell you. To your other question, no, under *no* circumstances would we ever issue or release a deliberately false diagnosis or medical record of *any* kind.'

'Yes. Okay. Thank you.' Rosalind hung up, mortified that she'd made a dork out of herself, but at least she'd asked and gotten the answer, leaving her last hope flat on the highway. No fake. Her mother had had the condition.

Back outside, she perched limply on the chaise she and her sisters used to fight over every time more than one of them was on the porch, until their dad finally set up a schedule of which of them could use it when, and thumb-tacked it to the beam above the chair. The tiny holes were still there.

Tears tobogganed down her face. Her mother wasn't her birth mother. Or Olivia's. Or Eve's. Which meant her father wasn't her birth father either. Or Olivia's. Or Eve's. She couldn't upset Dad over it without risking another brain bleed that might kill him, though earlier today that hadn't seemed like such a bad idea. He should have told them the truth. He had plenty of years to come through with it after Mom died. Plenty before, too.

This was not supposed to be happening. Not now, at age thirty-four. Not ever. Parents were supposed to tell kids they were adopted from the moment they were brought into the new house, so that when they were old enough to understand, the information was so deeply part of their identities, there could be no misery or trauma as a result.

This was miserable. And traumatic.

Fifteen sobbing, snuffling minutes later, Rosalind decided sitting on the forbidden chaise crying at the ocean was not going to get her anywhere. She had a house full of crap to go through before she could go back to New York and resume living the wonderfully scattered bits of her life. Two-bedroom apartment near Columbus Circle, one bedroom of which she'd transformed into a painting and design studio. One part-time job at Starbucks. One gym membership. Two book clubs. One endlessly fascinating city of dancing and eating and concerts and possibilities.

Her sisters were wrong. She wasn't hiding from life; she was living as much of it as she could.

Wiping her tears with the backs of her hands, she got up resolutely from the chaise and marched back into the house. She stared at the living room strewn with flattened boxes and bulging bags for about thirty seconds, then chickened out. She couldn't face it. Instead, she crept up to the second floor, to the small room in the back of the house, the non-ocean side, where Mom used to sleep. The room contained a twin four-poster bed, an antique dresser, a wooden chair and barely enough space to walk between them. Little-girl Rosalind had once asked Mom why she didn't sleep in the larger, sunnier front room. Mom had touched her cheek and said she felt cozier and safer tucked into the smaller one, like a little mouse snug in its nest.

Rosalind had loved that image, even though it made no sense to her at the time. Back in Beverly Hills, her mom's bedroom had been an enormous affair with pink-curtained French windows, a pink floral bedspread on the California king bed, a blue and pink striped settee and matching chairs, a table, an enormous teak desk, television, treadmill and a closet big enough to be an average person's bedroom. If you liked snug little nests, why spend most of the year in an airplane hangar?

Into the small, dim mouse-room she went, its smooth, cool pine flooring creaking occasionally. She sat gingerly on the bed, letting her feet swing, wishing her mother's ghost would show up and explain everything. Long ago, Jillian Croft's personal items had been packed up or given away, but since Lauren never liked this room, the furniture and wall hangings were still the same as when Mom stayed there. Feeling her mother's presence strongly, Rosalind looked around, from window to coastal watercolor by a local artist Mom loved, to dresser to chair to rag rug she'd bought at the Blue Hill Blueberry Festival one summer . . . and back to the dresser.

A sudden memory surfaced, of Mom showing the three girls the secret drawer at the bottom of that dresser, telling them how she kept the modest – for her – amount of jewelry she brought with her to Maine in that drawer so no one would ever steal it from her.

Pushing herself off the bed, Rosalind crossed to the simple three-drawer design, knelt and pulled on the bottom molding. The camouflaged drawer slid smoothly out.

No forgotten jewelry, just notebooks, three of them, in dull shades of blue, red and green. She opened the blue one. An old ledger, containing rows of numbers written in her father's hand. She scanned the figures, flipping through pages. Payments, every month, starting in 1980, going through to December 2003. Then nothing. She flipped back to the beginning. On the first entry there was something written under 'payee' – a name? A company? – but it had been solidly crossed out.

That was weird.

She pulled out another book. Another ledger. Another record of payments, also every month, starting in 1989, ending in April of 2002. Under payee, a name: Helen Phillips.

In the third ledger, payments again, again every month. This one from 1984 all the way to the previous month, dated a week before Dad had his stroke. Payee: Leila Allerton. The amounts in all three were fairly substantial, increasing modestly over the years.

Employees? In what capacity? Why keep ledgers here, when

Dad had accountants and bankers at his beck and call all year long? Why would he need to employ someone in Maine anyway? As far as Rosalind knew, he and Lauren had lived here simply, as had the Braddocks during their summers on the point, in reaction to the excesses of their LA life.

It didn't make sense.

Something illicit? Mistresses? *Three* of them? Rosalind couldn't imagine it. Dad had been slavishly devoted to Mom, even during the times she went off her meds and became a nightmare to live with. He seemed equally devoted to Lauren.

She wrinkled her nose. Blackmail? That seemed so melodramatic, the stuff of TV shows.

Unless maybe the blackmailers had known about Mom's condition. Maybe they were nurses or doctors from the office where Mom had been treated, or others who had enabled the fake pregnancies in some capacity.

But why had two stopped receiving payments, one only recently, one a while back? Why was one name crossed out? Did two of the women die? Settle for a lump sum? Give up? Did Dad have them offed?

She started to laugh, then abruptly stopped.

Finding out your parents had lied to you about the most basic facts of your existence opened up a whole new world of horrifying possibilities.

No, not murder. The instinct that had more or less immediately allowed the possibility of Mom's diagnosis clamped down and refused that idea entry.

She stared again at the figures in each ledger. The same amounts for each woman each month, adjusted upward over time. Inflation? Increased demands? Had the three women – could she even assume the crossed-out name was also a woman? – been operating together? Separately?

Over and over, the same circle of thoughts leading only to a pounding headache and a wave of acid nausea.

She dropped the ledgers, scrambled to her feet and took deep breaths until her stomach settled, then headed across the hall to her room facing the bay, the one she'd always shared with Eve, while Olivia had the bedroom next to Mom's. Dad, and eventually Lauren with him, had claimed the big ocean-side room at the end of the hall.

Feeling slightly saner – wishing she could take sanity for granted again – she changed quickly into running shorts and shoes, gulped a glass of water and headed out the front door, breaking into a jog when she reached the road through the thick pine woods. The air was cool, dry, the sun making dappled shadows on the sand and gravel surface; the only sounds were songbirds and her thudding feet.

Gradually her pace quickened as her body and mood lightened enough to enjoy the run. It felt good to be working out after so many days crouched over boxes, after so many emotions yesterday and today. And always so pleasant to be running here instead of on concrete and asphalt or on a treadmill going nowhere.

A horsefly appeared, buzzing threatening circles around her as she jogged. Rosalind growled at it. The beast's bite was painful, the inch-long body hard to swat. The insects made persistent escorts. Only Eve had been able to bring herself to smack one hard enough to kill or stun it, usually while Olivia and Rosalind shrieked with nervous laughter. The instant one of the creatures made an appearance, the two of them would start yelling for her.

A mile or so later, the fly finally gave up, allowing Rosalind to run in peace, ending her workout with an impetuous sprint down the driveway. Panting, she charged up the stairs to the deck and let herself into the screened porch for mosquito-free stretching. Her headache was gone, though the mystery of the ledgers still buzzed around her, horsefly-like. Too bad Eve couldn't swat that one away.

After she'd stretched, a burst of energy took Rosalind into the living room, where she dragged the lawn and leaf bags out to the edge of the driveway for collection, loaded the boxes of recyclables into her rented Silverado pickup, and hauled them the eight miles to the recycling center. Back at the house, she neatly stacked the boxes to be saved or gone through, and vacuumed the dust and paper scraps off the worn Oriental rugs and varnished pine flooring.

There. In less chaotic surroundings, she would be able to process everything she'd been through more calmly. At least that was the plan.

After showering, she mixed leftover lobster with mayo and piled it into a couple of toasted white hot dog rolls, following that with a peach and a slab of the Betty Crocker gingerbread topped with a squirt of canned whipped cream. In Beverly Hills they'd had a cook who made their meals, everything healthy, everything from scratch, decades before healthy had become such a buzzword of the kitchen. Maine had been the only place the sisters were allowed to indulge in convenience foods and artificial ingredients. Kool-Aid drink mixes loaded with sugar, Pop-Tarts for breakfast, Oreos at lunch. Kid nirvana.

After finishing her solo dinner, she did the few dishes and hung the drying towel back on its rack. The house was too quiet, too empty. While growing up, being alone in their house in Beverly Hills had been a rare treat. Being alone in her New York apartment with her books, paints and fabrics was delicious indulgence. Up here, alone felt wrong. Maine was about other people. Maine was about ditching the southern California movie star crap and coming together as a normal family. Or at least what Rosalind had considered normal.

Oh, the irony.

Now she was stuck in limbo between one family stripped of even that naïve definition, and another one that so far had no characteristics at all.

She considered going out to the Anchor Bar for a drink, then rejected the idea. Chatting with strangers generally appealed to her, but tonight she didn't think she could have a casual conversation. What was really on her mind was too anxious to spill, pressing out like the air in an overinflated balloon. 'Nice day today, so great when the fog lifts, lobster prices gone up a bit this year, my mother had no uterus.'

Resigned, she went upstairs and got ready for bed, hoping last night's pathetic attempt at sleep would make tonight's easier. She was about to climb under the covers with a book for a book club meeting she'd probably have to miss, when the ledgers she'd found earlier started yelling from her mother's room, demanding she take another look.

No! Enough emotional upheaval today.

After ten minutes rereading the same paragraph over and over, she gave in, stomped to her mother's room, gathered up the little brats and took them to bed with her instead.

Again and again she pored over the pages, dates, amounts, three names, one crossed out. She had no idea what it meant.

Finally, she put the books on her bedside table, turned out the light, pulled up the blankets and closed her eyes, listening to the waves lapping at the shore, the leaves whispering to the breeze.

Dates, amounts, names . . .

Names, dates, amounts . . .

Out on the bay, the eerie, echoing call of a loon, then the

answering trill of another. An animal walked through the woods not far from the house, scuffing leaves, snapping twigs. Probably a porcupine.

Names, dates, amounts . . .

Amounts . . . names . . . dates . . .

Rosalind's eyes flew open. *Dates.*

She turned the light back on, grabbed the ledgers and frantically started counting the months on her fingers, over and over, making sure, making absolutely sure.

1980 through 2003.

1984 to the present.

1989 through 2002.

Those first payments started a year and a month before Olivia was born. The second payments started roughly a year before Rosalind's own birthday. The third set of payments, ten months before Eve's.

The correlation could be a coincidence. She could be completely wrong. The dates could have no significance whatsoever.

But if she was correct, and if the crossed-out name was also that of a woman, she could be looking at records of payments to the three women who had given birth to her and her sisters.

Chapter 4

March 2, 1967 (Thursday)

I have cancer. They have to operate. I have it in two places, one on either hip. Not cancer exactly but some tumors that might turn into it. Sometimes I want to scream, sometimes the feelings are so huge I'm afraid I'll go crazy. At the public library I snuck away from Mom and Christina to look up books on cancer. It's so disgusting and so evil. They had pictures and everything, horrible bulgy growths on people's bodies, and holes that looked like the insides of your skin coming to the outside. I nearly fainted. I had to put my head down on the smelly carpet. I wanted to die immediately so I would never ever look like that.

This can't be happening. I've prayed to God all my life and have always felt like it was not just my plan to be somebody important someday, but His plan too. Now He lets this happen! Worse, He makes this happen?

Why? What did I do to deserve it? What if I die before I get out of this little nothing town? I begged Mom to let me have the surgery right after the show this spring, but she doesn't even care that the tumors could kill me. She wants to wait until summer so I don't miss any school. Who cares if I miss school? Waiting could let the cancer spread. I don't think Mom loves me that much. Not as much as she loves Christina, who is not as pretty, talented or smart as me, so why why why? Am I not worth it to her? Dad barely notices either of us. The only time I feel normal and happy is when I'm on stage.

Please, God, don't let me die from this.

Rosalind jolted awake from a nightmare in which she'd been a small girl in a huge crowd, separated from her mother, trying to find the flash of red from the dress Mom had been wearing. Her mother kept turning, beckoning, but no matter how fast Rosalind was able to push through people in her way, her mother kept getting farther and farther ahead.

Didn't take a dream expert to figure that one out.

Most of the night she'd lain awake thinking about the names in the ledgers: Leila Allerton, Helen Phillips, and whoever had been crossed out, see-sawing from being sure these were the Braddock sisters' birth mothers, to being sure that was impossible. Because it was just too weird that Dad would still be paying them for handing over their daughters decades ago.

An hour before slipping into a final restless doze, she had reluctantly decided to tackle Lauren again, probably upsetting her even more deeply.

Ugh.

She pulled the sheet up over her face, breathing in the sleep-clouded air. Lauren had never been one of her favorite people, though Rosalind recognized that at least some of her coolness towards her stepmother stemmed from what Lauren represented as Mom's replacement instead of who she was. Now that it was apparent she had been complicit in the plot to keep the truth from the three people who most deserved to know it . . . well, it didn't help.

Still, Rosalind hated the idea of torturing her with more questions.

She pulled the sheet down with a groan. Who actually *did* such bizarre things? Secret ledgers and lifelong lies, mysteries and malice. Not normal people. Not sane people. Certainly not people with a shred of empathy, compassion and/or good judgment. Mental illness had been her mother's burden, but not Dad's. Not Lauren's. At no time in the past nearly twenty years since Mom died did either Dad or Lauren think, *hey, wait a minute, maybe it's a bad idea to keep lying to the girls. They deserve to know the truth, even if it reflects badly on us.*

Obviously Rosalind and her sisters were never supposed to find out. Obviously Mom and Dad thought they'd committed the perfect crime. Obviously as the years went on and the lie took firmer and firmer root, Mom and Dad, and then Dad and Lauren, had found it easier to let the falsehood flourish than have to yank it up by the roots.

Cowards, all of them.

She threw off the blankets and thudded over to the window. Another perfect, serene day, sunlight sparkling on the water, leaves fluttering cheerful hellos from their twigs. A pair of gulls flew past. A lobster boat slowed as the fisherman bent over to haul up his trap.

Today there should be howling winds and lashing waves. A full-throttle tropical storm.

You have your father's chin.

The memory dropped in for a surprise visit. Mom up here, sober and calm, taking hold of said chin and inspecting it proudly. Rosalind had gone into the living room and stared at her father's beard, touching her own smooth jaw, trying to figure out what her mother meant, until Dad told her either to say what was on her mind or stop bothering him when he was trying to work.

Hope rose. Maybe he was her father after all.

Her next thought sank it again. Mom had also said Rosalind had her mouth. Olivia had her figure. Eve had her height and her cheekbones.

Lies. Who knew how far back they went, how many more had been told?

Throat tight, she stepped back from the window and went around the room giving the other shades a sharp yank so they rolled open with a satisfying snap.

Downstairs, she toasted a piece of wholegrain bread and spread it with crunchy peanut butter and jelly, grabbed a banana and a peach from the fruit basket under the window, then made a cup of coffee dark enough to match her mood.

Out on the porch, she forced herself to eat, watching passing clouds turn trees on the bay's three islands from yellow-green to dark and back.

A hummingbird buzzed up to the screen to investigate her, wings a blur, silvery body jerking side to side. Her namesake.

Christmas Day, when Rosalind had been six or seven, flitting from one unwrapped present to another, unable to settle, Dad had called her a hummingbird. Curious, she had insisted on seeing a picture, and had gazed at the plate from Dad's well-thumbed book of eastern birds, entranced by the creature's beauty. The following summer, Mom had put up a hummingbird feeder and Rosalind had gotten her first live view. Look at her! All iridescent grace! She'd felt desperately sorry for her plodding, earthbound sisters.

And what a thud to the ground when she had overheard her father using the term in exasperation – *She can't stick with anything* – and a further thud when she'd started to notice her supposedly inferior sisters getting all the compliments from strangers and all the attention from boys.

'Hello, little guy.'

True to his nature, the hummingbird zoomed away, on to other things, maybe better, maybe just different. Stuck with this complicated and painful mess her parents had left, Rosalind envied him. It would be easy enough to finish packing the house and go back to New York, pick up her life again and tell herself nothing had changed. Nothing really had. Not yet. Unless she pursued this, nothing would.

Too late for that. Rosalind was unlike her sisters in other ways, too. For one, she couldn't decide facts didn't exist and then believe herself.

She finished breakfast with an hour to spare before the library opened. The Internet there would at least allow her to begin looking for Leila Allerton, whose payment dates in the ledger correlated with Rosalind's birth year. Unlikely that she'd find a way to connect her parents with whoever turned up owning that name, but at least it was a place to start, before she tackled Lauren.

Hyper from coffee and adrenaline, she did a speedy wash of the dishes and went into the living room, where she folded her arms and stared at the pile of unpacked boxes the way she imagined a teacher would stare at her most loathed pupils.

'You. Come here.' She dragged a victim toward her, ripped off the tape – a sound she was coming to hate – and unwrapped the tissue-paper bundle on top.

'Aww!' She broke into a wide smile. Here was the rest of the Heart Family's wonderful, uncomplicated world. The kids' school and playground set, the family's camper, the bicycle built for two with kid seats on the back. The grandparents – how could she have forgotten the grandparents? – the Disneyland Dumbo ride, and of course, the Heart's primary residence: The Loving Home.

She giggled, gazing at the flimsy blue plastic structure, open in front and at the sides, back walls hung with pastel wallpaper illustrated with cartoons of paintings, plants and furniture. When had she first gotten this doll empire? Birthday or Christmas? She remembered her mother's lips pursed in disapproval and her unresponsive body when Rosalind had thrown her arms around her in passionate gratitude: 'Don't thank me.'

Rosalind had instinctively looked to her father, the one the girls counted on when Mom wasn't making sense. He'd smiled and asked her a question about her brand-new family that had her scurrying back to unpack more treasures, the hurt forgotten.

Now it occurred to her that Mom might have been off her meds, and experiencing a bout of paranoia. She might have felt the perfect-family gift was a personal attack, a dig at her inability to conceive her own.

She retrieved the dolls she'd unpacked earlier and arranged Mommy and Daddy Heart opposite their children in the Loving Home living room.

'Kids, your mommy and I have something to tell you.'

'Okay, Daddy.' The adorable twins were all ears.

'We're not your real parents. Daddy bought you from other women, and we have lied about it all these years. Hahahaha!'

Mommy joined in because it was so very funny! 'Hahahaha!'

The kids did not find this amusing. How could Mommy and Daddy Heart be so cruel? What kind of Loving Home was this anyway? A big fat fake!

Rosalind sighed. Some lucky girl should have these dolls. She'd pack them up and donate them before she had Mommy downing pills and vodka, and gave Daddy a Heart attack.

After the dolls were put away, Rosalind showered, dressed and headed for the Blue Hill library. Besides researching the two names in the ledgers, she was curious whether the shock of her mother's infertility could have triggered or exacerbated her mental illness. She had heard of trauma setting off schizophrenia in people who might otherwise have remained healthy.

An hour later, Rosalind emerged from the pretty brick building on Main Street and stood on the front steps trying to decide her next move. She found it inconceivable that the world looked the same as always, that people were still going about their business normally, because she felt like an astronaut sent out on a space walk without a tether.

At the library's computer, she'd confirmed that bipolar disorder could be brought on or worsened by shock or trauma, but that people and conditions varied so widely, Rosalind could never be sure what impact the diagnosis had on her mother.

She'd also learned that Google could find way too many people named Helen Phillips, the woman she'd picked out as Eve's birth mother, but only three named Leila Allerton. One nurse in Waco, Texas, one retired social studies teacher in Spokane, Washington, and one opera singer in Princeton, New Jersey, home of Daniel Braddock's alma mater.

At least Rosalind had places to start. If she got desperate, she could hire a private investigator, but that would be a very last resort. The fewer people who discovered the truth about Jillian Croft's past, the better. The public furor over her unexpected death, the speculation that she'd committed suicide, the fans who still wrote pleading for pictures, interviews, facts about her life, the occasional weird phone call that would make one of the family have to change his or her number *again* . . . it was a miracle the press had only camped outside Pine Ridge for two days after Dad's stroke. But then, in spite of his illustrious career as a drama coach and teacher, Daniel Braddock was famous mostly through his late wife.

Someone came out of the library behind her, forcing Rosalind to move aside. She was still sick at the thought of having to confront her stepmother again, but if Lauren could confirm Rosalind's theory about the names in the ledgers, and point her toward which Leila Allerton could be her birth mother, Rosalind would take the investigation from there.

Lauren met her again at the Pine Ridge café, clearly apprehensive. The nervous flush already colored her skin as she crossed the red-carpeted corridor between the booths and the cafeteria-style serving counter, and pulled out the chair opposite Rosalind. 'What is this about?'

Nice to see you too. 'How's Dad today?'

'Same.' She looked toward her right. 'What's going on, Rosalind?'

'I had a few questions about things I found at the house.' Rosalind pushed over one of the coffees she'd bought, keeping her voice breezy, as if she were about to ask if her stepmother had her heart set on a recently unearthed stapler.

'Oh.' Lauren's shoulders relaxed, but her hands stayed tightly clasped on the table. 'What things?'

'Payment ledgers.'

Lauren's head snapped straight again. 'Payment—'

'Who are Leila Allerton and Helen Phillips?' She watched Lauren's features contort, feeling utterly sick. This was a monstrous thing to do.

'I don't know them.'

'Their names are obviously familiar.'

'Rosalind . . .' Lauren looked away again, lips tightening.

'Was Leila Allerton my birth mother? Was Helen Phillips Eve's? Do you know whose the crossed-out name was? Was she Olivia's—'

'*No.*' She lifted a trembling hand to her throat. 'I won't do this, Rosalind. I can't.'

'Please.'

She shook her head in quick jerks, pale eyes wide and distorted behind her thick lenses. 'This is not a subject I can discuss.'

'You have to understand how difficult this is.' Rosalind tried to speak reasonably, when really she wanted to shout and shake her stepmother until the information came out. 'I was raised by a mother who died eighteen years ago. Then you took over, mother number two. Now there might be a third in the picture, even if she and I were in contact not much longer than nine months. Don't you think I deserve to know who that is?'

'Your father is the one to—'

'My father is out of commission for who knows how long. You were right that this could upset him, maybe dangerously. You're all I have, Lauren.' Her voice cracked, an effect worthy of actress Olivia, except that her distress was genuine. 'Obviously you know something.'

'It's not my place.' Lauren stood, bumping the table, making coffee slosh over the rim of her cup. 'It's not my place, Rosalind. You're over the line here.'

'*Please.*' Rosalind rose and grabbed her stepmother's sleeve, afraid she *would* start shaking her. 'At least tell me about Leila Allerton. At least tell me what town she lives in. You don't have to tell me anything else. Please. Spare me having to hire a private detective, who'd probably turn up things no one wanted him to know, including me.'

'You can't do that.'

'Actually, I can. There's nothing to stop me.' She had never spoken to her stepmother like this. Calm, in-your-face-rebellion was Eve's forte. Olivia's was shrieking. Rosalind, typical middle child, always tried to smooth conflict away. 'I deserve to know, Lauren. This is information basic to who I am.'

'You were fine without it. For decades.'

'And that makes it okay?' Rosalind's voice rose; she made

an effort to keep it under control. 'Let's sit. Please.'

She sat back down, praying Lauren would join her again, that they could talk this out without her stepmother fleeing back upstairs.

To her immense relief, Lauren grudgingly lowered herself into the chair. 'I can't tell you anything.'

'Why not?' When she didn't answer, Rosalind leaned forward, anger giving her the courage to stare right into Lauren's eyes. 'I was lied to, first by the two people I trusted most, and then by you. Now I'm in the position of having to hire a stranger to find the truth my own family still won't tell me. A truth that if this stranger turned out to be the information-selling type, the media would be willing to pay him plenty for. More even than I could afford for his silence.'

'You wouldn't do that.'

'I absolutely will if I have to.'

'Rosalind.' Lauren covered her face with her hands. 'Don't ask me this.'

'Too late. I have. You need to help me.'

Lauren's shoulders hunched. For a second, Rosalind was terrified she was having some kind of health crisis, and was on the verge of standing to investigate when Lauren brought her hands slowly down to meet in a prayer position under her chin. 'Do your sisters know?'

The question made Rosalind flinch. As much as she wanted this information, a stupid part of her had obviously still hoped she was wrong, that this was all an easily explained misunderstanding. 'Both of them saw the paper that said Mom had complete androge—'

'Shh.' Lauren darted glances at the tables around them, most empty.

'That's all Olivia and Eve know. They didn't see the ledgers, and I haven't told them. Right now, this is just for me.' Rosalind had to force the words out of her throat. 'I need a town. A state. Somewhere to start so I don't go knocking on doors asking women if Daniel Braddock hired them to—'

'*Shh*.' Lauren glanced behind them again. 'I promised him, Rosalind. I gave my husband my sacred word that I would never, ever tell anyone. You don't know what this cost him. What it *would* cost him.'

Rosalind's rage deflated. The last stupid spark of hope faded and went out. This was no longer even possibly a ludicrous idea from the depths of her overactive imagination. Her father had bought his three daughters from strangers, for some reason choosing to pay their mothers in installments over time. For their silence? For their upkeep?

She waited, throat cramping with the effort not to cry, not wanting to push too hard, but also terrified she hadn't pushed hard enough. 'Please.'

Lauren pulled a lace-bordered handkerchief out of the pocket of her beige pants, dabbed her eyes and blew her nose. 'Try New Jersey. Princeton. But please, dear God, be careful.'

Princeton. The opera singer, a performer like Mom. A woman who was living proof that the glamorous, complicated Jillian Croft, adored mother for Rosalind's first sixteen years of life, had not given birth to her. Rosalind shared more genes and traits with the total stranger smiling online from a publicity shot than with the woman who'd raised her, a woman she had known intimately by sight, sound and smell.

'Why didn't they tell us?'

'Why do you *think*?' Lauren stood and stared down at her with pity. 'They didn't want you to know.'

'But that's sick. And it's wrong.' She stood and moved toward her stepmother, lowering her voice when she intercepted a concerned glance from a staff member serving the table next to them. 'They lied to us. Both of them. About where we came from. About who we *are*. About who *they* are.'

'Daniel will always be your father. He'll always be Eve's father, and he will always be Olivia's father. I need to get back to him now.'

'I know that. But you—'

'Never talk to me about this again, Rosalind. I mean it. You'll get nothing else from me. Nothing. No matter what you threaten.' Lauren was trembling, her breath coming in little gasps. 'This has devastated me. I gave Daniel my word, my promise, and now that means nothing. Mark my words, you are not the only one who suffered over this.'

She walked away, leaving her untouched cup of coffee sitting in a spilled puddle on the table. Rosalind watched her go, wanting to put her head down and sob. She'd made a terrible and painful mess of a mess already so terrible and painful she wouldn't have thought it possible to do worse.

There was no going back to speculation, no way to secretly assure herself deep down that this wasn't really happening, no way ever again to look at the discovery as an intriguing mystery. And though none of the past had changed or could ever change, there was no way to view her childhood the same way either.

She could only go forward in trying to redefine and reclaim her sense of family, decide whether or not to track down this beautiful stranger in New Jersey, who might be as reluctant as Lauren to discuss what she'd done or what she knew.

But who also might be the missing piece from a puzzle Rosalind hadn't even known existed.

Chapter 5

May 14, 1967 (Sunday)

Guys and Dolls *ended today, with the matinee. It was the greatest, most amazing experience of my entire life. Someone told me I was as good as Jean Simmons, who played Sarah in the movie. Everyone applauded so long and loud when I came out for my bow, it was the greatest, most incredible high. I didn't ever want it to stop.*

I drank vodka at the cast party at Debbie Binger's house Saturday night. Ben Jacobs, my Sky Masterson, asked me to go outside with him, and I did! He kissed me and we made out. He is so cute! He said I had the best chest in the whole school. I wouldn't let him put his hand down my pants, though. He'd find out I don't have hair yet.

I hate writing that sentence. Why don't I? Why don't I? Is it the cancer?

Today after the matinee was over, I cried all the way home, because it might be my last show ever. All Mom did was tell me to get hold of myself. She doesn't care that I might die of cancer. I couldn't stop crying, even in bed, and Christina made some crack about how yeah, I'm a drama queen all right. Sometimes I want to hurt myself. Sometimes I want to hurt other people.

I think I might be going crazy.

* * *

Rosalind let herself out of the front door of her new temporary housing in Princeton, New Jersey, a pretty white colonial on Laurel Road, which happened to be across and down the street from a house owned by Zaina Allerton. Zaina Allerton happened to be the mother of Leila Allerton. Leila Allerton might very likely happen to be the mother of Rosalind Braddock.

After that difficult café-table conversation with Lauren back in August, Rosalind had discovered Leila's address ridiculously easily – two minutes searching Whitepages.com. Further research – another three minutes reading Leila's Wikipedia article – turned up that she was a USC Thornton School-educated mezzo-soprano who performed with opera companies around the country. Ten minutes of targeted googling revealed that Leila lived with her mother, a widow of Lebanese origins, and that she had a daughter, Caitlin, six years younger than Rosalind, who was engaged to Princeton alumnus Emil Christopher.

Those fifteen minutes had gained her a third mother, a third sister and a third grandmother. Rosalind had walked out of the library exhilarated and terrified. Half of her had wanted to take the next flight to Newark. The other half recognized that she probably needed more time to adjust emotionally, and that she'd be a lot more at peace trying to get to know a new family if the job organizing and selling the property in Maine was completed first.

She'd finished work on the Candlewood Point house as fast as possible, aided one more time by Eve over Labor Day weekend, until the place was empty, all the furniture and possessions Dad and Lauren didn't want at Pine Ridge sold, absorbed by the sisters into their own homes or put into storage. Rosalind hadn't told Eve about the ledgers. She wanted to wait until she had more to go on.

Back in New York, having tearfully turned the keys over to

the delighted Maine real estate agent – a house owned by Jillian Croft could be priced through its own roof – and with September well underway, Rosalind had begun to formulate her next move.

The first plan had been to travel to Princeton, knock on the Allertons' door, announce herself and see what happened. Luckily she'd saved herself from that idiocy. Far better would be to establish a relationship with the family gradually. To that end, she'd scoured real estate rental listings in Princeton, and stumbled over this miracle situation down the street – a family had to move suddenly for a job and was – eventually – willing to rent the house to her for two months or until it sold, whichever came later.

All she had to do now, on this crisp and beautiful first day of October, was walk across the street, knock on the door and introduce herself as a new neighbor. The only way Rosalind had decided she could stomach going through with this was not to lie unless it was absolutely necessary, but also not to volunteer information about herself or her family unless someone asked. Or until it became ridiculous not to bring up her real reason for being there. Or until something completely different happened that she had no way of anticipating. To put it mildly, she was new at this business of confronting previously unknown parents.

One foot in front of the other, across the street, the lawn, under an enormous oak and a maple that would probably start turning color in a week or so, across the Allerton driveway, and up the path to their front door, past rhododendrons and azaleas waiting for spring, and asters, chrysanthemums and ornamental kale adding color now. The garden, like most Rosalind had seen around Princeton, was impeccably kept.

She climbed the last step to the door, adjusting her relatively tame outfit – purple leggings and tunic with a riotously flowered puffy scarf – trying to be completely in the moment, to take in her surroundings, the swish of Route 206 traffic a few streets away, the soft fall-smelling air, the breeze touching her cheek. It was very possible her life would never be the same again after she rang this doorbell. The moment deserved a pause to recognize its importance.

Her fingers, when she reached out, were trembling.

Before she could make contact, the door swung open, revealing a beautiful older woman, probably late seventies or early eighties, about Rosalind's height, with dark eyes and impeccably styled white hair, breathing as if she'd run to answer the summons of the doorbell Rosalind hadn't pressed yet.

Rosalind caught her breath. 'Hi.'

'Hello, hello. You're early, come on in. Caitlin isn't home yet. I'm Zaina.' She spoke in a rich, musical voice, her English so impeccably pronounced it gave her away as foreign.

This was Rosalind's grandmother.

Maybe.

Rosalind blinked. 'No, I'm not . . . her.'

'Her?'

'Whoever you're expecting.'

'You're not Angela? Caitlin's florist friend?'

'I'm Rosalind.' She waited a beat to see if Zaina would stagger back from the shock of hearing her name, which she didn't. 'I'm renting across the street for a few months, the Gardners' house. I thought I'd come over and introduce myself.'

'Ah, I'm sorry, my mistake. It's nice to meet you.' Zaina extended her hand, which Rosalind took, trying not to gawk too obviously. The older woman had faintly olive skin and hooded eyes ringed by the dark circles that often went with that complexion. On her full lips, a deep rose lipstick, her only makeup. 'Where did the Gardners go?'

'The husband got a job offer in San Francisco.' Rosalind

71

wouldn't mention that she'd practically had to threaten the realtor, who initially refused even to suggest the arrangement to the Gardners, and had agreed to pay an exorbitant rent. She prided herself on living modestly for the most part, but couldn't deny that having ridiculous amounts of money came in very handy at certain times. Jillian Croft had split her considerable fortune equally between her daughters. If Dad had objected to being left out, he'd never showed the slightest sign, most likely because he came from plenty of money himself.

'I see. Well, come in, come in.' Zaina gestured impatiently, as if Rosalind was stalling after several earlier invitations. 'Come have some coffee.'

'Thank you.' Throat dry, Rosalind stepped past her into a house that smelled vaguely of orange blossoms, hardly able to believe that her best possible outcome had happened – the worst being a door slammed in her face.

'I was making ma'amoul, you know those cookies?'

'No, I don't.'

'They're Lebanese, like me.' She put a hand to her ample chest. 'Fantastic. You must try some. You will love them.'

Rosalind followed her into the house, an exotic mix of colors and styles, floor surfaces covered throughout by richly hued Oriental rugs. A peek into the living room showed a deep burgundy sofa, green love seat and cream armchairs decorated with colorful, intricately embroidered pillows. An etched brass tray became a table by squatting on carved wooden legs. Plants spilled from pots on the windowsill.

Around the corner, she stepped into the kitchen, done in bumblebee colors, deep yellow walls, light cream cabinets and black countertops and appliances. A tray of ripening pears and persimmons sat on the counter next to a bowl of sesame candies wrapped in cellophane. Black chairs with yellow cushions were pulled up to one side of an island on which were cooling beautifully patterned domed cookies next to a box of powdered sugar and a sifter.

A home with a warm, comforting personality. Rosalind would have loved to grow up here.

'I like coffee strong. Is that okay with you?' Zaina gestured to one of the chairs at the island. 'Sit down, sit down.'

'Yes, I like it that way too.' Rosalind sat, trying not to grin like a fool. So many times she'd gone over what this first contact might be like. Never had she imagined it this warm and sweet-smelling.

Zaina filled a bright red kettle with water and put it on the stove to heat. 'What brings you to Princeton?'

'I needed a break from the city.'

'New York? I assume New York; around here "city" can mean nothing else.' She measured whole beans into the grinder. Enough for several cups.

'Yes. I like to explore new places, try living in different parts of the country.'

'Really.' Zaina glanced over from the stove. 'I can think of nothing worse. Wait now, I'm going to grind.'

Rosalind waited until the noise had subsided. 'My dad calls me a hummingbird. Never too long in one place.'

'A nomad, eh? You can't put down roots that way.' Zaina dumped the grounds into a coffee filter. 'What do you do that you relocate so often?'

'A lot of things.' Rosalind fidgeted on the stool. 'I paint, I design clothing, I work at a coffee shop part-time . . .'

'Ah.' Zaina's tone made it clear Rosalind had a long way to go before her career was worth discussing further.

She was used to that.

'Your home is lovely.' She gestured around the kitchen and

out toward the living room. 'How long have you lived here?'

'Oh my goodness.' Zaina crossed over to the powdered sugar box and lifted the flaps, transferred a couple of heaping tablespoons into the sifter. 'A long time, almost sixty years.'

'Princeton's a beautiful town.'

'Yes.' She picked up the sifter and turned the crank. Sugar snowed on to the perfect gold hue of the cookies. 'A nice place to raise children. Only an hour to New York or Philadelphia and a lot going on. But it's changed so much. So crowded! So expensive! It used to be a sleepy college town. Now it's jammed with people, and the stores are all so fancy. You can't even buy a pair of sheets downtown; you have to go to the malls. Those have exploded too. There used to be just one, Quaker Bridge, out on Route One. Now there are about a thousand. Malls and housing developments and corporate headquarters all around where there was just forest and farmland.'

'That must be hard.' Rosalind put her elbows on the island and leaned toward her possible grandmother, wanting to sit there all morning and listen to the musical, vaguely foreign sound of her voice, watch her comfortable and economical movements around a kitchen where she was clearly at home and in charge. This was a real grandmotherly grandmother, the stuff of children's stories, slightly plump, welcoming and smelling of cookies.

'It's a big change.' Zaina put down the sifter and shuffled over to answer the tea kettle's whistled summons, then poured boiling water into the French press. 'I'm lucky I was able to be here when the town was unspoiled and uncrowded. The old Princeton.'

'How many children did you raise here?' Rosalind made herself look politely interested, so she wouldn't betray how starved she was for information on the woman who might be her birth mother.

'One daughter. Leila. She'll be back soon with my grand-daughter, Caitlin.' Zaina walked over to a cabinet, where she got out a small plate. 'You have brothers and sisters?'

'I have two sisters.' She'd been prepared to hear Leila's name, but the syllables still shot her with adrenaline, much more real coming from Zaina's lips than written on a ledger or viewed on a computer screen. 'Can I help?'

Zaina put the plate in front of her, white china with a multicolored floral border. 'You can put a few cookies on the plate. Thank you.'

'Sure.' Rosalind formed two concentric circles with cookies while Zaina wiped off the sugar-dusted counter and put away the sifter.

'Here we go.' Zaina brought over two mugs and the French press, breathing hard again. 'Have you ever had Lebanese coffee?'

'I don't think so.'

'I'll make you that sometime. Najjar is the best. It's thick and dark. Puts hair on your chest.' She laughed and settled on the chair at the end of the island, as if standing had exhausted her. A stab of alarm went through Rosalind. Was she asthmatic? Ill? 'My sister used to read fortunes in the grounds. You finish drinking until there's only sludge in the bottom, turn the cup over for a minute or so, then back up. The shapes formed inside suggest your future. Of course it's all nonsense, but good fun. Samia had a great imagination. She never let on she was making it all up. Oh, she told such stories.'

'Is she still in Lebanon?'

Zaina gave a quick shake of her head, closing her eyes briefly. 'She is with God.'

'I'm sorry.'

'Don't be sorry. We all die. It was her time. Have a cookie.' She lifted the plate toward Rosalind. 'These are filled with walnuts, flavored with orange blossom and rose waters. My grandmother's recipe. I also make them stuffed with dates.'

The rich pastry crumbled in Rosalind's mouth, giving way to a heavenly flavor of perfumed nuts. Exotic and addictive. 'These are amazing.'

'Yes. They are.' Zaina chuckled, depressing the plunger on the French press, and poured out two cups. 'The date ones are my favorite. We'll have to make you a Lebanese dinner. A feast.'

'That would be so wonderful.' Zaina had no idea how wonderful. Rosalind had spent less than an hour in this house, and already her maybe-grandmother was treating her as part of the family, without realizing that she probably was.

Daniel Braddock was the child of older parents, both dead by the time Rosalind came along. Her mother's parents, Betty and Arnold Moore, lived in a tiny house in a tiny town, Jackman, Maine, about a hundred miles west of Millinocket, nearly to the border with Canada's Quebec province. They were severe, taciturn, and clearly bewildered as to how their daughter Sylvia had turned into Jillian Croft, the toast of Hollywood. On every visit, Rosalind's mom brought gifts she thought her parents would need or like – clothes, kitchen appliances, furniture, decorative art. None of them were ever seen again. Dinners were brief and awkward – food appeared on the table, they ate it, boom, done. Every invitation to visit California was refused, though several times Grandma and Grandpa did make the three-hour trip to the summer house on Candlewood Point, visits that made their departure like the release from holding one's breath. After Jillian's death, the girls had kept in polite contact – birthdays, holidays, occasional phone calls – but hadn't visited more than a few times.

To discover that all along Rosalind had – might have had – a fantasy grandmother like Zaina made her ache for what she'd missed. Stories read to her sitting on Zaina's lap. Treats snuck out from under her apron when Mom wasn't looking. Feasts to celebrate meeting a new neighbor who'd only be there for a short time.

Zaina pushed a mug over to Rosalind and lifted hers in a toast. 'Cheers and welcome to the neighborhood.'

'Thank you.' The coffee was even stronger than Rosalind made it. 'Did you grow up in Lebanon? Your English is excellent.'

'I did, yes. Have another cookie.' She looked so pleased when Rosalind reached for another, Rosalind couldn't regret the calories. 'Everyone in Lebanon learns English and French. Or they did in my time.'

'When did you come over?'

'In 1961. I graduated from AUB, the American University of Beirut, where I met a very handsome American named Cecil Allerton. I came here with him when he was accepted to Princeton's PhD program in archeology. He died in 1975. Cancer.'

'I'm sorry.'

'No, don't be sorry.' She winked mischievously. 'Everybody dies. It was just his time.'

Rosalind laughed. 'You know, I've heard that somewhere before.'

'Ah, here they are. My daughter and granddaughter.' Zaina's eyes drifted to the kitchen window at the same time Rosalind heard a car door close, then voices and footsteps. Her heart started pounding. She stood involuntarily, still clutching her cup of coffee.

The back door opened. Zaina turned expectantly.

First into the kitchen, carrying a paper grocery bag, was a young woman who must be Caitlin, blond and beautiful in a cheerleader way, a Reese Witherspoon type. Thick, professionally highlighted hair, subtle makeup and flawless skin, she was the kind of woman who made Rosalind feel clumsy, heavy and hideous, the same envy and exasperation she felt around Olivia and Eve.

Rosalind Braddock, doomed to a lifetime of supermodel sisters.

Behind Caitlin, bringing with her a cloud of fresh fall air, or so it seemed, was Leila, very like her picture, but so much more alive. Rosalind noticed the hair first, restrained in her photo, now loose, tight chestnut waves having their way with the space around her head before drifting past her shoulders. Then the eyes, deep brown like Rosalind's own, not as dark as Zaina's, filled with laughter and warmth. After that, the way she moved, quick, light steps, following her daughter's sensible stride, not setting her bag gently on the counter but letting it go, trusting its fall, then turning to face the room.

Having seen her picture online, knowing they shared few physical traits beyond coloring, Rosalind had still hoped she'd recognize Leila instinctively, that she'd connect, on a bone-deep level, to the essence of herself in another generation.

Nope. She was drawn to this beautiful, seemingly carefree person as she would be to any attractive stranger.

'How was it?' Zaina asked.

'Terrible.' Caitlin glanced at Rosalind. 'We couldn't find a single decent place that was free on the date we were hoping for.'

'We were *quite* picky, though. We'll find something.' Leila took off her jacket, warm brown suede that draped fashionably around her slender body, then unwound a scarf printed in strong fall colors, looking directly at Rosalind. 'Hello, I'm Leila.'

Rosalind nodded, flustered and blushing, annoyed at herself for being so unprepared, after weeks dreaming and fantasizing about meeting this woman.

'This is Rosalind. She's renting the Gardners' place. Rosalind, my daughter Leila and my granddaughter Caitlin.'

'Hi, Rosalind, welcome to Princeton.' Leila's voice was smooth, musical like her mother's, but more focused, accustomed to projecting from a stage. Her gaze was a force to be reckoned with. 'Do you know how to plan a wedding?'

'Oh . . .' Rosalind gave a nervous blast of laughter, too loud in the small kitchen. 'I could try.'

'Good. We're all set.'

'*Mom.*' Caitlin appeared from behind the left-hand door of the enormous side-by-side refrigerator where she'd been putting away groceries. 'She's kidding, Rosalind.'

'I am kidding. Mostly.' Leila pulled her hair back into a ponytail, then let it go. 'Not yet desperate enough to recruit strangers, anyway.'

'We're going to be fine,' Caitlin said. 'As soon as we find a place. Speaking of which, Judy's friend Angela texted me, the flower lady.'

'She never showed up.' Zaina frowned. 'I was having so much fun chatting with Rosalind, I forgot to notice.'

'She's swamped. We'll reschedule.'

'Caitlin was going to be married next year.' Zaina smiled affectionately at her granddaughter. 'But then I found out I'm dying.'

Rosalind couldn't help gasping.

'Jeez, Teta, I wish you wouldn't freak people out like that.' Caitlin sent her grandmother a scolding look. 'Sorry, Rosalind.'

'What's the problem?' Zaina looked genuinely confused. 'Everyone dies. This is just—'

'I know, just your time.' Leila gave her mother a brief hug. 'It's wonderful that you're at peace with it, Mama. You have to give us more leeway. We're still adjusting.'

'I'm so sorry.' Rosalind's throat thickened. She was furious with herself for not running right down here in August, screw the house, screw everything. She'd been blessed with the perfect grandmother and now she was going to lose her.

'I found out a couple of weeks ago that I have entered stage three heart disease.' Zaina sipped coffee as if she were discussing the weather. 'The doctor said I'd have anywhere from a few weeks to a few months left. I want to see Caitlin married to this young man of hers before I join my husband.'

'So instead of a year, we're trying to plan a wedding in a month.' Caitlin widened her eyes and mouth in mock panic, carefully smoothing the creases of the grocery bag she was folding. 'Which is why we're a little crazed right now.'

'This may be out of line, but . . . I'm not working while I'm here.' Rosalind tried not to sound too eager. Helping plan this wedding would put her in regular contact with the family. She wouldn't have to be one of those annoying neighbors who kept dropping by. 'I make most of my own clothes, I can draw and paint. I worked as a decorator for a while, and a hairdresser, and for a catering company. Plus I know the names of two excellent affordable champagnes.'

The three women blinked at her.

'You're hired,' Leila said.

'*Mom.*' Caitlin laughed uncomfortably. 'She doesn't want to help plan my wedding. She doesn't even know us.'

Zaina was laughing. 'Forgive my daughter, Rosalind. She gets right down to business.'

'Actually . . .' Rosalind gestured with her cup. 'I'm happy to help if it's okay with everyone. I wasn't sure what I'd do while I was here. My life is in New York. I just knew I needed to get out for a while.'

'If you can sew, you can fix my dress.' Zaina beamed at her.

Caitlin shook her head, lips pressed together. 'You're not wearing that dress, Teta.'

'Of course I'm wearing that dress. It's the perfect dress. I wore it to every wedding, and every wedding I've been to, the happy couple is still a happy couple. I'm wearing it to yours.'

'Mama.' Leila spoke gently, exchanging glances with her daughter. 'It's a thousand years old and shows it.'

'I could take a look,' Rosalind offered. 'If you tell me whether your name is Zaina or Teta.'

'Ah.' Zaina raised her brows. 'Understandable confusion. "Teta" is Arabic for grandmother. Zaina is my given name.'

'Then I will definitely look at the dress.'

'Trust me, you can't fix it,' Caitlin said. 'It's a ruin.'

Zaina leaned in to whisper to Rosalind. 'Tomorrow you can sneak over and we'll have a look together.'

'I'm standing right here, Teta,' Caitlin said.

Zaina smiled affectionately at her granddaughter. 'I'm dying. I get to do whatever I want.'

'You're getting a lot of mileage out of that one.' Leila came up behind her mother and looped her arms around her neck.

'I'm going to milk it like a dairy girl.' Zaina pulled Leila's forearms more tightly around her, and her expression lost its cheerful warmth for the first time that afternoon. Leila leaned down and pressed her cheek against her mother's. Rosalind had to look down to keep from misting up.

'We found baby artichokes at Wegman's.' Leila pulled away and headed for the refrigerator. 'To roast with the chicken.'

'My favorite.' Zaina patted Rosalind's hand. 'You must stay for dinner. Leila is a fabulous cook.'

'She's not kidding.' Leila winked at Rosalind. 'I'm a miracle.'

'Everything she does well she learned from me. Except singing. God taught her that.'

'Good teachers helped.' Leila bent to open the vegetable bin, waves of hair shifting over her back.

'You must come. Caitlin's fiancé, Emil, will be here, and his friend Bryn.'

'Bryn's coming?' Caitlin's smile was wide and immediate – her mother's smile. 'I didn't know that.'

'Bryn is a sculptor. A brilliant man, kind and polite, also very handsome. Thirty-two years old and never married.' Zaina lifted an eyebrow. 'Are you single, Rosalind?'

'Stop, Mama.' Leila rolled her eyes. 'Rosalind, she'll try to match you up with every straight male in Princeton.'

'I am single, yes.'

'Then it's settled. You'll eat with us.'

'You should.' Leila poured herself a cup of coffee. 'A welcome to the neighborhood.'

'Lebanese can't help inviting people to dinner.' Caitlin glanced over her shoulder at Rosalind from where she was refilling the kettle at the sink. 'It's genetic, this urge to feed people.'

'To feed people way too much.' Leila came around the island and settled into the seat next to Rosalind. This close, though her energy and lively gaze projected eternal youth, Rosalind could see the lines around her eyes and mouth, a loosening of the skin at her throat. 'Where did you grow up, Rosalind?'

'Los Angeles.'

'Oh, no kidding.' She laughed in delight. It was hard not to laugh with her, even though nothing seemed funny. 'I *love* that town. I went to the USC Music School, so I know it fairly well. Where in Los Angeles?'

'I grew up in Beverly Hills.'

'Ooh, *Beverly Hills 90210*.' Caitlin turned on the stove under the red kettle. 'I was madly in love with Jason Priestley. He wasn't in your class, was he?'

Rosalind pretended to consider. 'Not that I noticed.'

'What did your parents do that you got to live in Beverly Hills?' Leila asked.

And there it was. Rosalind had prepared herself for this moment so many times, had practiced the offhand tone she'd use, had imagined how strong and resolute she'd be about not showing her distress.

The reality made that nearly impossible.

'I . . . My mother . . . was an actress. My dad was a teacher. Acting teacher.'

'Really.' Leila turned abruptly, so close her hair brushed Rosalind's arm. 'What's your last name?'

She had to work so hard to break through the tense block in her throat that she ended up practically shouting. 'Braddock.'

'Good God.' Leila swallowed and looked down at her coffee. 'Braddock.'

'Braddock as in *Daniel* Braddock? Oh my God!' Caitlin's mouth dropped open at Rosalind's nod. 'Mom! Your hero.'

'Yes.' The word was barely audible.

Caitlin gasped. 'Wait. That means your mother was *Jillian Croft*!'

'This is incredible.' Zaina's eyes were open nearly as wide as Caitlin's mouth. 'Right here in our kitchen.'

'Amazing.' Leila laughed, not taking her eyes off her coffee. 'Your mother was lovely, and so talented. And I was a huge fan of your father's, Rosalind. I still am. He was a deep, important inspiration to me, and to many young actresses. I was sorry to read about his stroke over the summer.'

'He's recovering, thank you.' Rosalind had to hold herself rigid so her trembling wouldn't show. 'Did you ever meet my parents?'

'I did.' Leila lifted her head and looked Rosalind straight in the eyes, hers crinkling into a smile. 'At a bookstore in Santa Monica. I waited in line for hours. Your dad was signing one of his books.'

'You *met* him?' Caitlin's shock practically lifted her off the floor. 'You never told me that. Why didn't you ever tell me that?'

Leila shrugged, knuckles white around her coffee mug. 'I don't know. It was sort of unreal, and very special meeting someone who had such a big influence on my art. I guess I felt talking about it would make it ordinary somehow. So many of us were there that day. I was just one of them. Maybe that's ridiculous.'

'Totally ridiculous,' Caitlin said.

'Well, that was my over-romanticized reaction at the time.' Leila put down her coffee and stood resolutely. 'Back to work. We need to get that florist pinned down and research more locations. Rosalind, we eat around seven thirty. Why don't you come back around six thirty? Emil and Bryn will be here and we'll have drinks and get to know one another. Okay?'

'Yes.' Rosalind got to her feet, terrified her knees wouldn't hold her. 'Sure. Can I bring anything?'

'Oh . . .' Leila glanced at her mother's picture-perfect cookies. 'You want to freeze the ma'amoul for Christmas, right, Mama?'

'Yes. For Christmas.' Zaina touched the edge of the plate. Silence hung. It hit Rosalind that no one knew if Zaina would still be around in three months. It didn't seem possible. Except for the shortness of breath, she seemed vital, robust and full of humor.

'Dessert would be super, I hadn't planned anything. Thank you, Rosalind. We'll talk more tonight, okay?' Leila turned to her daughter. 'First let's see if we can trim the guest list to a more manageable size.'

'Oh, no problem,' Caitlin said sweetly. 'We can cut all your friends.'

'Ha . . . ha . . .'

'Bye, Rosalind.' Caitlin gave her a little wave. 'Nice to meet you. See you later.'

'Yes.' She stepped away from the black-topped island, grateful for the chance to escape and regain control of her emotions and perspective. 'Nice meeting all of you. Thank you for the coffee, Zaina.'

'You're welcome.' Zaina pushed herself to standing. 'I'm off to take a nap.'

'Need help with the stairs, Mama?'

'I'll use the back bedroom. Very comfortable.'

Rosalind walked to the hall, aware after a few steps that someone was behind her. She turned at the front door.

'Thanks for stopping by.' Leila reached past her to open it. 'See you tonight, Rosalind.'

'Yes. Thanks again for inviting me.' Rosalind hesitated, trying to smile blandly as she watched Leila's expression, hoping to see something that would give away the truth of their relationship.

But Leila's beautiful face wore a calm, serene smile as she waved, a smile that didn't slip once as she turned, closing the door behind her.

Chapter 6

June 25, 1967 (Sunday)

I had the surgery last week. It still hurts, but not so bad as before. They said there was no cancer yet. Before the operation they had me stand against a wall and took pictures of me naked. That was so horrible. I stood there, freezing and trying very hard not to cry, but I couldn't help it. I was so scared, and so embarrassed. I tried to remember some of Sarah Brown's lines from Guys and Dolls, *tried to sing her songs in my head, but it was still so humiliating. I asked the bitch nurse why they were doing that to me, and she said the doctor ordered the pictures, and that was all she would tell me. Is that normal before surgery? I don't understand. It made me feel like a circus freak.*

It's so good I didn't have cancer. I can still do everything I wanted to. But where is my period? I'll be seventeen in four months. Seventeen! What is wrong with me and why won't anyone tell me? Mom just says there's nothing to worry about, and we don't have to talk about me all the time. I hate her, I hate myself more.

My body has changed in most ways like it's supposed to. I look like a woman. I have boobs and hips.

But I'm not a woman unless I get my period.

So if I never get my period, and I'm not a woman, what am I?

* * *

Rosalind stood again in front of Zaina, Leila and Caitlin's house, balancing a still-warm apple pie in her left hand. In her right dangled a shopping bag containing vanilla and cinnamon ice creams, plus a box of chocolate mints, all purchased from Thomas Sweet, a fat and sugar paradise in Princeton's Palmer Square. She would have to avoid the place while she was here unless she wanted to blow up like a sumo wrestler. She'd also brought a creamy wedge of extra-sharp Vermont Cheddar purchased from Bon Appetit, a store in the Princeton Shopping Center crammed so full of gourmet deliciousness that she had trouble leaving. Stuck in next to the ice cream, chocolates and cheese in her bag was a bouquet of spray roses in a cheerful mix of colors.

She was out to please. Tonight would be an important next step in cementing what she felt had been a positive first impression. Eventually she wanted to get to the point where it felt natural to get Leila alone and imitate the baby bird in P. D. Eastman's book: *Are You My Mother?*

Shopping bag swinging from her arm, she reached for the bell, only slightly less nervous than she'd been earlier that day.

The door was opened by a tall, strikingly handsome blond man, about Rosalind's age. She immediately recognized Emil Christopher from the online picture in his and Caitlin's *New York Times* engagement announcement. He was the type of gorgeous that tended to become irritating – the personality could never live up to the perfection of the features. Blue eyes, smooth skin, strong jaw, classic nose tending toward sharp. The kind of California-beautiful guy who was all over the Beverly Hills school system, none of whom ever gave Rosalind a second look. His type was genetically programmed to go for women like Olivia and Eve. And, obviously, Caitlin.

None of which objective and sensible judgments stopped Rosalind from feeling a deep, zigzagging shock of attraction.

'Hey, you must be Rosalind. I'm Emil, Caitlin's fiancé. Let me take those for you.' He reached for the pie and bag without waiting for her response. 'Mm, that looks excellent. Did you make it?'

'I did.'

'A work of art.' He grinned at her too long, perfectly casual in just-worn-enough jeans and a teal polo shirt. Rosalind dropped her eyes, annoyed at herself. Getting flustered would only validate his conviction that he was irresistible. 'Come on in, Rosalind.'

'Thanks.' She followed him toward the kitchen, inhaling its beckoning fragrances. 'Something smells amazing.'

'This house always smells amazing. Leila and Zaina are fabulous cooks. Hey, everyone, look who's here. Complete with a very fine Rosalind-made pie.'

A chorus of welcomes, oohs and ahhs rose, as if the family had known Rosalind a lot longer than a few hours. Zaina sat at the kitchen island, eyes bright with happiness. Leila stood at the stove, wearing black oven mitts that went up to her elbows. Caitlin stood next to her, holding a glass of water. Another man leaned on the kitchen island, close to Zaina. He straightened when Rosalind walked in.

'Rosalind, this is my buddy, Bryn Griffiths.' Emil put her pie on the counter. 'Bryn, the one and only Rosalind Braddock.'

'Hello, Rosalind.' Bryn didn't respond to her smile, but he didn't seem hostile, just reserved. He was only a few inches taller than she was, nicely built, with wire-rimmed glasses and tousled curly hair. The exact person you'd picture if someone said *Irish poet*. 'You're the talk of the house.'

'Oh.' She nodded a few times, unsure what to say to that. 'Well.'

'Bryn's a sculptor.' Caitlin looped her arm affectionately around his neck, leaning against him. 'A brilliant one.'

He scoffed. 'Brilliant in your mind, maybe.'

'Whose else matters?' She kissed his cheek with a loud smack.

'Bryn and Emil were roommates at Princeton.' Leila smiled distractedly, pushing back a lock of hair from her forehead that didn't want to be pushed back. She'd wrestled the rest into a bun that exposed the slender length of her neck and emphasized her cheekbones, bright pink from the kitchen heat. Over her jeans and burgundy sweater she had on an adorable red and white polka-dot apron with tiered skirts made to look like a fancy halter dress. 'Oh, *look* at that pie. My God, you can't have made the crust yourself. It's factory perfect.'

'Just luck.' And years of obsessive practice. Pie had been her father's favorite dessert. 'Hope you like apple.'

'Who doesn't?' Leila pulled off her oven mitts, smiling warmly. 'Thanks, Rosalind. This will be a treat.'

Rosalind felt absurdly pleased. 'There's ice cream in the bag. Two flavors.'

Emil was checking. 'And sharp Cheddar. How did you know about that in California? I thought cheese and apple pie was a northeastern thing.'

'Mom was from Maine.'

'Jillian Croft was from Maine?' Caitlin had on her by now familiar wide-eyed-astonishment face.

'Sort of.' Rosalind smiled, annoyed at herself for bringing up her mother. She wanted to talk about *this* family. 'Sylvia Moore was from Maine. Mom became Jillian when she and Dad moved to Los Angeles and launched her career.'

'What are we all doing talking in here?' Zaina made shooing

motions toward the living room. 'We have eating to do.'

'Yes.' Leila clapped her hands twice, teacher commanding a class's attention. 'Emil, you pour the arak. Bryn, help me with this stuff. Rosalind, we're not going all-out Lebanese tonight, but we figured we'd share a few tastes you might like. Arak is common in Lebanon. It's licorice flavored, like French pastis or Greek ouzo, only better.'

'And lethal.' Bryn picked up a tray of small bowls holding various nuts, olives and other things Rosalind didn't recognize.

'No kidding,' Emil said. 'A couple of those and the world is a Hallmark card.'

'A Hallmark card?' Bryn gave him a look over his shoulder, leading the way into the living room. 'Like, "So sorry for your loss of motor control"?'

Caitlin gave a shout of laughter.

'Wait, I've got one.' Leila was still chuckling. 'How about, "Glad to hear you're in recovery"?'

'Sweet, Mom!'

Rosalind couldn't resist. '"Drinking of you . . ."'

'Ah, Rosalind.' Leila applauded. 'Another score.'

'Okay, okay.' Emil laughed good-naturedly. 'Maybe not a Hallmark card.'

'Bryn, you can put the tray on the coffee table. Why don't you and Rosalind sit on the couch together?' Zaina smiled extra sweetly. 'Close to the food.'

'Sure.' Bryn lifted a sly eyebrow at Rosalind. 'Okay?'

She shrugged, and sat next to him. Zaina lowered herself into a chair by the window while Emil and Caitlin appropriately shared the love seat. Leila headed for the overstuffed wing-back chair and plunked down on the floor in front of it, leaning against its cushioned seat, stretching and crossing her long legs in front of her.

'Eat,' she ordered Rosalind. 'Try everything. No shyness allowed.'

Several bites later, Rosalind decided that if matchmaking meant she got premiere access to the food, it was absolutely fine with her. Dishes of olives, pistachios, roasted chickpeas, bright pink pickled turnips, and a bowl of thick, tangy cream they called labneh, served with za'atar, a fragrant, slightly tart spice mixture. Following instructions, she spread a small triangle of pita – they called it khoubz – with labneh, garnished it with a slice of tomato and a sprinkle of za'atar, and practically saw God. She'd have to go easy or she'd have no room left for whatever smelled so good in the kitchen.

Emil expertly filled highball glasses with ice and arak, a clear liquid that clouded when mixed with water. It was beautifully dry, refreshing and, as Bryn had said, very strong.

'Here's to our new neighbor.' Zaina paused for a breath, hand to her chest, then lifted her glass. 'Rosalind, we are glad to have you.'

'Hear, hear.' Emil toasted her warmly. 'We want to know all about what it was like growing up with famous parents.'

'Emil.' Caitlin smacked him lightly on the shoulder. 'We are not going to spend the evening fawning over Rosalind.'

'Who's fawning?'

'Bambi's mother?' Bryn asked quietly.

Rosalind suppressed a giggle. 'Oh deer.'

'Nosy then,' Caitlin said. 'You're being nosy.'

'Nope,' Rosalind murmured. 'That was Pinocchio.'

Bryn snorted. 'You tell the truth.'

'I'm not being nosy, Cait. I just want to know every detail about her mother and father, and every famous person they knew or came into contact with the entire time she was growing up.' Emil ducked Caitlin's next smack by getting up and crossing to the food, turning his lazy, magnetic grin on Rosalind as he stood in front of her, helping himself to a handful of pistachios. 'I'm sure everyone asks you about your parents.'

'Actually, you're the first.' She grinned back, having to work not to blush. Damn the man for being so hot. 'My stock answer is that it was like growing up with regular parents, only mine were famous.'

'Come on. It had to be more exciting than that.' Emil split a pistachio shell and tossed the nut into his mouth. 'Parties, drugs, orgies . . .'

'Leave her alone, Emil.' Caitlin patted the cushion next to her. Emil obediently went back and sat.

'If that's the stock answer, what's the real one?' Bryn asked.

Rosalind took a sip of arak to buy time. She'd become adept at dodging stupid questions, but the disarming simplicity of Bryn's seemed to require a better answer, though she'd stop short of a totally truthful one. Her mother's illness made for poor cocktail conversation.

'I suppose it's the same. I didn't know any other family.' Rosalind made herself glance at Leila, who looked back placidly. 'Mine felt normal to me, though of course I was aware that we were the subject of a lot more attention than other kids or families. At times it was great, at times difficult. Like anyone's life, I guess. I can't really judge.'

'Same problems, same dynamics, different context.' Bryn got up with the tray of food and offered it to Zaina.

'Aren't you sweet, Bryn.' Zaina selected an olive and tucked it into a triangle of pita with labneh. Rosalind immediately decided to try that combination next. 'Bryn's father is a federal judge in Massachusetts. His mother is a prominent lawyer.'

Bryn's face shut down. He turned and offered the tray to Caitlin.

'That's impressive.' Rosalind felt for him. Zaina was overdoing the pimping. 'So you grew up in the Boston area.'

'I did.'

'Brookline on the B line.' Emil grabbed more pistachios.

'And you're a sculptor? Do you show your work?'

'Here and there.' He bent down to Leila with the tray.

'Oh, right.' Caitlin snorted. 'He had a solo show last year in a gallery in SoHo. His stuff sells for big bucks.'

'Wow.' Rosalind didn't have to fake being impressed this time. 'That's fantastic. Congratulations.'

'Thanks.' He put the tray back on the table and sat next to her again. 'It beats being shot out of a cannon.'

'A cannon?' She gave a startled laugh. 'Are you serious? You used to work in a circus?'

'Nope.' He sipped his drink serenely while the room erupted. Rosalind blushed. 'Then what?'

'He's teasing you.' Leila was still giggling, fingers curled in front of her mouth.

'It's his weird sense of humor.' Caitlin beamed at him, hand on her fiancé's long thigh. 'He's hilarious.'

'Nah.' Bryn glanced at Rosalind, then away. 'Sorry about that.'

'No, it's okay. It was funny.' A little weird, but funny. 'What do *you* do, Caitlin?'

She made a face. 'I work for Jersey Insurance. My title is Assistant to an Asshole.'

'*Caitlin.*' Leila frowned at her.

'I don't even want to think about what that might entail,' Bryn said.

Zaina crossed herself. 'Kids these days.'

'Emil has the real job.' Caitlin patted his thigh. 'As soon as we're married, I'm going to quit and pump out a football team's worth of boys.'

Emil pretended to choke on his drink. '*Jesus*.'

'What?' She blinked sweetly at him.

'What do you do, Emil?'

'I'm in management consulting with Bain & Company in New York.' He winked at Rosalind, making her a bit shivery, in spite of hating the wink thing. 'I know, I know, when you walked in you assumed *I* was the artist and *Bryn* was the corporate guy. Am I right?'

'Uh, no.' She forced a polite laugh. 'I guessed that one. But I have no follow-up questions for you because I know nothing about that world.'

'Don't blame you.' He emptied his drink with obvious satisfaction. 'It makes for pretty banal conversation.'

'No kidding,' Caitlin said. 'I'd rather talk about the wedding, and how we can pull it off next month. The tenth is our target, right? November?'

Emil's features tightened. 'So you tell me.'

'What?' Caitlin pouted. 'You don't want to talk about it?'

'We talk about it constantly.' He gestured to Rosalind. 'I don't want to bore our guest.'

'Rosalind is going to help,' Zaina said. 'So Leila and I can laze around eating bonbons.'

'Really.' Emil turned his blue eyes on Rosalind. 'That's incredibly nice of you.'

Rosalind gave him a curt nod, refusing to feel fizzy.

'We'll talk bride and groom now so we can relax during dinner.' Leila searched the pockets of her apron and came up with a piece of paper and a pen that had a grinning face with fluffy rainbow hair at its non-writing end. 'Here's what I have, roughly in order of urgency. Venue, officiant, caterer, music, flowers, alcohol, cake, invitations, dress, hair and makeup. Who wants what?'

Emil raised his hand. 'I'll do makeup!'

'Oh, great idea.' Caitlin's face was flushing from the alcohol. 'A clown wedding.'

'No makeup.' Leila pointed her goofy pen at Emil. 'You do the booze.'

'Go with my strengths.' He peered into his empty glass. 'Speaking of which.'

'I can design the invitations.' Bryn raised his hand briefly. 'And I'm around if Caitlin wants company on errands.'

'Aw, thanks.' Caitlin batted her eyes at him. 'You're the best.'

'Hey, aren't you supposed to think *I'm* the best?' Emil gestured to himself.

'You know I do.' She pinched his cheek.

'Thank you, Bryn.' Leila made a mark on the paper.

'I'll make the cake.' Zaina took a sip of her drink and launched into a coughing fit. Emil's smug attitude vanished; he leapt up and poured her a glass of water. The room stayed tense and silent until she finished drinking, even while she waved to tell them she was fine.

'Are you okay, Teta?' Caitlin looked terrified.

'Of course, of course.' She patted her chest. 'My heart is the problem, not my drinking.'

'You sure making the cake won't be too much, Mama?'

'No, no.' Zaina dismissed Leila's concern. 'It's not too much. I will do it.'

'Thank you, Teta.' Caitlin raised her glass to her grandmother.

'I can do hair.' Rosalind raised her hand. 'I can try out a style, and if you hate it, you can hire someone else, no offense whatsoever. But you can't beat my price, which is nothing.'

'Wow. Thank you . . .' Caitlin gave her a quick, uneasy smile.

'I can also help with errands or whatever else you need. I'm just sitting around for the next few months.'

'Really?' Caitlin looked envious. 'You're not doing *anything*?'

'Rosalind, why don't you and Bryn check out venues tomorrow while Caitlin is at work?' Zaina sent a Cheshire cat smile toward the couch. Bryn gave a nearly silent snort of laughter.

'Oh no, they don't want to do that.' Caitlin shook her head emphatically. 'Bryn is crazy busy and Rosalind, you just *met* us, for God's sake, we can't ask you to do all this.'

'I don't mind.' Rosalind turned to Bryn. 'You?'

'No, really.' Caitlin's voice rose. 'It's too much to expect.'

'I wouldn't mind either,' Bryn said. 'I don't have anything big going on right now. I know of a couple of non-traditional venues that might work. I can call around the usual places, too, and keep on top of cancellations.'

Caitlin was looking desperate. 'But that's—'

'What's up, Cait?' Emil turned to her. 'Would you rather not have help? You keep complaining about how much work this is.'

'Of *course* she wants help. We all do. If I want to keep singing, I have to learn more old lady roles.' Leila grimaced. 'I'd set aside this month and next to work on a few new ones, and then the wedding date changed . . .'

'You absolutely should learn them.' Rosalind glanced at sulky Caitlin, feeling guilty sympathy. She'd be pretty upset, too, if a stranger barged into her wedding planning. But the opportunity for effortless Allerton time was too perfect. 'I can help out quite a bit.'

'Okay, then.' Leila lifted her glass. 'Thank you so much.'

'Yes, thank you, both of you.' Zaina smiled her grand-motherly smile. 'But especially you, Rosalind, taking this on for strangers. God had a good reason for putting you in our path.'

Rosalind felt herself blushing, hyper-aware of Emil's grateful smile. After a lifetime of criticism by her father, she had little practice handling such open appreciation.

'When you get back to your house, you might want to try walking on water,' Bryn said quietly. 'Maybe the tub.'

'I practice daily,' she answered as quietly. 'Sink every time.'

'Did you two want to share with the rest of the class?' Caitlin asked.

'Leave them alone, they're fine.' Leila pointed to the food. 'What did you think, Rosalind?'

'I think I gained a pound in the last half-hour.'

'You have excellent taste,' Leila said. 'We get nearly everything at Sahadi's in Brooklyn. When you're back in the city, you have to check them out.'

'Tell them I sent you,' Zaina said. 'They'll treat you like family.'

'I'd love that.' Rosalind would love a mother–daughter trip even more. 'Have you been to Lebanon, Leila?'

'A few times. With Mama.' She gazed fondly at Zaina. 'We spent one summer in the mountains when I was a girl. Then after I graduated college we spent two weeks in Beirut, and two weeks again in 2008.'

'My last trip home.' Zaina spoke matter-of-factly. 'I won't be there again in this body.'

'You're going to use someone else's?' Caitlin shuddered. 'Creepy.'

Zaina cackled. 'I'll take yours, then make you eat raw liver. For breakfast. With onions.'

Caitlin's horrified expression made them all laugh.

'Have you ever been?' Rosalind asked her.

Caitlin shook her head. 'The trips have never been at a time I could go.'

'You're scared.' Emil stood and waved his glass. 'Anyone need another drink?'

'I'm *not* scared.'

'The US put out a travel warning to Lebanon when we went in 2008, and she freaked out.' Leila looked at her daughter with pity. 'I felt completely safe there the whole time. The people are so lovely, so hospitable. Everyone treats you like you're family. And so good-looking, my goodness. Dark, dark hair, and gold skin with light gray eyes, oh my God. I even fell for some of the women.'

'*Mom!*'

'Schwing,' Bryn murmured.

Rosalind threw him a look and turned back to Zaina. 'Do you still have family there?'

'Oh yes.' Zaina flung out a plump arm as if bridging the distance to her homeland. 'Cousins and cousins once removed and twice and three times, both in Beirut and in Zahleh, the mountain city I grew up in.'

'You can't escape family even if you want to.' Leila laughed, re-crossing her legs. 'We were invited somewhere every day, often twice, sometimes three times. It was so wonderful, but I admit at times I felt I couldn't take a breath without someone asking me if it was a good breath and if I was happy with the breathing in Lebanon, and if there was anything they could do to make the next breath better.'

'Yes, yes, all true.' Zaina nodded, still smiling. 'Let's just say some of us emigrate for a reason. Especially at age twenty-five, when you have six aunts who think they know what's best for you.'

'I'd suffocate,' Caitlin announced. 'I love my family, but the two of you is plenty.'

'Nice, Cait.' Emil sat back down with his glass full.

'Yeah, thanks, kid.' Leila rolled her eyes.

'Family is very important in Lebanon. Maybe too important sometimes.' Zaina set her half-full glass on the end table next to her chair and folded her arms. 'But you Americans could learn a thing or two.'

'What's *that* supposed to mean?'

'Hey, what is up with you tonight, Caitlin?' Leila asked. 'You're bristling at everything.'

'I am *not*—' She broke off and gave a short laugh. Emil put his arm around her and hugged her, nearly making her spill her drink, but at least she kept laughing, her face turning a pretty shade of rose. '*What makes you think I'm bristling, Mom?*'

Leila was laughing, too. 'Mother's intuition. And all the *bristles*.'

'I'm sorry.' Caitlin straightened, glancing at Rosalind. 'I'm a little keyed up, I guess.'

'Don't blame you.' Leila blew her daughter a kiss. 'You have a lot on your mind. We all do. So let's go have some dinner, okay?'

There were enthusiastic murmurs, drinks finished in a hurry, people standing, picking up dishes to take back to the kitchen. Bryn offered Zaina his arm and escorted her into the dining room. Rosalind followed, infatuated by what had just happened between mother and daughter. A clear, direct message delivered calmly, understood, respected, and just like that the tension was over.

In the Braddock family, if they were lucky, the next day the grudge would be lifted. In the meantime, there would be hurt feelings, wounding words, hostile silences, strained conversation.

Eve would shut down, Olivia pout. Rosalind, stomach awash in acid, would try to put everything back to normal. How many times in her life had she felt she'd been dropped by aliens into that collection of clashing egos and neuroses?

Granted, the Allertons were probably on best behavior tonight with her and Bryn in their midst, and she and her family had certainly had plenty of good times together. But not the easy, supportive love and warmth she'd seen here, especially in a family facing terrible grief in the not-too-distant future.

'Rosalind, you sit there.' Leila pointed to a chair at the dark wooden dining table, set with colorful place mats and bright yellow plates. 'Bryn, you're next to her. Then Mama at the foot, Caitlin and Emil on that side.'

Rosalind went to her place next to Bryn.

'Did I miss something?' he murmured. 'Are we dating?'

'Apparently.'

'Strange.' He glanced at her, then away. 'Usually I'm aware when my relationships start.'

'This one popped out fully formed, like Athena from Zeus's head.'

He laughed, a rumble that crinkled the corners of his eyes and showed up surprise dimples. 'I might like dating you.'

'Better than being shot out of a—'

'What *are* you two whispering about?' Caitlin had taken her seat.

'State secrets,' Bryn said. 'If I told you, I'd have to kill you.'

'Hey.' Emil was at the sideboard opening wine. 'She's *my* fiancée. No one kills her but me.'

Caitlin rolled her eyes. 'Emil, you are *so* adorable.'

'Here's dinner.' Leila came into the dining room bearing a huge platter on which sat two chickens roasted to a mahogany shade, surrounded by mounds of tender-looking browned vegetables that must have been roasting with them. Emil stepped forward to take the load from her.

'Thank you, Emil. Just there is fine.' She pointed to the center of the table, then sat and unfolded her napkin. 'Zaina, will you say grace?'

'Of course.' Zaina put her blue-veined hands together and bowed her head. 'Thank you, God, for this superb meal, and for bringing us all together tonight. Special thanks for Rosalind, who we will make work so hard on this wedding that she'll wish she'd never knocked on our door. Amen.'

Rosalind looked up with a grin. 'Thank you. I guess.'

'Now.' Leila picked up a lethal-looking silver carving set with monogrammed handles and started slicing and dissecting the birds into serving pieces. Caitlin told a long story about her overbearing misogynist boss, occasionally interrupted by her fiancé with good-natured accusations of exaggeration and laughter all around. Rosalind sat eating her perfectly roasted chicken flavored with lemon and oregano, answering questions put to her, otherwise soaking in the family-ness with a combination of relish, envy and wistfulness. She'd had dinner with other close families, most notably her UCLA friend Becky, whose parents lived in Brooklyn and hosted the girls often. But this family was hers – probably – and it hurt that she'd missed thirty-four years among them.

After the chicken came a huge green salad with herbed buttermilk dressing, then Rosalind's apple pie, which everyone raved over as if it were priceless art. Then tiny cups of decaf espresso, and a silver plate heaped with dates and dried apricots. *Then* out came her chocolates, and Emil poured snifters of brandy.

By the time Rosalind had eaten her last bite and sipped her

last sip, she was a little drunk, a lot stuffed and happier than she'd been in a long, long time.

'Thank you all so much. I've really enjoyed meeting everyone. You were so nice to include me tonight.' She stood, smiling around the table, hoping she wasn't swaying or slurring her words.

'The pleasure was ours.' Zaina pushed herself to standing. 'I'll get your ice cream.'

'No, no, keep it, please, keep everything. They were gifts, and you fed me so well. Everything was delicious. And the courses kept coming. My God, I haven't eaten that much in one sitting in forever.'

'We loved having you.' Leila smiled up from her seat at the head of the table. 'Thank you for offering to help with the wedding.'

'I'll pick you up in the morning.' Bryn pushed back his chair. 'Ten o'clock okay?'

'That's fine. Caitlin.' She made her expression as friendly as possible. 'Thanks for the welcome. I look forward to helping out.'

'Sure.' Caitlin met her eyes briefly. She'd clearly be a challenge.

Reluctantly, Rosalind turned to Emil, feeling girlish and stupid and shy. 'Goodnight.'

'I'll walk you home.' He got to his feet.

'Huh?' Caitlin stared up at him. 'Across the *street*?'

'It's the gentlemanly thing to do.' He pushed his chair back in.

Rosalind practically panicked. 'No, no, don't be silly. I don't need an escort.'

'Bryn's leaving.' Caitlin pointed at him. 'He can go with her.'

'Bryn is staying to help me look at designs for a cake,' Zaina said.

'Hello?' Rosalind waved her hand. 'This is crazy. I'm fine alone.'

'No trouble. Let's go.' Emil headed for the dining room door.

Rosalind looked helplessly at Caitlin, who was staring after her fiancé with narrowed eyes. The last thing Rosalind wanted to do was piss off her new sister. 'Is there something I should know about this neighborhood? Gangs? Random shootings? People-jacking?'

'No.' Caitlin rolled her eyes. 'He's just trying to be impressive.'

'I *am* impressive. I don't have to try.' Emil walked back and gave her a loud kiss on her forehead. 'Don't start, Cait. I'm not going to elope with her.'

'Maybe you should,' she grumbled, but then, thank God, smiled up at him, though a bit unwillingly.

'Ready, Rosalind?'

'Ready. Thanks again, everyone. It was a wonderful evening.' Rosalind followed Emil's tall form through the kitchen, where he opened the door and gestured her through like the gentleman she still couldn't tell if he was.

The night air smelled sweet, chilly enough to feel like fall. Stepping into it with Emil felt much too intimate.

'Sorry about that. Cait gets a little possessive when she drinks. She's fine.'

'Oh.' Rosalind didn't want to touch that one. 'Well, she has nothing to worry about from me.'

'You mean I'm not even tempting?'

She sent him a look, which made him laugh. He really was disgustingly attractive. Even though she was on Caitlin's side in this matter, Rosalind was admittedly titillated. A good strong buzz, delicious evening air, and a ridiculously handsome escort. A nice combination. It had been a while since someone had flirted with her whose attentions didn't make her want to pull out a can of mace.

'It will be fun to help plan your wedding. I'm flattered the family trust me to be part of it.'

'Yeah, they're good people. Wait . . .' He stopped them at the curb with a hand on her arm, looked one way down the totally deserted street for a long moment, then the other way. 'Okay, *now*.'

He grabbed Rosalind's hand and pulled her across.

She ran with him, laughing. 'What are you *doing*?'

'Whew.' He grinned down at her. 'Made it.'

Rosalind yanked her hand away, trying to stop giggling. 'That was ridiculous.'

'Of course it was. Fun, though. Which house?'

'This way.' She started north toward the Gardners'.

Emil fell in step beside her. 'You know, Rosalind . . .'

When he didn't continue, she shot him a look. 'Know what, Emil?'

He stopped walking and turned to her, tall and sexy even lit too pale by the cold hues of the street lamp. 'It's pretty amazing that you're Daniel Braddock's kid.'

'People are usually more amazed that I'm Jillian Croft's kid.'

'Yeah.' He nodded slowly. 'She was truly hot.'

'Aw, jeez.' Rosalind waved him away and kept walking. 'She was my *mother*.'

'Seriously, I thought she was amazing.'

'I know, I know.' She lifted her arms and let them drop. 'You and every other straight male.'

'That time I meant talented.' He put a hand on her arm to stop her again. 'You don't look that much like her.'

'Oh, *thanks*.' She gave him a playful push, trying to keep the moment light, while her heart hammered. People had told her plenty of times that she didn't look like her mother. Now, knowing why, the subject felt dangerous.

'No, no. I didn't mean it that way.' He took her shoulders and held her firmly enough that she'd have to work to get away. 'Seriously, Rosalind. I did not mean that you weren't attractive. You are incredibly attractive, trust me.'

'No, no, that's just . . . no.' She made a slashing movement across her throat. 'Cut. Change of subject.'

'Okay. But you believe me?'

'Yes. *Yes.* Now stop.'

'Thing is.' He was looking at her curiously. 'Thing is, Caitlin told me that Leila was crazy about your dad. Like obsessed crazy. She had every one of his books, and would play this video lecture he gave all the time. Caitlin once found a Daniel Braddock file in her mom's desk, full of photos and clippings spanning decades. She always wondered what that was about. Seemed to me like more than just professional worship. I didn't realize they'd actually met until Cait told me tonight. A long time ago, at least twenty-five years, maybe more. In all her talk about him, Leila never mentioned meeting him, which seems pretty strange.'

Fear crawled up the back of Rosalind's throat. She felt suddenly stone sober. And absolutely positive that she didn't want to hear whatever Emil was about to say. At the same time, she couldn't make herself stop him. He was going to suggest – or God forbid prove – that Leila and her father had had an affair, that Rosalind was the result, and that Jillian Croft had adopted and raised her without knowing she was her husband's love child. Or worse, much worse: knowing.

There was no way Rosalind could take that news and act remotely normal. Even now, she wanted to start screaming, here in the street.

It had taken a lot over the last weeks to come to terms with the new facts of her life as she'd constructed them. Leila had most likely gotten pregnant by some guy in circumstances that made it impossible for her to keep the baby, so she'd given Rosalind up to parents who were desperate to have a second daughter. For reasons Rosalind was partly here to discover, payments were made, were *still* being made.

Now Emil was about to blurt out that Rosalind was the result of an affair, which would not only blow her previous relatively comfortable scenario to hell, it would also make it obvious that she was in Princeton to get to know her mother.

Rosalind was supposed to have plenty of time to prove or disprove the information she suspected, and to process it at her own pace, not have truths she wasn't ready to hear hurled in her face.

She swallowed. 'So?'

'I'm wondering if they had an affair.' He glanced back at the house and moved closer. In spite of her oncoming meltdown, Rosalind noticed that he smelled really good. 'I'm wondering if that affair produced a daughter.'

Her throat thickened. She wanted to speak, but could only shake her head.

'Which would mean you and Caitlin are half-sisters.'

Tears rose, and rolled down her cheeks. 'Emil . . .'

'I'm sorry, Rosalind. I'm so sorry to do this to you.' He brushed her tears away, and with warm, gentle fingers took her chin in his hand and made her look up at him. 'But I'm dying to know if Daniel Braddock is Caitlin's father.'

Chapter 7

September 22, 1967 (Friday)

I got the lead in the fall play, Harvey. *I play an old woman, the sister of a guy who is friends with a six-foot invisible rabbit. Sounds funny, but it's a good part. I've tried to pay attention to old women to see how they walk and act. But then when I say my lines at home, it's like I've got an old woman inside me who already knows how.*

I just have to survive this year and next, and I'll be able to graduate and get out of here. More than anything in the world I want to go to New York and study acting at the Stella Adler Studio. It's really the only place to go as far as I'm concerned. I don't know how I'll afford it, but I'm supposed to be there, fated to be there. I have no doubts about this whatsoever. I will find a way.

Mom is proud of me (first time ever?) working so many hours at Finch's Grocery. She thinks I'm getting ready to start a career there after I graduate. That makes me want to laugh. I'm just saving as much money as possible to get away from here. She doesn't know me at all. Like my kindergarten teacher used to say, 'Stop, look, and listen.' She never does any of those when it comes to me. I'm invisible except as an annoyance.

Once I saw a picture of Mom in a photo album. It was on

the shelf, and I was bored, so I pulled it out. She was so young and so pretty! What happened? Why do pretty young women let themselves turn into hideous old moms? I'm not going to do that, no matter how many kids I have. And I am going to have them.

They have better doctors in New York. If I don't get my period by the time I leave, they'll figure this out and fix me, I know they will.

Rosalind pulled the door of her rented house shut behind her with a weather-stripping whoosh and the click of the lock engaging. It was nearly ten. Bryn was due any minute, and she'd have to fake being eager to help figure out where Caitlin would get married, when really she wanted to run back to New York and hide from this suddenly ominous mess.

After getting away from Emil, Rosalind had spent a horrible night, her initial upset gradually replaced by rage, barely notice-able at first, then sprouting all over, like an emotional Chia Pet.

As usual, the dark hours turned small worries into huge ones, though these worries were pretty big even in daylight. Rosalind had established such a lovely fantasy myth about Leila's pregnancy. Her mother and father, wanting another bundle of joy after adopting Olivia, had heard about Leila's love child through whatever agency she had registered with. Their joy! Leila's joy! Her infant daughter would be well cared for, secure and adored. Rosalind had even concocted a generous and genteel reason for the continuing payments: Daniel and Jillian believed so deeply in Leila's talent, they wanted to give her every opportunity to pursue her dreams, free from the constraints of having to make money.

Yeah, that part had been a stretch, even for her.

Then a night of turmoil, anger and anxiety over a theory of

Emil's that was neither lovely, generous nor genteel. Her father had had an extended affair with Leila that produced two daughters. He took one and paid Leila to raise the other.

The worst part? Crazy as it sounded, it also made more sense.

Angry panic rose again. Rosalind took in a deep breath. Let it out. Tried to empty her mind, and when that didn't work, tried to focus on an image of flower petals opening. Closing. Opening. Closing. Open—

Did that mean Dad had also had affairs with Olivia and Eve's mothers? How many others? Did Rosalind have sisters and brothers scattered all over the globe? Did Mom know? How had she been able to bear it?

Had Daniel Braddock never heard of condoms?

She opened her eyes and took a flying leap off the top step to the walkway below.

Maybe her sisters were right. Maybe she should have left this alone.

Ten o'clock. No cars on the street, no impatient honking, furious cab drivers shouting, or banging of delivery people. She had no idea how anyone survived all this deafening peace and quiet.

At the sidewalk, another glance at her watch. She regretted being so cozy and cute with Bryn last night. He'd show up today quite reasonably expecting more of the same, maybe even buying into Zaina's matchmaking idea.

This morning he'd find out what kind of a hummingbird she was. There last night, zoom, nowhere today.

The thought made new anger sprout in her chest.

A car came down the street, a navy SUV. Rosalind squinted, then decided that wasn't the kind of car Bryn would drive, proven true when it zoomed past.

Maybe he wouldn't show. Maybe he was a flaky artist-type who'd sleep until noon and forget entirely. That would be perfect. Then she could take time to calm down and decide what to do next. Whether she could still ingratiate herself into the family knowing that Leila had been the other woman, that her father had not, as it had appeared to the girls all those years, tolerated and managed her mother's erratic behavior in the name of devotion, but in the name of God knew what – remaining in her limelight? – while he dipped into whatever female receptacle he could find.

She walked restlessly along the sidewalk, skip-jumping through a hopscotch game drawn in pink chalk by whatever kids lived nearby.

Did Mom insist on raising the three of them because it was the right thing to do, or because she wanted kids, or because Dad demanded it? Was the distance Jillian maintained from her daughters, which they'd ascribed to her illness, really a function of resentment?

Another car. A black Audi. Five minutes late. Rosalind followed it with her eyes as it sped past. Not Bryn, but still too soon to hope he wasn't coming. She turned around and did the hopscotch board backwards.

Maybe Mom never managed to accommodate Dad sexually; maybe the vaginal stretching hadn't worked. Maybe she understood that in order to keep her marriage intact, she had to let him go. In the game of infidelity, the deck was stacked against her the moment she was born. She could never have cheated on him in return.

Dad was always traveling for workshops, lectures, conferences; he was always in demand. Mom must have known what he was also doing while she stayed home alone and cursed her body.

No wonder she'd wanted people to think she was pregnant. Not only pride, to keep Dad's secret from humiliating her the way men everywhere humiliated their wives, but also to let the world know that she was fully female, in all the traditional, perhaps narrow, ways she defined it.

Too many possibilities, too many consequences, too much ugliness. Rosalind liked her original adoption fantasy infinitely better.

Third car, ten minutes after ten. A green Prius, slowing. Here he was, when Rosalind was at the height of her anger and confusion. She felt sorrier for Bryn having to spend the morning with her than for herself having to go through it.

The car pulled over. Rosalind sighed and opened the door, plastering on her best attempt at a smile.

'Hi.' He was wearing a dark green hoodie over a blue shirt, nicely worn jeans and sneakers. His smile was genuine, generous and dimpled. She felt like a puppy killer.

'Hi.' She got into the car and buckled up, staring resignedly through the windshield, aware of his gaze on her. 'What's our agenda?'

'Three stops. One, I found a cancellation at a place not far from town that does a lot of weddings.' He put the car in gear and pulled forward. 'Makes you wonder if there's a sadder or more complicated phrase than "cancelled wedding".'

'Probably not.' She caught him glancing at her again and told herself to be more polite. Not his fault her father was a lying, cheating whore. 'Those places take care of everything. Ideal for a quickie wedding.'

'Could be.' He slowed at the intersection with Route 206 and put on his left turn signal. 'Then we're seeing a house belonging to one of my collectors.'

'Collectors of what?'

Bryn seemed to find that amusing. 'That's what we artsy people call someone who buys our work.'

'Oh.' Rosalind felt as if she should have known this. But she wasn't planning to set the art world on fire with her canvases, so why would she? 'I'll get to see some of your sculpture?'

'You will.'

'Nice.' She let her head fall back on the headrest. That was about all the small talk she could handle.

'I'd rather see Caitlin married there.'

She turned to look at him, struck by something odd in his tone, and that he hadn't mentioned her groom. 'Why?'

'It suits her better.'

'What about Emil?'

He pulled out into a break in traffic. 'I think you're about to tell me I'm being sexist. Bride's the only one that matters.'

'I might be, yes.'

'It's more that Emil hasn't spent a lot of time discussing what he wants for the ceremony, and she has.'

'Ah.' From the little Rosalind had seen of Caitlin, she thought a swanky professional spot would suit her perfectly, but Bryn knew her better.

They drove on until the silence became awkward, and then more awkward. Rosalind stared guiltily out the window. Bryn shouldn't have to pay for her mood. But she couldn't think of anything to say that wouldn't sound horribly forced.

'You okay today?'

'Yes. Fine.' She immediately regretted the automatic response since it was so clearly not true. A rude cop-out after he'd been polite enough to ask. 'Just a garden-variety personal mess. Not life or death.'

'I'm sorry.' He sounded it. 'Want to talk about it with a stranger you have no reason to trust?'

'Ha. No thanks.' She softened her voice. 'But I appreciate the offer.'

'Sure.' He turned on to a residential street lined with homes and yards much larger and more opulent than those they'd been passing. 'So what do you need? Silent chauffeur? Cheerful tour guide? I'm too straight to do gay best friend, but I could try if it would help.'

Rosalind snorted, her crankiness ebbing. He was funny. And cute, if you liked curly-haired, twinkly-eyed guys with glasses. Unfortunately she'd always been a sucker for big bad boys until her latest, Don, the guy Olivia had been so crazy about. Don had been sweet, kind, loving . . . and eventually bored her to breakup. 'Just be the best gosh-darn Bryn you can be.'

'I can do that.'

More silence, Rosalind craning to take in one stately home after another, until Bryn started whistling. It took her a few lines to recognize the tune from *The King and I*, about whistling instead of giving into fear.

Rosalind eyed him suspiciously. 'Is that a message?'

'Not for you.'

'Okay.' She didn't know how to respond to that. 'So . . . how did you get into sculpting?'

The question was ridiculous, one he probably heard twenty times a day, but it was all she had.

'Oh, well mostly I—'

'Never mind.' Rosalind held up her hand. 'Don't answer that. I might as well have asked why you were born male, right?'

'I don't mind the question. That whole aura of mystery that artists and writers cling to is crap.' He slowed to a stop at a red light. 'You never hear a stockbroker say, "I didn't choose this career. It chose me."'

His earnest, breathy tone made Rosalind giggle, something

she wouldn't have thought possible ten minutes earlier. 'That is true.'

'Or a Major League pitcher, "The ball chooses its own path, I just stand aside and let it."' He gestured impatiently. 'Those people are attracted to certain kinds of work, learn the job and get it done. That's what I do, too.'

'Fair enough.'

The light turned green. 'Was I ranting?'

'You were. But it was interesting.' She wondered what that felt like, as an artist, to believe the tangible representation of your thoughts and feelings was so important that other people needed to share the experience. Her paintings were stacked in her apartment's extra bedroom, facing the walls. 'I do find it strange to finish a project, then look at it later and feel like it couldn't have been me who did it. For something so personal, it's a strange disconnect.'

Bryn pulled through the intersection, leaving behind the blocks of elegant homes and traveling through a more sparsely populated area, lots of grass, lots of trees. 'What's your medium?'

'Clothing design. I started sewing when I was a kid after I asked Santa for a machine. At first I made outfits for my dolls. I'd cut out two flat pants shapes and sew them together. Pretty awful. But I loved it. Later I bought patterns and figured out how it was really done. I made a lot of my own clothes.'

He gestured to her outfit, a bright yellow shirt and red shorts over plaid tights and black ankle boots. 'Still do?'

'Still do. Also . . .' She looked out the window, embarrassed to be admitting her truth, to an artist of all people. 'I paint some. Not good, nothing serious, but it's another creative outlet.'

'Yeah?' He smirked at her. 'So how did you get into painting?'

'Ha ha. I started when I lived in Denver. Hard not to with

those mountains all around. After I left Colorado, I started painting Maine.' She sent him an apologetic smile. 'I'm not looking to be *collected*. But I enjoy it.'

'That's what matters. When did you live in Denver?'

'From 2009 until 2012.'

'Where else?' He glanced over at her. 'When did you leave LA? Give me the whole life story.'

'All right. Let's see.' She started counting on her fingers. 'Graduated in 2007 from UCLA. Took me six years because I kept changing majors – psychology, then education sciences, and finally art history. Then I got sick of LA and moved to Denver, then got sick of Denver and moved to New York. What about you?'

'I've been on the east coast all along. Grew up in Massachusetts, which you know, went to Princeton, which you know, stayed in Princeton, which you might have guessed. What you probably don't know is that I took a gap year before college and traveled all over Europe.'

'Nice work if you can get it.' She relaxed into her seat, grateful to Bryn for providing distraction from her uncharacteristic brooding. The day looked sunnier already.

'Here we are.' He took a right turn into what looked like a long driveway up a gentle slope.

Rosalind gaped at a passing sign. 'You think Caitlin should get married at the Educational Testing Service?'

'What, you don't find SATs romantic?'

'*This* place is popular for weddings?'

'Nah.' He drove farther, following a long curve to the left, and pointed to a warm brown building with funky angles and lots of glass. 'That place. The Chauncey Hotel.'

'Much better.'

Inside they were met by Megan, a tiny, stylish woman with

enormous brown eyes who seemed to feel the chance to help organize Caitlin and Emil's wedding was the best thing that had ever happened to her. In Rosalind's view, fear of bad online reviews had given customer service a desperate friendliness even more annoying than apathy.

Chirping happily, Megan led them to the Brodsky Gallery, an attractive room colored in bright red, brown and orange, with a fireplace and multiple comfortable places to gather and sit. High tables, she assured them joyfully, could be arranged around the room for those preferring to stand.

'Of course it's unusual that we have the space available at so late a date, so I'm afraid you'll have to decide fairly quickly if you want your wedding here.' She beamed at them both. 'We have another couple coming this afternoon.'

'What do you think, darling?' Bryn made puppy eyes.

Rosalind gave him one of Olivia's stink eyes in return. 'I think we just met yesterday and it's not our wedding.'

'Oh, I'm sorry. I assumed . . .' Megan blushed and gave an adorable giggle. 'Well, who knows, maybe yours will happen someday.'

'Not mine.' Rosalind tried to match her perkiness. 'I'm staying single.'

'I'm sorry to hear that.' Megan winked at Bryn. 'Maybe not as sorry as he is.'

'I'll recover. Therapy. Drugs. Time.' He held out his hand. 'Thanks, Megan. We'll be in touch soon.'

Out in the parking lot, the morning had warmed enough that fall no longer seemed the appropriate season.

'You still up for stop two, or did all that cheer wear you out?'

'I survived it fine.' Rosalind met his eyes over the top of his car, and realized with a start that it was the first time that morning she'd looked right at him. 'And I feel better, thank you.'

'You don't strike me as the type to stay down for long.'

'Nah.' She got inside and buckled up. 'I bounce back. I'm lucky.'

They retraced their route back down the driveway. The silence felt more comfortable between them now. Ironic, since Rosalind was no longer so interested in keeping quiet.

'How long have you known Caitlin? You and Emil were roommates at Princeton?'

'Yup. Freshman year. She was still in high school when she and Emil started dating.'

'Wow. That's a long time.'

'Yeah . . .' Again that strange tone. 'They were on and off.'

'I see.' Rosalind clenched her hands in her lap and willed her voice to come out sounding normal for the next question. 'Does she ever talk about her father?'

'No.' He looked both ways at the drive's end, then turned back toward Princeton. 'Why?'

'I'm curious if there was ever a dad in the picture.'

'No. He's never been around.'

'Does she know who he is?' When he didn't answer, she laughed uneasily. 'Just being nosy.'

'Uh-huh.' He came to the intersection they'd driven through before, but turned left this time. 'Pretty amazing coincidence you coming to Princeton.'

Rosalind tensed and stole a look; Bryn was staring calmly through the windshield. 'Why do you say that?'

'Because of how Leila idolized your father.'

'Oh, that.' Rosalind clenched her hands tighter, trying to sound dismissive. 'My father gave lectures and did book signings all over the country. For decades. I'm more surprised when I *don't* run into someone with a connection.'

She deserved an Oscar. She really did. There should be a runner knocking on the car window any second to hand over the statue.

'How are you liking your other neighbors on the block? Any of them get you to plan weddings, too?'

Crap. He was going to make her earn another award. Did he suspect something, or was she classically paranoid because she had something to hide? Of course he'd think that if she'd knocked on the Allertons' door to introduce herself, she must have knocked on all the other doors too. Never occurred to her.

'Oh, sure, they all asked for help, but none was as nice as the Allertons, so I refused.'

'Gotcha.' He frowned while she held her breath and prayed he wouldn't ask any more questions. 'You're here because you couldn't take the city anymore?'

'That's right. Crowded. Noisy. It gets stressful after a while. I needed a break.' Truthfully, she thrived on the city's crazy energy and couldn't imagine leaving. Though she did tend to think she'd landed into happy-forever every time, whether with a man, a city or a hobby. Inevitably she'd get bored and take off again for greener pastures.

'How did you pick Princeton?'

'It's close by. Dad talked about the town fondly. The college was his alma mater.' She made herself stop fidgeting. 'Why? You think it's weird?'

'Which part? Dropping your life to go somewhere else, or helping plan a stranger's wedding?'

'Both.'

'Yup. Weird.'

Rosalind cracked up, loving his honesty. 'Weird maybe, but meant to be since the Allertons needed me.'

'I'm benefitting, too.'

'How?' The second she asked, she realized he'd been flirting. She had to remember what she was doing when she let herself get too comfortable around Bryn. She didn't want to have to smack him down.

'Do I really have to answer that?'

'No. You don't. Thank you, that is very nice of you.' She used her most formal voice, pretty sure he was smart enough to get the message.

He must have because he stayed silent while they climbed a long hill with fields on either side, grassy to the right and manicured for sports on the left.

'We're out of Princeton already?'

Bryn chuckled. 'You wanted a small town.'

'I did, I did.'

'I was just thinking . . . It must be strange to be a celebrity without having signed up to be one. Because of your parents.'

Rosalind liked the question. Much more interesting than the usual *What stars did you hang out with?*

'It is a little strange, but we're used to it. I'm careful what I say on social media, take basic security measures, et cetera, though creeps still find me occasionally. I stick with Dad's last name because I grew up with it and don't care that much if I'm recognized or not. My younger sister goes by Eve Moore, my mother's maiden name, to avoid as much publicity as she can. And my older sister goes by Mom's stage name, Olivia Croft, to *get* as much publicity as she can.'

'Olivia, Rosalind and Eve.' Bryn slowed for a stop sign at the top of the hill, where a sign marked the entrance to Princeton

Day School. 'Let me guess. Olivia de Havilland, Rosalind Russell, Eve . . . Arden?'

'You're good.' She was absurdly pleased. 'It goes further than that. Olivia's middle name is Claudette, mine is Greer, and Eve's is Grace.'

'Claudette Colbert, Greer Garson, Grace Kelly.'

Rosalind turned to him, grinning. 'You watched old movies. I mean old like the forties, not old like *Ghostbusters*.'

'My mom insisted. She loved them. Sunday night was movie night at our house. All homework for the weekend had to be done before dinner, and we ate in front of the TV. All of us complained when we were adolescents, because of course we were way too cool for anything our parents liked, but in retrospect it was a great cinematic education.'

'Absolutely.'

'Did any of you try to follow your mom into showbiz?'

'Only Olivia. She landed a few movie roles in her twenties and early thirties, but never got her big break. Now she hosts a TV cooking show based in LA. I did theater in college just for fun. Eve refused to go near the stage except as a techie on stage crew. She's an architect now.'

'TV host, architect . . . What would you call yourself?'

'A hummingbird. Little sips of everything, then on to the next flower. My dad came up with the nickname.' She laughed, but couldn't keep out the bitterness. 'I was thrilled at first. Thought it was a compliment.'

'Why wasn't it?'

'Because that's not the kind of personality he thought I should have.' She felt the rage building again, the resentment. 'What are your parents like?'

'My parents . . .' They started downhill again, the road now thickly lined with trees on both sides. In another few weeks

Princeton would be a stunning blaze of color. 'My dad is more into achievement than joy. Mom is more into money than depth.'

'Ouch.' Rosalind was apparently not the only bitter child in the car. 'They sound delightful.'

'They are. That was my ungrateful son act. Dad used to do woodwork in college, really beautiful stuff, but he didn't consider that real work and went to law school. He met Mom there. I don't think she ever loved being a lawyer, just the income that went with it. They're good people, they just operate under a different set of values than I do.'

'Do you have siblings?'

'I have two brothers and a sister. All lawyers.'

'*All* lawyers?' She gaped when he nodded. 'Wow. How happy were your parents when you decided to sculpt?'

'That's where the cranky child comes from.'

She grimaced in sympathy. 'Not at all.'

'Not at all. But they got used to it. My little taste of success has helped.' He turned left, pointing to a house on the corner. 'Emil grew up in that house.'

'Ah.' She peered eagerly as they passed a nondescript ranch mostly hidden behind trees, picturing adorable little Emil – of course he would have been adorable – shooting basketballs into the net at the back of the driveway, maybe sledding down the tiny hill in the front yard. What had his childhood been like? She was too embarrassed to ask.

'Here we are.' They pulled into the semicircular driveway of a white colonial with black shutters whose perfect rectangular symmetry was broken only by a brick chimney on one end and a garage on the other.

'Your collector?'

'Yup. Sharon's not here, but she said it was fine for us to

check out the house and yard.' He put the car in park, switched off the motor and climbed out with her. 'I used to come here to work when I was starting on bigger projects and didn't have enough studio space.'

'She's your patron?'

He tilted his head, waiting for her to come around the car. 'In a way.'

'Your girlfriend?'

'Definitely not that. I'm the wrong generation and gender.' He stooped and picked up a key from under the mat.

'She trusts you at least.'

'Yeah, and it's a good thing, otherwise I wouldn't be able to steal so much from her.' He grinned at her expression, then opened the door and led the way into the house. 'What do you think? Wedding?'

Rosalind's first impression was that if Caitlin was planning a traditional bridal gown, she'd disappear when she walked into the house. There was a *lot* of white. Most walls, carpets, even some of the furniture. The decor was spare but tasteful; not crammed with art as Rosalind had expected from the term 'collector', but pieces beautifully presented, their color popping against the snowy background. And yet, the more she looked around, in spite of being a fan of crowded, colorful spaces, the more she sensed the warmth in the place. More to the point, she could see it fitting Caitlin and Emil's wedding.

'I think this is fabulous.'

'Yeah?' His face lit. 'I thought so too, but wanted to run it by someone before I brought Caitlin.'

'And Emil?'

He rolled his eyes, dimples showing. 'Yeah, him too, I guess.'

'Where is your work?' She eyed a creepy metal statue that

122

looked like fingers coming off of fingers and hoped that wasn't his, because she would have no way of faking admiration.

'Outside.'

Whew.

They continued through the house, footsteps echoing on hardwood floors, padding across rugs and carpets and into the spacious – white! – kitchen, which they determined, after counting ovens, burners and outlets, would support caterers fine.

Rosalind smoothed her hand over a section of teal tile, the only color in the room. 'I think this place is it.'

'I agree. And the price is right. Sharon's charging whatever it costs to clean up after the party. Plus the date is flexible, in case they have to reschedule suddenly.'

'Nice.' She felt a jolt of sadness, understanding that he was talking about Zaina's health.

'Let's check out the back yard, though it's pushing it to think we can be outdoors mid November, even with climate change.' He opened the door off the kitchen, and they stepped into the gorgeously landscaped yard.

Sculpture in several places. 'All yours?'

'No.'

'Which?'

'Guess.'

She walked to the center of the flagstone patio, feeling nervous, not sure if the tension was coming from him or her. Maybe both.

Nestled in one area near some rhododendrons, a rusted metal silhouette of a rooster. Nearby, an odd plastic-looking animal without features, which appeared to be standing on its head. In the middle of a patch of pachysandra, a stone statue of . . . a man? Woman? Hard to tell. The form was fluid, twisted, reaching upward.

She pointed. 'That one.'

'Yes.' He exhaled as if he'd been holding his breath, and came up behind her. 'How did you know?'

'Lucky guess.' Except it wasn't. She'd known immediately and couldn't even begin to articulate how or why except to say that the work fit him.

'What do you see in it?'

'I'm not sure.' She studied the graceful arch of the piece, how the figure crumpled in on itself on one side, stretched long on the other, both defeated and defiant. It made her want to rush back to her studio, toss her paints and try sculpting. 'Exhilaration, but also sadness.'

He said nothing until she turned, worried she'd upset him.

'Uh, yeah.' He pushed his glasses up his nose, and looked past her. 'That's pretty much it.'

'I love it, Bryn.' And what joy being able to say that sincerely. 'I have no idea how you got that much emotion out of a piece of stone.'

'*You* got that much.' He bunched his mouth and raised his eyebrows. 'Not everyone does.'

'When did Sharon buy it?'

'That was my very first sale. Almost five years ago.'

'No kidding.' Rosalind was oddly delighted, as if she'd discovered a treasure no one else knew about. 'How did it happen?'

'During college I worked summers for a landscaping company. Grunt work, but I liked it and the owner, Craig. When I finished grad school I went back to him part-time so I could afford to do some of my favorite things, like eating every day and sleeping under a roof.'

'The luxuries.'

'Exactly. One day our crew was over here, landscaping Sharon's yard. She didn't like any of the plants or trees Craig suggested for that spot, and couldn't envision what she wanted instead. Everyone was getting a little frustrated. Finally I suggested a sculpture, and she jumped on the idea. Friends of hers saw my piece and wanted something similar for their gardens. Then one of them threw a party and invited a *New York Times* reporter, who did a piece for the business section on the partnership of landscape architect and sculptor, and my career was officially born.'

'Wow.' She thumped her hand to her chest. 'That is amazing. Just like that.'

'Yeah.' He looked rather ruefully at the statue and shook his head.

'What?'

'It's kind of like what you said about your painting. After all the sales, after getting a solo show in SoHo, I keep expecting someone to figure out I'm not a *real* sculptor.'

'For heaven's sake.' Rosalind looked at him incredulously. 'You have no business feeling like a fake. Look at that gorgeous thing.'

'Yeah, but there are plenty of people as talented as I am, or more, who didn't have my luck, who haven't sold a thing. People who were all about art from the time they could hold a pen or brush or chisel. I was going to be a good Griffiths kid and go to law school.' He shook his head. 'I'm still not sure how all this happened.'

'No, no.' Rosalind put a hand on his arm. 'There's no threshold for sculptor-ness. You sell this many, you sell that many, who cares? You could sell none and still be a sculptor, because you sculpt.'

'And you're an artist because you paint.'

'No, no, that's totally different. I do not belong in that category.'

One eyebrow went up. 'Because . . .'

'I do it for fun. I haven't sold . . .' She laughed at his skeptical expression and gave up. 'Okay, you suck.'

'Ha!' He cracked up, looking down, shifting his weight, dimples adorable in his cheeks.

She wished she knew someone to match him up with. 'Do you take lessons in how to make people feel better?'

He gave her a sidelong look. 'Well, Rosalind Greer Braddock. That has to be the nicest thing anyone's said to me in a long time . . .'

'No way.'

'. . . that I believed.'

She grinned. 'You're welcome. Bryn . . . something Griffiths.'

'Alwyn.'

'Bryn Alwyn Griffiths. I like that.'

'Thanks.' He held her gaze for longer than was appropriate, but she wasn't uncomfortable. It was a really good moment, the kind that probably went unnoticed most of the time between two people, and which Rosalind couldn't remember feeling this consciously before.

That moment when two people decide, purely on instinct, that they can trust each other absolutely.

Chapter 8

October 17, 1967 (Tuesday)

The one thing my mom did right in my opinion was have me on October 17, which is Rita Hayworth's birthday, 'the love goddess'! Such a good omen, I think. I wouldn't mind being America's love goddess, that's for sure and for certain.

Today will go down in history as my best, best, best birthday ever. I found out that in the state of Maine, I can legally leave school when I turn seventeen. Seventeen! Guess when that is?

Today!

All my plans have seemed like daydreams that might or might not come true. Now I know they can, and they will. I don't have enough money yet, but I will work myself sick at Finch's Grocery if it means I don't have to stay in this stinking town much longer! Right now I'm thinking I'll leave after the spring musical, which I better get the lead in because I've already decided it's my last non-professional show.

Happy birthday to me. I am already halfway to New York!

Rosalind stood in the second-floor hallway of the Allertons' house, listening to Leila practice. Bryn had dropped her back home after their trip that morning, and she'd arrived at the Allerton's a few minutes earlier, buffeted by the wind and rain, and was welcomed warmly by Zaina, who was bursting with excitement over Rosalind's promise to look at her dress for Caitlin's wedding. While they chatted in the living room, an operatic phrase had drifted faintly down the stairs, accompanied by the distant tinkle of a piano. One look at Rosalind's awestruck face, and Zaina had encouraged her to tiptoe upstairs to listen outside Leila's bedroom-studio door.

The voice was astonishing, rich and warm with golden overtones. It seemed impossible that such an ethereal sound could come out of an ordinary person in an ordinary body, standing in her ordinary house on an ordinary day. Rosalind had always pictured opera singers as people of grand, almost mythic proportions – and not just physically. Her father had adored the art form, blasting LPs of the old greats through their house: Beverly Sills, Joan Sutherland, Luciano Pavarotti, Leontyne Price, Ben Heppner, Donald McIntyre. Saturday afternoons without fail, the Metropolitan Opera broadcasts would be on the radio in every room, whether Mom was in the mood or not, which she often wasn't. In his later years, Dad discovered satellite radio and the Met's twenty-four-hour opera channel, which delighted him, and which Lauren seemed to tolerate fine, though she didn't share his passion.

With the strange lack of logic that often invaded the human brain, Rosalind had always considered movie and theater actors as everyday beings, while artists and musicians were creatures touched by miracle. Having grown up around stars, she could sit in the audience watching her mother and mother's friends and colleagues on film, and only in very rare instances lose the people in the pain or joy of their characters. But it seemed to her, standing outside Leila's door, that the ability to transform a pleasant speaking voice into a brilliantly hued musical instrument had to be handed down from the divine.

When she could finally tear herself away, she crept back down the hallway so as not to disturb Leila, and back to the living room. Zaina was ready, holding up a beautiful royal-blue dress in a style typical of the 1950s – wide neckline with cap sleeves, a fitted bodice and sharply flared skirt. On the bodice, tiny pearls in a swirling design caught the light, creating a delicate and refined accent. 'This is my dress.'

'Oh Zaina, that is gorgeous.' Rosalind came over to touch the smooth silk, admiring its quality and characteristic subtle sheen. Unfortunately, the closer look showed discoloration under the arms from perspiration, the telltale outlines of water stains on the skirt, and a tear near the right shoulder.

'It was my wedding dress.'

Rosalind looked up from the garment. 'You got married in blue?'

'No, no, it was traditional white.' Zaina smiled at the dress with affection. 'After our wedding I had it shortened and dyed so I could wear it as an evening dress.'

'Very practical.'

'Sentimental, too. I loved the dress. I didn't want to put it away forever.'

'Did you get married here or in Lebanon?' Rosalind did a quick comparison of the dress's shape and Zaina's, partly hidden under her loose flowered shirt and skirt. The waist would have to be let out quite a bit.

'In Lebanon. July eighth, 1961, at the Tiger restaurant, a few weeks before we moved to the United States. It's still there, an old restaurant in the mountains with a balcony that comes right out of the rock. That's where we had the ceremony and the reception.' She looked off into her past, smiling dreamily. 'A breathtaking view of Beirut in the distance and the Mediterranean beyond. It was such a beautiful day. We danced and drank champagne and ate ourselves sick. After dark we stood watching the sea turn navy then black, and the lights come on to define the city. We were so happy.'

Rosalind's throat thickened. So much emotion, so many stories, so many chapters opened and closed, with Zaina's final one almost over. 'Do you have pictures?'

'Oh, yes, yes. But I'll only bore you with one of them.'

'I'd love to see whatever you want to show me.'

Zaina hauled herself to her feet. 'I know just the one.'

'Is it upstairs? I can get it for you if you'd like me to.'

'No, no. It's in the back bedroom. I'm sleeping there now. I moved the photo to be by my bed.' She shuffled over toward the opposite side of the living room from the kitchen.

As soon as Zaina's form disappeared through the doorway, Rosalind jumped to lift the skirt and examine the interior of the dress. French seams, which left a beautiful clean line inside, but which meant when she let out the waist, there would be color difference when the now-protected fabric was exposed, and wear where the double stitching method had been used. Hard to tell if there was even enough material to compensate for Zaina's larger size. The stains were impossible to fix unless Rosalind covered them with something. Scraps of lace? More pearls? The hole could be mended, but the fix would show. A corsage could cover at least part of the darning she'd have to do, but . . .

She hated to admit it, but she agreed with Caitlin and Leila that the dress wouldn't be wearable. Especially for an event this important. Zaina would want to look her best.

'Here.' Zaina walked slowly back in, breathing hard, holding out a picture in a gold frame, glasses dangling from a silver chain around her neck. 'This is Cecil and me, standing at the balcony.'

Rosalind straightened. 'Why don't we sit down?'

'Yes.' Zaina let herself drop on to the burgundy sofa and patted the cushion next to her for Rosalind. 'Tomorrow morning I get fluid build-up drained out of me. That will help me breathe better again. Such a nuisance, this dying.'

Rosalind's chest constricted. She still couldn't get used to the casual way Zaina talked about her life being over, but she'd like to think she'd be able to accept her own death that gracefully. Hard to imagine the courage it took, and the depth of faith. 'I'm glad it will help you be more comfortable.'

'Best of all, my waist will deflate like a balloon. You won't have to let the dress out as much as it looks now.' Zaina put on her glasses and held up the portrait. 'So. Here we are on our wedding day. You see how beautiful the place is.'

'Oh, yes.' Rosalind took the picture reverently, staring at the couple. A young knockout stared back with Zaina's dark eyes, skin smooth and neat brows dark, her nearly black hair pulled into a low bun around which cascaded her veil. The dress, easily identifiable as the one next to them, draped down and out of the picture, pristine white. Next to her, Cecil – Rosalind's grandfather – tall, blond and handsome, with a wide grin under a bushy mustache and kind eyes, a lovely Viking who'd conquered this beautiful woman. Behind them, the city of Beirut, a sparkling carpet at the edge of the nothingness that was the Mediterranean. 'You are movie-star beautiful, Zaina. And your husband is so handsome. What a view! You were right, it's a spectacular place.'

'It was a good day.' Zaina nudged her and pointed to the darkness at the edge of the frame. 'A good night, too. We conceived Leila after the wedding, I'm convinced.'

'Really.' Rosalind couldn't stop staring at the picture, at Zaina's exotic features, her dark hair and brows a dramatic contrast to her faintly olive skin. At Cecil's apple-pie face and erect posture, seeing hints of Leila's features in both. Nothing of her own. 'I wish I could have met him.'

'You would have loved him. Everyone did.'

'Was it hard coming here to the US? To Princeton? A big adjustment?'

'Oh, sure, sure.' Zaina nodded a little sadly. 'I missed my family. I missed the weather. I missed our summer house in Zahleh like I'd lost a limb. We lived in Beirut, but I always felt Zahleh was where I belonged.'

'Tell me about . . .' Rosalind didn't trust herself to pronounce the syllables so graceful on Zaina's tongue, 'that town and your house.'

'Zahleh is a small city in the mountains. We had a beautiful stone house there, very traditional, with balconies and arched windows, bright shutters and lovely carvings. We owned many acres. My parents grew apples, grapes, plums, figs and mulberries.' She paused for breath, hand to her chest. 'Also almonds and walnuts and olives. It was paradise. Truly.'

Rosalind thought of the tomato plant she'd tried and failed to grow in a pot on her fire escape. 'It sounds it.'

'We'd make our own olive oil, and dry grapes in the sun to make raisins. Local and sustainable as you'd say now, eh?' She laughed. 'Of course it was about more than food, though food is very important. Eating is how we Lebanese cement family and friend relationships and grow new ones. It helps build and maintain the community. We'd go en masse to a restaurant or one of the coffee houses. The kids would play, the grownups would talk. Who takes the time to do that here? Always so busy, all of us. We don't nurture relationships or community. Not that way. Not here.'

'It sounds so lovely.'

'Here you have to work much harder to find your tribe, especially in a big city. Here families are scattered like leaves in the wind. Is your family nearby?'

'California, Massachusetts and Maine.'

'And you move around so much.' She clicked her tongue in disapproval. 'No roots. No tribe.'

'You're right.' Rosalind resolved that when she got back to New York, she'd work harder to build her tribe. She had friends from her job, a few from her building, some from the gym and her book clubs, but she hadn't done much to try to bring them together. It seemed like a lot of work. 'No wonder you miss Lebanon.'

'It is a beautiful place. Of course Beirut was badly damaged during the civil war, and clumsily rebuilt.' Zaina took off her glasses and held them up. 'Leila will tell you I see the country now through a rosy pair of these.'

'Rosy lenses are not always a bad thing.' Rosalind touched Zaina's soft hand. 'I have many pairs myself. They're good for getting through hard times.'

'Very true.'

'Tell me about coming to Princeton.'

'Oh yes, you asked. I forgot. Princeton was a welcoming place for the most part. I made friends with other graduate student wives and eventually other faculty and their wives too, when Cecil started teaching. And there were a surprising number of Lebanese here. If I got homesick for Arabic food, we'd take a trip to New Brunswick or Brooklyn for supplies and cook at home.' She patted Rosalind's knee. 'We're planning a Lebanese meal for my birthday. You'll be able to taste the food made the way it's supposed to be made.'

For one thrilling second, Rosalind thought she was being invited to the party itself. Thank goodness, before she put Zaina in an awkward spot by enthusiastically accepting a non-invitation, she realized that she was still part of this family only in her own mind. Zaina must mean she could try leftovers. 'I'd love that, thank you.'

'Settled.'

Rosalind put the picture down on the coffee table so the happy couple smiled out at them, wondering what it was like to care so much about someone that you would leave your entire life behind for his sake. She'd left LA and Wolf when his bad-boy rock-star persona had gone from exciting to exasperating, though she'd also started to feel caged by the sameness of living in the place she grew up. She'd left Denver after Troy's tree-hugging spirituality became restrictive instead of refreshing. 'You were brave to leave your country and go overseas.'

'I was in love.' She said it as if there was no other option. 'Cecil made up for the loneliness. For everything. I never regretted leaving with him. Even in the hard times.'

'Did you consider moving back to Lebanon after he died?'

'Maybe for a few days, during the worst of the grief. But my life was here by then, and Leila's life was always here. It was traumatic enough for her to lose her father at thirteen without me changing everything else. They were very close. Like this.' She lifted crossed fingers. 'Daddy's little girl. Oh, did I have my hands full when he was gone. So much pain at such a young age. I sometimes wonder if it kept her from settling with a man.'

Rosalind nodded politely, wondering why people always assumed damage when straight women remained unmarried. As if it wasn't possible to be a happy, healthy female *sans* husband.

'So!' Zaina ran an affectionate hand down the luminous

skirt of her dress. 'Will I be able to wear this at Caitlin's wedding?'

Rosalind tightened her lips, hating to break the bad news. 'It would be very difficult to fix.'

Zaina's face fell. 'I see. Of course.'

'There are water stains, and the color has faded.'

'Yes.' The hand stroking the silk was wrinkled and spare, but the fingers were slender and still straight. On her fourth, Zaina wore a modest sapphire and diamond engagement ring, and the gold band her husband must have given her the day the picture was taken. 'I planned to be buried in this dress. I wanted to wear it one last time while I'm still living. To one more wedding.'

'I'm not sure I could let out the seams enough that it would fit you. There isn't much material to play with.' Rosalind had to clear her throat. 'The alterations would show brighter than the rest of the dress. Like a stripe.'

'Ah. Well then.' Zaina clasped her hands firmly in her lap, brave smile fixed in place. 'If it can't be done, it can't be done. It's my birthday two weeks from today, October sixteenth. One day before your mother's.'

Rosalind blinked, always surprised by how much celebrity gossip stuck in people's heads. 'So it is.'

'I'll ask for a new dress.'

'Wait a second.' The idea popped into Rosalind's head so quickly she nearly jumped off the couch in excitement. 'I just had an idea of how I can make this work.'

'Yes?' Zaina's expression lit hopefully. 'You think the dress can be fixed?'

'It won't be . . . exactly the same.'

'Would I embarrass Caitlin at her wedding by wearing it?'

Rosalind had to suppress a giggle of sheer delight. 'I guarantee you will not.'

'Oh! Can you really do this?' Zaina clasped her hands to her chest, color flooding her cheeks, eyes shining. 'I knew God brought you here for a reason. Maybe Cecil sent you to us!'

'Maybe he did.' Rosalind grinned affectionately at her grand-mother, wishing she could acknowledge the link right then, claim both her and Cecil as family. Instead, she stood. 'I should measure you so I can make the alterations. Do you have a tape?'

'Yes, upstairs. Though my waist will change after the pro-cedure tomorrow.' Zaina leaned forward, preparing to get up.

'No, no. You stay there. I can get it.'

'Thank you. It's in my room.' She pointed over her shoulder toward the stairs. 'Last door on the left. In the top drawer of my sewing table, by the closet.'

'Sure.' Rosalind climbed the stairs, pausing again to listen to Leila singing something vaguely familiar, something Rosalind's father must have played. As a child Rosalind had been disdainful of the full-throated sounds of classical singing. Now she wished she'd paid more attention. When she got back to New York, she'd start going to operas at the Met. It would be lovely to share that obsession with her birth mother.

Opening Zaina's door, Rosalind smiled. Exactly the warm, tasteful look of Zaina herself. More bright Oriental rugs on the hardwood floor, an old-fashioned sleigh bed in dark wood with a floral bedspread. A vanity that looked like it had been made in the 1950s, its mirrored lid open, exposing makeup and half-used bottles of perfume cluttering the interior. On every surface, vanity, dresser, desk, there were knick-knacks – some clearly valuable, some trinkets – and, among them, framed photographs.

At the sewing table, Rosalind stopped and reached for a picture. Leila. Young, beaming, standing on a beach at the edge of the water in a flowing sundress the wind had plastered to her rounded body.

Pregnant. With Caitlin? Or Rosalind?

Not Rosalind, born in April, unless the beach was in the tropics.

Sweat pricked her forehead and under her arms. How many times as a little girl had she stared in wonderment at the picture in her mother's pregnancy bible, imagining herself curled up safe and warm in that enormous belly? How many times had Mom talked about feeling Rosalind's insistent kicking, about how she couldn't wait until her second little girl decided to come out? That she knew Rosalind had picked the eighth day of April because it was the day she'd be at the peak of her perfect infancy?

Rosalind put the picture down abruptly, opened the top drawer and took out the measuring tape, white plastic with black markings.

She still didn't understand how her mother could have brought herself to go through faking *three* pregnancies. Did she want to? Or did Dad have to force her, to protect his cheating from being exposed?

'Did you find it?' Zaina's voice came up the stairs.

'Yes.' Rosalind hurriedly closed the drawer and ran back downstairs. 'Sorry, I got caught looking at pictures. The one of Leila, pregnant on the beach. She looks so beautiful.'

'Yes.' Zaina smiled tightly. 'I love that one.'

Rosalind stayed standing, clinging to the measuring tape as if it were a lifeline. 'How pregnant was she?'

'Let's see. I think about six months.' Zaina fingered the glasses around her neck. 'More than halfway through.'

'So Caitlin was born . . . ?'

'June fourteenth.'

June. No help figuring out which child was *in utero*. For either daughter, at six months pregnant, Leila had to be standing on a beach somewhere warmer than the northeast.

'Shall we start?' Rosalind helped Zaina to standing, and measured her waist. 'Thirty-two now . . .'

'After tomorrow's procedure it will be thirty again. I'll make sure to get drained right before the wedding.'

Rosalind covered a wince. Such an indignity. 'I'll put down thirty.'

After finishing the measurements, she was pleased to note the pattern wouldn't have to be radically altered to fit Zaina's older body. A little more room in the bust, a little more in the waist – the full skirt would hide the rest.

'That should do.' She picked the dress up carefully by its hanger. 'I'll get right to work on it.'

'No, no, not now.' Zaina gestured to the space beside her, still beaming. 'Stay and have more of a chat. We're already making you work too hard.'

Rosalind hesitated, wanting to start calling fabric stores immediately, but tempted by the chance to spend more of the precious time left with her grandmother. 'I can stay a bit, thank you.'

'So.' Zaina waited until Rosalind had sat back down. 'We got talking and I forgot to ask. How was your trip with Bryn this morning?'

'Productive. We looked at three places – a hotel, a house, and a funky old barn that was totally cool, but not right for—'

'Yes, yes. Bryn texted Caitlin, and she told Leila and me already. It's ridiculous how fast information flies around these days. Like a rocket bird.'

'You already knew.' Rosalind was obviously missing something.

'Forgive me.' Zaina gave her a look of pure mischief. 'I wasn't asking about the venues.'

'Ah. I see.' Rosalind hated to disappoint her. 'Bryn is very sweet. We had a good time.'

'But . . . ?'

She spread her hands helplessly. 'No spark.'

'Is that all?' Zaina smiled indulgently. 'Give it time. The spark will come when it's ready. You two would be good for one another.'

'I'm not—'

The front door flew open. Steps sounded, then Caitlin appeared in the doorway, her beige raincoat dotted with drops, cheeks pink from the chill.

'Hi, Teta, I'm meeting Emil— Oh.' She stopped. 'Hi, Rosalind. What are you doing here?'

'Caitlin, did I teach you those manners?'

'Sorry.' She shook her head, as if coming out of a trance. 'I was just surprised. Thanks for spending your morning on my wedding, Rosalind.'

'Sure.'

'She's here to look at my dress. She thinks she can fix it.'

'Oh.' Caitlin's mouth snapped shut on the word. 'Really.'

'Really. And what are *you* doing here?'

'Who taught you those manners?' Caitlin shook her head, smile back to genuine. 'I'm meeting Emil. We're taking the afternoon off, going to taste champagne and wine, and interview a minister.'

Zaina pretended horror. 'Not in that order!'

'No, no, don't worry. Is Mom here?'

'She's—' On cue, Leila hit a rich, trilling high note.

'That answers that. I won't bother her.' Caitlin came a few steps into the living room. 'So, Rosalind, you thought Sharon's house was the best place?'

'Yes.' Rosalind struggled to think how to describe it. 'It's the perfect mix of homey and impersonal. Comfortable, but you won't feel like you're having your wedding in a stranger's house the way you would if you were a stranger coming here, for example. This house very much embodies the personalities of the people in it. Hers not so much.'

'Okay.' Caitlin frowned. 'Bryn said something similar. I'd always pictured a church and traditional reception hall, so I was leaning toward the Chauncey.'

'Oh dear. My death is interfering with your wedding.' Zaina was only half teasing.

'Teta, don't be silly.' Caitlin waved her grandmother's concern away, looking suitably abashed. 'I'm having a Bridezilla moment, is all. It's been so crazy. I will happily do without the fantasy wedding if it means you can be there.'

'In my blue dress.'

Caitlin glanced at Rosalind and bunched her mouth. 'We'll see what Rosalind can do.'

Rosalind's stomach sank. Apparently offering to fix the dress had not felt like a generous gesture to everyone. Where her sister was concerned, she seemed to be making every wrong move possible. 'Caitlin, when do you want to talk about hairstyles?'

'Oh . . . God, I don't know. I'm so frazzled.' She put a hand to her perfect smooth forehead. 'How about next . . . God, I don't know—'

The door sounded again, open, then shut. Emil appeared beside his fiancée, also pink-cheeked, hair shining with raindrops, blue eyes blazing from his impossibly handsome face. Rosalind told herself not to react.

Too late.

'Hi, Zaina.' He lifted a hand, then his gaze lit on Rosalind. '*Hey!* What a surprise. Nice to see you. Hear you had a good trip this morning.'

Rosalind nodded, intensely annoyed at herself for starting to blush. Bryn would dive into a burning building to rescue his love. Emil would back slowly away, wishing he could have done more. And which one set *her* on fire?

She forced herself to sound nonchalant. 'You and Caitlin should visit Sharon's house and the Chauncey Hotel. The barn not so much.'

'That's what Bryn said. You saved us time, thanks.'

Caitlin and Emil looked in unison toward the staircase, so Rosalind wasn't surprised when Leila spoke behind her. 'Caitlin, hi, I thought I heard you. Hi, Rosalind. Thank you for spending your morning in service to the Great Event.'

'No problem.' Rosalind turned on the couch to watch her mother enter the room. She looked stunning today, her flyaway chestnut curls pulled back into a loose bun, her lean body perfectly framed by an olive-green sweater dress she'd accessorized with a scarf in fall colors secured by a gold pin. Rosalind felt a jolt of longing. 'You sounded beautiful up there.'

'Oof, I'm not in good voice today. You're easy to please.' Leila smiled and put her hands on her mother's shoulders, then her face fell. 'God, not the dress, Mama. Please let us get you a new—'

'Rosalind can fix it.' Zaina patted the material. 'It will be perfect again.'

'Really?' Leila raised a skeptical eyebrow. 'You can work a miracle like that?'

'I can't promise. But I can try. It will be ready in plenty of time for you to find something else if you don't like it.' Rosalind's face reheated. She planned to remake the dress from scratch for Zaina's birthday in a slightly larger size, replacing the existing pearls on to new material. She didn't want to spoil the surprise and, in case she couldn't find appropriate fabric, didn't want to get Zaina's hopes up any higher.

Leila and Caitlin exchanged a glance that made Rosalind squirm.

'Am I the only one besides Zaina who believes in Rosalind's superpowers?' Emil winked at her.

'Emil.' Caitlin tugged at his arm. 'Stop flirting. We have to go or we'll be late.'

'I'm coming. Thanks for taking all this on, Rosalind. Will we see you at dinner tonight?'

'No, no.' She held up her hands, double stop sign, glad to be given the chance to emphasize that she did recognize boundaries. 'I've invaded plenty in the past couple of days. I'm not here to camp out.'

'Another night maybe.' He drilled his eyes into hers.

Along with the fizz, Rosalind felt a prickle of annoyance. Why was he doing this to his fiancée?

'We're off.' Caitlin tugged on his arm again. 'See you later, Mom.'

'Bye, you two, have fun.' Leila looked in concern at her mother, whose bloom of color had faded into pallor. 'Mama, let's get you down for a nap.'

'Down for a nap! Like I'm three years old.' But she let her daughter help her to her feet.

Rosalind picked up the dress. 'I'll see you later.'

'Why, do you have plans right now?' Leila asked.

'Not particularly. I was going to go back and call my sister. Then start work on—'

'I have to find a mother-of-the-bride dress.' Leila took Zaina's arm. 'I need another opinion. Feel like hanging around a bit longer?'

Rosalind's heart started thumping. This woman with

exquisite taste did not need an opinion from she-who-dressed-like-a-clown.

Leila had something to say to her: *Stay away from my mother's dress*, or, *Stay away from my daughter's fiancé*, or, maybe, *I am your mother, welcome to the family*.

'Happy to help.'

'Back in a second.' Leila tenderly escorted her mother to the back bedroom, then led the way into the kitchen.

Rosalind gestured to her own outfit. 'You're trying to find something like this, I assume.'

'Exactly the look I'm going for.' Leila smiled, and their eyes met; hers shifted quickly away. 'I'm going to make a cup of tea, want one? Or coffee?'

'Tea is fine.'

'Tea it is.' Leila started filling the bright red kettle. 'I use a black tea and make it strong, that okay?'

'Absolutely. Can I help with anything?' Rosalind stood in the center of the room, feeling like her arms were in the wrong place no matter where she put them.

'Not a thing.' Leila put the kettle on the stove and turned on the flame. 'So you and Bryn got along okay?'

'Sure. Yes.' She pretended annoyance. 'Is there something horribly wrong with him that everyone is trying to foist him on me?'

'Besides the leprosy?' Leila opened a cabinet and brought down a clear jar filled with black twiggy leaves. 'No, he's fabulous. A little lonely, though, Mama and I think. We want him to be happy.'

'He can't be happy single?'

'Perfect point, but you know what I mean.' She grabbed down a teapot. 'It's harder for men. We women are much better at it. Being happy and single, I mean. I'm living proof.'

'Me too.' Rosalind felt herself practically glowing. They had this in common, this trait that no one else in her family understood.

'People always say it, don't they? "I don't understand why you're single! You're so pretty!"' Leila imitated a critic with a high snarky voice. 'Like there's obviously something deeply wrong with me. Like I'm secretly gay or in denial.'

'Don't forget emotionally damaged.'

'Ha! Emotionally damaged for sure.' She spooned tea into the pot, then leaned against the counter, waiting for the kettle, arms braced loosely behind her, gazing up into middle distance. 'I have had some great loves. But after a while, enough is enough. I'm ready to be on my own again.'

'Yes.' Rosalind's chest felt heavy with emotion. Leila was tilting her world on its axis. 'I am the same way.'

'No kidding.' For the first time, Leila really looked at her. Rosalind stood holding her breath, waiting for her mother to state the obvious, desperate for her to say it and terrified at the same time. 'It's funny. Caitlin wanted the whole white picket fence thing from the moment she was born.'

'Really?' Rosalind's voice caught.

'I used to wonder if that was in reaction to me never settling down with anyone.'

'Oh, but she's had you and Zaina her whole life. She's had this beautiful home her whole life.' Rosalind ached with envy. What she wouldn't have given for that experience of family.

'True. I guess people are born the way they are. I had two parents who adored each other. You did too . . .'

Rosalind froze, horrified by the gall of Leila saying such a thing if she and Rosalind's father had been lovers.

Maybe lovers. Emil's theory, one that made a tremendous amount of sense, but still only a theory.

She remained speechless, caught between wanting to bond with this beautiful, talented woman by admitting to the battles and rages in her childhood house, during which she'd cower in her closet, clutching her Heart Family dolls, telling them not to worry, that she'd keep them safe. But it wasn't up to her to expose that truth when her parents had taken such extraordinary measures to maintain the image of the perfect family. Exposing that truth to her father's mistress? Unthinkable.

'Well.' Leila abruptly turned back to the counter. 'Caitlin's getting her perfect life now. I just hope she knows what she's wishing for.'

'They seem happy together.' Sort of.

'I wouldn't have picked him for her. But she loves him. He . . . Well, you saw how he is.' She got down two mugs. 'I think he's afraid marriage will turn him ugly. Hence the flirting. To reassure himself he's still attractive.'

Rosalind couldn't help the jolt of disappointment and shame, chiding herself for not realizing the truth sooner. 'Yeah, I didn't think it was about me.'

'I'm not saying it isn't. You're adorable.'

Rosalind laughed uncomfortably. 'Thank you. But I promise I'm not out to score with your daughter's fiancé.'

'Well, *that's* a relief.' Leila glanced over with a smirk to show she was teasing. Rosalind hoped she was. 'Emil . . . had a tough childhood, he and Bryn both. Alcoholic parents. Bryn's mom, Emil's dad. It's not an ideal way to grow up, though I think it bound them together in some way. Well, you know something about that, too.'

Rosalind inhaled slowly, started counting to ten, then told herself Leila only knew what everyone else did. The publicity her mother adored had meant her weaknesses became as public as her strengths. Though even when the press found out about

145

the second stint in rehab, Jillian Croft's popularity had remained intact. Her father's had only been further burnished as the saint who supported her through the toughest of times.

Rosalind had bought into that as deeply as anyone.

'Anyway, I figure either Emil and Cait will stay together, or they won't. I can't see him staying true to her, and I can see her looking the other way when he strays. She's as much in love with his credentials and the life she imagines they'll have together as she is with him.'

'God, Leila, that's so depressing.'

'Only if you decide it is.' The kettle shrilled. Leila poured water into the teapot, peering to check the level while waving away vision-obscuring steam.

'You know, Rosalind . . .' She covered the pot with its lid and a floral tea cozy. 'When you have a daughter, you think you're going to have a carbon copy of yourself. A child you can teach about what you believe a woman is.' She spoke slowly, with uncharacteristic gravity, then turned and smiled wistfully at Rosalind. 'And then you give birth to this fully formed person who has no interest whatsoever in what you want her to be. I've learned to respect that. Caitlin is a grownup. She's made her choice. I will support her. Oh my God, I've made you cry, I'm sorry.'

Rosalind wiped away tears, laughing. 'No, forget it. I'm being ridiculous.'

'What did I say?'

She couldn't think how to broach the topic, waiting so long for her whirling brain to settle on an explanation that she half expected Leila to change the subject. But her birth mother stayed still, cool as always, eyebrows half lifted, waiting for an answer with no sign of impatience.

Finally Rosalind hit on what she wanted to say. 'I adored

my mother. She was every bit as remarkable as people expected her to be. But she would never have made that speech about me.'

'Ah.' Leila folded her arms across her chest. 'I didn't know your mom. Not that I knew your dad well, but from his writings and teachings it was hard not to feel I did.'

Rosalind felt her heart speeding again. 'And you met him . . .'

'Yes.' Leila stared at the wall next to Rosalind's head. 'But I can imagine your mother had demons that made it hard for her to be there for her daughters the way your dad was.'

Rosalind locked her jaw to keep the next wave of fury down, not trusting herself to speak until it had passed. She'd always been protective of her mother; not as blindly as Olivia, but instinctively she'd felt Mom's vulnerability and need. This time it was unbearable to hear her criticized by the woman who had probably been her father's mistress, a woman who knew nothing about Mom's true nature except whatever self-justifying bullshit Daniel Braddock might have told her.

Her anger deflated, leaving her exhausted by the teeter-totter of emotions. Empathy would help her through this. Jillian Croft had not been Mommy Heart, apparently part of the reason Rosalind was standing in this kitchen. Leila had doubtless succumbed to the notorious Daniel Braddock charm, in the same way Olivia and Eve's mothers most likely had, in the same way the world had, and always would, succumb to his type. 'Dad had his own issues.'

'I'm sure he did. Most people do.' Leila swept up an escaped strand of hair and tucked it into her bun, looking thoughtful. 'Is it too whiny to say I would have loved to have had my dad around longer, even with issues?'

Rosalind wrinkled her nose, calmer, but unwilling to bend into sympathy yet. 'Yeah, it's pretty whiny.'

Leila gave her a startled glance, then laughed, came across the kitchen and gave Rosalind a quick hug that stunned and nearly undid her.

'All right, you. To the computer. Let's look at some dresses.'

Chapter 9

January 1, 1968 (Monday)

Happy New Year. I had an awful thought today. What if the reason I am not having my period is because my mom had them do that surgery on me so I couldn't? She said so many times she hopes I never have to deal with a kid like me. Maybe she made sure of it. My scars are near where my ovaries are supposed to be. I looked that up. Is that what they took out?

I'd ask but she would just deny it, whether she had it done or not. I think not being able to trust someone who is supposed to love you must be the worst sentence ever.

Really, though, it seems too horrible even for her. I'm not sure I deep-down believe she could do something like that to me. And I was late late late *even before the surgery. But I hate that it worries me. I should feel safer than that.*

Tryouts for the spring play are in a few weeks. It's going to be South Pacific. *I am going to get the part of Nellie. Or else!*

I'm feeling blue today. Even the thought of New York isn't much help. It's so cold and gray here, the dazzle and freedom of the city seems so far away. I can't imagine how I'll survive the wait.

* * *

Back across the street after the strange episode with Leila, Rosalind laid Zaina's dress across the blue-covered king-size bed in her rented house's large master bedroom, and paced over to the pair of rain-streaked windows overlooking the street – mostly obscured by the large oak in the house's front yard – then back to the bed. She was sleeping in the room down the hall on the north side of the house, more comfortable in the smaller space. This room, however, would make a perfect sewing project room. Downstairs in the basement she'd noticed a large folding table, ideal for her machine, which she'd ask Ruth, the friend and neighbor watering her plants in New York, to overnight to Princeton. She could set that up next to the double windows for light and view. On the smooth hardwood floors she could lay out and trace the dress pieces to make a new pattern, which she'd alter, then re-cut in the new material. The suede recliner by the southern window would be a cozy, relaxed spot for the tedious tasks of hemming the dress and sewing pearls back on its bodice.

None of which she wanted to embark on now. She was still jittery after the talk with Leila, roiled up and bouncing from emotion to emotion without any idea how to process the feelings. Angry, happy, bitter, yearning . . . such a peaceful combination.

She should call Dad, see how he was doing. It had been a week. Maybe more than a week.

Not now. She scrubbed her fingers through her hair, barely an inch long, dark roots showing under the blond.

Maybe she should try meditating. She'd gotten into the habit when she lived in Denver, dating Troy, who'd introduced her to the concept. Rosalind had enjoyed the calming effect, finding it seeped into the rest of her day, even though her sessions lasted all of ten to fifteen minutes, the maximum she could manage to hold still. Troy could probably have spent the rest of his life motionless and concentrating. Rosalind had kept up the practice for a while after her move to New York, but had admittedly gone back to her old habits. The city swept her up in its energy from the moment she got out of bed until she dropped back into it.

Maybe she'd be able to succeed here, surrounded by the peaceful charm of this little neighborhood and town. On a throw rug by the window, she positioned herself in a half-lotus – her knees wouldn't contort enough for the full one – closed her eyes and focused on her breathing.

Tried to clear her mind of the chatter that had invaded it.

Tried to free her body of the tension keeping relaxation hostage.

Observed her body's rhythms, gently pushing thoughts out of her mind as they occurred, without blame, without judgment or—

Argh! She couldn't do this.

Okay, shh. Rosalind allowed herself to have that thought, then determinedly settled in again, relaxing her muscles one at a time, breathing in, breathing out . . .

In. Out.

Did Leila have an affair with her father? How could Rosalind negotiate this new relationship with Leila if her birth mother had betrayed Mom?

Relax. Breathe.

In. Out.

A gust of wind rattled the windows.

In . . . Out . . .

Maybe it was best for Rosalind to go agnostic on the issue, acknowledge that she didn't yet know details or truths, so it was better to approach Leila as an innocent until proven otherwise.

Her shoulders, which had crept back up, relaxed again. This made sense. This she could do.

Her breathing deepened. Her muscles began to unwind in earnest. Now she was getting somewhere!

No, don't think that.

In. Out.

From her bedroom down the hall, her phone started ringing. Rosalind had forgotten to turn it off.

One eye opened. She should ignore it. Take advantage of this growing peace and see it through.

In. Out—

What if it was important? What if something had happened to Dad and she hadn't been in touch?

Crap.

She scrambled to her feet and rushed down the hall, grabbed the phone off the unmade bed and peered at the display.

Eve.

Did she want to talk to Eve? She had nothing to add to what she'd already shared with Eve except that she was bouncing around new horrific possibilities. Didn't make much of a story.

While she hesitated, the call went to voicemail and Rosalind was hit with an absurd sense of loss. Eve was part of the family Rosalind knew, the part she could still count on. Eve hadn't wanted to hear anything about her own birth family and adoption, but she'd been interested in if not always supportive of Rosalind's search so far.

She dialed her sister back. 'Hey, Eve, sorry, just missed you.'

'Not a problem. How are you? We haven't talked in a while. What's going on? Are you in New Jersey?'

'Yes. I'm here.' She wished she'd been able to get further into meditation before having this conversation. 'In Princeton.'

'Have you met Leila?'

'Yes. And her family.' She felt stiff, like her mouth was having trouble moving.

'*So?* Is it awful? What's happening? Why aren't you telling me everything?'

'No, it's not awful.' She roused herself to sound typically cheerful. 'Let's see. Leila's daughter Caitlin is getting married. She's a bit of a princess, and I don't think she's quite sure what to make of me, but she's friendly enough.'

'Does she know who you are?'

'No. Her fiancé is Emil, gorgeous, a player, total preppy Princeton guy, exactly the stereotype.'

'Does *he* know?'

'No. Then Zaina, Leila's mom, Lebanese, warm, lovely. I wish you could meet her, you would love her. We should have had a grandma like that.'

'Does *she* know who you are?'

'No. Then Leila is . . . she's beautiful.' Rosalind found herself getting choked up. 'Very lively, kind of a free spirit, I think.'

'That's familiar.'

'Exactly.' She put a hand to her chest. 'Yes, exactly. A lot like me in many ways, and—'

'How did she react when you told her?'

'I haven't yet.'

Silence. Rosalind's stomach started churning.

'How long have you been there, Rosalind?'

'Two days, Eve. I met her yesterday.'

'Okay, so . . . what's the plan? When are you telling her?'

Rosalind put her hand to her forehead, anticipating a headache. 'There is no plan, and I'm not sure.'

More silence. 'You're not sure.'

'I'll do it when it feels right.' She started pacing, hallway to master bedroom doorway, to stairs and back. 'This isn't like announcing to Leila that she won a sweepstakes. I want her – all of them – to trust me first, and like me. I want to get a feel for how this will go, or if it's even the right thing to do.'

'I guess it is pretty complicated. What are you doing in the meantime?'

'Helping them plan Caitlin and Emil's wedding.'

'You're . . . Are you *kidding* me?' Her sister was being unusually sharp. 'How did that happen?'

'They asked me to help. Or, I volunteered, and they accepted. They're having to hurry because—'

'They know already, Rosalind. They have to. Why else would they let a total stranger into the house and ask her to help plan a major family event?'

Rosalind closed her eyes. She didn't want to think about this. Not now. She didn't want another thing to turn out nothing like she'd expected. 'Because I'm adorable?'

'No one is that adorable.'

Nausea threatened in earnest. Rosalind stopped her pacing opposite the bathroom, just in case. 'Excuse me, I am exactly that adorable.'

'Rosalind. Come on . . .'

'They are desperate for help, and I not only showed up at the right time, but my talents are exactly what they need. I'm helping remake a dress for Zaina, and I'll be doing Caitlin's—'

'Leila knows who you are. Maybe all of them do.'

'Why wouldn't she say anything?'

'Most likely she's waiting for you. So do it.'

Rosalind put a hand to her queasy middle. 'It's been *two days*. I will when I'm ready. Calm down.'

'It's why you're there.'

Something was definitely bugging her sister. This was more

like talking to Olivia than Eve. 'They have some big events coming up, Zaina's birthday, the wedding . . . I don't want to add to their stress.'

'They already know, Rosalind. At least Leila must. What could you possibly gain by . . .'

Rosalind waited a few beats for her sister to continue, then frowned. 'Eve?'

'Rosalind . . .' Eve's voice was gentler now. 'Is this about wanting them to be your family?'

Rosalind's stomach turned over. 'For God's sake, Eve, they *are* my family.'

'No. We are. Dad, Olivia, me – even Lauren. These people are total strangers.'

'Which is why I'm getting to know them.'

'I think it's a bad idea.'

'You think everything I do is a bad idea.'

'No. That is not true. Remember when you snuck me to In and Out Burger after Mom decided we should all go vegetarian? *That* was a good idea.'

Rosalind managed a smile. 'That *was* a good idea.'

'Listen, big sister. You know I just want to keep you from getting blown up by your own enthusiasm. I love you and I don't want you getting hurt by this. Mom and Dad obviously had their extremely twisted reasons for doing what they did. I'm just afraid if we try to untwist them, it'll open a Pandora's box of other horrors.'

Rosalind leaned against the wall and slid down to a squat. Eve was right there. Some had come flying out already. 'It's already happened.'

'What's happened?'

She braced herself, eyes closed, hating to do this to her sister. 'I think Dad might have had an affair with Leila.'

'That wouldn't surprise me.'

Rosalind's eyes shot open. Whatever she'd been expecting Eve to say, that wasn't it. 'What? What do you mean, it wouldn't surprise you?'

'Just that. It wouldn't.'

'Why not?'

'You know what Mom was like. He probably needed a break.'

Rosalind gasped, struggling to make words. 'How can you talk about this like it's nothing?'

Her sister sighed. 'Because, Rosalind, I've been thinking about this a lot. Not just since we stumbled over that paper. Before, too.'

'But . . . Dad was devoted to her.'

'He was also a man, and she was a bigger star than he was and a pain in the ass who might not have had a vagina. Men find those pretty indispensable.'

Rosalind recoiled. 'Stop. Stop talking like it's . . . it's some kind of . . .'

'Fact?' Her sister's pragmatic tone was infuriating. 'They wanted kids. Dad decided to go out and get them, happy-ever-after for everyone.'

'No.' She struggled back up to standing. 'There is no way Mom would be in on this. She was crazy jealous, especially in her worst moments. Let him have sex with another woman? That's completely nuts.'

'I don't know, Rosalind.' Eve sounded world-weary. 'I just don't know. Neither of us does. And since we don't, and our lives are fine, it seems to me digging up the possible ugliness is pointless. But you're already ass-deep in it, so I don't know what to tell you. Just be careful.'

Rosalind opened her mouth to let her sister have it, then

backed off. Olivia had turned lecturing her sisters on her version of truth into an art form. Eve not so much. In fact, almost never. 'I *am* being careful. I promise. How are *you* doing? How are things at home? At work? You don't sound quite like yourself.'

Silence. Then a long sigh. 'I'm sorry, Rosalind. I'm PMSing. Plus work is driving me crazy. Plus . . .'

Rosalind twisted her mouth. 'You? Mike?'

'No, I'm fine. He's fine. I mean, not fine, but not injured or sick. School starting up again has helped. He's at least forced to get up and out. I've managed to convince him to try group therapy. I'm still working on getting him to see a psychiatrist for meds, but I don't know if he'll do that.'

Rosalind managed to relax a tiny bit. 'At least he's taking some action.'

'Yeah . . .'

She tensed again. 'There's something else.'

'Lauren called me. I guess I was bitching to her about work at some point. Apparently she has a childhood friend who lives on this tiny island in Wisconsin. She's considering adding a guest house on to her property for when her kids and grandkids visit. Then *she* has a friend who wants a patio made into a three-season room. Lauren recommended me for the jobs and they're interested.'

'Eve, that would be awesome!' Rosalind couldn't understand why her sister didn't sound excited. 'You're always complaining that all you get to design is bathrooms. Can you do it?'

'Not from here.'

Rosalind waited. Olivia blasted everything she was feeling until you envied Wonder Woman her shield. Eve took patience and pulling. 'So you're considering going up there to check it out?'

'I haven't decided yet. They'd pay expenses but I wouldn't make much beyond that.'

'Yes, but talk about a win-win situation. They get free design and you get a change of scene and something more substantial in your portfolio. It sounds perfect.'

'I don't know.'

Rosalind rolled her eyes. Granted, she could be impulsive, which came with its own set of hazards, but her sister's caution drove her crazy. 'Could you take leave or vacation from your job now?'

'Maybe.'

'It sounds perfect. Get outta Dodge, try something new. It's exactly what you need.'

Eve sighed heavily. 'Mike is convinced this is part of some greater plan to leave him.'

'Oh.' By some miracle Rosalind managed not to blurt out what she was thinking, which was: *Great idea!* 'He's making an exciting career move for you all about him. He should be supporting you.'

'It's more complicated than that. He's my other half. We've been together almost three years. I have to take his emotions into account.'

'Well, I think you should jump at this. Mike will get over it. Though I don't recommend you phrase it to him quite that way.'

'I'm thinking it over. I'm swamped here right now. I couldn't get out there until after the holidays. And frankly, going to the ends of the earth in January doesn't appeal much either. Maybe February or March . . .'

Rosalind grinned. Her sister was going to do it. She might not even have admitted it to herself yet, but if she was talking like this, she would. 'Well, it does sound promising.'

'Yup. Oh, Mike's home. I gotta go. Love you. Be careful.'

'Love you too. You talked to Olivia lately?'

'Last week. If she doesn't kill her husband soon, I'm going to.'

Rosalind barked out a laugh. 'Everything as usual, huh?'

'Exactly. Oh, call Dad, okay? He was asking about you.'

'I will. Bye.' Rosalind ended the call and tossed the phone on to the bed next to the dress. Yes, she should call her father. But before that, she'd have to meditate again, and think about the good times. About Dad's kindness and his patience with their mother. The way he'd sit at the table while the sisters did their homework and do work of his own. How sometimes when Mom was in a bad way he'd take them to Bennett's for ice cream and make them laugh at the silly way he licked his cone.

The way he'd comment every time Rosalind put on a couple of pounds or had a zit on her forehead. The way he'd cut her down if he thought she was angling for more attention than she deserved, or bragging when she reported some success at school. The way he might have been out screwing every woman who was willing, while Mom sat home . . .

Oops.

She picked up the phone again. Before she dialed her father, she should call Ruth and ask for her sewing kit and machine, along with any accumulated mail they'd already arranged Ruth would send.

Blatant procrastination.

The call took thirty seconds. Rosalind told Ruth where to find the items and gave her the Princeton address and her FedEx account number; Ruth said a package had arrived and she'd send that too, then wished her well before Rosalind could stretch the call longer by asking about her husband and kids.

Darn.

She brightened. The perfect solution had just occurred to her. She'd call Lauren. After all, Dad might be sleeping or not up to a phone call. That would be easier.

For her.

She selected Lauren from her favorites list and waited, free hand clutching the arm holding the phone.

'Hi, Rosalind.' Lauren sounded disapproving. But then she often did. 'Haven't heard from you in a while. Your dad has been asking—'

'Hi, Lauren. I'm calling to see how Dad's doing.'

'He's sitting right here. We're doing a crossword puzzle. You can call him. Or I'll pass my phone over.'

'I don't want to interrupt anything. I only have a second. How is he doing?'

'Ask him yourself.'

'I . . .' Too late. Rosalind closed her eyes, listening to the shuffling sounds of the phone being passed to her dad, wondering not for the first time how Lauren could stand the slow rhythms – now a lot slower – of a much older man's life.

'How's my hummingbird?' His voice sounded deeper again, stronger, not the weary whisper he'd used last time they spoke.

Her throat locked. She took a deep breath and swallowed. 'Fine. I'm fine, Dad.'

Except that I don't know who you are anymore, or what you're capable of.

'No, you're not. Your voice funny. Sounds funny.'

'I'm not feeling well, nothing serious. How are you?'

'Weak. Old. Pissed off.'

'Sorry, Dad.' She gritted her teeth, suddenly seeing a scene she thought she'd finally put out of her head. Mom sobbing into her plate in their lavish Beverly Hills dining room, chandelier overhead a custom copy of the one in the ballroom scene of *My*

Fair Lady. It had been New Year's Eve 2001, the night Mom died.

For the first time Rosalind could remember, their father had made no attempt to calm or console her. The girls – Olivia twenty, Rosalind sixteen and Eve eleven – had sat frozen around the table, flicking glances at each other, unable to understand what had changed.

Finally Rosalind stood and put her arm awkwardly around her mother's shoulders, bending to kiss her hair. Mom had recoiled and shoved back her chair, her head hitting Rosalind's chin, making her bite her tongue hard enough that it stayed swollen for days. Mom had run upstairs, leaving shocked silence, broken by the slamming of her bedroom door.

Dad had moved first, told them not to worry, that Mom was upset but would get past it and be fine. They'd miserably picked at the rest of their dinner – Rosalind would never eat steak Diane again – then Dad had sent college girl Olivia off to party with friends from high school, and doled out sodas, pretzels and candy to Eve and Rosalind, who'd sunk down in front of the TV, unsettled and scared.

Just after midnight, as the Pacific Coast joined the worldwide celebration of the new year, Rosalind had been shakily dialing 911, frightened, but with a teenager's confidence that doctors would fix whatever was wrong with her mother. Eve had been standing by Mom's bed shouting, *Stop it, Mom, stop it! Wake up*, now! as Dad frantically performed CPR.

Hours later, at Cedars-Sinai, Olivia showed up drunk off her ass, crying hysterically before she even knew the worst, to the point where Dad had pleaded with the ER people to sedate her.

Back home, Dad had sat his stunned, silent daughters in the kitchen over mugs of Swiss Miss hot chocolate, and poured a large glass of whiskey for himself.

Overdose, he'd said. Mom had been upset about not getting a movie part, and about the state of her career in general, and had inadvertently taken too many of the pills she used to relax.

All her life, Rosalind had accepted her father's explanations and his interpretation of her mother's behavior. Now Mom's sobbed words at the dinner table came back to her, and hit hard.

I'm too old. I'm not enough anymore. It's all over.

Maybe she hadn't meant her career.

'Rosalind? Still there?'

'Yes, Dad . . . I'm sorry . . .'

She barely made it to the bathroom, threw up everything in her stomach and then some.

I'm too old. I'm not enough anymore. It's all over.

Her phone rang again, making her jump. She'd forgotten she was still holding it, even while puking.

It was Lauren.

Rosalind slumped on the tile, slightly dizzy, determined to sound as normal as possible. 'Sorry. I had to hang up. Upset stomach.'

'Are you home?'

'Oh . . . yes.'

'Get into bed. Eat sugary things, lollipops, hard candies, clear popsicles. The sugar helps settle you. Don't skimp liquids, but wait until your stomach can tolerate them.'

'Okay.' She got up shakily. Mom had always said *tummy*, even when the girls were older, which alternately soothed and mortified them. *Eat things that are kind to your tummy. No meanie food to make it more upset.* 'Tell Dad sorry. I'll call again soon.'

'I'll tell him. He sends love and hopes you feel better.'

She couldn't send love back. If indeed that was what her dad

162

had said. More likely Lauren was providing the proper fatherly sentiments. Dad's affection for them was palpable but seldom verbalized.

Rosalind rinsed her mouth with mouthwash to get rid of the loathsome taste of bile, then brushed her teeth to rid herself of the loathsome taste of mouthwash.

Now what? After a lifetime believing her mother was distraught over her career and careless with her meds, it was now possible her mother had died in despair over her husband's affairs. Maybe even killed herself.

Dear God.

Rosalind all but staggered back into the front bedroom and collapsed into the recliner, staring at the ceiling, rain hammering the window over her head, her stomach gradually settling, even if her mind refused to.

In her family, why was it never about things like tax evasion or lying about having a college degree? The traumas cut deep, left scars, the drama was as over-the-top as it was damaging.

Impossible not to wonder who she would have become if instead of across the country in Beverly Hills, she'd grown up across this street.

Chapter 10

February 4, 1968 (Sunday)

I went to see the movie Fantastic Voyage *today, with my friend Sarah and her parents. It finally made it up into this horror of a wasteland. Raquel Welch is so beautiful, it makes me furious and impatient that I can't be her yet! I would love to meet her. I bet she is a very cool person. I would love to meet anyone famous at this point. Countdown to leaving: one hundred and five days.*

When I am in New York, I will see one movie every week. If I can't afford it, I'll find someone to take me. That's where being pretty is very helpful. I feel sorry for uglier girls. They have to work twice as hard for things I take for granted. It seems so unfair, but that's how the world works, so there's no point pretending it doesn't.

If I wasn't having so much fun at rehearsals, I would leave this place now! I have stopped working hard at my classes. Just enough to stay in school so I can be in the show. There is no point anymore!

My real life will be starting soon.

Several torturous minutes later, Rosalind was tired of her own misery and made the effort to think logically instead of emotionally, in hopes of buoying her spirits again. Whether Mom had killed herself or not, she was still dead. Whether she took the overdose because of a dwindling career or a cheating spouse . . . Rosalind couldn't change that either. As for Rosalind's relationship with her father, there was nothing she could do now. He was too sick to confront with any of the details she was discovering, and she certainly wasn't going to share with Lauren that her husband might be a serial cheater.

Rosalind was in Princeton to find out if Leila was her birth mother, which instinct currently told her was more than ninety-nine percent likely, and to get to know her and her family. Once she felt comfortable, she would bring the topic out in the open, and attempt to forge some kind of relationship if it seemed right and mutually desirable. The story of how she came to be conceived and adopted would, she hoped, come to light as part of that relationship.

In short, the more she knew, the more power she'd have to make good decisions all around.

There. Better.

She launched herself out of the recliner, and got a drink of water, which her stomach received calmly. Back in the master bedroom, she went over to Zaina's exquisite dress. Taking it apart without her seam ripper would be even more tedious than usual, but it was something constructive to do, and frankly, after the day's upheaval, tedious sounded pretty enticing.

In a bathroom drawer she found a decently sharp pair of nail scissors, returned to the recliner and got going, gradually absorbing herself in the repetitive task, snipping seam threads, separating the two pieces of material, half an inch, an inch, then snipping more threads, over and over, with the goal of releasing the garment's right sleeve from its decades in bondage to the bodice.

The doorbell rang, startling her so badly she poked her finger with the scissor tip.

What time was it? She squinted to see the clock next to the bed. Only seven thirty. Hadn't this day already been going on for twenty-nine hours?

Over at one of the wet west windows, which she hoped would give her a clear view of the front stoop, she smushed her nose and cheek against the glass, noticing it had stopped raining.

Bryn. Hands on his hips, head bent, shifting his weight.

Oh dear.

He wasn't going to turn into a pest, was he? Sweet guy, but . . .

Doorbell again.

Rosalind sighed and went downstairs, foggy-brained and exhausted, suddenly aware that she was shaking with hunger. Might as well see what he wanted, then get him out of here so she could eat.

'Hi.' He glanced at her, then away, held out a red plaid scarf. 'I was across the street showing what I'd come up with for the wedding invitations. Zaina said you left this.'

Rosalind glanced at it. 'Not mine.'

'I had a feeling.' Bryn shook his head. 'She's determined.'

'Determined?' Rosalind couldn't get her fog-brain to clear.

'To get us together. Sorry about that.' He looked straight at her, then all but recoiled. 'Rosalind.'

'That's me.'

'Do you . . . need a . . . drink?' He gestured randomly. 'Or a . . . food?'

Rosalind started laughing, and once she started, bizarrely she couldn't stop.

'Okay. Okay.' He moved her gently into the house and closed the door behind them, patting her back awkwardly while she got her currently nutty self back under control. 'What's going on?'

She glanced up at him, embarrassed to meet his eyes fully. 'It's been kind of a day.'

'Sorry to hear that.' He patted her once more, then put his hands down like a kid caught touching. 'Have you eaten yet?'

'No, but I'm—'

'What do you feel like?'

'Shit.'

'No, you don't want to eat that.' He was grinning now, wider when she giggled – sanely this time.

'You don't have to feed me, Bryn.'

'What if I want to?'

'Why would you want to?'

'Because you're my soulmate.'

'Oh.' She laughed again, uncomfortably. 'Right, I forgot.'

He gave her shoulder one more pat. 'All better now?'

'Better now. Thank you. Believe it or not, I'm generally a stable person. Today was . . . unusual.'

'If you say so.' His exaggerated expression of disbelief made her giggle again.

He really was adorable. She should find some way to fix him up with Eve. 'I only came downstairs to tell you to leave me alone.'

'Yeah?' He gestured toward the door. 'You still can if you want me to go.'

'Bryn.' She gave him an incredulous look. 'Aren't you ever obnoxious? Selfish? Manipulative? A beer-drinking, ass-grabbing caveman, anything like that?'

'Not since I became perfect.' He grinned, his blue eyes dark in the dim light of the foyer, dimples deep. Adorable. 'Have you ever had a Conte's pizza?'

She hesitated, wavering, then decided what the hell. Eating pizza with Bryn sounded much nicer than whatever lonely frozen dinner she had waiting here. 'No. Am I about to?'

'Yes.' Bryn pulled his cell out of his pocket. 'I'll order, then we'll pick up. Any toppings you hate?'

'None.' She headed for the kitchen, feeling less shaky, though still as hungry. At least she was now looking forward to the evening. 'I've got beer, and stuff for a decent salad.'

He followed her, phone to his ear, already waiting for Conte's to answer. 'Perfect.'

Less than an hour later, Rosalind was sitting with Bryn in the house's bright, comfortable kitchen, all ultramarine paint and blue and white tile, inhaling piece after piece of the fabulous pizza. Just the right tang vs sweetness to the sauce, just the right thin chew to the crust, and the cheese – who could argue with cheese? Her mood had improved a hundred percent, and not just because of the fat and white flour intake.

'It was good you showed up when you did, Bryn.' She lifted her beer in a toast. 'I would have been in a corner banging my head against the wall by now.'

'Thank Zaina. She sent me over. I would have waited to stalk you for at least . . .' he tilted his head, 'another half-hour.'

She smiled, noticing how long his lashes were, and how they formed the perfect roller-coaster swoop over his very blue eyes, and how he had the perfect number of laugh lines at the corners of those eyes, then noticed that she was gazing at him for way too long and he might get the wrong idea. If Eve ever got the nerve to walk away from Mr Dreary, she'd definitely try to introduce them. 'What's next on the wedding chores list?'

'Our next assignment, should you choose to accept it . . .' Bryn pushed forward his plate and leaned back in his chair, 'is to go back to Sharon's and start making serious plans for what goes where, which rooms will be used for what, et cetera. Caitlin and Emil are getting closer to picking the day. One of the ministers they spoke with today can manage their target date.'

'Which is?'

'November tenth. Strange timing, he's only free in the morning, but at least he can do it. That morning's possible for the caterer as well.'

'Wow, they'll be able to pull this off.' She felt a burst of anticipation, until she realized she wouldn't be on the guest list unless she came out to the family as Leila's daughter. Even then, she couldn't count on it. 'That's great.'

'Yup.' He looked almost as not-excited as Leila had earlier in her kitchen.

'You're not in favor of this wedding—' She almost said *either.* 'You don't think they'll make it?'

'Stranger things have happened.'

Rosalind put down her Sam Adams. Same depressing news from two sources in the same day. 'Ouch.'

'Nah, I was being flip. Sort of.' Bryn stared down at his plate. 'I'd love to see them go the distance. Whether they do or not is anyone's guess. I know couples I thought were perfectly suited who practically tore chunks out of each other with their teeth during the divorce. Others do fine when I would have given them worse than even odds. So who knows?'

'Nobody.' She scraped up a gooey bit of cheese that had flowed on to the cardboard. 'How about you? Do you want to get married someday?'

'If I can find someone utterly perfect in every way, sure.'

'Well, yes, of course.' She grinned at him. 'Entirely reasonable.'

'You're not . . .' He held up his hand when she looked startled. 'Getting married, I mean.'

'Ah. Nope.' Rosalind tipped her head back and lowered the cheese into her mouth.

'Why not?'

She shrugged, using wet kisses to degrease her fingers. 'I'm not against the idea, but I couldn't commit to anyone in good conscience. I can see myself totally into the marriage for three, four years, then, "Gosh, ya know, I got other things to do."'

He narrowed his eyes. 'A hummingbird.'

'I've always been that way.' She got up to rummage for the box of Thomas Sweets chocolates she'd hidden from herself in a cabinet. 'What were you like as a kid?'

'Wild boy.'

Rosalind turned back to face him. 'No way.'

He rolled his eyes. 'Yes, me, the boring one.'

'No, no, that's not what I meant.'

'I was different then.' He pushed back his chair and crossed his legs. 'Before the lobotomy.'

'Bryn!'

He laughed, and she laughed too, and decided laughing with a new friend in a warm kitchen was the best way to end an exhausting day. Plus chocolate, which she pulled out from behind a canister of flour and put on the table between them.

'I looked up your sculptures online after we got back from the trip this morning.' Which felt like at least a week ago. 'On your website, but also Google showed a bunch on exhibit in various galleries and museums. I was impressed how many.'

'Yeah?' His face assumed the careful position of someone waiting to be judged. 'What did you think of the pieces?'

'Honestly? I loved them. And . . .' She opened the box of chocolates and pushed it over to him, feeling vulnerable and anxious about answering truthfully. 'I'm guessing that you're working something out.'

His hand paused over the chocolates. 'What makes you say that?'

'Well, I mean, I don't know. I'm hardly an expert, and I'm probably—'

'No, no, we went through this already. You're an artist too. I want to know what you felt.'

Rosalind sat blinking at him in dread. How often had her father told her, *Think before you speak, Rosalind, you shoot your mouth off more and faster than a semi-automatic.*

Deep breath.

'Okay. Your work has this . . .' She tried to coax the perfect word out of her mouth by circling her hand. Happily, it worked. 'Euphoria about it. But also pain. Like you'll have a figure leaping into the air, which seems joyful, but the features are contorted. Or you portray someone whose expression is rapturous, but his body is twisted and miserable. I don't know, I'm probably reading way too much into it.'

'Actually . . .' Bryn cleared his throat. Abandoned the chocolates for another sip of beer. 'You nailed it.'

She watched him curiously. Unless she was wrong, he was feeling something keenly. 'Is there a story there?'

'There's always a story.' He spoke slowly, eyeing his beer. 'So yes, in this case, there is as well.'

'Something from your feral childhood?' She squeezed her eyes shut. 'I need to shut up now. I'm sorry. That was horribly nosy. You do not have to tell me anything.'

'No, it's okay.' He leaned forward, forearms on the table, bottle clasped between both hands, his face so somber, she almost told him not to put himself through this. Certainly not for her sake. 'I don't tell many people, but I'd like to tell you.'

'Oh?'

'Oh.' He lifted his head, his eyes so open and vulnerable, she started to panic.

'Bryn, you really don't have to.'

'First, tell me what you paint, and why.'

'Sure, sure.' She jumped at the chance to lighten the mood. 'I started painting in Colorado, the mountains, I told you that. Being an ocean girl, I found them beautiful certainly, but also claustrophobic when I got up into them. Always another peak blocking any long view. At the same time, they pointed up toward an even bigger view than the sea, the mystery and rather terrifying freedom of space. I could never capture it. I felt . . . I didn't know it well enough. Does that makes sense?'

'Absolutely.' He was nodding, eyes alight. 'What about when you came to New York?'

'Since then I've been painting Maine. Our house, the area around it. People enjoying the coast.' She shifted in her chair, feeling the familiar reluctance, but determined to share because she wanted to know Bryn's story, and it seemed only fair. 'There's so much beauty, of a different nature, calmer, more comforting. The sea, the islands, the rocks, the trees, the ferns and moss underneath them, the way the sun shines through, and the patterns it makes on the ground. It seems very simple, but it has incredible depth to me.'

'Good times there?'

'The best.' Her voice caught. 'Our family was happy there, and . . . whole.'

'There's nothing simple about that.' He was watching her intently. She found it hard to return his gaze. 'They say people only have one story to tell. Maybe two. You can find different ways to present it, dress it up, dress it down, populate it this way or that, use one medium or another, but it's all the same story.'

'Do you agree?'

'Sometimes.'

'Tell me yours?'

'Okay.' A tiny smile curved his lips. 'My childhood was kind of rough. Mom was an alcoholic. Dad dealt with her drinking by staying at work. Emil and I both had alcoholic parents, by the way, only the demon got his dad much worse. My mom was able to stop after my senior year in high school.'

'Good for her. I've seen how hard that is.'

'Right. Your mom . . .'

'Yes.' Rosalind grabbed a chocolate. 'My mom.'

'So you know everyone in the family reacts differently. My brothers went straight, like if they became perfect children, maybe she'd have no reason to keep drinking. My sister and I went the opposite direction, acting out our pain in broad daylight. Kim exercised her alcoholic gene early. I didn't touch the stuff when I was younger.'

'Good choice.'

'Yeah, smart me. *I* wasn't going to get caught by any pesky addiction to alcohol.' He thumped his chest proudly. '*I* did massive amounts of drugs instead.'

Rosalind tried unsuccessfully to hide a snort.

Bryn smiled and waved her on. 'Go ahead, I meant that to be funny. You have to laugh. There is no point making melodrama over something that far in the past.'

He had no idea how true that sounded tonight. 'My sisters and I coped differently, too. Eve withdrew. Olivia pretended nothing was wrong. I hid during the worst emotional storms and tried to fix everyone when there was calm. Needless to say, that didn't work.'

'No, none of it works.' He moved restlessly in his chair. 'Unless the drinker takes responsibility.'

Rosalind nodded. Her mother had tried, but the responsibility had proved too heavy for her to lift off. 'Did your mom hit bottom your senior year?'

'Yeah.' He straightened and clasped his hands behind his head, gazing into the distance. 'In a way, I pushed her there.'

Rosalind felt prickly and edgy, wasn't sure she wanted to hear this. 'What happened?'

'I was out with friends one Wednesday night in April; we were high and messing around. We'd gotten into college already, and had pretty much checked out of high school. We all had messed-up home situations in one way or another, were in a lot of pain. Of course back then we just thought we were too cool for the real world.

'That night we'd been at my friend's house in Somerville doing mushrooms, and decided to continue the party in downtown Boston. We went to the Central Square T stop – T is the public transportation nickname – to wait for the train. My best friend, Jake, went manic on the platform, jumping, shouting, pretending he was trying to fly. We all copied him, laughing, probably terrifying everyone around us.'

Rosalind let go of the beer bottle, which she'd been white-knuckling, and folded her hands in her lap, absurdly wanting him to stop talking, as if suppressing the story's end would mean one of those sad and angry kids might still be okay.

'A train comes, we can see the headlights down the tunnel. Jake was laughing so hard he could barely talk, yelling, "Look at me, I'm flying, I'm flying." Then, like it's part of the same joke, he shouts, "This train's going to make me fly!" He backs up to the wall, takes a running start toward the tracks. It happened so fast I didn't even have time to think of grabbing him. His face was wild, joyous; he was still laughing when he jumped.'

Even knowing it was coming, Rosalind couldn't stop her gasp. 'Oh Bryn.'

He shook his head. 'I still don't know if he knew what he was doing.'

It was a while before Rosalind could make herself speak, and then she could do so only when she put together what he was saying.

She laid her hand on the table toward him. 'You're sculpting Jake. You're sculpting that moment.'

'Yeah.' He released his arms from behind his head, lifted his Sam Adams almost to his lips, then put it down. 'Seems like sometimes life gives you gifts in pretty strange packaging.'

'I'm so sorry.' She could only manage a whisper.

'Thanks.' He looked up from the table, quirking an eyebrow. 'You know, when I came over here, I saw that you looked really upset. I figured that story would cheer you up.'

Rosalind cracked up, reached further for his hand and squeezed it. 'Yeah, thanks, I feel *much* better.'

'Seriously, anytime.'

They smiled at each other until Rosalind felt uneasy and dropped her eyes, trying to remember where they'd been in the conversation so they could get back there quickly. 'I'm guessing that's what made your mom quit drinking.'

'The aftermath, yes. I lost my shit for quite a while. Didn't go back to high school, had to finish over the summer. I took a gap year before starting at Princeton, traveled all over the world and went to museums everywhere I could, found artists, and hung out with as many as would let me, working whatever jobs were available so I could support myself.

'When I came back, I entered college as an art major instead of pre-law. And that is all I'm going to say about me tonight, because enough already. It's your turn.'

'My turn?'

'If you want to talk about your . . . mom.' His ears turned red. 'You probably don't.'

'Oh, thanks.' Rosalind felt herself closing up like a poked mussel. As much as she trusted Bryn, years of instinct, protecting her family by not revealing the chaos behind their pink stucco walls, were too hard to overcome. A word here, there, could trickle into the press through the cracks and crannies of people's open mouths, innocently or not. She'd found herself telling him too much already. 'I don't think so. Nothing personal.'

'No offense taken.' His smile was genuine. 'But the offer stands if you're ever ready.'

'Tell you what.' She pointed a finger at him. 'I'll call you up six years from now and spill it all out.'

'Sure, that works.' He mimed talking on the phone. 'Uh-huh. Oh, that's awful. Yeah, wow. That must have been so hard. Who is this again?'

Rosalind laughed, amazed that he could bounce back so quickly from the emotion of his story – and yet wasn't that her method, too? Why stay miserable? 'When I was a girl I'd fantasize about what it must be like to live in a normal family. No cameras in your face, no whispers behind your back, no suspicions that people who want to be your friend really want to be your mother or father's friend, or colleague or whatever else.'

'No such thing as a normal family.'

'Maybe.' Rosalind put her hands on her hips. 'I still have hope.'

'I bet you don't give up easily.'

'No! Why would I want to? Why would anyone want to?' She fingered the label on her beer. 'What upset me most today . . . without really going into it . . . I found out information that challenges who I believed my father was, or at least the nature of his relationship with my mother.'

Bryn's face reflected his concern. 'That's pretty intense.'

'Yeah, it was. It is.' She was suddenly achingly tired. 'I don't know what to think. I finally decided it was probably better not to.'

'Not to . . . ?'

'Not to think.' She suppressed a yawn by inhaling and exhaling noisily. 'So that's all there is to that.'

'Ah.' Bryn got to his feet. 'That's my cue.'

'Me trying not to think?'

'You trying not to yawn.'

'Oh.' She stood, feeling irrationally disappointed that he was leaving. She didn't want him to stay, but the idea of the still strange house making lonely creaks around her tonight didn't appeal. And she did truly enjoy his company, more than anyone she'd met in a while. 'Thank you for your support tonight. And for Conte's. And for bringing me my not-scarf.'

'Zaina knew you'd need me.'

'What do you mean?' She followed him to the dark foyer, where he opened the front door and turned back to her.

'She's psychic.'

'You believe that?'

'Nah, not really. But she's a remarkably intuitive person.' He stood smiling at her. Rosalind turned to look for a light to flip on. It was too intimate standing there in a small space lit only by light spilling faintly from the hall. Way too intimate when he reached and touched her shoulder. 'I'm sorry you were having a rough time today, Rosalind. Supposed to be gorgeous and sunny tomorrow, that should help.'

'Yeah, that sounds nice, thanks.' She spoke with high energy, trying to break the mood. 'What are you doing tomorrow? More sculpturing? Sculpting? Sculptipating?'

'Yes. If you'd like to come over and watch, you're welcome to.'

She'd started to decline when what he'd said hit her. 'You can work when someone's watching?'

'Nope.'

'Bryn!' Rosalind burst into helpless giggles. 'You crack me up.'

He slid his hand around the back of her neck and pulled her in for a soft, sweet kiss she was completely unprepared for. 'I'll see you . . . whenever. Later this week? We'll have to find out when Sharon's okay with us coming over.'

'Uh . . . yes. Okay. Sure.' Her voice came out way too high. She sounded terrified. But he was acting as if the kiss hadn't happened, so she would as well.

'Good.' He opened the squeaky storm door and stepped outside. 'Sleep well.'

Rosalind watched him through the glass as he strode down the front walk, then jumped forward and closed the door in case he looked back and caught her staring.

The emotional evening had brought vulnerabilities to the surface, that was all. She didn't want to encourage him. She did not want to have any kind of romance with an adorable, funny Irish-poet-looking sculptor who lived in a different city and who had a personality pretty much opposite of hers.

And she definitely did *not* want to feel this crazy giddiness over anyone as sweet and talented and long-ago damaged as he was. Given enough time, she'd get bored and break his heart, just like she had all the others.

At the same time . . .

She was no longer quite so sure about setting him up with Eve.

Chapter 11

March 28, 1968 (Thursday)

Mom got a call from the principal's office asking why I haven't been working at my usual level. She was so angry she threatened to take me out of the show. I told her she might as well rip my heart out with a fork. Then I yelled that she'd already taken out my ovaries so I wouldn't have kids just like she wanted, so she had lots of practice mutilating me. She looked like I had hit her. At first I was happy finally to score a point, but then she started crying. I have never seen my mother cry. Not even when Grandma died. I didn't know what to do. Dad came in later and gave me a beating.

I think I will leave immediately after the last performance of the show.

Rosalind poked her seam ripper's sharp metal tip under linked loops of blue thread between folds of blue material, then tipped the tool up to engage its sharp blade. The thread snapped, the material separated another inch. She did it again, pulling the skirt pieces gently apart. Another inch. Spread on the hardwood at her feet lay the other pieces of the carefully deconstructed dress, waiting to be made into new pattern pieces after this last seam was finished.

She'd ended up having to go back into New York to find material. Scouring the Internet was an option, but when it came to quality and color, Rosalind trusted only her hands and eyes. Wednesday, waking up full of pizza and a little giddiness hangover from dinner with Bryn, she'd spent the day checking out the local possibilities. Fabric stores in Princeton and its environs were stocked almost exclusively for interior decorating, so Thursday she'd taken the train into Manhattan and her favorite store, Mood, on West 37th in the garment district. With her she carried a piece of Zaina's original dress, carefully folded into her bag, to see if she could match the material's weight and sheen.

While the vivid royal blue would have made a stark, stunning contrast to Zaina's youthful dark hair and unlined, dewy skin, the same color in a new dress would only accentuate her fade into age. Rosalind's goal had been to find fabric in a darker, more restrained shade to suit Zaina's present coloring, but one that retained enough shine and body so the new dress would drape as elegantly as the old, and look as identical as possible. Also in her plan was to include an extra yard or so of either the same or complementary material for a shawl-scarf to drape over arms doubtless not as smooth and toned as they once were.

The fabric gods had been kind. She had found exactly what she was looking for in a deep lagoon silk duchesse satin. The material draped sensuously, with enough teal in the blue to dim but not dull the shade, and enough glow to capture the luster of the original fabric.

Sold, done, and back to the NJ Transit train to Princeton by early yesterday evening.

It had felt strange leaving the hectic bustle of her home city to come back to the clean, uncluttered but still foreign serenity here. Strange, but not unpleasant. For the first time, the rush of energy she always felt in New York had jarred instead of energized her. The tall buildings, sidewalk crowds and inching-along traffic had seemed more claustrophobic than vibrant. Instead of limited and one-note, Princeton had seemed fresh and soothing. Most likely she was just worn out. She certainly was now, having slept an hour or two at most the previous night.

Her sewing machine had arrived safely the day before, ironically while she was in the city and could easily have picked it up herself, along with mostly uninteresting mail and the package Ruth had told her about. A fairly mysterious package, paperback-sized, no return address, postmarked Saratoga Springs, New York. Rosalind had nothing on order and knew no one who lived in that city.

Intrigued, she'd ripped off the tape and opened the box to reveal a wrapped book. Not a paperback, a diary. A diary written by Sylvia Moore during her years in high school, ending with her visit to Dr Winston in January of 1969 when she received the devastating diagnosis.

Rosalind had spent a good five minutes staring first at the worn pink vinyl cover, then at the first entry, her mind spinning. Who could have sent this? Where had it been before now? How much did she want or need to know about her mother's most private thoughts? Just opening the cover felt like an appalling invasion of privacy, especially now that Mom was gone.

In the end, of course, Rosalind had to read it. At least she'd been sensible enough to get something to eat before she started, to avoid a repeat of Tuesday's low-blood-sugar melt-down. Tired from the day's errands and travel, she'd introduced a sandwich and banana to a stomach already jittery with nerves, then poured herself a glass of wine and curled up in bed to read.

It had taken hours to finish the diary, written in her mother's loopy handwriting, which Rosalind had always loved but which Mom insisted was clumsy and uneducated. Hours more before she could get to sleep.

This morning, the horror lingered. All her reading at the Blue Hill library about the careless and neglectful treatment suffered by girls of that era who had the same condition – their fear, their self-hatred, and the utter lack of support offered even by those closest to them – became even more outrageous and unforgivable when the victim was her own mother. The idea that Sylvia had been left to cope with this staggeringly traumatic condition all by herself . . . Grandma Betty's cruelty was impossible to fathom.

Undoubtedly not deliberate cruelty. Fear, shame, ignorance – but the result as far as Sylvia was concerned had been the same. Grandma was pushing ninety. As much as Rosalind was tempted to confront her, she hadn't visited her grandmother in years, and, really what was the point? Betty would have to work out the details with God.

If I'm not a woman, what am I?

The line had pierced her. Reading the diary had confirmed Rosalind's theory that complete androgen insensitivity was responsible for her mother's insistence on being absolutely and ultimately feminine in all she did, often pushing the boundaries of her sensuality past where her feminist daughters thought it belonged.

No longer could Rosalind attribute her mom's desire for attention solely to her bipolar disorder or to a raging prima donna ego. The yearning stemmed at least partly from her desperate need to convince the world of what she was so unsure herself, and what was taken so easily for granted by an over-whelming majority of human females: that she was a woman. In Mom's era, that was the only option. Yes or no, you were or you weren't. The concept of gender fluidity had yet to make its mark on mainstream consciousness.

If only Mom was still around to forgive for all the complexities Rosalind had misunderstood. Her sometimes embarrassing overt sexuality, the topless painting that hung in their living room, her insistence that she dress in skirts or dresses every time she left the house, even to go to the supermarket, the way she flirted with every man she came across, not to attract them as Rosalind had always thought, but to reinforce her own desirability.

Only at their house in Maine did she let herself relax, as if coming to her home state took away the awful burden of being the icon she'd created and demanded people recognize. There, at least, she wore pants – though never blue jeans; she didn't own a pair as far as Rosalind knew – and less or no makeup.

For their annual feast on Candlewood Point, she'd put on what her girls called the clambake outfit, a pair of her father's tattered overalls over a bathing suit, adding a sweatshirt as darkness – and/or mosquitoes – gathered. She'd help dig the pit, gather stones to line it, and driftwood for the fire. While the rocks heated, depending on the tides, she'd lead the girls in a hunt for sea glass or starfish, or hold pebble-throwing contests.

When Mom and Dad weren't up for the whole production, they'd simply light a fire in a safely pebbled area between rock ledges, then layer the clambake ingredients with seaweed in a giant pot, its metal exterior burned nearly black by the licking of previous flames.

Insert seam ripper, pull up, gently pull apart, on and on in hypnotic comfort, the simple repeated action keeping the rest of the world at bay.

Rosalind would like to think that later in life, when Mom had access to therapy through her regular psychiatrist or during one of her rehab stints for addiction to Valium and alcohol, she'd been able to talk about the syndrome, gotten professional help, and exorcized at least some of the demons. Since her diary ended so abruptly with the diagnosis, Rosalind was unlikely to find out, short of asking Dad, which wasn't yet possible. Unless there were other diaries somewhere . . .

So many questions.

The last bit of seam came apart. Rosalind rose from the recliner and put the final piece of Zaina's dress, the skirt side front, flat on to the floor, the shape curved and full at its bottom, narrowing to the waist. To make the new pattern, she'd trace the newly dismembered pieces on to interfacing, add extra room where needed, and transfer markings for darts and decoration. For all the dress's elegance, the pattern was fairly simple. The only time-consuming part would be the painstaking job of sewing on the intricate swirls of pearls. Still, she should be able to finish it easily in the week and a half until Zaina's birthday on the sixteenth.

Rising from her crouch, Rosalind stretched her too-long-constricted body, then headed downstairs for a can of flavored sparkling water. All morning she'd been haunted by the diary, by her mother's isolation from her family, by her cancer fears, by her shame at being photographed naked before surgery, and on and on. Her only consolation was that at least Mom had met Dad by the time she finally learned of her condition. Daniel Braddock would have relished being her rock and her hero during that awful time, as he did so many times later.

A rock and a hero and a cheater.

Rosalind shook her head, as if to fling the thought away, and opened the refrigerator for her favorite: LaCroix, grapefruit flavor. A memory suddenly surfaced, of her mother writing in a diary when Rosalind was probably ten. She'd gotten out of bed, having forgotten to ask for a parent signature on a field trip permission slip. Surprised by the sight of a blank book under her mother's pen, she'd asked if Mom was writing a story.

Mom had drawn her close with an arm around her waist and said she liked to think about her days and how she felt about what had happened during them, and that she liked to write those thoughts down so she wouldn't forget, because forgetting your life was as good as not having lived it. Then she'd closed the book before Rosalind had been able to read anything, which of course she'd been trying her best to do.

Back in her childhood bedroom, with the multicolored striped wallpaper she'd been allowed to pick out herself, Rosalind had immediately written down the details of the episode in a notebook she'd decided would be *her* diary – one that ended up being used primarily for sketches – and had spent a few days pondering the mystery of how forgetting your life could erase it.

Eventually she had decided the concept was another of her mother's random important-sounding phrases, doled out with Mary-Poppins-like precision, containing little practical wisdom. Like, 'If you can't be happy, be clean', and, 'Too many soups bloat the cook.' And Rosalind's favorite, when she was impatient for her supper, 'Food wasn't built in a day.'

She popped the soda top and took a sip before heading back upstairs. Maybe there *were* other diaries. If so, where? With Lauren and Dad? Who else knew Mom well enough to have ended up with them? As far as Rosalind knew, Mom's two closest friends, one from her early years in LA, one from grad school, still lived in southern California and in Maine. None in New York, though the sender could have routed the package to make him or her impossible to trace.

Most importantly, why would whoever-it-was hold on to the

diary for nearly twenty years and send it *now*, mere months after Rosalind had learned the truth about Mom's condition?

Unless it was a coincidence – which seemed unlikely – that should narrow the suspects down to the very few people who knew that she had become aware of her mother's syndrome: her sisters and Lauren. Rosalind couldn't imagine Eve or Olivia not sharing something this important.

She could ask Lauren, but if her stepmother had taken such trouble to have the package show up anonymously, she would never admit to sending it. Rosalind was in enough trouble with her already, just by having traveled here to contact Leila. It seemed best for now to accept the diary as a gift – of a kind – and not question further until the opportunity arose.

Whenever that might be.

A gust of wind sent the branch outside the window scratching at the screen to be let in. Rosalind shuddered and reached for her iPhone, wanting to fill the room instead with sounds of her childhood. Not her father's music, her mother's. She cast her mind back, trying to remember what bands or tunes her mother had loved.

Immediately a picture popped on to her memory screen, one of the many nights Dad had been away for a conference, Mom home with her daughters, a common occurrence, except that this night they hadn't been shuffled off to be taken care of by their nanny. This was during one of Mom's really good times, duly recorded by eleven-year-old Rosalind in her soon-to-be-abandoned diary. They'd held a girls-only sleepover in her mother's enormous pink room, the four of them clustered on her poufy couch around bowls of ice cream and cheesy popcorn, alternating warm salty fat with cool creamy fat.

Mmm.

On Mom's custom movie screen, they'd watched her

selections – always Jillian's choice from among her favorites, though she'd sometimes give in to a request if they begged hard enough. That night it had been *The Lady Eve*, then *Wuthering Heights*, which had made them all cry, so they'd followed that with *Bringing Up Baby*. By the end of that movie, with Katharine Hepburn teetering rather unconvincingly on top of a ladder, all three of the girls' heads were nodding. Mom had herded them into her big pink marble bathroom to brush their teeth, then snuggled them into their sleeping bags on her thickly carpeted floor. While they drifted off, she'd put on a CD of the *Wuthering Heights* soundtrack, played frequently when she wanted to invoke a mood of relaxed nostalgia.

On her iPhone, Rosalind easily located a recording of the Alfred Newman score, and in the fabric-strewn master bedroom, the tree-scratching was soon overwhelmed by lush string sounds evocative of the period and of her mother's passionate love of the film. Laurence Olivier at his handsome finest, and Merle Oberon living large and dying oh-so-tragically and rather melodramatically.

The music was soothing and friendly, for all its bittersweet associations, exactly what the room and Rosalind's mood needed. She moved aside the dress pieces and unfurled yards of interfacing on to the hardwood surface, leaving the length-wise center fold intact, then covered that with a sheet of dressmaker's tracing paper. Accompanied by shimmering string tremolos and syrupy harp glissandos, she arranged pieces of the old dress on to the paper so that they were lined up straight along the grain of the fabric, using the space as efficiently as possible, pinning the pieces in place when she was satisfied with their arrangement.

Using her tracing wheel and a chopstick found in one of the drawers in the kitchen, she transferred all lines and markings to the fabric underneath, making the necessary adjustments for Zaina's fuller figure.

The chime of a text made her raise her head and crawl over to where she'd left her phone by the recliner. She hadn't texted much for the past few days, and had only received a few. One from a co-worker at Starbucks, relaying that another worker had been caught having sex in the bathroom with a customer.

Ew.

And a group message from Olivia to her and Eve with a chicken recipe she'd just invented. Rosalind had responded only to a text from Bryn, with a brief *Sure*, when he suggested the following Wednesday afternoon for their repeat trip to Sharon's house. She'd decided his kiss after their pizza dinner had been a slightly-more-than-friendly good night, and had refused to allow herself any daydreaming or fantasy.

This text was from Leila: *Hey. Want to come mother-of-the-bride dress shopping?*

Rosalind froze, heart thumping. Dress shopping. With her birth mother.

As soon as her excitement lifted, it crashed again. She couldn't. Not today. Not after spending the night in her mother's shoes, devastated by what she'd gone through. Not now, when she could imagine so much more vividly the effect her father's affair – still unconfirmed, but by now factual in Rosalind's mind – must have had on the so-very-vulnerable Jillian Croft.

Shopping with Leila, a woman who had everything Jillian lacked, a woman her father had turned to as cruelly as Grandma Betty had turned away, would feel like a betrayal. A cheap one at that.

You there? Leaving in five.

Five minutes.

That settled it. Rosalind hadn't showered since the previous day. She couldn't get ready that quickly anyway.

Standing, she entered her password and typed, *Sorry, not a good time, good luck!* Ready to hit 'send', she hesitated, screwing her face up in a misery of renewed indecision.

Getting to know her birth mother was the entire reason she'd come to Princeton. A chance to spend extended alone time with Leila might or might not come again. If Rosalind turned this invitation down, then she needed to admit that she was effectively giving up her quest. She should pack her bags and go back to New York. Spend the rest of her life the way it had started, with the dysfunctional family she'd been given. Leave behind Leila, Zaina, Caitlin, Emil. Bryn.

Rosalind turned abruptly, as if she were expecting the solution to be behind her. What was the right thing to do?

That was the problem. There was no right thing, there was only this option and that one, a yes or a no. She was free to choose. Refuse to go with Leila and retreat to New York, where she'd continue in uncertainty, staying true to a beloved mother who could no longer care whether she was loyal or not.

Or risk rejection and disappointment in order to explore the ranks of a new family, not hers yet, with no guarantee it ever would be.

She thought of her friend Becky, one of the few good college friends she'd rediscovered in New York. Becky had the unfortunate characteristic of being wildly attracted only to unavailable men. The one single guy she'd dated was emotionally closed off and had many other flaws that she was always happy to discuss. The married ones – all perfect in her eyes – never quite managed to leave their so-called unbearable marriages in order to give her the relationship she was convinced she wanted.

Becky was a mess, but Rosalind still cherished her for the other values and tastes they shared, and the strong friendship they'd built on those. Yes, she recommended counseling instead of agreeing when Becky moaned about there being no decent single men in New York, but she was admittedly fascinated by Becky's ability to compartmentalize. Guilt in one box. Love in another. Seldom the twain shall meet.

If Rosalind condemned Leila, she'd be judging Becky by one set of rules and her birth mother by another. When Leila met the illustrious Daniel Braddock, she'd been practically a kid, still in college or just out, depending on how long the affair lasted, an age where she was easy pickings for such a handsome, charming and important older man.

A long breath, then she erased her text and tapped out another. *Fifteen minutes okay?*

The answer came immediately: *Done. See you then.*

Chapter 12

April 4, 1968 (Thursday)

Today I had to meet with Mr Carter, my history teacher, after school – my cutest teacher. He went on and on about the importance of not letting my academic performance slip. I know I know I know, it just isn't important for me. Mostly while he was talking, I was wondering what it would be like to kiss him. I bet he is really good at it.

Then he said maybe he and I could come to some understanding that would improve my grades. And he put his hand on my thigh, watching me really closely with those big green eyes.

I felt very hot and very shaky and very excited. But I am not a real woman. So even if I wanted to let him touch me down there, I couldn't, because he might find out.

I did let him kiss me, though. Yes, he was really good at it. I bet if I let him keep doing that I could at least get a C. But I know that while you can tell a boy kissing is enough, men need more. Sarah told me that.

I will really miss Sarah. She's the only friend I have who likes me for me instead of for what I look like and can do.

But I haven't even told her my secret.

* * *

As Rosalind stepped out of the house, determined to put the diary out of her mind for the morning and enjoy this time with her birth mother, Leila was just pulling up in her bright yellow Volkswagen Beetle, a car so cheerfully impudent it made Rosalind long to own one.

Leila reached across the seat and pushed open the door, most of her abundant hair flying loose behind a section drawn up to clear her face, skin tones warm against her scoop-neck ivory sweater and floral-patterned silk scarf. 'Hey there. Hop in.'

'Thanks.' Rosalind climbed in and buckled up, smoothing her skirt over her tights, picking off a blue thread from Zaina's dress, arranging her sweater. The small space enclosing them seemed awkwardly intimate. Or maybe there were still vestiges of guilt in her exhausted brain.

'Thanks for coming with me.' Leila shifted into first and executed a neat U-turn. 'I want to try on a couple of the dresses we found online and see what else is out there. Caitlin's at work and I thought you might feel like an adventure.'

'Absolutely.'

'There's a Lord & Taylor fairly close by, at Quakerbridge Mall, but if you have time I'd much rather go to Bridgewater Commons. They have a Lord & Taylor *plus* Macy's *and* Bloomingdale's. Dahlink, it is to *die* foah!'

Rosalind giggled, Leila's energy and enthusiasm, so like her own, winning her over. Coming with her today had been the right choice. 'Bring it on. I've got nothing planned.'

'Groovy.' Leila pulled up at a red light, blinker on for a turn north on to Route 206. 'The big, enormous, spectacular news is that Caitlin and Emil have an official wedding date. They got a decent caterer and a minister they liked who were both free on the same day, so they're set. They couldn't get the jazz combo they wanted, and couldn't find any others they liked, so they're just going with a digital playlist, which is fine by me because it's *beaucoup* cheaper.'

'Cheaper is good.'

'Saturday, November ninth!' Leila hit the horn in a series of celebratory toots. 'My baby's big day.'

'That is wonderful.' Rosalind felt a rush of empathetic joy. 'So exciting.'

'I know.' Leila dabbed at her eyes. 'I get teary just thinking about it.'

'I love weddings. Your mom showed me a picture of her and Cecil on their day.'

'Yes! I love that picture. My mom is so gorgeous, isn't she? Dad used to say he took one look and that was it, he knew he'd found the love of his life.' She slowed to keep pace with a black SUV in front of them. 'I don't believe in that stuff – there are just as many people in divorce court who felt the same way at first sight – but in this case he turned out to be right.'

'It makes a great story anyway.'

'God, I wish Dad was still here. He'd love to be part of all this. You would have adored him, Rosalind. He was kind of shy and awkward, but so charming and well-mannered, with this sly humor. He used to make Mama laugh so hard.' Her face clouded. 'He loved celebrations. He loved his family. His family loved him!'

'I'm sorry. I know what it's like to lose a parent early. It leaves a big hole.'

'It does. Let's have some music.' She reached down next to Rosalind's leg for her purse, and dragged out her phone, alternating glances between the road and the device as she poked at it. 'It's about half an hour drive depending on traffic. What do you like?'

'Anything.' Rosalind cringed as the car veered toward the center line. 'Can I help?'

'Sure.' Leila handed the phone over. 'Choose whatever you want.'

Rosalind scrolled quickly through the choices, a mix of classical, opera, and older pop and rock artists. 'Did your mom and dad listen to music in the house?'

'Oh yes, constantly. Always classical. That was my childhood soundtrack. They took me to the symphony too, here in Princeton and in New York. And opera. They *loved* opera. Before I was old enough to sit still for that long, they'd describe their evenings at the Met. It all sounded so magical.' She lifted a hand from the wheel to paint pictures in the air. 'The red and gold theater, the twenty-one chandeliers that rose up to the ceiling at the beginning of every performance, the incredible costumes. I couldn't *wait* to go. I imagined it as a fairyland of perfection. It was close, anyway. Did your parents play music?'

'Some. Dad played mostly classical. Mom liked folk music, Joni Mitchell, Judy Collins, James Taylor. But she *loved* big band tunes; she had a huge collection of vinyl and CDs.' Rosalind's voice warmed. She'd honor her mother this way. 'She'd move furniture to the walls in our den and announce that the ballroom was open. Then she'd put on music loud enough to fill the house and we'd dance all over the place.'

'That sounds so fun. Your mom was always so untouchable, so beautiful and, I don't know, so intimidatingly perfect. I love hearing the more human stories about her.' Leila seemed as comfortable talking about Jillian now as she had in her kitchen. Decades had elapsed since the affair. She must have made peace with it. Or she was able to compartmentalize as effectively as Becky. 'Did she ever dance in a movie?'

'No. I think she probably wanted to, but in a movie made in the forties, not the seventies and eighties. She hated disco.'

'Oh, true confessions time. I went through a disco phase.' Leila started singing 'Night Fever' in a hilariously good Bee Gees falsetto, bouncing in her seat.

Rosalind cracked up. In spite of her worries, she was falling for her birth mother, greedy to find out more, to catch up on so many years of lost time. Or maybe she, too, was enjoying the power of compartmentalizing. 'What did you think of your first trip to the Met? How old were you?'

'Uh . . . twelve? I was bored mostly. Annoyed that the Carmen was fat and old because I'd always pictured the character looking like Ava Gardner. But I liked it enough to go again. And again and *again*.' She turned to Rosalind, face flushed and lit so that she practically glowed. 'Then I was hooked.'

'I should listen to more opera.'

'No, no, *watch*. Opera is meant to be experienced with both eyes and ears. Go see it live or watch a DVD, or one of the Met Live in HD broadcasts at a movie theater. It's really sublime, you know, this extraordinary mixture of theater and singing and spectacle. Plus, unlike when I was a kid, there are line-by-line translations, so you know exactly what's going on. And the singers are such better actors now than a generation ago, when it was all stand and deliver.'

'Did you ever perform at the Met?'

'God, no. I was never that good. Good enough, though. I'm proud of what I've accomplished. It's been the perfect career for me. Different houses, different shows, different productions, different casts.' She gestured, rotating her forearm in a circle. 'It's never bored me, not for a second.'

Rosalind found herself grinning, unable to stop. A fellow

hummingbird. Someone who could understand and validate the life Rosalind had chosen, the person she was. 'Give me a good beginner opera to play right now.'

'We have twenty minutes!'

'A scene. An aria . . .'

'Okay. Let's see.' Leila slowed for a stop light. They'd passed through a residential area, then a mile or so of thick woods, and emerged into a highly developed area, passing car dealerships, the tiny Princeton Airport on the west side of the two-lane highway, and strip malls galore. 'How to convert a willing newbie in three notes . . . I know! Find Strauss, *Arabella*. There's an unbelievable duet in the first act, between the sisters, Arabella and Zdenka. Look for "*Aber der richtige, wenn's einen gibt*" and play that track.'

Rosalind peered at the list of music on Leila's phone, and found the opera, then searched the tracks for something that might represent *Ahbber dare rish-teesh* . . . whatever she'd said. 'Yes. Here it is. Track four.'

'Good. It is to die for. Mama wants this played at her memorial service. She's a Strauss fanatic.'

The track started with swooping lush soprano phrases, and ended with the most sublime intermingling of female voices and orchestra that Rosalind had ever heard.

She was breathless. 'Leila, you can't play that at a memorial service; no one will come out alive!'

'I know, I know. It's rapturous.' Leila turned her glowing smile on Rosalind. 'I'm so pleased you liked it! You'll be an opera natural. Now, because you like that, more Strauss, then we can do something more traditional on the way home, Mozart or Puccini. Search for *Rosenkavalier*, the von Karajan recording, and play the final trio, last disk, first line "Marie Theres" . . .'

'*Rosenkavalier* . . . my dad loved that opera, I remember

him talking about it.' Rosalind searched eagerly under Strauss, found *Rosenkavalier*, found the last disk. '"Marie . . ." – here it is, track nineteen.'

Four minutes and thirty-nine seconds later, she was again catching her breath, fighting tears. Not two female voices this time, but three, singing individually and together, joining for exquisite harmonies, then separating, each voice coming forward and receding from the other two and from the orchestra in purposeful, carefully structured, harmonically devastating chaos.

She was pretty sure she'd heard the same music blasting from her father's speakers, undoubtedly more than once, and been unimpressed. Maybe it was having Leila with her, maybe it was her mood, maybe her age . . . She pressed a hand to her chest, feeling as if she needed to contain the emotion or it would burst through her bones and skin, like the creature in *Alien*. 'What have you done to me? I'm a mess.'

'Torture, isn't it?' Sniffling, also laughing, Leila reached across to squeeze Rosalind's wrist. 'I'm so, so happy that you're miserable.'

That broke the spell, making Rosalind giggle. 'It's *awful*! It's like the car shrank and I needed to run somewhere to escape.'

'Yes, yes, yes, Rosalind. Exactly. I call it "jump off a building music". It's too beautiful to want to keep *living*.' She squeezed once more, then pulled her hand back to the wheel. 'Luckily the death wish is only temporary.'

'Good thing.'

'Yes, because we're almost at the mall.' She pointed to her left, where they were passing thick green woods . . . and passing and passing and passing. 'The Duke estate. It's about a gazillion acres – believe it or not, this is the short side. Tobacco money.

Doris Duke inherited the fortune from Daddy and left every penny for her foundation. Big into art and environmental preservation. I'm a huge fan of wealthy people with a social conscience.'

'Same.' Rosalind felt vaguely embarrassed that in spite of the recommendation of her financial guru, she had yet to start such a foundation herself, either alone or with her sisters. In her case, predictably, the problem was choosing the focus. There were so many causes she supported. And to that list she'd now add an interest in the plight of women with complete androgen insensitivity.

Maybe she should also start a foundation for children of parents who turned out to be liars.

'Now, we join Route 202 and head for a capitalist Mecca instead of using our money for social good.' Leila pointed triumphantly ahead, then raised a fist. 'Because we are just that shallow.'

Rosalind raised hers as well. 'Hear, hear.'

Bridgewater Commons featured an enormous center court with escalators in its middle, surrounded by three floors of stores, all geared toward higher-end clientele. Leila and Rosalind started at Bloomingdale's, Leila tearing through the racks, trying and discarding outfits with dizzying speed, even some Rosalind thought fit and flattered well.

At Macy's the same.

At the entrance to Lord & Taylor, she paused, smiling at the name in its distinctive black script. 'Mama and I used to go to Lord & Taylor on Fifth Avenue every year in December to see the Christmas windows. We'd take the bus or train into Manhattan, then a taxi to the store – one of the very few times I ever saw Mom or Dad spring for a taxi.

'In the morning, we'd shop for me. One year it was a natty

brown wool three-piece pantsuit.' She nudged Rosalind. 'Vest included.'

'Ooh.' Rosalind fanned herself. 'So hot.'

'That was the seventies.' Leila sighed. 'Such a pity the fashionistas chose the ugliest clothing era ever to bring back.'

'No kidding. But what a great mother–daughter tradition.' Rosalind peered wistfully into the store. 'When my mom went shopping, it was about theater, not commerce. She'd be absolutely swamped by people. She had a personal shopper for the real transactions. We had things brought to the house and chose what we wanted.'

Leila made a horrified face. 'That's not shopping.'

'I know, I know. My life was weird.' Rosalind went with her into the store, their energetic strides matching. She wished she could have grown up shopping every Christmas with this woman. Not Mom's fault she was mobbed by fans, but then she refused to dress down or otherwise camouflage her identity so that her daughters might enjoy such a trip.

Consumed by the experience of being Jillian/Sylvia, with all her worries and struggles, the half of which Rosalind hadn't understood until lately, her mother probably didn't have spare energy to consider what her daughters might have needed from her, outside of what she decided to give them.

'On our trips into the city, Mama and I would always have lunch inside the store, in the Birdcage Restaurant.' Leila scanned her surroundings, as if hoping to find a similar luncheonette had magically appeared. 'Back then it was this little place with classic ladies-who-lunch food. You know, cottage cheese. You'd line up outside the door in two lines – one for single diners and one for larger parties. As a girl, I felt sorry for the ladies alone, like maybe they didn't have any friends. Ha! They were probably having the time of their lives. Kids still in school, taking themselves out shopping and for a meal they didn't have to cook themselves—'

'Wait, wait.' Rosalind stopped walking and held up a finger. 'Are you about to say "Those were the days"?'

'Saucy wench.' Leila cracked up, linked her arm with Rosalind's and headed them toward the dress section.

After the same lightning round of dress-trying and one hundred percent rejection, Leila put her hands on her hips and stared thoughtfully at Rosalind, seemingly unfazed by the failure of their trip so far.

'I expected the right outfit to jump out at me. It's not jumping. I think that's because I don't have any idea what that right outfit is. So.' She poked Rosalind's shoulder. 'Here's where you can help. What would *you* wear if you were going to your daughter's wedding?'

Rosalind's brows shot up. She was pretty much never consulted for her fashion advice. Except for the occasional fellow kook who stopped her in the street asking where she'd gotten some article of clothing, always disappointed to discover Rosalind had made it herself. 'You mean what would I wear if I were you?'

'No, no.' Leila shook her head emphatically, chestnut strands swirling. 'What would *you* pick?'

'Oh.' Rosalind scanned the racks, taken aback by this sudden responsibility, but thrilled Leila was asking for her opinion. 'I'd go . . . conservative, I mean, for me. But I wouldn't go with a traditional gown or cocktail dress, and I wouldn't stick with muted shades. For one, this isn't going to be a super-formal wedding, and it's a really happy occasion, which in my mind calls for big color.'

She took a few quick steps away from the dressing room, looking for the jumpsuit and coat she'd been lusting over while

Leila was trying on outfits, both of which Leila had passed without even a glance. Over by the mall entrance, then to the left . . . or right?

A flash of bright purple caught her eye.

'There.' She made a beeline, yanked a size eight off the rack and held it out to her birth mother. The jumpsuit, belted in its own fabric, was made of soft drapey material that would cling, but not too tightly. It had spaghetti straps, and was cut low in front and back. 'This.'

Leila looked alarmed. 'That?'

'Yes.' Rosalind shook the garment insistently until Leila took it, then she crossed the section to pull the other garment from its place, a sheer black full-length coat with floral embroidery on the sleeves that featured enough violet to match beautifully. The fine mesh material would soften the frank lines of the jumpsuit that were clearly making Leila anxious.

'Oh my God. That is gorgeous.' Leila laughed nervously. 'But I don't know. I'm fifty-seven. This isn't exactly what I'm used to wearing. It's made for women ten feet tall with neither boobs nor butt.'

Rosalind shrugged. 'You've looked fabulous in half the stuff you tried on already, and you didn't like any of it. Obviously it's time for a change. Besides, you're slender and in great shape, and the color will be perfect with your hair.'

'Well . . .' Leila looked dubiously at the two garments, then smiled, her face flushing. For a crazy second, Rosalind caught a glimpse of herself in the pretty features, a glimpse that disappeared the second she tried to analyze it. But the resemblance had been there. 'Okay. I'll try. But come into the room with me this time, because I might be too embarrassed to model it in public.'

'Sure.' She followed Leila back to the dressing room and waited outside the stall, nearly giddy with excitement and happiness. This had been such a wonderful outing, one that had vindicated not only her decision to stay in New Jersey, but also her decision not to spring the are-you-my-mother? question on Leila yet. Maybe Leila had come to the same conclusion, which was why she hadn't acknowledged Rosalind either. Growing closer, spending time together like this could only make the eventual unveiling easier and much more natural.

'Oh. Well. Hmm.' Leila's voice came through the door of the room. 'This might actually work.'

Rosalind perked up. 'Let me see.'

'Hang on, let me try the jacket, too . . .'

Thirty seconds later, the door swung open.

She looked dazzling. Chic, elegant, feminine and sexy without being obvious. The bright jewel purple was perfect with her hair and skin.

Rosalind grinned and nodded. 'Oh yeah. That's it.'

'Are you sure?' Leila turned back to the mirror. 'It's nothing like what I was picturing myself in.'

'You look amazing. The color is perfect for you, and the material hangs gorgeously.'

Leila peered over her shoulder. 'Butt good?'

'Butt great. No butt worries at all. You don't even have to wear control panties.'

Leila patted her abdomen. 'These pleats hide a multitude of sins, as Mama would say.'

'You don't have any sins; you're slim, like my sisters.'

'Oh, come on, not like you're dumpy.'

'Next to them I am.'

'So stay away.' Leila turned and looked at herself one more time. 'I don't know if I'm just sick of looking for anything else or if this is really as great as it looks. How did you manage on the first try?'

Rosalind rushed to answer. 'It's what *I* wanted.'

Leila turned. Her eyebrows rose.

'Well, then,' she said softly.

Rosalind had trouble breathing. 'Well, then . . . what?'

'Well, then *you* should buy it too.' She gave a sassy toss of her head and threw open her arms. 'Why not?'

Rosalind shrugged, deflated and relieved at the same time. 'I don't have the height to carry it off.'

'That's what heels are for. Go get one.' She pointed imperiously. 'I insist.'

Rosalind started to protest, then realized there was absolutely no reason to.

Half an hour later, mother and daughter were heading happily home with matching Lord & Taylor purchases wrapped up in the back seat, sucking on Diet Cokes and sharing a bag of popcorn. Rosalind wasn't generally a fan of mall shopping, but today she could have stayed there the rest of the day. Caitlin had no idea how lucky she was.

'Thanks for coming with me, Rosalind.'

'You're welcome. Caitlin didn't want to go? I feel like this is a mother–daughter thing.' Rosalind froze, handful of popcorn halfway to her mouth. *Crap.* Now she'd done it.

'Sure it is.' Leila didn't seem to miss a beat. 'But Caitlin is busy, Zaina's not up to the trip, and I needed a girl pal.'

'I had a great time, thank *you*.' Rosalind finished her popcorn, thinking she could say just about anything and Leila wouldn't react. Maybe this was the next step, edging closer without actually saying anything. Kind of like playing chicken.

'I forgot to tell you. Mama said she promised you a Lebanese feast, so we're having it on her birthday, Wednesday the sixteenth. Are you free that night?'

Rosalind gaped. 'She wants *me* at her birthday party?'

'She does.'

'But . . . I feel like I'd be barging in on family time.' She waited, semi-breathlessly, though by now she knew better than to expect a reaction.

'You wouldn't be.'

'That's really nice of her.' She followed the popcorn with a swallow of Coke, feeling braver by the minute. 'I'm so grateful how you've all embraced me like this.'

'No problem.' Leila patted her hand. 'We like you.'

'Good. That's good. I like everyone as well.'

'Here's what I'm curious about.' Leila grabbed a handful of popcorn, touched her tongue to the kernels and drew those that stuck, lizard-like, into her mouth. 'What kind of girl you were. What did you want to do with your life when you were little?'

Rosalind couldn't help a smile. 'I was pretty ordinary, I guess, or as ordinary as the kid of a mega-celebrity can be. At least in Beverly Hills my life was more normal than it would seem to people here, since LA was all about movies and the people in them. For a while I wanted to be a gymnast. I took it pretty seriously for a few years. I loved the tumbling, I loved feeling my body leave the ground, everything upside down and shaken up. I loved the power of it. But I wasn't good enough to be competitive, and then puberty hit and I sort of lost interest.'

'That's remarkable. What else?'

'Let's see. I loved sewing, embroidery, girlie stuff like that. I loved to dance, I took lessons in ballet and tap.' She started counting on her fingers. 'I took tennis and diving lessons, I played the flute for a while.'

'You did it all, huh.' Leila slowed behind a knot of traffic. 'Any theater?'

'Sure. For fun. I loved it but never took it seriously.'

'You're smart. What kind of parts?'

'I got a couple of leads junior and senior year. The funny girls, Adelaide in *Guys and Dolls*, and Ado Annie in *Oklahoma!*'

Leila bounced in her seat, swaying her head to 'I Cain't Say No'.

Rosalind cackled and scooped up popcorn, stuck her tongue into it experimentally, and felt the strange pinch of kernels grabbing on for the ride to her mouth. 'That's the one.'

'So what stuck from childhood to now? What's your overriding passion?'

Rosalind felt the familiar jolt of irritation. *Et tu*, Leila? Judgment from a fellow hummingbird? 'I liked to draw when I was a girl. I still do that. I paint, actually.'

'Do you take that seriously?'

Rosalind growled silently. Leila was acting like such a *mom*. 'Sort of. I'm not brave enough to put it on display. But it makes me—'

'Why do you think that is?' Leila took a sip of her Diet Coke and put it back into the cup holder between them. 'Fear of failure? Fear of success? Different sides of the same thing, you know.'

'Yeah, I'm not sure.' She was not having this conversation again. 'Did you know what *you* wanted to do from the beginning?'

'Oh yes. Either singing or writing. I always thought it would be wonderful to write an epic love story. Like *Gone With the Wind*, only without going on so long and with a happier ending. Unfortunately, every time I started a story, I'd get stuck or bored. I stayed with singing, though, so there was my answer.'

'That's wonderful.' Rosalind folded her arms peevishly. Apparently she didn't have an answer for anything. Her life was randomly dispersed. Like rabbit pellets.

'I'm not implying you have to have a single-focus career. You know that, right?' Leila turned worriedly, searching Rosalind's expression, which Rosalind tried to bolster back into cheerfulness. 'There are plenty of other things that make a woman's life valuable. Marriage, children, volunteer work . . .'

Rosalind scooped up more popcorn. Yeah, and she didn't do any of those either. Which made her what? Worthless? Not any more of a woman than her mother, but for different reasons?

She couldn't accept that was what Leila meant.

They were passing back through strip-mall land, near the airport, about five too-short minutes from home.

'Here's another question.' Leila's announcement made Rosalind tense. What now? 'Have you noticed how headlights have turned mean?'

'Uh . . .' Rosalind glanced over in confusion. 'Mean?'

'See?' Leila pointed at an oncoming car, whose headlights, when you thought of them as eyes, did look angry.

Rosalind laughed, grateful for the change of subject, even to something so silly. 'You are *right*. They're terrifying.'

'You keep doing what makes you happy, girl.' Leila slowed for a stop light and turned to face Rosalind. 'You know who you are, and you clearly have plenty of power to go after what you want. Ignore anyone who tries to bring you down. Ignore me, too, in fact.'

'I'd love to.'

Leila burst into her beautiful rich laughter. 'There you go.'

The next five minutes recaptured the day's fun, Rosalind rebounding into her natural cheer. By the time they pulled into the driveway on Laurel Road, she was grieving the end of the trip.

'Hey, Caitlin's here. Uh-oh.' Leila pressed the garage door opener and glanced at her watch. '*Ugh*, I had no idea it was so late! I was supposed to meet her at five thirty to go look at flowers, and it's nearly six.'

Rosalind followed her out of the car and into the kitchen, body heavy with guilt. She'd stolen her sister's mother when her sister needed her.

In the kitchen, Caitlin was standing, arms folded, tapping her foot. '*Mom.*'

'I know, I know. I'm sorry. I lost track of—'

'You are never on time. *Never.* This is incredibly important.'

'I know, I know.' Leila strode toward the dining room. 'Where's Mama?'

'Visiting the Khalafs. They picked her up. Can we go now? Angela's waiting.'

'I'll freshen up and be ready. Two minutes, I promise.' Leila fled, leaving Rosalind not much in the mood to have a pass-the-time chat with Caitlin, which feeling was undoubtedly mutual.

'Argh!' Caitlin pressed her hands to her temples. 'She is late *all* the time. I have no idea how she manages to live her life.'

'I'm sorry. I wish I'd—'

'Where did you go?' She glanced at the bag in Rosalind's hand. 'Shopping at Quakerbridge?'

'Bridgewater Commons.'

Caitlin made a sound of impatience. 'That's a hell of a trip when there's a Lord & Taylor twenty minutes closer.'

'We went to a bunch of stores.'

'She never takes *me* shopping there.' Her eyes narrowed suspiciously. 'What were you looking for?'

'Your mom wanted to get her wedding outfit.'

Caitlin's mouth opened into an O, for outrage. She took a step back, hand to her chest. 'She took *you* to get a mother-of-the-bride dress for *my* wedding?'

Crap. Crap. Crap. Rosalind held up a placating hand.

'Caitlin, I am so sorry. I wasn't thinking. I should have said I couldn't go.'

Caitlin closed her eyes briefly. Let out a breath. 'Okay. I know. It's not your fault.'

'What's not her fault? I'm ready to go. Did Rosalind show you my fabulous wedding outfit?' Leila strode toward the bag and lifted out the purple jumpsuit and flowered coat. The jumpsuit's color popped brilliantly against the yellow walls of the kitchen. 'Check this out. I'll wear my strappy black pumps with the—'

'Mom.' Caitlin was clearly horrified. 'That's not at *all* what we talked about for you.'

'I know.' Leila smiled admiringly at the outfit. 'I like this much better. Rosalind picked it out for me. She got one too.'

Rosalind wanted to bury her head in her hands. *Oh, Leila.*

'You got *matching outfits*?'

'Not matching.' Rosalind couldn't get the words out fast enough. 'I mean, yes, they're the same, but it's not like we're ever going to wear them at the same time.'

Caitlin heaved a breath. 'Mom, this is a *wedding*. You're supposed to look like a *mother*.'

'Oh, really? And what exactly does a mother look like, Caitlin? June Cleaver? Donna Reed? Sister Margaret? A long-sleeved, high-necked dress with orthopedic shoes? No other look qualifies me for maternity?' She flung out her arm toward Rosalind. 'How about Jillian Croft? Is she not a real mother because she was the most beautiful and sexy woman on the planet?'

'No. No.' Caitlin lowered her voice. 'But—'

'Last time I checked, there are mothers of all kinds out there, Caitlin. This . . .' she shook the outfit at her daughter, 'is the kind *I* am. Okay?'

'Okay. Okay, fine.' Caitlin slung her purse over her shoulder. 'Can we *go* now?'

'Yes. We can. Rosalind, thanks for an incredibly fun afternoon that I'm sorry my daughter has chosen to ruin for both of us.'

Rosalind wanted to sink through the floor. Worse and worse and then worse. 'Actually, I get it. Caitlin should have gone with you so that you two could have agreed or at least compromised on—'

'No. She needs to learn that she doesn't always get her way. Somehow I never managed to get that message through to her. Come on, Cait. Let's go.' Leila banged through the back door, Caitlin stalking behind her.

Leaving Rosalind alone and miserable in the middle of their kitchen.

Chapter 13

May 12, 1968 (Sunday)

The last performance of South Pacific *was today, the Sunday matinee. I sang my heart out, while inside, I was thinking, I'm gonna wash this town right outta my hair . . . tomorrow!*

I have money for the bus. I have a suitcase that I stashed under some branches near school. It's not supposed to rain.

I'm so tired, but I suppose I won't sleep much. It's been a hectic few weeks. I got a room at the Taylor Apartments in New York, the cheapest women's residence I could find – still a lot of money, but meals are included, which will help, and it will be safe. I bet there will be other girls there who want to be actresses too. Maybe I'll find friends who will star with me in movies later. It could happen!

I had to provide a letter from a doctor stating that I am in good health, a character recommendation, and proof that I have a job. Sarah covered for me while I went to Skowhegan to the doctor. I told them to bill my parents. I will send them money when I make more, I promised myself that. I am no thief. Mr Carter gave me the recommendation. I let him think it was for a college summer program. I also let him kiss me again and touch my breasts – at least those are normal. He made all these noises and I think he . . . well, it was gross. At

least I thought so. But I didn't feel dirty because this is for such
an important cause! I lied that I had a job. Who would hire a
nobody from Maine sight unseen? I wouldn't. I am sure I can
find something quickly once I'm there.

Goodnight, me, sleep well if you can, I am so proud of you!
Real life starts tomorrow!

'I'm stuffed.' Rosalind pushed away the nearly empty container
of sushi she and Bryn had taken out from Ajitan, a tiny
downtown Princeton restaurant. The day had turned out to be
freaky-warm for October, one of those gift days it was hard to
enjoy anymore because of its implications for the planet. They
were sitting around a fire pit in the back yard of his cute
Victorian house in Lawrenceville, the next town over from
Princeton. 'How can white rice and fish be so filling?'

'Anything's filling if you eat enough of it.'

'That can't be true; what about celery?' She sat back in her
chair, pulling around her a blanket Bryn had supplied. It was
beyond blissful to be able to relax and put the rest of her
problems on hold, watching the fire throw wavering ruddy
shadows on Bryn's face.

This wasn't the first time they'd hung out since the pizza
dinner at her house. The previous Sunday afternoon, Bryn had
invited her out for ice cream. Earlier that same day, Rosalind
had made a point of spending time with Caitlin, talking wedding
hairstyles, showing her Internet pictures of some ideas, and
sketching a few others. Her intention had been to help, of
course, but also to make more progress bonding with her sister,
not only as an investment in their future relationship, and to
smooth over the shopping trip mess two days earlier, but also
to pave the way for asking questions about Caitlin's father.

She'd made some progress, but Caitlin was clearly still

keeping her at arm's length, and Rosalind had been spent. It was an enormous relief later that day to hang out with Bryn, eat ice cream, and chat about something other than weddings and families. Her worries about him becoming too intense had been unfounded – he hadn't so much as touched her – leaving her free to enjoy their time together.

Today they'd spent a few hours at Sharon's house, plotting the flow of bodies at the wedding, taking pictures and making sketches of rooms and where furniture should go in them, then lists of signs that would be needed when deliveries started showing up – alcohol, chairs, tables and presents – and plans for how the garage could be cleared to accommodate most of the stuff.

During the entire enterprise, they had talked. And talked and talked and talked, an increasingly addictive rush of seeking and finding connections. Politics, movies, books, each other's favorite cities, favorite ice cream flavors, favorite times of day. The easy meshing of their ideas and rhythms had made Rosalind realize how in thrall she'd been to men she'd dated previously, and how much passive time she'd spent with them. Listening to Wolf talk about the best ways to record sound, listening to Troy discuss the importance of alternative power sources, listening to Don pontificate about healthy eating and cautious investing. Three experts in their fields, at least in their own minds, eager to share knowledge, passions, points of view, and to be validated in all of them.

Since Rosalind had spent her childhood listening to her father be brilliantly correct about everything, it wasn't a big intellectual stretch to understand why interacting with those men felt familiar and right. But how seductive instead to be not merely a vehicle for reflecting back male glory, but the object of as much interest as she showed.

She had a crush. Unlike the one on Emil, this had only gotten deeper the more time she spent with Bryn, and the more of himself he revealed.

'What I don't understand . . .' He picked up a tiny piece of pickled ginger with chopsticks and brought it to his mouth. She was kind of into how gracefully he used them. A pretty serious crush, because, really, chopsticks? '. . . is how Asians eat quantities of rice and rice noodles and the French eat almost exclusively white bread, and Italians gorge on pasta, and all of these are thin, healthy cultures, while in the US white flour and rice are supposed to send you straight to obesity and death.'

'Different body chemistry? Different grains? Who knows. Maybe it's sugar, which none of them eat a lot of and we do.' She took a sip of the sake he'd suggested they buy, nursing a deliciously balanced buzz to keep it either from slowing into fatigue or accelerating into drunkenness. 'My dad used to make fun of health reporting. "A team of scientists gave ten Americans nothing but corn flakes for a week, and ten French people nothing but Cheerios. At the end of this period they gave both groups a French grammar test, which proved that Cheerios are superior at helping you speak French."'

Bryn chuckled, giving a slow up-down nod of approval. 'Your dad sounds great.'

'He could be.' She tipped the sake glass again, barely letting any between her lips, unsure how to phrase her next thoughts, though around Bryn she felt no pressure to be perfectly brilliant and/or competent with every word. 'What do you do when you discover someone you love has parts you really, *really* hate?'

'Hmm.' His brows drew down. He started to push up his glasses before he remembered he wasn't wearing any. Rosalind liked him in contacts, loved the immediateness of his blue eyes, though she was also becoming a sucker for the wire-rimmed scholarly look. 'I'd say you accept that you love the person and also really, *really* hate parts of him.'

'That sounds like a therapy answer.'

'There's a good reason for that.' He tossed back his sake and poured them both more. Rosalind didn't object, though she probably should. 'I've been through years of it. Plus I understand what you mean. My mom was a smart, dynamic and hilarious person caught up in a disease that turned her into a nightmare at regular and increasingly close intervals. In a true cliché of denial, the family tiptoed around pretending hers was normal behavior and we were all fine with it.'

Rosalind winced. 'Very familiar.'

'It makes no sense, but I never stopped feeling like I was letting her and the family down by not being able to fix her. And in an equally stunning lack of logic, I resented her for that.'

'Yes, yes. God, yes.' Rosalind was nearly breathless with the thrill of connection. She raised her glass. 'Here's to crazy begetting crazy, and to us for breaking the cycle.'

'Amen.' Bryn drank with her. 'So I get the love–hate thing.'

'Are you close to your mom now?'

'Closer than I was. Her sobriety helped. But she took time to come around to the sculpting thing; actually, both my parents did. Same with my siblings, but I didn't care so much what they thought. It's been hard not to feel Mom and Dad value me only for my success. Parents have such power. If you don't separate from them, they can still make you feel like a kid whose behavior disappointed them.'

'By separate, you mean go through the rebellion phase, loathe everything they stand for, et cetera?'

'Et cetera.' He stood to get another log for the fire. 'I imagine life with your mom was even more complicated by celebrity.'

'You could say that. She was either avoiding it or indulging it, depending on her mood.' Rosalind put her drink down and watched him. 'She liked to be off her meds when she worked. She claimed she could feel emotions better. Though I will say, when she was manic, she was great, at least to us girls. Probably harder on Dad. But we adored her energy and humor and how nothing was out of the realm of possibility.'

He dropped the new log on the fire, creating a shower of sparks. 'Your mom was an amazing presence on screen. Riveting.'

'She was like that in person, too. So beautiful and graceful and talented that people flocked around her, wanting some of her joy to rub off on them. Then she'd crash and have to be coaxed back on to her meds or she'd relapse into pills and drinking.' Rosalind pulled the sleeves of her sweater down over her chilled hands, waiting for the fire's warmth to reach her. It felt right to trust Bryn with the childhood truths she'd kept from so many others. 'In many ways Dad was an amazing father, especially given what he had to deal with. We knew he'd do anything to protect us. But . . . for example, when he was proud of me, or complimented me, it was like a huge weight taken off, because for that moment I wasn't found lacking.'

'Do you know about the chicken study?' When she shook her head, Bryn sat back down and leaned toward the fire, giving her a clear view of his fine profile. 'Three chickens in three cages, each with a lever. One chicken pecks at the lever and always gets a treat. One pecks and never gets a treat. Those two get bored and stop pecking.'

'Yeah, sounds pretty unfulfilling.'

He grinned at her, making her heart beat just a bit faster. 'In the third cage, when the chicken pecks, sometimes it gets a treat, and sometimes not. That one never stops pecking. Never.'

She narrowed her eyes. 'You calling me chicken?'

'Both of us. Keeping on with the pecking because sometimes we'd get a reward. It's not consistent so there's nothing you can control or count on or understand. You're stuck.'

'Argh, Bryn!' Rosalind let her head drop back on the chair, gazing up at the faintly starry sky. 'You're making me feel so sorry for young me. I want to reverse time and grow up in some family that goes through life peacefully, whose healthy, intelligent parents have normal jobs they love, and kids they love, none of whom have major issues. Where do you sign up for that?'

'I'm not sure it exists.'

She lifted her head and pouted at him. 'It has to. Somewhere. Not everyone gets hit by crime or major tragedy or mental illness or cruelty. Someone must get a peaceful, happy ride through life. I have to believe that.'

'Why?'

Her pout turned into a frown. She'd always been shut down over her position, never challenged to explain. 'I guess because then I can dream about that life as something real. Too late for me, but maybe for my children.'

'You want children without getting married?'

Rosalind blinked, taken aback by her own words. 'No. I mean, no. I was just talking about . . . general human experience. I don't know why I said that.'

'Okay.' He held her gaze, a smile barely curving his lips. Even annoyed by his smug amusement, Rosalind had to look away, at the logs carved into red and gray arches by fire burning their centers. Because if she kept staring at Bryn in the near darkness, attraction was going to turn her harmless buzz into something potent.

He'd seemed different to her today from the moment he came by to pick her up, and not just because of the contacts. As he'd stood outside her door, solid and masculine in jeans and a blue T-shirt under a black canvas coat, something inside her had shifted.

'I have another question. If you don't mind.' She loved this intimacy between them, loved that he didn't seem to find any topic off bounds, that the dysfunction and tragedy of her family was familiar to him instead of threatening. 'Then we can talk like normal people again.'

'I like hearing what's in your head, Rosalind.'

His gentle words flustered her just enough to confuse the question she wanted to ask. She'd been thinking for the past several days, considering her mother's courage in leaving her life and family behind, her utter confidence in her own acting talent. Leila's lifelong determination and devotion to her singing. Rosalind's courage had brought her to New Jersey, but she was discovering a troubling pattern to her behavior, finding herself drawn forward by longing, then tossed back nearly as far by anxiety.

'How do you find out if you've been living your life making choices out of fear? What if it means opinions you've discounted might have been right all along? How do you change?'

'That's three questions.'

'Then I have three questions.'

'Those are harder. I may have to charge double.' He put his glass on the edge of the fire pit to glisten orange and yellow. 'First, you're definitely not alone in that fear, especially as the child of an addict. You survived something that crushes a lot of people. Second, you thank God – literally if you believe, figuratively if you don't – that you have people around you who care enough to tell you that you're fucking up.'

'Like, "Ouch, that hurt, tell me more?"'

'Something like that.' He clasped his hands together between his thighs. She wondered how he could not be cold in his thin coat. The air around them was damp. 'Third, the hardest part, you decide to stop living that way and then do it.'

'Come on.'

'I'm serious. It takes a lot of energy and a lot of work and you'll screw up half the time – more than half at first. Just tell yourself from now on that when you want to draw back from something, go forward instead.'

'Even if I'm faced with a mugger?'

He gave her a look. 'Yes, Rosalind, even if you're faced with a mugger. Invite him home. Make him hot chocolate. Offer to polish his gun.'

'Stop!'

His eyes crinkled into a firelit grin. He leaned toward her and put a hand on her knee long enough to transfer warmth, then took it back. 'I had to do the same thing. I lost it after Jake killed himself. Everything messed up about me that I'd been suppressing emerged in an explosion of rage and ugly misery. I had to start over, reinvent myself, free from the strait-jacket of my parents' expectations. But it was terrifying. I still struggle. I still have to remind myself to move forward, not retreat.'

'What's something you did recently that you were scared of?'

'Hmm.' He rubbed his hands together. 'I kissed you. That was terrifying.'

Rosalind laughed, more startled than amused. 'Why?'

'You could have vomited from revulsion. You could have grabbed a knife from your boot and stabbed me. You could have followed me home and set my house on fire.'

'Uh, Bryn?'

'See? Fears are in your head. Just tell them to get the hell away from you.'

A warm feeling spread through Rosalind's chest, accompanied by a wistful ache. Bryn was sweeping her off her feet, a completely new kind of seduction. Nothing like Wolf's guitar serenades or Troy's poetry or Don's flowers and expensive dinners.

'So where would you start?' he asked.

I'd kiss you back.

But he might take it to mean too much when she wasn't sure herself how much it would. The urge could add up to no more than sake, intimacy and firelit darkness. Bryn was a wonderful, earnest guy, but the two of them had enough baggage to crash an Airbus, and he was looking for someone who wanted forever, while she . . .

Was scared of it.

'I'm going to ask you a question now, okay?' He was back to facing the fire. 'I would like an honest answer.'

Rosalind caught herself moving to the very back of her chair. 'Okay.'

'What are you really doing here?'

Her mouth opened. No sound. Then it came out, without planning or forethought. 'Leila is my birth mother.'

'Holy shit.' He shook his head as if he were waking up from a confusing dream. 'Holy shit, Rosalind.'

She couldn't believe she'd told him or that she didn't immediately regret it. 'I know.'

'Holy sh— Okay, I already said that.' He got up from the chair, as if the news was too huge to take sitting down. 'Who knows besides you?'

'I'm not sure.' She ducked her head. 'Nothing's been said. I'm pretty sure Leila knows. Zaina might, too.'

'Caitlin doesn't.'

Rosalind hunched her shoulders. 'Caitlin probably doesn't.'

'Jesus.' He sounded angry for the first time since she'd known him. 'You need to tell her, Rosalind. She deserves to know.'

'Yes.' Rosalind looked up at him, guilt spreading a weight in her stomach. She deserved this. She'd been playing a stupid game for her own purposes and needed to make it stop before she hurt someone. 'You're right. It's not fair to her.'

'Is this why you brought up the fear thing?' He was speaking gently again, but his face was still grim. 'Because saying anything about this will be scary.'

'Big scary. But . . .' Rosalind tried a smile, 'I've been told all I need to do is move forward.'

'So you're adopted then?'

'Yes. Just found out.'

'Jesus.' He moved restlessly. 'Now what? Who is your father? What are you going to—'

'I don't know any more than I told you, Bryn.' She held out her hand in a plea for him to understand, swearing to herself that would be the first and last lie she'd ever tell him. 'That's all I have.'

He pivoted back to the fire.

'I need to tell you something, too. Since it's apparently give-up-the-big-secrets night.' He shoved his hands in his jeans pockets, weight planted on both feet. 'I was obsessed with Caitlin for years. Watching her and Emil, waiting for her to wise up that he was not what she needed . . . it was torture. The way she related to me, depended on me – you've seen it.'

Rosalind stood and moved next to him, equal parts jealous and sympathetic. 'I sort of suspected by the way you talked about her. Sounds like she was your lever that sometimes gives treats.'

'She was exactly that.'

'I'm sorry, little chicken.' She gave his shoulder an awkward pat.

Bryn made a sound of derision. 'Hey, I might be a nice guy, but my ego demands that you call me something more manly than little chicken.'

'Big chicken?'

He gave a sigh of exaggerated patience and took her hand. 'I guess that'll do.'

'Are you still in love with her?' Her heart beat faster than it should have waiting for his answer.

'I don't think I ever was really, but no. Believe it or not, you *can* kick a puppy enough times that it will go away.'

'A *big* puppy.' She got a smile from him that time, and a squeeze of her fingers, though he still stared into the fire.

'Three years ago, she and Emil had a huge fight and broke up. She came right to me.' He pursed his lips, blew out a breath. 'I knew I should tell her to go to hell, but, well . . . dream come true and all, and I am a guy.'

'Seems like none of you can help it.'

'Guess not.' He turned to look at her, his face close in the dancing firelight, and Rosalind felt another flutter of attraction. No, a big flutter. No, a flap.

His swallow was audible. Then he looked back down. 'After that first night, it started unraveling pretty quickly. I wouldn't sleep with her until we told Emil. She refused to, which made me feel as if we were having an affair instead of seeing each other legitimately. I couldn't take the guilt and ended it. After years of wanting her, the relationship lasted all of two poisoned weeks, and was never consummated.'

'Tell me she didn't go right back to him.'

'She went right back to him.'

'Ouch.' If Caitlin had been in the yard with them, Rosalind

would have been tempted to punch her. 'I'm sorry, Bryn.'

'Yeah, it was bad. But an important lesson. First, do not bother with fantasies.'

'Except for my perfect family.'

'Yes, Rosalind.' He spoke in a syrupy be-kind-to-the-patient voice. 'Except for that family.'

'Second?'

'Second, I learned that I couldn't be with someone who denied her pain like that. At times I can barely stand the frustration with Emil.'

'Does Emil know that you were together?'

'I don't think so. I agonized about it, then decided she and I had been an aberration, not worth sacrificing such a long friendship or messing up their relationship for. In the end, Caitlin and I both got what we wanted. She got a warm body while she wasn't with Emil. And I got her out of my system.'

'Or . . .' Rosalind tipped her head to see his features better. 'She had real feelings, but wasn't willing to give up the Emil Total Package.'

'Huh?' He looked mystified. 'Something wrong with *my* package?'

'No!' She giggled, relieved that he was shaking off the gloom already. 'I mean I don't know . . . I mean that's not what I—'

'You're off the hook. Emil *is* the total package, and that is important to her.' He turned to face Rosalind, took her hand in both of his, and played lightly with her fingers, watching her intently. 'I've been thinking . . . I'd like to sculpt you.'

'Huh?' Whatever Rosalind had thought he was going to say, that wasn't it. 'Me?'

'Yeah.' He was still looking toward her, but now objectively, sizing her up, mentally transforming her into what he saw as an artist. She recognized the look from having worn it herself. 'Ten years sculpting my pain, Jake's pain. I want to start something new.'

'Scared woman with goofy clothes?'

'Beautiful scared woman.' His eyes warmed. 'With *really* goofy clothes.'

'You must learn to appreciate the finer points of kook fashion.' She tilted up her chin, stretched out her arms, let him examine her a few seconds longer.

'Try this.' He tipped her face to the side, ran his fingers through her hair, now impossible to control and showing a half-inch of dark roots, but under his hands she felt precious. Gently, he bent her at the waist, twisted her so her torso faced upward, and curved one of her arms like a ballerina reaching out, pressed her other hand against her heart. Then he stepped back and assessed. 'Like that. Sort of.'

She held the pose. 'How long does it take you to make a sculpture?'

'Depends. Anywhere from a week to a few months.'

'I'd have to stand like this for a few months?'

'Is that a problem?' He moved forward and repositioned her arm slightly higher.

'Of course not. But shouldn't you choose someone who'll be around town longer than I will?'

'Nope.' He put her arm lower again, studied the effect. 'You're the one.'

'How come?'

'Because I'm falling in love with you.'

Rosalind gasped, dropping the pose, then caught his smile and was immediately mortified. 'Oh, you're joking again. I thought—'

'No, I'm not.' He drew her to him. 'Not this time.'

223

His mouth was warm, his body solid, and he was a really, really good kisser.

Help.

'Bryn.'

'Yes, Rosalind.'

'I'm not . . . I'm not there . . .' She stopped before she added 'yet'.

'That's okay.' He pressed his forehead against hers. 'I'm a patient guy.'

'I might not ever be there.'

'I get it.'

'So . . .' She closed her eyes. 'What are you going to do, wait around and see?'

'Yeah, it's this new thing called dating.'

'Bryn . . .'

'Shh, stop stressing. Men have fallen in love with you before, it's not going to hurt.' He enveloped her in his arms. For one second she thought she should pull back, but he felt really, really good, and it wasn't like she was unavailable. Or not attracted. She was just . . .

Scared. And hadn't ever been scared before, had rushed headlong into love-love-*love*! every single time. Did that mean she was older and wiser now? Or something much more frightening?

'Move away from fear, Rosalind,' Bryn whispered. 'Fo-o-or-ward, into the li-i-ight.'

'I ca-a-an't,' she whispered back.

'Why no-o-o-ot?'

'Because the light is fi-i-ire and it would ki-i-ill me. Plus you're standing so close I can't move anywhe-e-ere.'

'True.' He bent to kiss her again. Desire rose sharp and hot, until she was all but decided to give into its pull.

'Hang on.' Bryn lifted his head and settled her against him, breaths quick and heavy, in time with hers. 'I need to get the man-beast under control.'

'Why?' She asked without thinking, drugged with passion-stupidity.

'Because I still have enough functioning brain left to know that taking this further tonight is only going to give you exactly the reasons you need tomorrow morning to wish it hadn't happened. I'm going to take it as a good sign that you didn't vomit the second time I kissed you either, and leave it at that.'

'That is just *so* romantic.'

'I can be very romantic when I'm not terrified of rejection. Hang around and find out?' He didn't wait for her answer, but stepped back and lifted the screen to cover the fire.

'C'mon, Rosalind. I'll drive you home before I change my mind.'

Chapter 14

May 26, 1968 (Sunday)

So much has happened, my goodness! I'm a New Yorker now. I have a place to live and I have a job! I got it pretty quickly. What happened was, I told Mrs Colfax, sort of the dorm mother of this girls-only apartment building, that the job I was counting on had fallen through, and here I was all fresh from backwoods Maine in the big city, alone and unemployed, and I cried the most beautiful tears I knew how. She was lovely, felt so sorry for me and said she'd see what she could do about letting me rent a room anyway. Worked like a charm. The other girls seem pretty nice. My room is tiny and basic, bed, chair, desk. There's a public room with a kettle where we can entertain visitors, and another room with a television where the residents gather. As I expected, a lot of the other girls living here are also trying to catch a break in theater. The competition! I have sized them up and decided I'll do fine.

I have a job at the little Italian restaurant around the corner. I think the owner is sweet on Mrs Colfax. I get huge tips by smiling at the gentlemen. It's kind of sad how easy they are to manipulate. You'd think they'd have more pride.

I love love love New York! It's loud and smelly and bigger than I ever dreamed it could be, and I am in love to the death.

As soon as I get settled in a little more, I will go to the Stella Adler school and see about taking the acting world by storm. It's my destiny after all.

Rosalind sat in her newly adopted sewing chair, the suede recliner by the window, hemming Zaina's dress. The old one, still in pieces, she'd folded carefully into a drawstring bag made from one of the skirt panels as a keepsake. Zaina had mentioned wanting to be buried with the dress. Now she could.

Over and over again, Rosalind drew a length of blue thread through silk of the same color, collecting the tiniest bit possible of the skirt and pulling the thread snug. She'd learned to blind-hem by machine, but still preferred the slow, hypnotic rhythm of the handwork, feeling connected to generations of women sitting in chairs, drawing needle and thread through cloth, creating, mending, updating or repurposing. A woman's art, maybe a dying one. She relished her part in keeping it alive.

The Allertons hadn't contacted her for wedding help in recent days. Rosalind hoped that was because preparations were going smoothly and not because Caitlin had put her foot down. She'd used the time to work on Zaina's dress, piecing it together with loving care, neatly finishing seams that would never show, installing interfacings, facings and a zipper, luxuriating in the fine weight, drape and rich color of the fabric. With experimental dips into opera repertoire warming the room, she had steeped herself in fantasies of sights seen by the original dress, its first wearing during a sacred ceremony in the ancient country of Zaina's birth, then dances and dinners and concerts two oceans away in an unfamiliar new one.

As the days passed and the dress neared completion, Rosalind had also experienced an increasing feeling of foreboding. Given that she was someone who could lie tied to tracks with an oncoming bullet train ten seconds away and stay confident she'd be freed in time, this was distressing, though understandable. Bryn had been right, and Eve before him. Rosalind needed to stop stalling and acknowledge to the whole family who she was, and why she was there. Caitlin's face after the shopping incident should have made that immediately clear.

She would talk to Leila first. Assuming that went well, Zaina and Caitlin after. If the conversation with Leila went badly, Rosalind could slip back to New York with apologies and without doing any more damage.

She couldn't imagine it going badly. She and Leila had been talking around the obvious since the first day they met.

Her phone's ring made her smile. The part of being in a relationship she'd missed the most was the simple connection to another person that transcended the business of everyday living. The hi-how-are-you and how's-your-day-going calls. The goodnight-sleep-wells. The sorry-to-hear-your-life-has-been-upended-like-a-harvested-carrot.

She and Bryn had seen each other twice since their picnic in his back yard – the weather had turned decidedly autumnal in the meantime – and her feelings and attraction were only deepening. He was clearly one of the nice guys, but with enough spice, humor, and complications to be challenging.

In short, she couldn't find a reason not to fall for him, which made her feel she was hurtling toward a fate utterly out of her control. A ridiculous thing to worry about, given that every person on the planet was doing exactly the same thing, even the few who'd deluded themselves into thinking they had power over their destinies.

She secured the needle and reached for her phone.

It wasn't Bryn. 'Hello?'

'Rosalind, it's Caitlin. I'm sorry to bother you. Mom said I should call you. I need . . . No one's here, and I have to . . . Mom's in Brooklyn with Teta, Emil is working, and the invitations *have* to go out tomorrow or I'm going to lose it.'

'No, no, it's fine.' Rosalind glanced at the length of thread trailing the needle, adrenaline rushing. This was the call she'd been anticipating for the last few days, dreading it would never come, terrified it would – but from Leila, not Caitlin. 'I'll be over in about five minutes.'

'Thank you *so* much.'

'No problem.' Rosalind punched off the phone and kept hemming until she ran out of thread, securing the end with a tiny knot, then hiding the tail by weaving it under the seam facing. She put the dress carefully back on its hanger, brushing a snipped thread from the skirt with shaky fingers. The material hung, lustrous and elegant, part of the past coming back to life.

Seemed like that had been happening a lot lately.

By the time she arrived across the street, she was forcing herself to breathe low and deep, determined not to give in to the tiny voice telling her to get on the next train back to New York and leave this highly charged mess alone.

'Thanks so much for coming over.' Caitlin's hair fell from a high ponytail nearly to her pink sweater, which matched her flustered coloring. Glasses perched on her nose, making her look younger and more serious, emphasizing the size of her blue eyes and the heart shape of her face. She ushered Rosalind inside with a glance at her plaid miniskirt and yellow striped leggings. 'Mom *promised* she'd leave Brooklyn well before rush hour, but of course she didn't, so they're stuck going twenty on the Jersey turnpike.'

'I get it. Living in LA you just assume traffic is going to be a nightmare.'

'This didn't *have* to be a nightmare, Mom *made* it one.' Caitlin led the way to the kitchen, pink-slippered feet making sliding sounds, syncopated to the clump of Rosalind's red flowered ankle boots. 'She does whatever she wants whenever she wants to and too bad for anyone who's counting on her.'

Uh-oh. Rosalind's red flowered ankle boots were now required to walk across eggshells. 'Some people have a really bad sense of time.'

'I understand that.' Caitlin yanked back one of the yellow-cushioned chairs from the kitchen island. On its black surface lay sloppy piles of envelopes, invitations, pens and stamp rolls. 'But it seems to me by the time you're near sixty, you should have figured out ways of controlling it so you don't keep letting people down. Have a seat.'

Rosalind sat obediently, tempted to say, *Or maybe by the time you're near thirty, you should have learned not to count on your mother*, but decided that would not get them off on the right foot. 'That must be hard.'

'And the closer we get to the wedding, the harder Emil suddenly has to be working, which was not the deal *at all*.' Caitlin sat, leaving one empty chair between her and Rosalind, and picked up a sheet of paper dense with typing, notations and pen lines. 'The addresses are on this list. I've crossed off the ones I've done. You can start from the bottom and work up.'

'Sure.' Rosalind reached for an invitation. The single card was cut from turquoise stock, with black calligraphic decoration scrolling down from the top right corner, thinning to a delicate single swirl near the bottom margin. Caitlin and Emil's names were printed in a plain font, along with Zaina and Leila's as the wedding's hosts. 'These are really nice.'

'Bryn did them. He's brilliant.'

Rosalind nodded, pierced by retroactive jealousy, a doubly

useless emotion. 'If it's any consolation, I think it's pretty normal to get frazzled over weddings.'

'I guess.' Caitlin picked up a pen with a resigned sigh. Her skin was enviable, small-pored, all peaches and cream – no doubt she'd never had a zit in her life. Rosalind had enjoyed a regular zodiac of them throughout young adulthood. If that wasn't bad enough, Caitlin's figure was of the patently unfair variety – long legs, sexy even in sweatpants, tiny waist, slender hips, breasts a-plenty; the kind of woman Rosalind wished fervently would blow up like a hippopotamus later in life. 'Thanks for helping. I assume your handwriting is legible? Even a little?'

Rosalind wrote down the first name – *Mr and Mrs John T. Winwood* – in her freakishly perfect script, and held up the envelope. 'A sample.'

'Ha!' Caitlin did her over-the-top gape of astonishment. 'That is ridiculous. How do you do that?'

'I have no idea. Drove my sisters crazy.' She put the envelope down and kept writing: *93 Cleveland Lane*. 'They told me it was prissy and unnatural. They were both scrawlers, of course.'

'Jealous then. I wish I'd had sisters. Or at least one.'

Rosalind lifted her pen so she wouldn't make a mistake, desperately hoping she wouldn't make a worse one when she opened her mouth. 'Does Emil have siblings?'

'One sister, Danielle. Two years older. She and I don't get along.' Caitlin wrinkled her nose. Even that looked adorable. 'Emil was dating Danielle's best friend when he and I met. Or when we met again.'

'When was the first time?' Rosalind put pen to paper again, calm enough with the new topic to keep working.

'Princeton High School. He was a senior, I was a freshman. I fell for him on sight. We had a fling over the summer before he went to Princeton. Then we both dated other people, but I don't know, I couldn't get him out of my head.' She rested her chin on the hand holding the pen. 'He was always the prize, you know? The one you compare all the others to.'

Rosalind slid an invitation into her envelope. She didn't know. When she left her boyfriends, they were gone, from her heart and head. 'I haven't had one of those.'

'Oh, well anyway, then I went to college at Rutgers, and we lost touch.' Caitlin went back to her writing. 'After graduation, I moved here and got an apartment in West Windsor with some girlfriends. Real estate in Princeton is ridiculous.'

'I can believe it.'

'I knew I'd find him at some point, whether by accident or looking him up. In the end, I bumped into him at a party. He was there with this other girl, Danielle's friend, but I don't know, something in me felt really strongly that he and I were meant to be together. So I pretty much got in his way as much as I could. And it worked, I mean of course it did. He and I are just . . . *it*. But his sister doesn't understand that. She thinks I'm a spoiled gold-digger who takes what she wants no matter what. Her exact words. Emil told me.'

'Ah.' Rosalind was not risking any comment. Getting and staying on Caitlin's good side would be tricky enough without blundering through that minefield. Bad behavior all around. 'Do you get along with Emil's parents? Where are they, by the way? They're local, right?'

'Yes, a really old Princeton family. His dad went to Princeton, his granddad went to Princeton, et cetera, et cetera, and they all lived here their whole lives, too. Right now his mom and dad are off in the Galapagos Islands, one of those cruises you book years in advance, so they couldn't cancel. They're great people. This is, his mom and stepdad, don't know if you knew that. His dad drank himself to death.'

Rosalind lifted her head, appalled both at the news and at the matter-of-fact way Caitlin spoke, as if she were reporting that he preferred three-ply tissues to two. 'That's awful.'

'Yeah. His mom remarried pretty quickly, though. Always made me wonder, you know? I think she cheated a lot. It was her coping mechanism. But they're happy, I guess.' She crossed out another name on the list. 'Emil gets along with his stepfather really well. Emil gets along with everyone, actually.'

Rosalind forced a smile, aghast at the miserable content of her sister's chatter. 'He seems like a great guy, Caitlin. I'm so happy you found him, and that the wedding is working out at such short notice. It's going to be really beautiful.'

Caitlin glanced up sharply, then back down. 'Okay.'

Okay? What crap could she have stepped in by being happy for a bride? 'Did I say something I shouldn't have?'

'No. No, of course not.' Caitlin kept staring at her envelope. 'It's just you say it like . . . like you're more part of this than . . . you are? Or no, that's not right, I don't know what it is. Maybe it's me. I'm a little out of my brain these days.'

Rosalind peeled off a stamp, trying desperately to seem nonchalant as she frantically searched for ways to put Caitlin at ease, hating her cowardice for not having talked to Leila already so she could acknowledge their relationship right now. 'I know it probably feels weird that I showed up and insinuated myself into your family like this.'

'Yeah.' Somehow the kitchen seemed quieter than it had been, as if the cabinets were suddenly listening. 'Actually it does.'

'I just want you to know that I don't have any strange agenda or anything that will threaten you or your relationship with any of your—'

'What? What are you *saying*? You've been here like two *weeks*.' Caitlin looked incredulous. 'You think I'm worried you'll threaten my relationship with my family?'

'No, no, of course not.' Ka-boom, wrong *again*. She was back to batting zero. 'I am not handling this well. But after the shopping trip . . .'

'Oh, *that*, okay. No, don't worry. That was on Mom, not you. She can be so totally clueless.' Caitlin rested her elbows on the counter, shaking her head. 'It's just hard right now, with Teta dying and all this wedding stress. Really, it's great you showed up. You're helping, and that's really nice.'

'You're welcome.' Rosalind touched Caitlin's shoulder, body relaxing, relieved to have made it over another bump. 'If I ever make you feel uncomfortable, please tell me.'

'It's a deal.' Caitlin sat back abruptly and grabbed a new envelope. 'So . . . you and Bryn scoped out Sharon's on Wednesday?'

'Yes. It's going to be a perfect place. We figured out all kinds of cool areas people can congregate, how the food stations will fit in, the best place for the bar . . . It will flow really well and look gorgeous.'

'Uh-huh.' Caitlin answered absently, pulled the address sheet closer and scanned it intently. 'Is something going on between you two?'

Rosalind re-tensed. Another bump. A bigger one. 'Sort . . . of. What made you ask that?'

'I'm getting a weird vibe from him about you.'

'Ah.' Rosalind put another envelope on the stack, with no idea what she'd written on it. 'We've been hanging out.'

'Romantically?'

She crossed a name off the bottom of the list. 'Recently. Yes.'

They each wrote another address, pens dragging across the paper, Rosalind's hand unsteady.

'He's a good guy.' Caitlin's voice cracked. 'One of the best.'

'Seems to be.' Rosalind wrote 'Pincestown', and had to toss the envelope on to the recycle pile.

'So . . . did he tell you? About . . . you know . . .'

Rosalind froze with her hand on top of the envelope stack and had to force her muscles to pick one up. Easier to pretend she had no idea what Caitlin was talking about. But she was determined not to foul up any future relationship with her by lying now. 'About you? Yes. He did.'

'Wow. That's . . .' Caitlin might as well have finished the sentence: 'a betrayal.' 'He did. So you know.'

Rosalind lifted an eyebrow, hoping her sister still had a sense of humor. 'That would be how it works, yeah.'

Caitlin let out a giggle, face blushing, looking so beautiful and vulnerable, Rosalind's heart ached for her. Crazy girl, letting Bryn go for someone like Emil. 'I'm not proud of it. But it sorta *had* to happen, after all those years knowing each other. I guess it was building for him, and it was for me, too, and I guess . . . anyway, we worked it out, and it's all good now. So I'm glad for you, and for him.'

Rosalind had to give her credit for trying, but the words came out as another starring-Caitlin episode of *Please Get Away From Everyone I Love*.

'Thanks.' She stuffed another invitation in another envelope, desperately searching for a safe conversation topic. 'I'm looking forward to Zaina's birthday party. All that Lebanese food. I bet it's going to be incredible. I'm not the greatest cook but—'

Caitlin was looking at her in horror. '*You* are coming to my grandmother's last birthday party?'

Rosalind's stomach started churning. Again. She'd done it *again*. 'Zaina asked to have me there.'

'Oh. Well, if Teta wants you there, then you should be there.' Caitlin practically hurled the envelope on to the finished pile, and crossed the next name off the list with a vicious black stripe. 'And yes, the food will be really good. You'll love it.'

Rosalind gave up, staring blankly at the address list. There was nothing she could say to repair this until she talked to Leila.

One trauma at a time.

She forced her eyes to focus on the list and began writing the next address. *Mr and Mrs John R. Pine.*

Caitlin sighed and put down her pen, plunked her forearms on the counter and bent her head so her ponytail curled over one cheek.

'All right.' Her voice came out muffled. 'I wasn't going to bring this up, but I need to know. Emil thinks that your father and my mother had an affair. I already asked Mom and she denied it, which I totally expected her to do, because she'd never admit the truth. Do you know?'

Mayday, Mayday. Rosalind wanted to take cover in the nearest closet. How was she going to get out of this? 'I don't know. No.'

Caitlin turned to look at her, head still resting on her crossed arms. 'You haven't tried asking Mom?'

'No.' Rosalind hid a guilty wince. 'I was planning to tonight.'

'Oh, good luck.' Caitlin turned her face away again. 'She'll say, "Of course not", or, "I don't know what you're talking about", and there you are, right back where you started. Mom does what she wants.'

Rosalind unlocked her fingers from around the pen. 'That could happen.'

'Emil thinks I could be Daniel Braddock's daughter, but in case you were also wondering that, I'm definitely not. I don't know why he doesn't believe me, but I know this for a fact. Mom was pregnant another time, a bunch of years before I was born. She lost that baby, and never got over it. I heard her talking about it one night with Teta, a long time ago, when I was like fourteen. This *void* that she couldn't get rid of. So she met some guy and got herself pregnant again to fill it. That was me. The void-filler.'

Rosalind's throat was cramping as hard as her fingers, both in sympathy for Caitlin's poignant misery, and because she had a feeling she knew who that baby was. Not lost, born healthy and surrendered. Any second now, Caitlin would put the obvious together with the obvious and come out with, *Hi, sis.*

'Anyway, I know who my father is, and it's not Daniel Braddock. So if you were thinking we might be half-sisters, you can rethink. Mom might have had an affair with your dad, but I wasn't the result. I just wanted to make that clear.'

Rosalind managed to croak out two words. 'Thank you.'

'What a mess, huh?' Caitlin sat up, picked up her pen and drew another envelope in front of her. 'I can't tell you how often I've wished I was born into a *normal* family.'

For once, Rosalind could totally relate. 'I know what you mean.'

'Teta raised me, really, you know.' Caitlin glanced up at Rosalind as if to judge the effect of her words. 'Mom was always off doing this and that, her career or who knows what, probably other affairs. She might have thought she wanted to replace the baby she miscarried, but when it came down to the work involved, not so much.

'Her generation had this idea that women had to have careers *and* babies, and that if you didn't want to or couldn't do both, you weren't living up to your total female potential.' She laughed bitterly. 'Thank God our generation has calmed that down. You pretty much can't have it all. If you want to stay sane, you have to choose. I'm choosing kids and family.'

Rosalind murmured something non-committal, reaching for

a stamp, still astounded that Caitlin hadn't put two and two together to reach the gigantically obvious conclusion flashing neon in her own brain. But Leila's 'lost' first baby would of course still be dead. And in her Caitlin-centric thinking, she hadn't questioned the outrageous coincidence of Rosalind showing up across the street.

'All right. Well.' Caitlin peered at the address list, pen still poised. 'I'm glad we got that out.'

'Same.' Rosalind dared a shaky smile. 'Kind of like barfing when your stomach is really upset.'

Caitlin burst into unexpected laughter, slightly maniacal, but rich and contagious, strikingly like her mother's.

'What's so funny?' Emil strode into the kitchen, his harried face brightening when he saw Rosalind. 'Rosalind! You're a sight for sore eyes. Hey, Cait.'

Caitlin's giggles faded. 'You are so late, Emil. Mom is stuck in Brooklyn. I had to call Rosalind to help.'

'I know, babe.' He rounded the corner toward her. 'I couldn't get away.'

Caitlin lifted her face for a kiss, and her expression darkened. 'You've been drinking.'

'Had to take a client out. Rosalind, you are a goddess, thank you for coming over.' He stepped back to the cabinet above the refrigerator and brought down a huge blue bottle of Bombay gin. 'Let's all have a drink. Rosalind? Cait? How 'bout it?'

Rosalind waited for Caitlin's reaction, desperate not to ruin their fragile truce. She was not going to say yes and end up drinking with Emil while Caitlin sat temperately alone.

'I'll have a small one.' Caitlin wagged her pen at him. '*Small.*'

'One small.' He brought down two tumblers and waited, hand on a third. 'Rosalind?'

She couldn't handle straight gin. 'Maybe with tonic?'

'Absolutely.' He plonked ice into their glasses. 'So, Rosalind, seamstress, hairdresser, location picker, and all-around amazing woman . . . how's the dress coming?'

Caitlin stiffened, already aggressively vertical in her chair.

'It's coming along fine.' Rosalind touched Caitlin's arm. 'I should have it finished in plenty of time for you to find a replacement if you don't like what I've done.'

'She'll like it.' Emil poured generously from the gin bottle. 'I'm feelin' it in my bones.'

'Teta has her heart set on the dress, so she should wear it.' Caitlin didn't even glance at Emil, probably a good thing because the second serving of gin was anything but the small amount she'd asked for. 'If you promise it won't be embarrassing, that's good enough for me.'

Rosalind put her hand to her heart. 'I promise.'

'Okay.' Caitlin's features relaxed. 'It will make her so happy. Thank you.'

'Once more we are in your debt, Ms Braddock.' Emil winked, reaching for the refrigerator handle, missed, and had to try again. 'We'll find some way to repay you. What would you like? Money? Jewels? Tickets to the latest show on Broad— What *is* the latest show? I don' even know.'

'You don't owe me a thing.'

'That's good.' Emil tossed a lemon, a lime, and a bottle of tonic on to the counter, righting the bottle when it fell over, and started searching in another drawer. 'Where's that thing? The one that makes the li'l—'

'In the back behind the spoons,' Caitlin said.

'Spoken like a true wife, right? I didn't even have to finish my own sentence. It's a freakin' miracle.' He slammed the drawer shut and yanked the blade of a small tool over the peel of the lemons, forming curling strips that he plopped into his and Caitlin's gin. Then he squeezed a wedge of lime rather violently in the third glass, added tonic, and handed out the drinks. 'So, Rosalind, whatcha been up to when you're not stitching or writing invites?'

'That *you* were supposed to be doing,' Caitlin snapped.

'That *I* was supposed to be doing.' He gestured toward the pile with his glass and sloshed gin on to the top invitation. At Caitlin's horrified gasp, he picked it up, keeping it level to avoid further spillage, and carried it over to the trash. 'No harm done. We have plenty extra.'

'Just be *careful.*'

'Yah.' He leaned against the island and looked expectantly at Rosalind. 'So?'

'Besides sewing? I've been . . . reading. Exploring a little. And—'

'Hanging out with Bry-y-yn.' Caitlin's sing-song held a note of triumph. 'Nudge nudge wink wink . . .'

'Really?' Emil's face turned impassive. He took a swig of gin, ice cubes tinkling against the glass, swallowed wetly. 'The guy has the heart of a Romeo, huh?'

Rosalind kept writing, pretending she hadn't heard. Instinct and Emil's sharp, tense movements told her he was not a drunk to mess with.

'What are you talking about? Romeo?'

'You should know all about that, Cait-bait.' Barely suppressed anger bled through Emil's gentle tone.

Caitlin jerked, then held herself rigid again. 'What's *that* supposed to mean?'

'He's been in love with you forever.'

'Well *apparently* not anymore.'

Rosalind cast her eyes down at her drink, held tightly in her hands, wishing she could turn herself into a tonic bubble and disappear into the air.

'I'm happy for you, Rosalind. Happy for you both.' Emil lifted his glass. 'Long live romance!'

The kitchen door opened to admit Leila and Zaina just when Rosalind was thinking she'd have to jump in to avoid a fistfight. 'Caitlin, darling, sorry, sorry, I am so sorry.'

'Whatever, Mom.'

'Rosalind, thank you so much for coming over.' Leila had her arm around Zaina, who was smiling determinedly but looked exhausted. 'I'm going to get Mama to bed.'

'For heaven's sakes, Leila.' Zaina rolled her eyes. 'I can go to bed by myself. It's not like I'm an old, sick woman.'

Emil was the only one who laughed.

'Mama, you need rest.' Leila looked miserably guilty. 'I kept you out much too long.'

'It was a lovely day.' Zaina patted her daughter's hand. 'Seeing the old stores again, Sahadi's, being in that neighborhood. It was like a youth tonic.'

'I'm so glad you got to go.' Caitlin got up and hugged her grandmother. 'Rosalind was just telling us that your dress is going to be beautiful.'

'Oh?' Zaina beamed at Rosalind, losing years off her face. 'That is wonderful.'

'Looks like you're making progress.' Leila gestured at the envelopes.

'No thanks to you.' Caitlin returned to her seat.

'I'll help now, and if we don't get to them all tonight, I'll get up early and finish.' Leila looked as weary as her mother. 'We'll get this done, Cait. I know it's not happening exactly when you wanted, but they'll go out tomorrow.'

'That's not—' Caitlin closed her eyes briefly. 'Okay. Yes.

You're right. I'm sorry. Teta's day was more important.'

'Come on, Mama, let's get you to bed.'

'I *am* tired. Goodnight, everyone.' Zaina shuffled out of the room to a chorus of goodnights, leaning heavily on her daughter's arm.

A few beats of silence remained in the kitchen, silence even Emil was sensible enough not to break.

'We . . . we have to go.' Caitlin cleared her throat, took one more sip of her drink, and got down from her chair. 'We're meeting Joe and Deborah at Blue Point Grill, and I still have to dress.'

'I'll make sure the invitations are finished,' Rosalind said.

'Thanks, Rosalind.' Caitlin gave her shoulder a brief pat. 'Come on, Emil.'

'I haven't finished my drink.'

'I think it's better that you don't.' She folded her arms and stared him down until he pushed away from the counter, glancing over at Rosalind.

'You're the boss.' He went to the sink, held his glass as if he was about to dump it, then casually brought it up to his mouth and drained it.

Rosalind caught herself just before she gasped.

'There we are.' Emil put the glass in the sink. 'Finished my drink and ready to go.'

'Aw, thanks, *sweetheart*.' Caitlin grabbed her coat from the hook by the door. 'I'm *really* looking forward to spending another evening with you shit-faced.'

She stomped out of the house.

Slam.

Emil met Rosalind's eyes and raised his eyebrows. 'I'm gonna get my ass kicked. You wanna go to dinner with her instead of me?'

'Huh.' She tried to look regretful. 'Not so much.'

'All-righty, then. Goodnight, beautiful.' He swaggered out, whistling the Bridal March, leaving a dense silence behind him.

Rosalind picked up her pen. Put it down again. She wanted to sneak out the back, go home and let the poison of Caitlin and Emil's exchange leach out of her before she had to talk to Leila.

Alcohol had killed Emil's father. The same disease looked to be taking hold in the son, following the common, always tragic pattern. Rosalind and her sisters had been on the lookout since they took their first drinks, needlessly as it happened. She was sad for Emil. Sad for Caitlin. And if he didn't get it under control, she was sad in advance for their children.

Footsteps made her grab up her pen again.

Leila appeared in the kitchen, grim smile in place. 'God, what a day. What are you drinking? Where is everyone?'

'Gin and tonic. Emil and Caitlin had a dinner date.'

'What? They left *you* with all that?' She gestured to the pile of envelopes, clearly appalled. 'I need to talk to that girl.'

'No, no, she's fine.' God forbid Leila made it sound as if Rosalind had complained. 'She has plenty to cope with.'

'True. Emil was late, I was late.' She pulled a bottle of white wine from the refrigerator, unscrewed the top and poured herself a glass. 'She's feeling overwhelmed. What bride isn't? Cheers.'

'Cheers.' Rosalind took a big gulp for bravery, panic already tugging at her.

'I should have known better than to stay so long in Brooklyn today. But it was Mama's last trip, and she was having so much fun. Of course the neighborhood's changed from when we used to go. Sahadi's has to cater to a different crowd now. Still fabulous, though. We got a late start, then had late lunch, and well, you know. New York traffic.' She hoisted her drink, took a sip and exhaled in pleasure. 'That's better. So I hear you and Bryn are an item.'

A startled laugh burst out of Rosalind. 'That got around quickly.'

'It's big news. For our family anyway.' Leila kicked off her shoes and sat in the chair next to Rosalind, making her want to edge hers away, needing defendable airspace. 'Watch out, or we'll be taking wedding bets on the two of you.'

'Ha!' Rosalind caught her drink just before she dropped it. 'Not going to happen.'

'No, of course not, I knew that much. He'll disappoint you at some point, or bore you. They all do. The curse of women like us. No man can ever live up to the fantasy of what we want him to be.'

Rosalind forced a chuckle, surprised by a dark burn of protest in her chest.

'But it will be good fun while it lasts. He's a great guy. Just stay easy with him, don't let him fall too hard. I'd hate to see his heart get smashed, poor guy.'

Rosalind picked up another envelope, needing time to regroup, recharge, re . . . something. The angry heat in her chest had grown with Leila's words, fighting now with the closing-in-walls feeling of what she needed to do.

'Oh, leave that, leave that.' Leila made shooing motions at the piles. 'I'll do it in the morning. Really, everyone we're inviting knows about the wedding already. It's not that big a deal.'

To Caitlin it obviously was.

Rosalind put the pen down.

'So the dress cleaned up well?' Leila kicked the next chair farther away and rested her feet on it. 'You're happy with how it's going to come out?'

'Leila.' Rosalind gripped the edge of the island. 'Did you have an affair with my father?'

Leila spluttered into her wine, taking her feet down from the chair and turning to face Rosalind. 'Good God, at least give me a segue, huh? A nice intro? A little warning?'

'Sorry.' She bent her head. 'It wasn't an easy question.'

'Of course not. There is, however, you will be happy to know, a very easy answer.' When Rosalind's head jerked up, Leila smiled radiantly and relaxed again in her chair, gaze clear and direct. 'No, honey. I absolutely did not.'

Rosalind took a deep breath, gripping the table harder. 'Then why is he paying you?'

Leila's smile shut down. No more warmth, but neither was there anger or fear. There was simply nothing. 'I have no idea what you're talking about.'

'I saw the record of the payments.'

'No.'

'I deserve to know what's going on.'

'Why?'

'Because I'm his daughter. And because I'm also—'

'*No.*' Leila slammed her hand down on the counter. 'This topic is off limits. My mother is dying, my daughter is marrying an asshole, and I do not need this right now, Rosalind. Okay?'

Under Leila's hostile stare, Rosalind could feel her anger and strength deserting her. 'I need to know.'

'No, you need to leave.'

'Leila . . .'

'Now.' She pointed to the door so hard her elbow joint popped. 'I will not answer another question. Not a single one. Go. I'll see you at Zaina's party on Tuesday.'

Rosalind got down from the chair and headed for the door, stumbling into the jamb as she went through, exactly as Emil had, only her clumsiness was fueled by anger and grief, not alcohol.

Outside, the clean, bitter wind was welcome on her heated face. She'd made a mess tonight. Another one.

She dialed Bryn with shaking fingers. He picked up on the first ring. 'Hey there.'

'Listen, I'm . . . Would you mind if I came over?'

'Mind? Are you serious?'

Her panic started dissolving at the sound of his voice. 'You're not busy?'

'I'm watching season three of *Mad Men*, which means I am definitely not busy. You sound a little off. Something happen?'

'The conversation with Leila . . .' Rosalind swallowed convulsively. 'Did not go well.'

'Oh Rosalind.' His voice dropped into sympathy. 'You need me to come out there?'

'No, no, I'll come to you. Thank you, Bryn.' She ended the call and practically ran toward the garage and her car, thinking about the light and warmth in Bryn's little house, the quirky art on the walls that had been gifts from his talented friends, the good smells of coffee brewing, the warmth of the man, who hadn't hesitated to offer himself up at the slightest hint that she needed him.

Solid. Lasting. Her opposite.

She got into her car and drove, haunted by Caitlin's expression of grief over not being able to count on her hummingbird mother. With a sudden intensity that alternately thrilled and terrified her, Rosalind wanted to be worthy of Bryn's feelings for her.

And she wanted to be worthy of her feelings for him.

Chapter 15

June 3, 1968 (Monday)

Today I went to the Stella Adler school. Bad news. My first bad news here. It's expensive. Too expensive unless I get a scholarship, and even then I will have to do endless turn-on-the-charm waitressing to get lots of tips. I might have to get a loan or a second job. Not only that, but it's too late to audition for the main program for the fall. I nearly cried when they told me. I guess I am a little hick from Maine because it never occurred to me I wouldn't be able to start right away. This is very discouraging, but I'm trying to look at it that at least I'll have time to save more money. That won't be easy either. I just paid rent for June, and there isn't much left until I get paid again. I'll have to be really careful.

The only good news is that they offer single classes at Stella Adler, and those are ongoing, so I signed up to audition for one. It's better than nothing, and if I keep taking them, I'll be a familiar fixture when I apply for the main program, and will have learned enough to make me a stronger candidate.

My audition is Thursday. Very excited. I'm doing Katherine's monologue from The Taming of the Shrew, *which I've been practicing so much the girl next door knocked and told me to cut it out.*

* * *

Rosalind lifted her head from Bryn's chest, keeping her wet face ducked. 'Don't look at me. I think I might have cried a little.'

'No, no.' He squeezed her tightly, then loosened his sanctuary arms. 'Well, maybe. But only for fifteen, twenty minutes.'

She let out a slightly insane giggle, feeling both heavy and hollow. The emotional storm had been intense, but brief. 'C'mon. Thirty seconds tops.'

'Let me see.' He tipped up her chin and examined her thoughtfully. 'You're right about one thing.'

'What's that?'

'You look like hell.'

'No, no.' She wiped at her cheeks. 'You're supposed to say I look beautiful no matter what.'

'Oh, *right*. Right.' He ran his hands up and down her arms, communicating affection and support even while teasing her back from her meltdown. 'Sorry.'

'I forgive you.' Rosalind let out a cleansing sigh, feeling calmer and stronger. Bless Bryn for taking her outburst in stride, as loving and calm as if she'd come in chattering about the weather instead of raining all over his shirt. Tears had blindsided her the second he opened the door. 'I could use about a case of tissues. Got any?'

'I do.' He took her hand and led her back toward his warm, fragrant kitchen.

Rosalind accepted the tissue box he offered and set to work mopping up her emotional mess, knowing that when she was ready to talk about what had set her off, he'd be ready to listen. The Allertons had been fuel, but what set off the explosion had been her first glimpse of Bryn when he opened the door, forehead wrinkled in concern, arms open wide to welcome her, as if she were someone he'd known and adored his entire life.

Rosalind finished blowing her nose and sniffed the air. 'Something smells fabulous.'

'Chicken with chickpeas, tomatoes, ginger and spices. From one of Madhur Jaffrey's Indian cookbooks. Are you hungry?'

She suddenly was. 'That sounds so good.'

'No problem. I'll heat it up for you.' He opened his refrigerator and took out a covered glass container. 'Beer?'

'I don't think so. A glass of water, though. I'll get it, just tell me where you keep glasses?' She swept her finger side to side, indicating his row of cabinets.

'There.' He pointed to the middle one. 'Fresh green chutney, mango chutney or both?'

'Mmm, both, please. Thank you, Bryn. For dinner, and for that.' She gestured back toward the foyer. 'I'm pretty sure you weren't sitting around tonight hoping someone would show up and snot all over you.'

'Actually, I was.' He put the chicken into the microwave and pushed buttons. 'It's why I wore my lucky snot-proof sweater.'

It took Rosalind nearly half a minute to stop laughing, about as long as she'd been crying, two sides of the same release. 'Thanks for that image.'

'Seriously, I'm glad I was here when you needed . . . someone.'

'You.' She wasn't going to let him think otherwise. 'I needed you. Either you or a vacation in Paradise, but you're cheaper.'

'And legal.' Bryn threw her a warm smile that made her insides squirm happily, like worms in dirt, only more romantic. 'So the talk with Leila went badly?'

'Not disastrously. It was . . . complicated. Is your garbage under the sink?'

When he nodded, Rosalind threw away her tissues, rubbed sanitizer on her hands and reached for a glass from the cabinet he'd indicated. She loved his kitchen. It was small and comfortingly old-fashioned, with scuffed black and white checkerboard flooring, white appliances, scarred butcher-block countertops and cabinets painted lima-bean green. In the center of the room, a Formica table in a slightly darker green shade, on which Bryn arranged a place setting while Rosalind got her drink.

'In short, Leila said she didn't have an affair with my dad.' Putting her glass on the table, she pulled out a lima-bean chair with chrome legs and sat. 'Caitlin said her dad isn't my dad and Emil drank too much. That's about it.'

'I knew about Emil.' Bryn's face darkened. 'He's not happy.'

'About . . . ?'

'Anything.' He set a bowl of green sauce and a jar of mango chutney on the table in easy reach of her plate. 'You think Leila and Caitlin were both straight with you?'

'How would I know?' She leaned over to inspect the chutney. 'Did you make this?'

'It's not hard. You chop cilantro and a chili in the food processor, then mix in yoghurt, cumin and salt.' He took the steaming chicken dish out of the microwave and set it in front of her. 'I like good food, so I learned to follow recipes.'

Rosalind inhaled rapturously. 'Even through my red and swollen nose I can tell this is going to be good.'

'Bread?' He held up a naan. 'Store-bought.'

'I'd love some, thank you.' She spooned green chutney on to her plate, cut a piece off a chicken thigh, loaded her fork with that and a few chickpeas, then swiped the bite through the sauce. The rich, spicy flavor made her groan with pleasure. 'Oh, that is delicious.'

'Good.' He opened himself a Founder's All-Day IPA and sat across from her. 'Do you cook?'

'I'm like you. I follow recipes.' She ate another bite, incredibly grateful that he wasn't pressing her about the scene on Laurel Road, trusting that she'd talk more when she was ready. 'When I was a kid, I used to beg to make dinner for my family. I'd serve elegantly balanced meals, like pigs in blankets with rolls and potato salad.'

'Oof.' He snitched a chickpea from her plate. 'I have indigestion just hearing that.'

'No kidding. I'd think I had the work planned out, but everything always took twice as long as I expected. We'd end up eating hours late.' She tore off some naan and soaked it in the sauce from the chicken. 'The amazing thing was that neither of my parents ever complained. Even Dad. They thought it was great.'

'Good memories.'

'Yes.' She frowned at her plate. 'I haven't been thinking so much about the good times lately, with Dad anyway.'

'When you have a difficult parent, those moments are harder to remember than the bad stuff.' He dragged his chair closer, and pressed his thigh against hers. 'Which gives us a pretty skewed version of our history, doesn't it.'

'Yes.' She added mango chutney to her plate, not liking that idea at all. 'So our kids will only remember the awful things we did to them and not the good?'

He put on a comic look of panic. 'We're having kids?'

Rosalind rolled her eyes, annoyed to find herself blushing. *Second* time she'd mentioned having kids around Bryn. Freud would have something to say about that. 'When did you learn to cook? When you moved out after Jake . . . died?'

'Before that. I cooked as a teenager, too.' He poked himself in the chest. '*My* most famous meal was leftover chicken breast chopped into a white sauce, poured over Pillsbury crescent rolls. I served that with boiled cauliflower. My dad called it "White on White" after the painting by Kazimir Malevich.'

'White on white, fat on fat, we had the same mono-menu philosophy.' Rosalind gestured to the drumstick, feeling nearly normal, though still slightly hollow from her cry. 'Fingers allowed?'

'Encouraged.'

'Thank you.' She picked it up and took a bite. 'Did your mom cook?'

'Yeah, but she worked crazy hours, so I'd step in sometimes. She made good food, but not imaginative. A throwback to what she ate growing up. Meat, starch and vegetable at every meal. Lasagna was big excitement in our house.'

'*We* had a cook.' Rosalind rolled her eyes and had another bite.

'Was she awful?'

She looked up in surprise. 'No, she was great.'

'Then what?' He mimicked her eye-rolling. '"*We* had a cook."'

'Oh.' Rosalind shrugged, so used to apologizing for her privilege that she did it without thinking. 'It's just so . . . rich people.'

'And?'

'And we were such *rich people*.' She brightened at new memories. 'Mom cooked when we were in Maine. She had a good knack. Her turkey meatloaf was killer. Her clambakes were the highlight of our year.'

'Nice.' Bryn smiled crookedly, then held her gaze, his blue eyes so open that she became fidgety, finished her chicken bone and got up to wash her hands.

'I'll have to try again with Leila. Ask her directly if she's my birth mother.' She hung the kitchen towel back on the oven handle, shivering involuntarily. 'Which will probably be even more fabulous fun than it was today.'

'Yeah, I envy you.' He stood and gathered her against him. 'Maybe she'll say yes and be done with it.'

'That would be so nice.' She sighed blissfully. 'Because then everything in my life will become – and stay – perfect forever.'

'Uh . . . yeah.' Bryn locked his arms around her. 'Whatever happens, you'll manage.'

Rosalind leaned against him, eyes closed, and tried just to be, without the weight of the day pressing in on her.

It didn't work. There was too much. Too much to be fixed, even by standing blissfully with Bryn in his fabulous kitchen.

'Bryn?'

'Yes, Rosalind?'

'What do I do if Leila keeps denying that she's my mother? What do I do if she turns out not to be? Because if either one of those happens . . .' Her throat cramped again; she felt she was stepping out into a bottomless black void. 'It's like I won't really belong to a family. I mean, I know my adopted family is my family and will always be my family, but I guess I wanted . . . I don't know what I wanted.'

'Ah, Rosalind.' His kiss was so sweet and gentle it started a dangerous melty feeling throughout her body. 'You wanted that perfect family with no trouble and no tragedy.'

'Oh God.' Rosalind dropped her head so that it thudded on to his chest. 'The Hearts.'

'The whos?'

She lifted her head and reached into her pocket for her phone, opened Safari and typed *Heart Family dolls*, then pressed *Images*. The pictures came up. She handed the phone to Bryn. 'Go ahead. Laugh. You know you want to.'

He had the decency to force himself sober before he handed the phone back. 'Thank you for sharing. That was terrifying, but instructive.'

Rosalind sighed, feeling bruised. 'Embarrassing.'

'Understandable.' He moved close again and stroked her hair back from her face. 'Let me tell you something that will sound like the cheesiest line ever.'

'I like cheese.'

'No matter what Leila says, you will not stop belonging. You will start belonging, in new places and in new ways. With your old family, redefined as it may be. With your new family, flawed as it will be. Someday with a new family you'll create yourself.' He looked suddenly queasy. 'No, not yourself. That would be weird. With a guy. A great guy. A fantastic guy. A guy who by definition will not be as great or as fantastic as me unless he *is* me, and then you will deserve him absolutely.'

She managed a smile, as grateful for his comedic kick to her self-pity as for his profound words. 'You're right. I was being melodramatic. Ignore me.'

'It bothers you some or you wouldn't have said it.'

'Oh yeah?' She lifted her eyebrows, poking him gently. 'And the part about me starting a family with you?'

He looked adorably sheepish. 'You got me.'

'Well then. We're even.' Rosalind put a hand to his chest, tip of her longest finger just below the hollow at the base of his throat. 'Thank you for listening to my whining, for being a lovely solid person and for helping me through this craziness.'

'You are welcome.' He rested his forehead against hers. 'It's pretty intense stuff.'

'True.' Rosalind looked up, pitching her voice to a low whisper. 'You know, Bryn? When I look at you like this, up super close?'

'Yes?'

She slid her arms around his waist. 'Your eyes . . . they merge. You look like an extremely handsome Cyclops.'

'Mmm, so do you.' He swayed them back and forth. 'It's kind of a turn-on.'

'It makes me want things.'

'What . . . kind of things?' He sounded as if he were being strangled.

'It makes me want . . .' she kissed him lingeringly, then drew back until he became two-eyed again, 'to do the dishes.'

'Oh, for—'

Giggling, she moved briskly toward the sink before he could grab her. If anyone had told her after she left the Allertons that in a little over an hour she'd be laughing, flirting and feeling euphoric and rather amorous, she would have told him to stop smoking the funny stuff.

She was crazy about Bryn.

While he put away the food, Rosalind did the dishes, enjoying the comfortable silence between them. When the kitchen was neat, she hovered, wiping the sink unnecessarily, not sure whether she should offer to leave or offer to stay.

'What do you say we go into the living room and talk about nothing for a while?'

'Huh.' Rosalind dropped the sponge and dried her hands. 'Is that guy-talk for "Let's go make out"?'

'Absolutely.'

He held out his hand and she followed him, sat next to him on the too-firm brownish-green sofa and rested her head on his shoulder, both of them adjusting a few times until they got the positions exactly right. Within about twenty seconds, Rosalind had decided Bryn's body must emit a potent happy-relaxation drug, because she was no longer even considering leaving.

Dangerous, since she was still vulnerable from the evening's turmoil. Dangerous, since spending the night with Bryn wouldn't only be about sex, which had never frightened her before. She'd jumped happily into Wolf's den, eagerly battled Troy's spear, and dutifully doffed clothes with Don.

This would be different. Significant. A stab at a new level of commitment from a hummingbird who'd spent her life avoiding it.

She turned to kiss the skin at the open V of Bryn's shirt, spreading her hand across his chest. As she looked into his eyes, she felt not only the pull of attraction and desire, but the emotional equivalent of a swelling string melody from the climax of one of her mother's movie love scenes. 'Bryn?'

He covered her hand with his, bending to kiss her fingers. 'Yes, Rosalind?'

'May I spend the night?'

He looked up sharply. 'In . . . what capacity? Woman who needs nice guy to help her through a difficult time?'

Rosalind swallowed, closing her eyes for courage. 'No. Woman who found a great guy and is willing to try, even though she's petrified.'

His chest rumbled with laughter that held a dry edge. 'Why do you think I'm the funniest person you've ever met?'

She opened her eyes, caught off guard by his response. 'Because you're the funniest person I've ever met?'

'Because I'm petrified, too, Rosalind. Being oh-so-clever and adorably quippy around you is a matter of survival. Otherwise I would follow you on my knees until I died of dehydration or got run over.'

She made a teasing face. 'That would freak me out.'

'And spending the night won't?'

This time Rosalind didn't allow her gaze to waver. 'I'm thinking no.'

Bryn bowed his head for a beat, then moved her aside, stood and held out his hand. 'Okay, then.'

He led her into his bedroom, which looked exactly as a Bryn bedroom should – queen bed with a navy spread, a scuffed three-drawer oak dresser, bookshelf bursting with books, art on the walls, and a sculpture of a bird on a table by one of the windows. A few shirts were draped on a chair, and a pair of running shoes had been tossed carelessly over by the closet. Rosalind felt as at home there as she felt in his kitchen. As she did, increasingly, with Bryn.

Slowly, they took time to get to know each other's bodies. For once, Rosalind didn't feel shame or fear of judgment exposing her physical imperfections – the slight softness around her belly, the dimpled skin on her ass that no amount of jogging would eliminate. With Bryn it was easy to laugh at the clumsy moments – kisses that missed their mark, that extra arm always in the way, embarrassing stomach noises at the worst possible moments.

Afterward, they lay together, Bryn drowsy and replete, Rosalind awake and full of thoughts. Despite, or maybe because of, its imperfections – movies and romance novels aside, first-time lovemaking was never a couple's best – it had been the most satisfying sex of her life.

She'd once been puzzled by a friend who'd blissfully described her lover as perfect because he was 'always there'. Until tonight, Rosalind hadn't known what she meant.

Always there? Where else would he be?

Now she understood, and looked pityingly back through time on herself and her previous partners. None of them had understood what they were missing. How could they? What else, what other experience, could be so much richer than what she already knew?

Maybe that was what life was about. Not just having or not having kids or careers, attaining or not attaining the trappings of success, but finding and wallowing in transcendent moments, the 'jump off a building' experiences Leila had described, however long or brief they might be. Continually raising the bar on experiences you already had, as well as launching yourself toward new horizons.

'Bryn?'

'Mmm?'

'Do you think maybe you'd want to come into the city and look at my paintings sometime?'

'Uh-huh.'

'I'd love to know what you thought. Whether I should enroll somewhere, study with someone, or . . . I don't know, maybe you could tell me how I could improve, or . . .' She was babbling. 'Something.'

'Sure.'

'Thanks.' She settled, stroking the arm that lay across her chest, staring up into the near-total darkness. 'Maybe I could paint you.'

'Uh-huh.'

'Are you still planning to sculpt me?'

'Yup.'

'You're trying to sleep, aren't you?'

Bryn made a loud snoring noise, smiling faintly.

Rosalind giggled, feeling deeply content in spite of all the turmoil yet to be resolved. 'I'll shut up.'

''Kay.'

She lay quietly, absorbing the warmth of his body, envious of his solid, centered presence. How had this wild child learned to be this way? Through therapy? Through wisdom? Through self-control? Merely through distance from the traumas he'd experienced?

Maybe she could learn, too. Maybe once she had this whole

family thing settled, the rest of her life would settle with it.

Or was that another Heart-like fantasy? She didn't think so. Imagining being with Bryn, far into her future, didn't make her feel panicky. Maybe she was already changing. Maybe he was simply The One.

She hadn't thought she believed in The One. Not like her mother had.

Bryn's breathing slowed; the arm around her twitched. Rosalind smiled, chest expanding with so much feeling it didn't seem able to contain it all.

There was something infinitely beautiful about a lover falling asleep next to you. It spoke of trust and a deep willingness to be vulnerable.

His eyelashes flickered on his cheek.

Rosalind held still in the darkness, listening to him breathe, waiting to whisper his name until she was absolutely sure he was asleep.

Chapter 16

June 6, 1968 (Thursday)

I didn't get in. Not the traditional way. There was a very handsome man at the audition, Daniel Braddock, who said he'd never heard Shakespeare recited quite like that. The way he said it, I knew it was bad. I nearly fell apart. I have never failed at anything but being a woman and making my mother love me. Of course I didn't show how upset I was, one of the greatest acting moments of my life so far. I told him that was the way Shakespeare actually wanted the speech done, and I knew that because he was my great-great-great-great-etc. grandfather and he appeared to me every night and was my coach. And that if Mr Braddock wanted it done any differently, he'd have to tell me how by himself and I'd do it. I said it very politely, winking during the part about Shakespeare showing up so he wouldn't think I was just some crazy off the street.

He laughed and said fine, he'd try. He coached me through a few lines, not by telling me how to do it, like Mr McGregor did back in high school, but by telling me about Katherine, and what she was feeling, and who she was, and the journey she went on during the play. Then I understood, and I did the lines as a woman who is saying she now accepts that men rule her, but knows very well that she's still in charge, because she has eyes and lips and breasts and dark unknown places that plague a man's thoughts night and day.

I say this even knowing I'm only half that type of woman.

He told me to come back at five o'clock, so of course I did. We sat down to talk, and he said he'd seen something in me that was rich and important.

Of course what I was thinking was, Yes, I know that, but I couldn't say so without sounding conceited. Because it's a fact I've always known about me, who knows why. Like amazing violinists or writers know they have talent, and are driven to contribute. I find it humbling to be chosen like this, to be given this talent from God. It would seem unfair except that it seems He might have taken something away in return. Maybe that's His lesson: you get nothing for free.

Daniel took me out for dinner after that, oh my goodness, what a dinner! I had to do my best acting ever to keep from being bug-eyed and astounded by everything. Finally, my first taste of champagne. I knew I would love it. And such food! Such prices! I was born to live this way.

Best part: Daniel wants to do private coaching to get me where I should be, having grown up in backwater misery.

I told him that better not mean anything but private coaching. It is a distinct disadvantage only to be able to seduce men with my top half. Meeting him made me vow to get to a doctor as soon as I can afford it, to see what can be done to make me into a normal, menstruating female. They must know how to do it here.

He said yes, of course private coaching, actor to student, lines of propriety firmly drawn.

In my best upper-crust accent, I said that would be delightful.

'Birthday dinner is ready!' Leila's announcement from the kitchen brought the living-room party to its feet. Caitlin, Emil,

Bryn and Rosalind had been drinking arak and staving off hunger with pistachios, olives and vegetables sprinkled with olive oil and za'atar. In spite of the fact that it was her birthday, and that everyone worried about her tiring, Zaina had apparently insisted on making the meal herself. Leila had given in only when her mother promised to make most dishes in advance, freezing whenever possible, and to take a long nap before her guests showed up.

This Rosalind had heard from Caitlin shortly after she and Bryn arrived. Zaina had greeted them looking rested and moving easily, wearing a flattering blue wool dress just bright enough that Rosalind – in a moment of enormous relief – knew she'd been right to trust her instinct about the color silk she'd chosen.

After sharing a small glass of arak with the guests, Zaina and Leila had disappeared into the kitchen, refusing all offers of help.

Now the group wandered into the dining room, where the table had been covered with a cream cloth exotically embroidered in gold thread, a good deal of its beauty hidden under an impressive array of heaping platters. Candles flickered from crystal holders and a centerpiece of yellow and white roses completed the stunning picture.

Rosalind joined in the admiring comments, warmed by arak and the jovial atmosphere, enjoying herself thoroughly. All traces of tension and resentment among the Allertons seemed to have been worked through and discarded. The family members laughed and joked affectionately, as they had the very first night Rosalind ate with them. She could hardly wait to be an openly legitimized part of the tribe.

Zaina sat at the head of the table and gestured Bryn and Rosalind to the two chairs on one side, Emil and Caitlin to the two on the other, Leila at the foot. When all were seated, she bowed her white head and offered thanks for the meal, then they dug in, passing dishes and complimenting the chefs with words, moans of pleasure and second and third helpings.

Lemony hummus; smoky baba ghanouj; tabouli; kibbe – a mixture of ground lamb and cracked wheat flavored with onions and touches of cinnamon and allspice; a dish of grilled eggplant strips glistening with yoghurt and garlic; spicy lamb sausages drenched in sour-sweet pomegranate syrup; more of the delicious creamy labneh Rosalind had met her first night in the Allertons' house, here drizzled with fragrant fruity Lebanese olive oil; baskets of warm pita, thinner and chewier than the breads she could buy in her supermarket in New York, and totally addictive. With the feast, they drank glasses of rich, spicy Lebanese red wine from Chateau Ksara, which Zaina told them was founded in the mid nineteenth century, one of the country's oldest and finest wineries.

For dessert, a large tray of fresh fruit – pomegranates, persimmons, grapes, pears and mandarin oranges; a plate of dried fruit – apricots, peaches, and dates; and another silver platter of home-made pistachio baklava and ma'amoul cookies, date- and walnut-filled, still slightly chilled from the freezer, Zaina apologizing for having left them too late.

The conversation flowed effortlessly, bubbly like the Veuve Clicquot champagne Leila brought out to drink with dessert. The perfect meal, the perfect tribute to the sweet matriarch heading the table.

'Now, Mama.' Leila poured the champagne into six flutes and passed one to Zaina, then pulled an extra chair from against the wall so she could sit next to her mother. 'A speech. But remember, you promised not to make us cry.'

'No, no, no crying allowed, this is a joyous occasion.' Zaina lifted her glass, wrinkled cheeks pink from the wine, vivid dark eyes sparkling. Rosalind swallowed a lump in her throat, trying to hang on to her smile. She felt such deep affection for this woman who had so unconditionally welcomed her into this house from the very first. 'All I want to do is thank all of you for this lovely celebration . . .'

'Mama, you did most of it!'

'. . . which I, in my *infinite* wisdom, made possible.' Zaina beamed at her laughing family. 'This is the happiest birthday I've ever had. Including the one I thought could never be beat.'

'When was that, Teta?' Caitlin asked the eager question for all of them.

'Until tonight, my favorite birthday was back in . . . oh dear. Nineteen sixty-whatever. Early in the decade, though, because I hadn't been here long. Cecil and I had celebrated my first birthday here alone at home. In Lebanon, no one is alone on a birthday, ever. You are surrounded by family, generations deep. I was miserable. I tried so hard for Cecil, but I missed everyone so much. The next year . . .' She frowned in concentration. 'This old brain is so hard to pin down these days. The next year must have been 1962? Maybe 1963. Cecil was going to take me to Lahiere's, the best restaurant in Princeton, a big splurge for us. I was so excited. I put on my best dress, my wedding dress, the one you have, Rosalind, and my mother's pearls, which she'd given me when I left the country. I'll wear those to your wedding, too, Caitlin.'

Caitlin blew her grandmother a kiss. 'Go on, Teta.'

'Cecil wore a dark suit – oh, he looked so handsome.' Zaina clasped her hands to her chest, smiling fondly. 'We got in the car, it was some kind of Buick, I think, second hand. He started driving – back then we lived farther north, toward Kingston, by the canal. At one point he took a wrong turn. He said it was a shortcut. I knew the way to town – how hard is it when the place only has one street? – but you see Cecil had an impeccable sense of direction, and I was hopeless. Plus it was my birthday, and I was in a fine mood, so I only complained a little.

'Admirable restraint.' Leila toasted her mother. 'Dad could be such a know-it-all.'

'Yes, he certainly could be, in his own charming way. But this time . . .' Zaina lifted her brows, looking mischievous. 'Ten minutes later, we were late for the reservation, and he was taking one turn after another. I was getting more and more angry with him. No GPS in those days; all you had were gas stations with maps, believe it or not, but we were not in an area with anything like that.

'I can tell you, to my shame, it wasn't long before I was furious. He was ruining my birthday, the first one I had hoped to enjoy in this country.

'Finally we stopped in a strange neighborhood. He said he'd have to ask for directions. I wasn't speaking to him. I could have divorced him right there. A minute later he came back, complaining that the woman at the house could only speak French, and he couldn't understand a thing she was saying.' Zaina narrowed her eyes, letting out a growl of rage that made everyone erupt into laughter. 'I stomped out of the car, swearing at him in Arabic, calling him the biggest fool on the face of the earth. The front door of this house opened and everyone I'd met in Princeton was there to celebrate my birthday, not only expats but Americans too. It was the house of one of Cecil's colleagues. He'd mentioned to the wife that it was my birthday, maybe he told her I was lonely, I don't know, but she planned the whole thing. It was a lovely, lovely party.

'Until tonight, that was my best birthday. Because even though I no longer had Lebanon, and I no longer had my family around me, there was a new family here if I was willing to do the work to adopt it. So.' She lifted her glass, making eye contact with each member of the table in turn. 'Here's to being among family.'

Rosalind raised her glass, blinded by tears she refused to shed. 'Hear, hear.'

'Hear, hear.' Emil drew an obviously distressed Caitlin in for a hug.

'Hear, hear, Mama.' Leila kept her eyes on the table.

Everyone drank.

'And now,' Zaina took charge of the somber silence, 'I want to hear about everyone else's best birthday.'

'What about presents?' Emil asked.

'This first,' Zaina said firmly. 'Then presents. Then I will go to bed a very happy woman. Leila, my darling daughter. You start. Everyone else get ready.'

'All right.' Leila smiled bravely and grasped her mother's hand. 'My favorite is easy to choose. It was the year you and Daddy took me into New York to see Barnum & Bailey's Circus at Madison Square Garden. Three rings going all the time. I had never seen anything so amazing in my life. I took you when you were a girl, remember, Caitlin?'

'Of course.' Caitlin nodded, smiling politely. 'It was great.'

Leila scoffed. 'You kids grow up seeing all those special effects on TV screens and computer screens and phone screens. It makes it harder to appreciate people doing amazing things under their own power, using their own talent. Without any tricks.'

'Oh come on, what about the knife-throwing?' Caitlin asked. 'We did *Carnival* in high school, the circus musical, remember?'

'You had the lead,' Leila announced proudly.

'No, Katie Hostetler had the lead, I had the second lead, but anyway, the guy throwing the knife fakes the big throw, and then super quick hides the knife behind his back. A split second later, a knife pops out of the board the woman is standing in front of. It happens so fast your brain doesn't catch the switch.'

'Okay, okay.' Leila waved her daughter's correction away. 'Some tricks. Anyway, that was my favorite birthday.'

'We had fun too.' Zaina kissed her daughter's hand, then looked around the group. 'Emil. Your turn.'

'Okay.' He glanced across the table at Rosalind. 'My favorite birthday was the year my dad gave me a few hundred bucks cash and told me to blow it all doing anything I wanted in the city.'

Caitlin looked over as if she hadn't seen him before. 'You never told me about that. What did you do?'

'Uh . . . It was my twenty-first birthday, so I know it involved drinking, because I was finally legal. What was the name of that place?' He bent his head, pinching the bridge of his nose. 'Old bar . . . been around forever . . . in a hotel . . .'

'Bemelmans?' Bryn asked. 'At the Car—'

'Bemelmans!' Emil snapped his fingers and pointed at him. 'I went to Bemelmans at the Carlyle Hotel and ordered a martini. Just because I could.'

'I love that!' Caitlin beamed at him. 'So classy.'

'Then I took myself out to dinner and went to a show.'

Caitlin's face fell. 'Alone?'

'I had a blast.' He grinned uneasily and glanced at Rosalind again. Caitlin's eyes followed.

Rosalind kept on a polite smile, wishing Emil would stop doing that. She had no idea what he wanted from her. Sympathy? Approval?

Bryn put a hand on her thigh and squeezed gently. She smiled at him, grateful for and amazed by how much he picked up on her tension, and how he knew what would help defuse it.

'I think it was midweek, near exam time. Not a lot of college kids had that much money to blow on one night.' Emil lifted his half-full glass of champagne and took a conservative sip. Either he'd scared himself the other night, or Caitlin had, because so far he'd been drinking about the same amount as everyone else. 'Now you, Rosalind. What's your favorite? I bet it's wild.'

'Not at all.' She smiled at Zaina to avoid Emil's cocky grin. 'I have an April birthday.'

'What day?' Emil asked.

'The eighth.' She glanced at Leila, who, predictably by now, didn't react beyond a polite smile. 'My favorite was the year I turned twelve. Mom had just wrapped up a movie. Her career was sliding at that point, so it was kind of a crap movie. I think she had to play an older woman who has an affair with a young guy.'

'Who played him?' Caitlin asked.

'I have no idea.' She took in the surprised looks around the table. 'Mom made a lot of movies. My sister Olivia has seen all of them. But it was normal to us, it was her job. Seeing all of them would be like, I don't know . . .'

'Reading all your CEO father's PowerPoint presentations?' Bryn asked.

Rosalind laughed along with the rest of the table, looking around at each person, wanting to hold on to every moment as tightly as she could. 'Exactly like that. So the movie was over and Mom was both happy and relieved. She wanted to celebrate by visiting her parents in Maine, and then spending some time at our house on the coast.'

'She wanted to celebrate the movie being over or your birthday?' Emil asked.

'Movie. But we were at the cottage on my birthday.'

'Beginning of April, weren't you still in school?' Leila asked.

'Ha! Spoken like a mom,' Caitlin said.

'Go on, Rosalind.' Zaina gave her a nod.

'We were supposed to be in school. Mom took us out for a week. Unlike Dad, she wasn't a big fan of education, and if she really wanted something badly enough, he nearly always caved.' Rosalind stole another glance at Leila, who was listening calmly. 'April is usually pretty cold that far north, but that year my birthday fell on a magically warm day, up nearly to seventy. Mom, Dad, my two sisters and I were the only people on the whole peninsula. Mom insisted on having a clambake outside in the afternoon. We dug a pit on the beach, lined it with rocks, lit a fire, the whole deal.'

'Oh, what fun.' Zaina clapped her hands. 'I've heard about New England clambakes, though I've never been to one. I have had lobster in Maine, though. Spectacular.'

'Yes, it is.' Rosalind hesitated, unsure how much more detail to go into, then felt Bryn's hand squeezing again. 'There was something really magical about that day, just us five in this great unspoiled part of the world. To put it mildly, you can't go many places in LA and feel private. Especially when your mom is a superstar.'

'That's a lovely memory.' Leila's smile was brittle. 'I've been to Maine, I can picture it. Bryn, your turn.'

Bryn shifted beside her, draped his arm across the back of her chair. 'Mine happened the year I bummed around Europe instead of starting college. Mom and Dad flew over and surprised me on my birthday in Paris. They took me out to dinner. That's when I found out Mom had stopped drinking, about the best present I could have gotten. We managed to have a pleasant couple of days together after that, too.'

He coughed behind his fist. 'It was the first time I really

understood, as an adult instead of a pissed-off kid, that they loved me, in spite of how I turned out.'

Rosalind sniffled, holding back the sudden danger of tears.

'Oh, I know, Rosalind, me too.' Caitlin patted her heart.

'Ooh, me too.' Emil ground fists into his eyes. Everyone laughed rather dutifully.

'Of course they love you, Bryn, they're your parents. It's what we do.' Leila stood and clapped her hands. 'More champagne? We have plenty.'

'Absolutely.' Emil held up his glass, now nearly empty.

'Sure,' Bryn said.

'When *is* your birthday?' Rosalind asked him. There was so much she wanted to know.

'December nineteenth. Worst time of year to have a birthday. Everyone is so stressed out by Christmas they can't stand having one more thing to organize.'

'I have a friend like that,' Caitlin said. 'She picked a date in July and celebrates then.'

'Yeah, but . . .' Bryn was shaking his head over a grin. 'My birthday's not *in* July.'

A pop sounded from the kitchen.

'A most excellent sound.' Emil drained his glass and got to his feet. 'Time for presents. Caitlin is about to explode over what she got you, Zaina.'

'Yes?' Zaina smiled affectionately at her granddaughter. 'I hope it's *War and Peace*.'

'Ugh.' Caitlin wrinkled her nose. 'Why?'

'Because everyone should read it before they die, and since it's well over a thousand pages, I would have to stay alive for a very long time.'

'Oh, Teta. Wish I'd thought of that.' Caitlin pushed her chair back, sat helplessly for a second, then went to the head of the table to offer an arm to her grandmother. 'Sorry, it's not *War and Peace*.'

'What a disappointment.' Zaina pushed herself up without help, took a step and stumbled, her smile dropping into panic.

Bryn lunged in time to support her. 'You're okay. I've got you.'

'Of course I'm okay.' Her smile was back in place, but she was breathing hard, anxiety still in her eyes. 'Thank you, Bryn. I must have had too much wine. Ooh, but it was so good, wasn't it?'

'It was.' He escorted her carefully toward the living room, Caitlin stepping in to take her other arm, Rosalind and Emil following.

'Coffee, anyone?' Leila appeared with the champagne in an ice bucket. 'Or should we just stick to the bubbles?'

'Bubbles, of course, it's a party!' Caitlin sat next to her grandmother on the couch, face lit with excitement. On the coffee table in front of her were Zaina's presents, including Rosalind's, the dress and shawl carefully folded into a box, wrapped in bright yellow polka-dot paper, the bag containing the pieces of the original gown carefully tucked underneath.

'My goodness.' Zaina put her hands to her mouth. 'Look at all this! Is it all for me?'

'Of course, Teta. Who else would it be for?'

'What do I need with more stuff at this point?'

'Nope.' Caitlin shook her head firmly. 'None of that talk. Not tonight.'

'Yes, you're right.' Zaina lifted a hand to refuse her daughter's offer of a refill. 'No more for me, thank you.'

Leila poured for the rest of the party and sat on the other side of her mother. Bryn, Emil and Rosalind pulled up chairs to be closer to the bounty.

'What first?' Zaina scanned the gifts.

'Whatever you want, Mama.'

'This one.' She picked the polka-dot box. 'From Rosalind.'

Rosalind watched her untie the red ribbon, barely able to breathe. The evening had been so lovely, and she felt so deeply part of this wonderful group of people, she wanted desperately for her contribution to be received as the gift of love she meant it to be.

Zaina lifted the lid. Her face dropped into astonishment.

Rosalind stepped forward, unable to help herself, and lifted the dress from the box so it could be seen in its full glory. She'd finished sewing on the last pearls at nearly midnight, and had carefully ironed the gown so it would look as perfect as possible. It had turned out exactly as she'd hoped, very much the old, and very much the new. She could only hope Zaina felt the same way.

'Rosalind!' Zaina's face crumpled. 'What have you done?'

Rosalind's chest turned to ice.

'How did you manage this? How did you . . . what is this?'

'She made you a whole new dress,' Bryn said proudly. 'From scratch.'

'Except the pearls, which are from the original.' Rosalind stared anxiously, not sure yet of Zaina's reaction. 'The old dress is in a fabric bag underneath. I thought you might want the pieces.'

'Oh . . .' Tears ran down the old woman's face. She put her hands to her cheeks and spoke a few words in Arabic. Rosalind thought she caught Cecil's name. 'This is . . . magical.'

Rosalind allowed herself to exhale. Then she glanced at Leila, and her heart nearly stopped. Her birth mother was looking at her the way a mother was supposed to look at her daughter, mouth curved in a smile, eyes shining with pride and warmth. *Thank you*, she mouthed.

Rosalind managed a nod, putting a stop to the cascade of joyful tears waiting their turn. This evening was not about her.

'Oh my.' Zaina put a hand to her chest. 'I was the one who said no tears, and look at me! I'm ruined. Rosalind, darling. This is the most remarkable gift I could have gotten. Thank you, *habibti*, thank you . . . I have no more words. Thank you.'

She struggled to stand, opened her arms. Rosalind stepped swiftly toward her while Bryn dragged the coffee table aside. Zaina's embrace was soft and surprisingly strong, the perfect grandmotherly hug, smelling deliciously of floral perfume. She clasped Rosalind against her until Rosalind's throat was painfully tight with the effort not to cry.

At last she held her at arm's length and fixed her with an unwavering gaze. 'Thank you, my dear, from the bottom of my heart. You have given me my youth one last time. You have truly blessed this family.'

'You're welcome,' Rosalind managed to whisper.

'I will try it on first thing in the morning.'

'I hope it fits.'

'It will.' Zaina lowered herself back on to the couch; Bryn moved the coffee table back, beaming at Rosalind as if she'd won a trophy. Rosalind felt exactly the same way, until she caught the stony look on Caitlin's face, and her joy plummeted.

Good God. She'd done it again. How could she fix it this time?

'What's next, Mama? You don't want to get too tired.' Leila had caught Caitlin's expression, too.

Zaina turned with obvious reluctance from admiring the dress. 'Yes. All right. How about this one?'

The next present was from Bryn, a small, fairly abstract

sculpture carved from cedar – Lebanon's famous wood – of three women huddled together as if for warmth or support or strength. Rosalind had fallen crazy in love with it the second he'd showed it to her, again astonished how he could capture such clear emotion in so few lines and shapes.

'Oh Bryn. What a lovely piece. So much feeling, and so perfect for this house. I am so proud of you and what you've done.' Zaina fondled the smooth wood. 'Leila, we must put this in a place of honor.'

'Absolutely.' Leila stood and moved an antique-looking clock from the center of the mantelpiece, then replaced it with the sculpture. It looked a bit off. 'Hmm. Maybe not the perfect spot, but we'll find one. Thank you, Bryn, it's gorgeous.'

'You're welcome.' He tipped his gaze up to the ceiling, holding his mouth tight, making Rosalind's heart swell. 'I'm glad you like it.'

'Open mine next, Mama.' Leila sat back down. 'Save Caitlin's. She's been hinting for weeks.'

'Yes, all right.' Zaina tore the pink paper off a large, flat rectangular box. Bryn and Leila pried open the cardboard flap and eased out a painting so Zaina could have first view. 'Oh Leila. How lovely. How perfectly lovely.'

'I had a friend do it.' Leila turned the frame around to the rest of the room, so they could see the familiar wedding photograph made into a painting, Zaina and Cecil standing on a balcony, young and handsome, the twinkling of Beirut spreading behind them.

'It's so, *so* lovely. My darling child.' Zaina held up her arms; Leila bent to embrace her. 'What a perfect, perfect gift. To remember your father and me always. Thank you. All these gifts have been so wonderful, so meaningful. I'm so moved by all of them, and by how much love is in this room.'

'Now mine, Teta.' Caitlin pressed a small wrapped box into her grandmother's hand.

The paper came off to reveal the famous blue of Tiffany's. 'Oh my word. Caitlin, what have you done?'

'It's from Emil and me.'

'I just paid for it.' Emil got up to refill his glass. 'It was Caitlin's idea.'

Bryn and Rosalind exchanged glances. The way he spoke sounded ominous.

Zaina lifted the lid and gasped, looking more bewildered than pleased. 'My gracious. Child, I . . . My gracious.'

She held up a glittering diamond bracelet, a piece that must have cost thousands upon thousands of dollars if not more. There was a stunned silence in the room.

'Wow,' Bryn said.

For Caitlin's sake, Rosalind had to give it her best. 'How *gorgeous*!'

'Caitlin, my God.' Leila's eyes were huge.

Zaina gave a short laugh. 'I've certainly never worn anything like this before.'

Caitlin was looking carefully at her grandmother, a slight frown on her smooth brow. 'Well, now you can.'

'Yes, yes, of course, my goodness. Look at all this . . . but it is too expensive, Caitlin. This is . . . well, it's lovely. I love it. Of course I love it.' Zaina slipped it on to her wrist, where it glittered obscenely. 'It's perfect. Just perfect. My goodness.'

Caitlin looked down at her hands.

'Caitlin, such a lovely gift.' Zaina put her arm around her granddaughter. 'Do you remember when you were little? You wanted a bracelet like this. You had no idea what you were asking for, of course, but you thought you should get one for your birthday. Remember, Leila?'

Leila nodded flatly. 'I do, yes.'

'I will be the best-dressed woman at my granddaughter's wedding. The most beautiful bracelet, and the most beautiful dress. I'll outshine the bride!' She gazed rapturously at the dress Rosalind had made, reaching to caress the silk bodice. 'Cecil will be with me again, at a wedding, a family wedding. Thank you again, Rosalind. And everyone. I'm . . . I'm overcome.'

'No tears! Your rule!' Leila glanced anxiously at her daughter. 'You'll get the rest of us going, too.'

'You're right.' Zaina patted her chest, then smiled and took the bracelet off, put it back into its box. '*What* a birthday it's been. I can't thank you all enough for joining me at the meal, and for such gifts! The sculpture and painting will live on after I am gone. I would like to be buried wearing the new dress, with the one I wore to marry Cecil beside me. The bracelet is so very special, too special to go with me. I will leave that to you, Caitlin. To be given to you on your birthday in June, just like you wanted when you were little.'

Caitlin nodded tightly, wrapping her arms around herself.

Emil jutted his jaw forward. 'Glad you like it.'

'So.' Leila stood briskly. 'More champagne. And let's have some music. Mama, can you stay with us a little longer?'

'Bryn and I will do the dishes.' Rosalind turned to him, hoping he'd understand. They – especially her – needed to make a graceful exit, leave the core family the focus of the celebration. 'Yes?'

'Happy to.'

'No, no, Emil and Caitlin can—'

'Nuh-uh.' Rosalind held up her hand, already pulling Bryn toward the dining room. 'We'll do them. Family stay here. Keep the party going.'

'Thanks, you two,' Leila called after them.

In the kitchen, Rosalind turned to Bryn, no longer bothering to hide her misery. 'That was awful. I totally screwed Caitlin up. It never occurred—'

'You didn't screw up.' He was shaking his head emphatically. 'She did.'

'She won't see it that way.'

'She will in time.' He took her shoulders. 'Trust me.'

Rosalind took a deep breath, wondering how she could keep choosing to do what she thought was the right thing for the right reasons and end up spitting time and time again into her half-sister's face. 'I hope that's true.'

'C'mon, let's do this. We'll talk later.'

She nodded miserably and helped him tackle the job, clearing the dining table, then putting food away and washing up. Twice, Emil came into the kitchen. Once to the refrigerator to get another bottle of champagne, making Rosalind and Bryn exchange worried glances, and the second time, when they had nearly finished, to the liquor cabinet to extract the Bombay gin.

'Dude,' Bryn said quietly.

'What?' Emil turned, holding the bottle close to his chest. 'We're celebrating, lighten up.'

'Sure.' Bryn picked up another glass to dry. 'I get that. Think you might toss a glass of water in that lineup?'

'Don't start, Bryn.' He was slurring slightly. 'Don't you fucking start. Not tonight.'

'Okay.' Bryn nodded. 'I said my piece. You're on your own.'

'Appreciate it.' Emil leaned against the counter. 'Nice dress you made, Rosalind. Next to it our bracelet looked like a piece of shit.'

Rosalind turned from the sink. '*No*, it didn't. Are you kidding me? Tiffany? It was beautiful.'

'Caitlin's idea. A piece of shit.' He sighed and let the gin bottle drop to his side. 'I was embarrassed.'

'Don't worry about it.' Bryn put down the dry glass and reached for another. 'Zaina knows Caitlin loves her. They've been close her whole life. This is not a big deal.'

'It's a *huge* deal.' Emil lowered his voice. 'To me. She bought the damn thing for *herself*. What the hell am I supposed to say to that? Her grandmother's dying and she buys something she knows she'll inher—'

Rosalind gasped. Bryn cleared his throat. Emil stopped just in time.

'Zaina's going to bed. She wants to say goodnight.' Caitlin walked past her fiancé to kiss Bryn on the cheek and glance in Rosalind's direction. 'Thanks for doing the dishes.'

'No problem.' Bryn put down the towel. 'We'll come in now, we're pretty much finished.'

They filed silently back into the living room, where there were more hugs and happy birthday wishes, then Leila helped Zaina to her room, taking the dress with her at Zaina's request, leaving the other presents on the table.

'You guys wanna stay and party?' Emil pushed his hand through his hair, ignoring Caitlin's pointed look of fury.

'I'm heading home.' Bryn stroked Rosalind's shoulder. 'I have to get up early and go into the city for a meeting at a new gallery.'

'Loser.' Emil turned to Rosalind. 'You're not getting up early, right? How about it?'

Not in a trillion years. 'Thanks, but I'm beat. I'm going too.'

She hugged him, pulling away after he tried to keep the contact going longer than necessary, and went to hug Caitlin, who barely returned the embrace.

'You guys going to Bryn's house?' Emil followed them back into the kitchen, where they put on their coats.

'I'm going across the street,' Rosalind said. 'Bryn's going home. Thanks for the evening.'

'I didn't do anything.' Emil's voice followed them as they stepped outside into the miserable drizzle. 'I sat on my lazy ass.'

'Shut up, Emil.' Caitlin's reply reached them just before Bryn closed the door.

When it latched, Rosalind let out a breath that made Bryn chuckle. 'No more second-guessing. You did a really fine thing with that dress.'

'I'm now thinking maybe if I *try* to make her hate me, that will backfire, too, and she'll adore me.'

'You could give it a shot.' He put his arms around her and kissed her, his lips warm in the chilly air. 'But I think you're doing all the right things already. Caitlin will have to go through whatever Caitlin has to go through.'

'I guess you're right.'

'Of course I'm right.' He kissed her more passionately, pressing against her. 'You *sure* you don't want to spend the night?'

'Mmm, of course I want to spend the night. But I've spent several in a row with you and . . .' She made a face. 'I don't know. It's just how I am.'

'You need your space.'

'Yes . . .' She gave him a flirtatious look. 'But only a little.'

'I can handle that. I guess. Do I get you tomorrow night? Dinner?'

'How about I cook? You'll be back from the city?'

'I'd love that, thank you.' He grabbed her hand and walked toward his car. 'Need a hundred-yard ride to your house?'

'I think I can manage it.' She watched him drive off, heart sinking immediately into loneliness, a clear warning that the two of them had gone zero to sixty, spending too much time together too soon. She didn't want to feel dependent on him for her own happiness. Not him or anyone.

'Hey. Rosalind.'

She turned to see Emil striding toward her on the damp grass. Her heart sank further. 'Hi, Emil. What's up?'

'I'll walk you home.'

'I don't need you to walk me home.' She gestured toward her house and let her arm drop. 'It's right there.'

'I know.' He shoved his hands into his pockets. 'Actually, I need to talk to you.'

She stepped back warily. 'What about?'

'Please.'

She told herself not to get involved. She told herself it could only be a bad idea. But instead of his usual cocky, smooth stance, Emil was standing hunched, looking miserable and haunted, the first time he'd appeared human and sincere. Plus the drizzle was coming down harder, and she didn't want to stand there getting damp and cold arguing with a drunk. 'Okay. You can walk me home.'

Five seconds later, the rain turned from a driving mist to driving drops to driving bucketfuls, and they broke into a run. By the time they reached her doorstep, they were both soggy and shivering. Rosalind flung open the squeaky storm, then fumbled with her keys and opened the front door.

'Damn.' Emil stepped through. 'That was a deluge, huh.'

'Yup.' She found the foyer light switch and slapped it on. She didn't want to have a conversation with Emil in the dark. In fact, she didn't want to have a conversation with Emil at all. 'So what's going on?'

'Can we go in? Have a seat? Get comfortable?'

'Why?'

'Because this is really hard for me to talk about.' He was trembling slightly, but she couldn't tell if it was cold, alcohol, or emotion. 'I can't just launch into it.'

'Does Caitlin know you're here?'

'She's spending the night with her mom and Zaina. She's not going to care. Right now, she'd be happy if my car was wrapped around a tree.'

'I doubt that.' Rosalind took off her wet jacket, and hung it with his in the downstairs bathroom so it would drip on tile, not hardwood or carpet. 'Want a glass of water?'

'No. I'm good.'

'Okay.' She got one for herself and sat on the sofa, curling one leg under her, then gestured him over to a chair.

He sat, instead, at the other end of her sofa. 'Thanks for this, Rosalind.'

'Sure.' She considered if she could move farther away, but decided against it. 'So talk to me.'

'God. I'm just . . .' He put his hands to his temples. 'I'm freaking out.'

'About . . .'

'Getting married. I don't think I can do it.' He rested his forearms on his long thighs, then flung himself abruptly backward, head draped over the back of the couch, staring at the ceiling. 'I'm so fucked. I can't hurt her, I can't stand to hurt her. I just can't do it.'

'Why are you telling *me* this? Why don't you talk this over with Bryn?'

'Because you understand. Because you and I are alike.'

Of all the things he could have said . . . 'Huh?'

'We're hummingbirds.'

Rosalind gaped at him. 'Why did you use that word? Where did you hear that?'

'Bryn. He told me that's what your dad called you.' He looked at her aghast expression as if she needed medication. 'I'm his best friend. You're a big deal to him. He talks about you.'

'Okay.' She didn't like the feeling, having grown up hanging fiercely on to whatever shreds of privacy she could, but she should trust Bryn enough to know he wouldn't betray her confidence.

'People like you and me.' He sat up and gestured between them. 'We don't . . . we don't want to be caught. We don't commit to things that mean forever. I'm slowly stifling in this life, in this job, in this engagement. I need newness, I need stimulation, I need . . .'

'Therapy.' She bit out the word to stop him, to keep any more from coming out of his mouth. Because then she might have to face that he was spouting her precious philosophy back at her, and she wanted to tell him he was shallow. Immature. What did that make her?

'Are *you* in therapy?'

She shrugged, trying not to show how upset she was. 'I'm not engaged to someone I don't want to marry. Or in a job I hate.'

He scratched his head, twisting to look around the room. 'Is there any wine here? Or gin? Or—'

'No.'

Emil rolled his eyes. 'I know, I know, I have a problem. I need to face that. It hasn't been that bad until now, I could control it. It's just with all this stuff happening . . . You know I asked Caitlin to marry me two years ago because we thought she was pregnant? Did you know that? It was sort of a joke.'

His abrupt subject change startled her, but not as much as what he was implying. 'Come on.'

'No, you're right, you're right.' He held up a hand. 'Not a joke, but . . . Jesus, it was so far away, Rosalind. It seemed like the world's greatest idea when it was far away. I loved every minute of it. Then it got closer, and Zaina got sick, and instead of another year, it was weeks, boom, like that.'

'Emil, you need to be having this conversation with Caitlin, not me.'

He launched himself up, and started pacing, throwing his arms around. 'She wants things and then she's determined to have them. The guy with the Ivy degree and the big-bucks job. The house in Princeton. The fucking diamond bracelet, which she's been hinting I should buy her for years, and which she is visibly disappointed about not getting every birthday, every Christmas, no matter how hard I try to find something else she'll like.

'When I saw what she'd bought her grandmother, Rosalind . . .' His handsome face contorted. 'The voice inside me stopped nudging and started screaming, *"This is not the woman for you."*'

'Emil.' Rosalind stood and grabbed his arm. 'Look. I feel for you. I do. I get what you're saying, and it's all really complicated and really hard. But you need to talk to *her*, Emil. Not me. I can't do anything about this.'

'I'm not asking you to do anything.' He took her face in his hands, looking earnestly into her eyes. 'Just listen to me while I work this out. Please, Rosalind.'

He was gorgeous when he was a drunk raving lunatic. She hated herself for even noticing. 'I'm listening.'

He let go of her face and took her hands, held them as if they were reins. 'It's bigger than just Cait. Looking ahead, the rest of my life stretches out without any change, without any chance to follow any of the other dreams I had. Always in Princeton. Always in this job. Always with Cait. My oxygen is slowly being choked off.'

Rosalind tried to pull her hands back, annoyed when he squeezed them hard enough to prevent her. 'What is it you really want to do?'

'For one? Play jazz. Piano.' He laughed bitterly. 'I was good. Not that good, not like Bryn is good. Or Leila's good, or your mom or dad. People like them are lucky. People whose talent is enough to get them out of the rat race.'

She bristled. 'All of them worked incredibly hard.'

'Yes.' He swayed slightly. 'They did. Bryn especially, after the hell he went through. He clawed his way back, got himself together, and now he also got the girl. The guy is a rock star. My point is that I will never get the chance to work that hard at anything I care about because I'm stuck.'

'You can get—'

'I want to buy a motorcycle. Buy a motorcycle and just go. It would change my life, free me from this cute high-end prison-box I've made for myself.' He pulled her closer, took hold of her elbows, eyes shooting sparks, cheeks flushed. Rosalind gave up trying to respond. She might as well not even be there. Emil needed to talk and have his problems feel important to someone. She needed to get him out of the house as soon as possible. 'You knew enough not to go into the box, Rosalind. You've kept yourself free. I admire you more than you'll ever know.'

'Emil.' She took his shoulders and shook him, or tried to, but it was like trying to shake a steel tower.

'What?'

'Stop talking to me. Talk to Caitlin, tell her you can't marry her. Buy the motorcycle and go.'

He hung his head. 'I can't.'

'Why not?'

A few seconds went by, then he lifted his face, and she was stunned to see tears on his cheeks. 'Because I'm scared.'

Rosalind's heart melted. She put her arms around him, and petted him like a mother soothing her child. She understood fear. She understood claustrophobia. But it was as if Emil had been giving a lecture she'd written, and her words no longer made sense.

'Talk to Cait. Tell her what you told—'

The front storm door squeaked open. Loud female footsteps approached from the foyer.

Emil and Rosalind jumped away from one another an instant before Rosalind realized it was the stupidest thing they could have done.

Caitlin appeared in the doorway and jammed her hands on her hips. 'If you have finished with my fiancé, Rosalind, I would like to have him back.'

Chapter 17

July 18, 1968 (Thursday)

I am in love with Daniel Braddock. It didn't take long. I think I was probably a little in love with him after that first dinner together, but I was afraid it was the wine and the fancy place, and the fact that he paid me attention the way I wanted so much to be paid attention – as an actress. Now I also want him to see me as a woman . . . or a kind of woman . . . but he is completely professional, as he promised to be. We have worked on the Shakespeare monologue and Chekhov monologues (so dreary), and Gogol (more fun) and Mark Twain (most fun of all!), and on and on until my head is swimming with words and instructions and emotions.

But, but, but . . . when I am doing well, when I am doing really well, not just high-school well, his eyes get this look in them, this sort of ferocious pride that gets me all distracted and excited and shaky because I know I'm pleasing him and I think just maybe maybe maybe he might feel something too.

I'll die if he doesn't. And yet, how can I proceed into a serious relationship when I am not female the way any man would need me to be?

* * *

Rosalind closed her eyes, hoping she was dreaming, and that Caitlin would be gone when she opened them.

No luck.

'Caitlin—'

'We were just talking, Cait.' Somehow Emil managed to keep his voice calm. 'That's it. *Talk*-ing.'

'Oh yeah, right, and I'm a turtle from Mars.'

'They don't have turtles on Mars.'

'Shut up, Emil.' Caitlin advanced a few steps, hands on her hips, her pretty features a haunting combination of fury and pain. 'If you were just talking, why did you look so guilty when I walked in?'

'Because we knew you would jump to the stupidest and least likely conclusion and try to hang me for it.'

'Whoa, hold on.' Rosalind waved her arms for him to stop. 'Those would not be my words. But we *were* just talking. Not about anything romantic.'

'That's for sure,' Emil muttered.

Rosalind sent him a daggered look, and turned back to her half-sister. 'Really. There's nothing to be upset about.'

Too late, she realized there was *plenty* for Caitlin to be upset about, but for a change not because of anything Rosalind had done.

'I'll decide whether to be upset.' Caitlin advanced furiously. 'What were you talking about?'

'The wedding.' Mr Calm spoke again.

'Oh, sure. I believe that. Even *I* can't get you to talk about the wedding. Or did you mean hers to you?'

'Come on, Caitlin.' Rosalind appealed to her half-sister, desperate not to get in any deeper with her. 'It's all about Bryn for me, you know that.'

'Leave her out of this.' Emil took his fiancée's shoulders,

gazing down at her somberly. 'All she said was that I should be talking to you, not her.'

'About what?' Caitlin brought her arms up between Emil's and jerked them sharply outward, knocking his hands off her shoulders. 'How you shouldn't marry me?'

Rosalind was getting annoyed. 'It was not like that at all.'

'Then what *was* it like?' She strode up until she was two feet away, her beautiful face mottled with rage. 'And why were you talking about *my* wedding with *my* fiancé? My wedding is none of your goddamn business. Go back where you came from, Rosalind. Go screw up your own family. Stop doing it to mine.'

Rosalind put her hands to her temples, half tempted to blurt out that Caitlin's family *was* her family. But that was Leila's truth to tell her.

'Holy Mother of God.' Emil let out a guffaw. 'I can*not* believe I didn't figure this out sooner.'

Caitlin turned to include Emil in her scorn. 'Figure *what* out sooner?'

'You two.' Emil pointed between them, then smacked his forehead. 'All this time I was thinking *Caitlin* came out of Leila's affair with Daniel Braddock.'

'No, Emil.' Rosalind shook her head urgently. 'Don't—'

'But it was Rosalind.' He rounded on her with a wide grin. 'Of course it was you. That's why you came to Princeton. I *thought* it was a pretty big coincidence.'

'What the *hell* are you talking about?' Caitlin's voice was so shrill she was practically screaming.

Emil laughed again, an ugly sound. 'Leila is Rosalind's mother, babe. She's not just yours. And you're no longer an only child. Rosalind is your half-sister.'

'No.' Caitlin folded her arms. 'Absolutely not. I don't believe it for a second.'

'I'm so sorry, Caitlin.' Rosalind stepped toward her. There was no point denying it any longer. The situation couldn't get worse. 'He's right. That's why I came to Princeton. To find out if it was true.'

'It's *not* true.' Caitlin's breath stuttered. She stood glaring between Rosalind and Emil while they stared back, waiting.

'I'm sorry.' Rosalind couldn't bear the silence any longer. 'I'm the baby your mother had. She didn't miscarry. She gave me up.'

'Oh God.' Caitlin's face melted slowly into misery. Her hand crept to her throat. 'Mom took you dress shopping.'

'No, no. Do not go there.' Rosalind reached toward her, fighting nausea and panic. 'You will always be her daughter in a way I never, ever will be.'

'You . . . have . . . taken everything from me.' She spoke between heaving breaths. 'My mother, my grandmother, Bryn . . . and now you're working on Emil.'

'What do you mean, she took Bryn?' Emil sounded dumbfounded. 'When did *you* have him?'

Caitlin ignored him, jabbing a finger toward Rosalind's chest. 'I don't care *who* you are, you can*not* screw up my life like this. I will not let you get away with this.'

Rosalind shook her head. Useless to talk this out now. Caitlin was too angry to listen.

'*When* did you have Bryn, Caitlin?'

'Shut up, Emil.'

'No. I will not shut up.' He grabbed her elbow and forced her to face him. 'When we broke up? Three years ago or whenever it was? Goddammit. This answers a lot of questions I had decided not to ask. And you know why? Because I told myself you would never, *ever* do anything that horrible to me.'

'You and I weren't together, it wasn't cheating.' Her eyes

darted left, face contorting. 'Anyway, it doesn't matter.'

'It doesn't *matter* that you fucked my best friend the minute we broke up?'

'It wasn't like that. We didn't.'

'Let me guess. You wanted to, he didn't, or rather wouldn't.' She recoiled as if he'd slapped her.

'I know Bryn. He's a decent person who made the stupid mistake of falling for you. I'm just glad he finally found a real woman.' He stepped back, eyes narrowing into cruelty. 'You want to know what Rosalind and I were talking about?'

'Emil.' Rosalind spoke sharply. 'Wait until you're calm—'

'We were talking – no, actually, *I* was talking – about how I don't think I want to marry you anymore. And after this little revelation today?' He laughed and bent forward into Caitlin's stunned face. 'I'm sure of it.'

Caitlin staggered back, looking so wounded and helpless that it was all Rosalind could do not to go to her. 'You do not mean that.'

He laughed, a horrible cackle like a movie villain, which would have been funny if it wasn't so awful. 'Let me tell you something. One of these days I will meet a woman who will do two things you never did. *Listen* to me, and *love* me for who I am, not what I represent. Have a good life, Cait. I am gone.'

He strode out of the room.

The screen squeaked open.

Slammed shut.

Rosalind gave a slow blink of exhaustion. 'Caitlin . . . I'm so sorry.'

'You should be.' She sent Rosalind a look of pure hatred that made her shrink back. 'You've poisoned *everything*.'

'That's not fair.' Rosalind tamped down her anger and frustration, trying to speak gently. 'I had nothing to do with the implosion of your relationship. That's between you and Emil. As for the rest, last summer I found out that my mother didn't give birth to me. I came here looking for answers *anyone* would want.'

'Then why didn't you ask any questions? You just showed up and thought that would make you part of our family? That is so messed *up*!'

'It was a mistake, I can see that now, but I didn't mean to hurt anyone. I was trying to avoid exactly what I've caused.'

Caitlin's face crumpled into tears. 'God, what if Emil means it?'

Rosalind screwed up her courage and went to her sister with arms open. 'Please.'

Caitlin shoved her back. 'Do *not* touch me.'

'Okay.' She stood where she was. 'Okay.'

Kindness wouldn't work. Empathy?

'When my mother would—'

'Which mother? *My* mother? Are you talking about *my* mother? No, no, your *other* mother. The mega movie star. The one who made sure you were safe and had everything you wanted your entire life long. The one who made it possible for you to be in your thirties without a real job. Who left you the world as your oyster and the rest of us as your . . . your . . . cocktail sauce.' She gestured so savagely, Rosalind was able to tamp down absurd laughter. 'You'll never have to work in an office, you'll never have to save or stop yourself from buying anything you want because it's too expensive, and that, *even that*, is not enough for you. You have to come here and try to suck away everything I have, too.'

'For God's sake, Caitlin.' Rosalind's good intentions evaporated into contempt. 'Not everything is about money. And while I'm at it, not everything is about you.'

'Says she who has it all.' Caitlin paced three steps toward the fireplace, three steps back. 'You try having a mother who is so all about herself that you wake up every day not knowing if she'll be a real mom to you or not. Try having another parent who won't even acknowledge your existence. Try finding out your parent lied to you about the very foundation of your family.'

'I have all three of those. Jillian is the first. Your mother is the second. My father is the third. I know exactly how it feels.' Rosalind took a step closer. 'Like you're about to fall off the edge of the world. Right?'

Caitlin looked over at her, startled into silence, thank God. Maybe she'd start listening now.

The screen squeaked open. 'Caitlin? Are you in here? What's going on?'

'*Mom.*' Caitlin ran toward her mother and collapsed into her arms.

Leila stroked her hair, eyes narrowed at Rosalind. 'Emil just peeled out like he was being chased by cops. What happened?'

'He says he's not going through with the wedding,' Caitlin sobbed.

'Oh my God, Cait.' Leila hadn't taken her eyes off Rosalind. 'What brought that on?'

Caitlin lifted her head, sniffling. 'I don't know. I came over and found him and Rosalind looking all cozy. They were talking about the wedding. Then he got crazy and called it off.'

'What game are you playing, Rosalind?'

'*Game?*' Rosalind's shock came out as loud laughter. 'If I were playing a *game*, this would be *fun.*'

'What were you doing here with Emil?'

'Listening.' She made an effort to calm her voice. 'He asked to walk me home because he wanted to talk. We came inside because it was pouring. I told him that whatever he had to say about the wedding he needed to say to Caitlin, because it had nothing to do with me. That's when she walked in.'

Caitlin glanced at her mother, who was still staring evenly at Rosalind. 'Well . . . that's not what it looked like. They had just jumped apart. It was obvious.'

'Right.' Rosalind felt something hot and angry burst in her chest. 'I came to Princeton deliberately to screw up Caitlin's wedding. In fact, I am pregnant not only with Bryn's child, but Emil's too. I did them both at the same time on top of the stone lions in the middle of Palmer Square the very first night I was here. Okay? Happy now?'

Caitlin gave her zombie mother another glance before she spoke. 'That is not funny.'

'No? Then let me ask you this.' The entire road to this hell was paved with her good intentions; she might as well save herself another load of asphalt. 'In what universe would it make sense that at the same time I'm falling in love with a sweet, supportive, wonderful guy like Bryn, I'm also trying to seduce someone who is not only not my type and not available, but also an immature, shallow, commitment-phobic alcoholic?'

Caitlin gasped. 'He is *not* an alcoholic.'

Rosalind barely managed to keep back a snort.

'That's enough.' Leila's eyes flashed. 'Caitlin, go back to the house. Rosalind and I have something to discuss.'

'What, that you're her mother?'

Leila gasped. Rosalind expected to feel contrite, but only got angrier.

'What did you tell her?' Leila asked.

'I didn't tell her. Emil guessed.'

'You had no business telling her.'

'I *didn't* tell her.' An absurd image came of Rosalind's

293

kindergarten teacher instructing the distracted kids to put on their listening caps.

'You had no trouble confirming it,' Caitlin said smugly.

She could cheerfully vaporize her sister. 'I didn't want to lie to you, Caitlin. You've gotten the short end of the stick over and over since I've been here, because I didn't have the courage to say anything.'

'Oh, this was for *my* benefit?' Caitlin sneered. 'How generous.'

'Caitlin, be quiet.' Leila set her daughter away from her and took a step toward Rosalind. 'I think you should leave.'

'This is *my* house.'

'Leave Princeton.'

'No.' Rosalind's rage built further. 'I still have questions.'

'I'm not answering any—'

'If you had an affair with my father, how long did it last and how many kids did you have? Why is he still paying you? Are you blackmailing him? How could you have done what you did to my mother?' Her voice broke. 'Did she ever find out about where I came from? If she did, how did the two of you convince someone that proud to raise her husband's bastard?'

Caitlin backed away from Rosalind as if she'd turned toxic.

Leila took in a breath through her nose and relaxed her shoulders, which had been hunched nearly up by her ears. 'You will get out of Princeton and stay permanently away from my family. If you are still here the day after tomorrow, I will call the police for a restraining order.'

'A *restraining* order!' Rosalind hooted, sounding as hysterical as she felt. 'Bad enough I had *one* wack-job mother; now it turns out I have *two*! I must be the luckiest girl alive.'

Leila's eyes narrowed. 'No one asked you to come here.'

'Knowing who I was, which you did from the first day I

walked into your house, you were free at any time to tell me to leave.'

'I'm doing it now.' Leila turned and headed out, dragging Caitlin with her. For the third time that night, Rosalind got to hear the screen door squeak open . . . then slam shut.

Chapter 18

August 5, 1968 (Monday)

Best day of my life. Very, very, very best. Daniel got me into the Stella Adler conservatory program! Not just classes, the real program, with a full scholarship! I was so happy, so, so, so happy, that when he told me, right after our coaching session in his apartment – which is so remarkable, so many fine and expensive things, my goodness, apparently he is extremely wealthy on account of his father doing something industrial in shipping . . . now whatever I was going to write is clean out of my head, because I'm so excited.

Oh yes! After he told me, I was so happy I cried, and then I flung my arms around his neck and told him thank you over and over and over, with him laughing and holding me.

And oh how he held me. I knew right then. Right then.

He looked up at me with those deep, dark eyes – I'd always dreamed of marrying a man taller than I am, to help make me feel a normal female size, but how little that mattered. Both of us got very quiet and very still, and just when I thought I would die of the suspense, he kissed me.

And again, and again, and again, and because it was nothing like Ben Jacobs or Mr Carter or the men I smiled at and let touch me in the restaurant, and because my heart, my heart, *was every inch in the kisses, they were the most amazing kisses I've ever had.*

Then he said that I'd better get something straight. That I was his girl and no one else's. And that I better remember that.

I melted on to the floor then. Just a puddle. His girl! A handsome, wealthy man who can act. Am I dreaming?

PS I have written to my family every week since I have been here. I have sent my parents money to pay them back for the doctor visit I billed to them. I haven't heard back once.

Rosalind stood on the front stoop of the Allertons' house and rang the bell, waiting for Zaina to answer, remembering that morning not long ago when she'd rung the bell for the first time, in an agony of suspense over what she'd find.

Now here she was again, exhausted by having slept in fitful snatches, reducing the sheets and blankets of the now-familiar bed to a twisted mess. This morning, early, she'd been packing to leave, at the same time trying to choke down a bowl of yoghurt and granola, when Zaina had called to say she was alone in the house for the morning and wanted to talk.

The very last thing in the world Rosalind wanted to do today – her mother's birthday – was talk to anyone about the mess that Jillian's condition had caused not only to the Braddock family, but now, through Rosalind, to the Allertons as well. She hadn't even called Bryn yet. Zaina was probably the only person out of the seven and a half billion on the planet for whom she'd break radio silence today over the nightmare of the previous evening.

The door opened. Zaina made a soft exclamation. 'Ya habibti. You look as if you didn't sleep all night. Like everyone else in this house.'

'That's about right.'

She stepped back and opened her arms. '*Ahla w sahla*. Welcome.'

Rosalind crossed the threshold into those arms, and clung, eyes squeezed shut, trying to imprint the feel of her grandmother's warm, solid body and floral scent into her long-term memory.

'Come. I'll make you Lebanese coffee as I promised a long time ago. We'll have a chat. Try to make some sense of this big mess.'

'It's pretty big.' She followed Zaina into the bumblebee kitchen, dismayed to see her grandmother's step faltering, her breath coming hard. 'A lot of it is my fault.'

'Nonsense.'

'You're the only one who thinks that way.'

'*Malesh*, don't let it upset you. Everyone will calm down. Stand here so you can watch.' Zaina pointed to the stove and shuffled to the other side of the room, coughing briefly.

'Can I help?'

'No, no. You watch and learn.' She bent down and pulled open a cabinet, then came up with a long-handled copper pitcher etched with a floral design, its metal darkened with age and use. 'This was a wedding present to Cecil and me from my aunt Munira.'

'It's lovely.' Rosalind took the exotic piece from Zaina, who headed for the sink with a measuring cup.

'For each serving, you put in water, always cold, a little more than the size of the cup you're using. About the size of an espresso cup.' She came back with the water and poured it into the pot. 'Then a teaspoon of coffee, very fine grind. I use Café Najjar, from Lebanon, because of course it's the best.'

Rosalind managed a smile in response to her wink. 'I'm sure.'

'If you can't find that, use any coffee, but make sure you tell them Turkish grind. Very fine.' She stirred the mixture on the stove and turned on the flame. 'Now, we can talk.'

Zaina stood smiling expectantly, making no move to start, so Rosalind took the plunge. 'I'm . . . moving back to New York today.'

'You blame yourself.' Using the long handle, Zaina circled the pot a few times on the stove. 'This was not your fault. As I said, people will calm down.'

'More easily without me. I've done enough.'

Zaina shook her head. 'The wedding would have blown up anyway. Emil was starting to fall apart. Caitlin is too young to understand that loving someone doesn't make him right for you. Emil understands this. Maybe you gave him the courage to face it.'

'I don't see how I could have. I just listened.'

Zaina gave her a maternal smile. 'Maybe that was enough. Who knows? It doesn't matter how it happened, just that it did.'

'I suppose not.'

'I, for one, loved Emil, but did not want him married to my granddaughter. Leila feels the same. Look, we're going to boil. Watch.' She stared intently at the pot, which seethed upward. At the last microsecond, just before the dark sludge overflowed on to the burner, she pulled it off the heat and let the liquid settle. 'Now we put it back on the burner and do it again. Three times total.'

'You *boil* it.'

'Yes. Three times. Best coffee of your life. You'll see.' She waited, watching the dark liquid.

'Leila was furious with me.'

'Leila is mama-bear protective of her daughter, and Caitlin was in pain last night. She will be fine. Watch, here it goes again.' Again Zaina waited until Rosalind was positive this time there would be a lava-like flow all over the stove, and again, she pulled it back just in time, and the coffee subsided.

'Caitlin thought I was trying to seduce Emil.'

'No, no. She knew deep down that she was losing him, and she turned that fear into anger. Easier to get angry at you than the man she loves. When she calms down, logic will take over. Okay, third time.'

For a third time, the coffee was rescued from the brink of spillage. 'Now, done. We let the grounds settle a bit and pour. I'll get the cups from the dining room.'

'I can do it.' Rosalind started on her way, eager to spare Zaina more effort.

'Thank you, my dear. They're in the glass-fronted cabinet. White with gold rims. I meant to get them out earlier.'

'Sure.' She found them easily and brought two back into the kitchen. 'These?'

'Those are the ones.' Zaina took the cups and set them on the counter. 'Cecil and I bought these in New York for our tenth anniversary.'

'They're beautiful.'

'We had many happy coffees together.' She pulled off the dish towel hanging on the refrigerator handle. 'Now, my lovely girl, we get down to business. You came to Princeton to find us.'

'Yes.' Rosalind didn't even try to think through her response. 'I wanted to find out if . . . Is Leila my birth mother?'

'Yes.'

Rosalind exhaled as if someone had pulled a plug to deflate her. Finally, the blessing of a straight answer. 'Thank you. I really needed to hear that.'

'Which makes me your old grandma.' Zaina used the towel to wipe out one of the cups. 'I wanted to tell you that first day, when you said you were Daniel's daughter. But it wasn't up to me.'

Rosalind nodded and leaned against the stove, weak-kneed and heavy with relief and awe. 'I should have said something. There were several times I should have said something.'

'There is no point living in the should-haves. All any of us has is the now.' Zaina chuckled, putting the second wiped-out cup back in its saucer. 'Listen to me, sounding like the wise old grandmother with all the answers.'

'No, Grandma, I appreciate it.'

'Ah, no.' She lifted a warning finger. 'You must call me Teta.'

'Teta.' Rosalind tried the unfamiliar word out on her tongue, wanting to ask if they could bake cookies together, if she could learn all the Lebanese recipes stored in Zaina's head, if she could travel back in time and grow up around the skirts of this beautiful, big-hearted woman.

'The problem is that by the time you have life somewhat figured out, you're too old to live it the way you want to.' Zaina mumbled something in Arabic and reached for the coffee pot. 'But enough of that. You must have more questions.'

'Did Leila have an affair with my father?'

'I don't know what happened, *habibti*. She disappeared often during her pregnancy. In fact, she never actually told me she was pregnant. I guessed early on.' She poured coffee into two cups and brought them over to the island, where she and Rosalind sat. 'When she started gaining weight, she left. Lots of roles, she told me, all over the country. Very exciting. She wouldn't be home for several months.'

Rosalind could barely breathe. 'What did you do?'

'I told her I knew she was having a baby. That she had a home here, and a mother who loved her no matter what choices she'd made. After that, she did come home for Christmas, but she would tell me almost nothing. If it's any consolation, I suspect she was in love with your father.'

'Who is my father?'

Zaina lowered her eyes. 'I don't know for sure. My daughter was with a lot of men. Too many men, too many different phases in her life. But I always assumed that Daniel Braddock was your father, and with you here, I am all but certain.'

Rosalind's breath came out on an unintelligible syllable, somewhere between 'ah' and 'oh'. That was proof enough for her. Her father had cheated, but maybe he'd loved Leila enough to secure her future financially. And possibly two other women's as well . . .

Bizarrely, instead of filling her with the usual rage, the news quieted her, settled into her soul like bleak ballast. Acceptance? Or she was simply too exhausted to react. Maybe having used up her fury quota for the week, she'd have to wait for it to replenish.

'Now.' Zaina gestured to Rosalind's cup. 'You must not upset yourself any more. Try the coffee before it cools.'

Obediently, Rosalind lifted the cup and sipped. Bitter. Thick. Strong enough to make her sweat. 'Oh, that's delicious.'

'Yes.' Zaina nodded in satisfaction. 'I thought you'd like it. You're one quarter Lebanese, after all.'

'True.' She managed a genuine smile, astounded at her own calm, wanting to go back to something Zaina had said about Leila that had caught her attention. 'You said Leila had many phases of her life. I thought she was always about music.'

'Yes, but first there was Broadway, and then she wanted to be a pop star, and then a concert recitalist, and then an opera diva . . . She never settled long enough to work really hard at any of them. She'd get a role, then meet a man, opera would take a back seat for a while, then maybe another role would come along, or she'd try to write a memoir, and then another man would want to take her traveling, and off she'd go, on and on. This was my failing as a parent, I think. But after her father died, I didn't have the heart to force her in any one direction. His death crushed her.'

Rosalind frowned into her cup. 'Don't you think some people just get bored easily and have to keep trying new things? I mean genetically that's who they are?'

'Maybe.' Zaina took a sip of coffee and smiled appreciatively. 'When I was a girl, I read a short story. I can't remember what it was called or who wrote it, or very many details, but I do remember there was a girl – maybe more than one, but let's say one girl – tasked with going into a field of flowers and selecting the prettiest. The only rule was that once she passed a flower, she couldn't go back, only forward.

'So this girl starts walking, and she finds a beautiful flower. But as she's about to pick it, she sees another one farther along that is even prettier. So she goes to that one, but then farther off is one of the most exquisite blooms she's ever seen. This keeps happening, over and over. After a while she stops trying to pick and runs along while the flowers get more and more beautiful.

'Then she notices that some of the flowers aren't as beautiful anymore. She keeps going, thinking they will have to improve again. But they keep getting more and more faded and more and more ugly. Eventually she reaches the end of the flowers and has to settle for a tiny, half-eaten weed.' Zaina shrugged and took a second sip. 'Something like that.'

'It's a good story.' Rosalind bent her head, pushing her coffee cup handle back and forth in semicircles on the saucer. After last night's encounter with Emil, after her talks with Bryn, she was sufficiently confused not to have the usual I'm-doing-what-I-want protest in her. 'I wish I'd done everything differently here. Except for meeting Bryn.'

'Ah.' Zaina beamed at her. 'He is a gem. I always hoped he'd settle Caitlin down a bit, but they weren't meant to be together. Now he's with my other granddaughter, how about that?'

Rosalind raised her head, smiling affectionately. 'You're nothing like the grandmother I grew up with. My mother's mother.'

'What is she like?'

'Cold. Unsmiling. Uncultured. Narrow-minded. A terrible cook.'

'Gracious.' Zaina swirled her cup. 'She couldn't be *that* bad to have had such a lovely daughter.'

Rosalind shrugged, unable to share her resentment over how Grandma Betty had treated her mother, and why. 'We don't really have a relationship.'

Her cell phone rang. She pulled it from her pocket and glanced at the screen.

'Go ahead, go ahead. Answer.'

'It's Bryn. I'll call him later.'

Zaina glanced at the clock and pressed her lips together. 'Ah. Unfortunately for us, Leila will be back soon.'

'I'll go.' Rosalind picked up her cup for the last gulp.

'No, don't finish!' Zaina restrained her with a hand on her arm. 'You'll get a mouthful of grounds. Just sip until it's nearly gone. Then if my sister were here she could tell your fortune. I don't have that gift, of making stuff up. Not like Samia. She could talk your ear off.

'But I am quite sure your future is bright, Rosalind. A few bumps to come, but after that, smooth. Like the silk in my dress.'

'Which now you won't get to wear to a wedding.' Rosalind

put down her cup, utterly miserable at having to leave Zaina. 'I'll miss you.'

'Then don't go. Give Leila a few days, maybe a week, and talk to her again. You must be persistent.'

'I've done enough, Teta.' She smiled shyly, the word still unfamiliar in her mouth. 'I can't keep upsetting everyone. There will be a huge fallout here with the wedding cancelled. I'd become a constant reminder of everyone's misery. It was . . . naïve of me to think I could be part of a new family just by wanting to be.'

'You will always be family to me, *habibti*.'

Rosalind stood reluctantly. 'Maybe I could come see you again sometime like this? When you're alone. After things settle down a little.'

'Of course, of course.' Zaina heaved herself off her chair. 'I'll be in touch to let you know the best time. How's that?'

Rosalind nodded, unable to speak, cursing the unfairness of having been deprived of a lifelong relationship with this extraordinary woman whom illness would take away all too soon.

'Give me your New York address and your telephone number.' Zaina pushed over a pad and pencil. Rosalind wrote down the information, then let Zaina walk her to the front door.

'Goodbye.' She hugged her grandmother, fighting the sharp pain of grief in her throat. 'Thank you for . . . everything.'

'You don't have to thank me.' Zaina held her close. 'We'll meet again before I'm in heaven. This mess will be put right soon. I promise you.'

'Of course.' Rosalind made herself pull back, unconvinced.

'Have a safe trip. And don't forget to pick your flower before too much longer.' The old face was peaceful, smiling despite the tears rolling down her lined cheeks.

Rosalind turned resolutely and walked across the street

without looking back, in case Zaina was still standing in the doorway watching her. The sight would make her break down and howl.

Inside, she closed the door behind her with unnecessary force and with an angry burst of energy took the stairs two at a time, intent on finishing her packing and cleaning so she could get out of there, go back to the enormous, bustling anonymity of the city, where she was welcome to feel whatever she wanted, be whatever she wanted for as long as she wanted. Where her relationships were uncomplicated and undemanding. Back to her paints, to her dresses, to the diner around the corner and the hospital across the street, to where no one cared if she existed or not.

She waited to call Bryn until she only needed to close her suitcase and leave. His voicemail picked up, a relief. The events of the previous evening were too complicated to discuss quickly. Bryn didn't have that kind of time and didn't need that kind of worry today. Rosalind didn't relish reliving them either.

'Hi, Bryn. Hope you're having a good day and that the meeting went well. Listen, call when you can. I'm . . . Just call whenever.'

Seconds after she disconnected, her phone chirped to alert her to a text message. From Bryn.

Just talked to Caitlin. Sounds like a shit show last night. I'll call as soon as I can.

Rosalind slammed her phone on to the mattress and stood fuming, hands on her hips. Sweet little half-sister wasted no time. Single again, she ran straight to her backup boyfriend, and no doubt gave him a highly pro-Caitlin version of what had happened.

The familiar feeling of suffocation bloomed in Rosalind's chest.

She was outta there. Out of this mess of a family, out of the melodrama, out of this idyllic town, back to her scattered, crowded, entirely safe existence.

She closed the lid of her suitcase and pushed hard to wrestle the zipper closed.

The phone rang. Bryn.

She let it go to voicemail, texted instead.

Can't talk now. On my way back to the city.

I'm there now, want to meet up for dinner?

No, no, no. Rosalind closed her eyes. She did not want to see him. Not tonight.

I need to be alone.

Okay. When will I see you?

A flash of unwelcome irritation.

I don't know right now. We'll talk.

She tossed the phone back on the bed, leaned half her weight on top of the case, and managed to get the zipper closed.

There.

She loaded up her rental car, went through the house one more time to make sure she hadn't forgotten anything or left a previously undiscovered mess, then drove to the post office in Palmer Square to mail her boxed-up sewing machine back to herself. After that, she returned the car to the rental agency, where she suffered in seething silence the bewilderment and annoyance of the attendant for her sin of returning the car early.

The train to New York from Princeton Junction was on time, thank goodness – more than a minute delay might have sent her over the edge – and not crowded, so she was able to wedge her suitcase into the adjacent seat to make sure no one sat there.

Off the train, she maneuvered through the maze-like corridors of Penn Station, stalked out on to Seventh Avenue and stood in the cab line, breathing in the chilly, dusty city smell, exulting in the jostling crowds and impatient footsteps.

In a little more than half a grueling traffic-filled hour, she was back to her building on West 60th, being let in by Tim the doorman, all smiles at her return. Rosalind was so happy to be home, she nearly hugged him.

A short trip in the elevator with two blessedly silent people, and she was upstairs, unbolting her door, pushing into the familiar – if slightly stuffy – atmosphere, surrounded by her own colorful jumble of possessions, dancing around to see everything, to reassure herself that she was really there.

Her paints! An unfinished canvas stood in the center of her studio space, a birch forest in autumn, the shapes and colors vague and smudgy – one of her favorites.

Her fabrics! A dress in quilt-like patches of riotous colors draped on a dressmaker's dummy. It only needed sleeves – if she could decide what kind – and hemming to be finished.

Her books! Her music! Her exercise equipment! Her kitchen! She opened the refrigerator, mostly empty except for a bottle of Pierre Péters champagne, because Rosalind fervently believed it was important always to be ready for a celebration.

She unpacked quickly, changed into pink flowered sweats, then plugged in her Keurig machine and popped in a pod for peppermint tea. While the machine did its magic, she raided her bedroom for her comforter, intending to make this afternoon all about a fabulously cozy reunion with her couch. Not a family member anywhere within sight or sound.

Inhaling mint heaven, she sat and covered herself with the soft warmth, settling in to enjoy her own space for as long as she bloody well wanted to. In control of her emotions, her surroundings, and herself.

Alone.

Chapter 19

September 26, 1968 (Thursday)

I love the Stella Adler program, but I will have to work harder than I have ever worked in my life. Because I am tall and beautiful, every woman in the program hates me. I have to be twice as friendly to be accepted, even coolly. I will not make many friends here. A lot of the men are quite flirty, except for a few who I think must be homosexuals. At least I can be friends with them, which I appreciate or I'd be lonely.

Daniel and I are having to keep our relationship quiet so as not to make people hate me even more. The more I see of him, the more I love him, and the more terrified I am that when he finds out about me, he will not want me anymore. How can I tell him such an awful thing? That I'm deformed and not right, and who knows what can be fixed and what can't, whether I'll ever be able to have children, or any normal life that a man would want? It's hard to sleep sometimes, and yet he makes me so happy. I think I make him happy too.

Still no word from Mom or Dad, but Christina sent me a quick note saying Mom announced at dinner last summer that I was dead to the family and that they must never speak of me again. And she thinks I'm melodramatic? When I am a star, I will go back whenever I can to visit her and Dad, and I will lavish them with expensive gifts. That will show them what I'm worth. They'll talk to me then.

At least Christina is talking to me now. I forgive her for what a horrible sister she was.

Rosalind sat on her couch, under her comforter again, drinking another mug of peppermint tea. She'd been home a week. The manager had given away her job at the coffee shop, but she'd find another one soon, maybe at a place even closer to home. She'd done some work on her birches painting, but still wasn't satisfied and wasn't sure why. She'd gone to the gym regularly, had dinner with a college friend one night, and had gone to a movie with an ex-coworker the next day. She'd seen an exhibit of South American art at the Guggenheim, and had considered getting a dog.

Here and there she'd texted with Bryn, who seemed to be respecting her need for space by not pressing her.

All in all, a good week. The perfect antidote to her stressful time in New Jersey.

Distant traffic sounds floated up from the street, reassuring her that life went on, regardless of her experience of it. In Princeton's deathly quiet, the negative had so easily taken her over.

Another sip, hot, minty, soothing.

Toward the middle of the cup, she decided she should call Olivia. She'd been avoiding Eve, who'd be too full of questions about Leila, and even fuller of told-you-sos when she heard what a disaster the visit had been. Olivia wouldn't want to hear a word about any of it.

That made two of them.

'Hey, Olivia.'

'Rozzy! How's it going? I haven't heard from you in forever.'

She wouldn't point out that the phone worked both ways. 'I've been busy.'

'Doing what?'

'You don't want to know.'

'Ooh, that sounds wicked.'

'No, you literally do not want to know. You told me not to mention it.'

'Oh. That.' Her sister's voice went flat. 'You're right. I don't. Tell me something else. Weather? Work? Men?'

Rosalind choked on an answer. She didn't know how to frame her relationship with Bryn. And then it occurred to her she didn't have to frame it any way if she didn't want to.

'I have met someone.'

'Ooh, how *fabulous*! Who is he? How long have you been dating? Did you take my advice about your clothes and hair?'

'I did not.' She ran her hands through her bi-color do, making it stand up as obnoxiously as possible. 'He seems to like me anyway. Go figure.'

'Of course he does; you are awesome. Does he live in New York?'

'New Jersey. Princeton.'

'How did you meet him?'

'Can't tell you.'

'God, he's not, like, our adopted brother or anything . . . ?'

Rosalind nearly dropped her tea. 'No!'

'Thank God. What does he do?'

She grinned, anticipating her sister's reaction. 'He's a sculptor.'

'Oh no,' Olivia wailed. 'Please tell me he doesn't have a man-bun.'

'No man-bun.'

'Caveman beard? Piercings? Pot habit?'

'None of the above, Madame Stereotype. He's solid. Even you would approve.'

'Well, this is thrilling, then!'

Rosalind twisted her mouth wryly. 'It wouldn't be otherwise?'

Olivia made a sound of impatience. 'You know what I mean. He sounds wonderful. I knew you couldn't be single forever. Now *stay* with this one.'

'I will.' Rosalind made herself sound solemn. 'For a really, really long time.'

Her sister gasped. 'You mean—'

'Two or maybe even *three* months.'

'*Rosalind.*'

'I'm joking.' She suppressed the giggle that would annoy her sister further. 'How are things out there?'

'Nothing new or exciting. Derek is driving me crazy. I want to update our bathroom, and he is being such a *guy* about it. "As long as the toilet and shower work, there's nothing that needs fixing."' She imitated his grumpy voice perfectly.

'Ha!' Rosalind took a sip of tea, lolling against the back of the sofa. 'Marriage as usual. What else?'

'I talked to Dad last night. He was ranting about how you're the only daughter who hasn't been in touch with him regularly. What's up with that?'

Rosalind sat up stiffly. 'Busy. I told you.'

'Come on. You can't have been too busy for a phone call. He's having to fight to relearn everything, walking, talking, eating, reading, math, *everything*.'

'Yeah, that's what happens when you have a stroke.' Rosalind put her tea down on the Picasso coaster protecting her glass coffee table from rings. After a week of blissful retreat, the mention of her father made her hard-won relaxation succumb again to the burn of anger and guilt.

'Ouch. That was cold, Rosalind. Dad needs you right now.'

So had their mother needed him, to be faithful. So had his daughters needed him, to be truthful. Not surprisingly, Rosalind's calm acceptance in Zaina's kitchen of the all-but-proof of his cheating had merely been denial, a delay of the inevitable emotions to follow. 'He'll get better whether I call or not.'

'*What?* What kind of attitude is that?'

'Olivia, I need a break from Dad. A long one.'

'Why?'

Rosalind pushed the comforter down and off her lap, wishing she hadn't called. Avoiding her father was easier when she didn't have to think about him noticing her silence and being hurt. 'It's complicated.'

'You can't keep running away from everything in your life that gets tough, Rosalind.'

The vicious punch nearly made her gasp. 'That is *so* unfair. You have no idea what my reasons are.'

'It's part of the whole Mom thing?'

'Yes.'

'Well, whatever it is, get over it, please. It's cruel to abandon him. He's always been so powerful and forceful; now he's so weak and vulnerable. You know how men are, it's been devastating for him. Eve went to see him last weekend and said watching him struggle to read a simple sentence was agony. She said the nurses and the staff all treat him like he's a sick old man, like he's just anyone.'

'He *is* a sick old man. He *is* just anyone.'

'No, he's not! He's Daniel Braddock!'

Rosalind rolled her eyes. Exactly the attitude that had fed his arrogance. Put men in positions of power and they started to believe their own press. 'Okay, he's old, sick Daniel Braddock.'

'Promise you'll call him.'

'Olivia, I'm not going to promise that.'

'Promise you'll *think* about it.'

'Okay. I promise to think about it.' She changed the subject with a few more questions about upcoming cooking shows and the weather in LA, then hung up with relief and dragged the comforter back up, along with her cooling tea.

But no matter how much she tried to return to her blissful relaxed state, she could no longer banish the memory of her vigorous father's dull eyes and weakened body when she'd last seen him in Maine. Two months ago.

Sitting up again, she pounced on the remote lying next to her stack of partly read *New Yorker*s.

Maybe TV would help. Maybe there was a good movie on.

A few pointed, then aimless channel changes produced the expected there's-nothing-good-on result. Her mood went from bad to worse. What was she doing sitting here alone in the middle of one of the world's richest and vastest cities worrying about what she could watch on television?

Her hand stilled on the remote. A longing hit her, so powerful she knew she'd give in. Something she hadn't done in so long she couldn't remember the last time, the circumstances, or whether Jillian Croft had been still living or dead.

She wanted to watch one of her mother's movies.

Not just one. *The* one. Rosalind's favorite, *Dangerous Fall*, a sweeping romance filmed in the late 1970s, when Jillian's stardom had reached its peak.

She searched through the Netflix database with shaking hands, found the movie and set it up to play, clutching the remote to her chest like a shield. She was about to see her mother alive again.

Tears started during the opening credits, then Jillian entered the screen, tall, vital and so breathtakingly beautiful that Rosalind's tears turned into a smile of wistful delight. She played Maura, the strong, no-nonsense nurse with a heart of gold sent to the house of Curt, the manly, brooding hermit millionaire played by James Coburn. Maura's job was to heal Curt from temporary paralysis after, guess what, a dangerous fall.

Jillian Croft lit up the screen. There was simply nowhere else to look while she was on it, and too bad for whoever else made it into the movie. She inhabited Maura to such a degree that the oddly stylized dialog and unlikely plot gripped and wouldn't let go. Her chestnut hair tumbled and glistened, every strand where it was meant to be. Her hazel eyes telegraphed every emotion she was feeling, unless she was consciously hiding, in which case her flat expression managed only to be more evocative.

Fiercely proud of all her mother had accomplished with so many hurdles thrown in her path, Rosalind ate up the rest of the movie, frame after frame. Curt's gradual thaw; the growing love between the two characters despite their battles; Curt's eventual recovery, and then the devastating revelation that Maura was terminally ill.

Midway came Rosalind's favorite scene, in which Curt slumped to the ground, exhausted and defeated by his attempts to walk. Maura put her hands to her hips and chided him in her utterly convincing Southern accent: *My mama used to say, 'Don't stop bailin' 'til your boat's plenty dry.'*

The first time Rosalind watched the movie, the words had mystified her. At dinner, she'd asked her mother about the line. Mom had rolled her eyes and told them that as much as she loved the movie, that was one of the hardest lines she'd ever had to say, because Coburn thought it was awful. He'd start laughing, and that would set her off. They'd asked Sydney

Pollack, the director, to change the line, but he'd refused. The take that made it into the film was when the whole crew was so annoyed with the stars, and it was so late, that they didn't dare giggle again.

Rosalind had immediately asked what they'd wanted to change the line to. Mom had leaned her elbows on the table, eyes bright with mischief, and asked for suggestions.

From there, the meal had turned uproarious. Teenager Olivia had come up with, 'Don't stop shovelin' 'til the poopy stall's clean.'

Adolescent Rosalind had offered, 'Don't stop stirring or your mush will get lumpy.'

Even little Eve had piped up, 'Don't let your sunglasses get dirty or you can't see.'

On screen, Jillian managed to make even the cheesy line sound fresh and important, though Rosalind's enjoyment was diminished by the obvious parallels with her father's health. Learning to walk when you'd known how to run . . .

She shooed away the sympathy, focusing on Maura helping the all-but-broken Curt to his feet, urging him to continue training, promising him joy ahead. Watching her, there was never any doubt that she believed complete recovery to be the only result possible.

Of course, Curt improved; of course, they fell deeply in love, then her diagnosis threatened their joy. They picnicked together, red, gold and orange leaves drifting down around them, Maura showing clear signs of illness and fatigue. Taking her hand, trying to suppress his fear and his anguish, Curt stoically repeated her mama's line back to her, *Don't stop bailin', my love . . .*

A mess of tears, Rosalind couldn't even smirk. The movie ended with Coburn in a tuxedo, only a slight limp marring his stride, setting a bouquet of red roses on Maura's grave, then driving on to the church where he'd be getting married.

Glorious tear-jerking stuff, a Sydney Pollack classic, with a fabulous Jerry Goldsmith score and costumes by Theoni Aldredge.

Rosalind blew her nose and wiped her streaming eyes, pushing off the comforter, which emotion had made too warm.

For several minutes she sat watching the credits crawl up the screen. Her subconscious must have picked this movie for its message. Or her mother's spirit had done it for her.

Don't stop bailin' 'til your boat's plenty dry.

Her boat was still wet. Nearly up to the gunwales. And for the past week, while she'd told herself she was recovering, she'd stopped even trying to bail.

Bryn answered on the first ring. 'Hi.'

'Hi, Bryn.' Just the sound of his voice made her feel fluttery.

'You've been missing. And missed.'

'I'm sorry. I've been so—' A siren sounded over the line. 'Where are you?'

'On my way to your place.'

'Wait, what? Right now?' She stood abruptly, heart starting to pound, missing him retroactively with such force that she wondered if she'd just woken up from some kind of emotional coma.

'I had another gallery visit today, and thought I'd take a chance.'

'How did you get my address?'

'Zaina called me with it after you left. She thought I might want to come after you.'

Rosalind started smiling. 'And you do.'

'Yup. No pride whatsoever. Google says I'll be there in half an hour. I've got dinner. You hungry?'

Her smile spread. 'I am.'

'See you soon.'

Rosalind raised a fist – *yes!* – then realized that the guy she adored was about to show up after she'd treated him like crap for a week, and she'd greet him with a hideous I've-been-crying face, wearing sweatpants.

She owed him better.

In the bathroom, she washed her face with cold water over the stained sink, then ran wet hands through her hair to try to calm it down, succeeding beautifully at making it look worse. Sticking her head under the bathtub faucet only transformed her into a wet mess instead of a dry one.

This called for drastic measures.

In the cabinet under the sink she found the clippers she'd bought when she first took on this hairstyle, still with the number eight guard in place. An old shower curtain would protect the floor, another around her shoulders would protect her neck and shoulders. Twenty minutes later, both curtains bundled and stored, she used the hairdryer to hurricane off any loose hairs, and smiled at her reflection. A demure inch of her natural brown color remained.

Now, eyeliner, blush, mascara. Plum-colored yoga pants with a black floral tunic top she'd designed herself, which caught the purple in the pants. Black flats.

Tim called from downstairs. 'Mr Griffiths is here.'

'Send him up.' Back in the bedroom, she added gold earrings and a bracelet that had belonged to her mother, then gave her appearance another look.

Well.

Even Olivia would approve.

So she added a bright yellow cummerbund and changed the black flats for yellow ones with open toes and rainbow soles.

Smoothing her tunic, wishing she could calm her nerves as easily, she opened the door to Bryn's knock. Just the sight of him, curly-haired, smelling of the chilly city, blue eyes warm, holding up a shopping bag, made her wonder why she'd ever thought shutting him out of her life would solve anything. Why she'd ever thought shutting anyone out would solve anything. 'Hi.'

His eyes went over her. 'Wow. You look fantastic.'

'So do you.' She meant it. He could be covered in boils right now and he'd look fantastic. Despite her childish retreat, he'd been on his way to her. *He* had kept bailing.

'I love this look.' He pointed to her shorn head. 'When did you have it done?'

'Just now. In the bathroom.'

'You are kidding me.' He cracked up. 'What did you do, get a mini-mower and run it over your head?'

'Something like that.' She grinned, achingly glad to see him, not sure whether it was up to her or him to make the first move.

'I'm glad you called. I thought I was going to have to do manly battle with your doorman to let me up.'

'It was about time I did.' She laughed nervously. 'Called you, I mean.'

Another beat while they smiled at each other, then her step forward brought her in contact with his chest as he moved over the threshold, gathered her into his arms and kissed her soundly, the dangling shopping bag resting on her butt.

More kisses. Lots of them. Passionate, sweet, floodgates-bursting.

It had been a long time.

'Bryn.' Rosalind kept her arms around his neck, anxious to say everything the right way. 'This past week was a mistake. Shutting you out . . . was wrong. It's how I've always coped.

But it's . . . not so much hummingbird as chicken. I'm sorry.'

'You saved me my lecture.' He rubbed his cheek against hers. 'It's fine if you need space sometimes, Rosalind. We just need to talk it out first, so I don't spend a hundred and fifty-three hours thinking I'm about to lose you.'

'I know. I know.' She squeezed her eyes shut. 'It was really selfish.'

'Shh, it's okay, we're good. No guilt.'

Rosalind's eyes flew open. 'Wait, you *counted* the hours?'

'Nah. I'm not that pathetic.' He released her with a final kiss. 'Let's get you fed and have some fun. Nice address, by the way. Great apartment.'

'Thanks for bringing dinner.' She led him over to the kitchen, bubbling with relief and happiness that she'd wised up in time, that they could move on, that he'd give her another chance. 'I was just going to have soup.'

'You're still having it. I brought chicken soup, but also a pastrami sandwich big enough for four people, coleslaw, and salted caramel brownies.' He hoisted the bag on her counter.

'A Nyoo Yawk feast.'

'Plates are . . . ?' Bryn started opening cabinets. 'Here. Tell me what changed your mind about calling me.'

Her heart went soft at how he made sure to ask the important question so casually. 'My mom told me I was being an idiot.'

He stopped with two plates in his hand. 'Leila?'

'Jillian. A message from beyond the grave.' She grinned at his confusion, taking down a couple of glasses for beer. 'I watched one of her movies.'

'Which?' He divided the typically enormous deli sandwich between the plates. Rosalind's mouth started watering.

'*Dangerous Fall.*'

'Missed that one, though I saw a few. She was so remarkable.' He put the soup in the microwave and programmed it to heat. 'What was her message?'

'*Don't stop bailin' 'til your boat's plenty dry.*'

He cracked up, turning to look at her. 'I guess if someone said that, I'd call me too.'

'The movie is corny, and I'd like to think I would have figured it out on my own. But it helped.' She got down a couple of bowls for the soup, then remembered something Bryn had said earlier. 'You had a gallery meeting today and I haven't asked you a thing. How did it go? You said the owner you met last week was sort of "meh" about your work. Tasteless swine.'

'He was. But today was a good day.' Bryn grabbed the container of soup from the microwave, then dropped it back, shaking his hands.

'Yes?' She passed him a pair of crimson silicone potholders resting against the toaster, and opened the silverware drawer for forks and spoons. 'Tell me!'

Bryn carefully poured soup into the two bowls. 'Clyde, the owner, was not only interested in doing a solo show of my work, he was also excited about the new stuff.'

'*Bryn!*' She dumped the silverware and attacked him with a hug and kiss. 'Wait, what new stuff?'

'The sculptures of you.'

'You've *finished* them?'

'Just sketches. He liked the concept.'

'But this is fantastic! I'm so proud of you.'

'Plenty of work ahead.' He brought the soup to the table. 'Which reminds me, I want to see your paintings later.'

'Oh. Sure.' She brought napkins and silverware over, already embarrassed at the thought of him judging them. 'I'm over the moon about your news. Congratulations.'

He set a bowl at each place. 'You should know how grateful

I am to you for getting me out of what had become an artistic and emotional rut. I was stuck grieving Jake's death. You helped me move on.'

'I'm so glad.' Rosalind touched his cheek on her way to the kitchen for the beer glasses. 'Though really, all I did was show up and screw up your closest friendships.'

'True.'

'Emil! I can't believe I forgot.' Rosalind rushed back to the table, clutching the glasses. 'Did Caitlin mention what she let slip that night? About you and her?'

'Emil told me.'

'Oh God.' Rosalind set the glasses down. 'I should have warned you. I've been so self-centered this week.'

'This is not your mess.' He took her shoulders and made her look at him. 'It's mine. I've wanted Caitlin to tell him for three years. Maybe not in that context, but . . .'

'It was a bad context.' She winced, remembering. 'Was he angry?'

'There was some pretty good yelling. But I had it coming, and let him get it out of his system. Then he calmed down and we got to talk. He quit his job and is buying a motorcycle.'

Rosalind gasped. She hadn't thought he had it in him. 'Is that a good idea?'

'Maybe. Might do him good, might also be a disaster. Most likely somewhere in between. But if it's in his soul that he has to do this, he might as well do it while he's young and single.' Bryn shrugged. 'Much more importantly – we need a bottle opener.'

'I have one. I'll . . . Wait! I just thought of something.' She snatched the beer glasses back from the table and headed for the refrigerator. 'We should have champagne to celebrate.'

'What, Emil's motorcycle?'

'Your show.' She grabbed the bottle, twisted off the wire cage, popped the cork and poured the champagne into two flutes, handing one to Bryn, who'd followed to watch. 'Here's to your success.'

'And to yours.'

'Mine?' Rosalind raised a skeptical eyebrow. 'What did *I* do?'

'You successfully remembered that I am the man of your dreams.' He laughed at her expression and raised his glass. 'Here's to both of us, Rosalind. I'm so glad you called.'

'Me too.'

They clinked and drank, then sat and devoured the soup, rich and just salty enough, with chewy noodles and big chunks of meat that made it almost a meal in itself. They shared only half the sandwich, putting the rest away for later, and decided they'd trade the calories in the brownies for the rest of the champagne.

After a quick cleanup, Bryn refilled their glasses and Rosalind led the way to her studio, feeling kinship with people about to be executed.

'Huh.' Bryn stopped just inside the door and looked around at the backs of the paintings lining the walls. 'You keep them facing away from you?'

'I don't like to look at what I've done. Just what I'm doing.'

'Okay.' He walked toward her birches, stooped to put down the bottle, and stared. Took a sip of his champagne. Stared some more. Rubbed his chin thoughtfully.

Rosalind felt her face grow hot with humiliation, and he hadn't even said anything yet.

'I really like this one, Rosalind.' He took a step back. 'I like it a lot. May I see more?'

'Of course.' She walked around the room, turning canvases

for him, drinking her champagne too fast out of nerves, remembering her mother's absolute belief in her talent from an early age.

More proof they were not genetically related.

Bryn did a slow tour of the room, stopping now and then to pay more attention to a painting, passing others with only a glance. 'These are all the Maine scenes?'

'Yes. Colorado is in storage.'

'I like them very much, Rosalind. You have a great eye for proportion and color, and you obviously care a lot about your subjects. They have a wistful, sentimental feel. Really interesting.' He came back to her and clinked her glass with his nearly empty one. 'Here's to you. You are very talented. Thank you for letting me see.'

'You're welcome. And thank *you*.' She drained her champagne, absurdly deflated, apparently having hoped to hear they were the best things ever on canvas, even knowing they couldn't be.

'What?'

'Nothing!' She smiled as genuinely as she could and took his empty glass. 'I'm really glad you like them.'

His eyes narrowed. 'But . . .'

Curse his mind-reading. 'But . . . I don't know, how could they be better?'

'Better?'

'More professional.'

'What does that even mean?'

'I don't know.' She held the flutes up to her burning cheeks. If she thought she'd turned hot before, she must be volcanic now. 'Just . . . better.'

'I think I see.' He kissed her gently, looking amused, but in such a tender way that she couldn't feel annoyed. 'The bad news is also the good news. The only person who can make you believe you have enough talent is you. What other people think does not matter. Last week one gallery thought I was a hack. This week another thinks I'm brilliant. Same portfolio shown to both places. So is it crap? Or not? It's neither; it's simply what it is, and people either like it or not. Worse, people might like it now and in two or three months, or decades, change their collective mind. But if *I* don't believe in it, the work never gets done.'

'I don't have that kind of confidence.'

'You do, because you keep painting. I'm not talking about getting rid of your demons, which is impossible unless you're a raging narcissist. Just get them to where they are the annoying gerbil squeaks in the back of your mind, not the roaring lions in front.'

Rosalind nodded, listening raptly. 'How?'

'Uh . . .' He scratched his head. 'I don't know that one. Lie to yourself?'

She cracked up, gazing at him without censoring the emotion in her eyes, not caring if he could tell she was well on her way to falling in love with him. 'Thank you, Bryn. You talked earlier about me freeing you from pain you've carried around for a long time. You're doing that for me, too, only *I'm* the pain I've been carrying around. Pain in my own ass.'

He took the glasses back from her and put them on the floor under the legs of her easel. 'Sounds to me as if we're good for each other.'

'You may be right.'

'Of course I'm right.' He moved closer until their bodies touched, chest to thighs. 'I was thinking we might want to continue this tour of your apartment.'

'Ah.' She slid her arms around his neck and rocked against him suggestively. 'Any particular room you had in mind?'

'You pick.'

She gave what she hoped was a seductive chuckle, kissed him, and ambled toward her bedroom, languidly shedding clothes as she went. In the doorway, she turned to discover that Bryn was also naked, which suited her just fine. They fell on to her bed and made love as if they'd been apart for months instead of days, the familiar actions enhanced and made new by lingering gazes, whispered words, and emotions that were deep and thrilling.

And only slightly terrifying.

Coming down from the high, lying next to Bryn, hand on his chest, the comforting thump of his heart under her fingers, Rosalind felt as if she were on the brink of some huge and important discovery, as if something was bursting to get out of her that she hadn't yet been able to identify.

Relaxing, she let the emotions and thoughts and memories swirl around and through her, not trying to force them into coherence, hoping it would come in time.

Bryn's stroking of her hair slowed, his breathing slowed, his heart rate slowed. Still she lay, patient for once in her life, until she was able to put together what she needed to do.

Like Emil, off on his motorcycle, like Leila ordering Rosalind out of the house, when life got sticky and difficult and complicated, Rosalind either moved away, in a vain search for a situation that would never get difficult and complicated and sticky, or she retreated.

Going forward, she wanted to live differently. Calling Bryn today had been a good first step. Now she had to take another, much harder one.

Oddly, instead of fear, she felt calm resolve, even contentment. Beside her, Bryn shifted, swallowed. His eyes fluttered open.

'Bryn,' she whispered. 'I've decided something.'

His hand resumed stroking her hair. 'Mmm?'

'Day after tomorrow, I'm driving up to Boston to see Eve, then I'm going on to Maine.'

'Yeah? Maine? What for?'

She pressed against him, warm and happy, wanting to purr like a tigress. 'I need to talk to my dad.'

Chapter 20

December 15, 1968 (Sunday)

I am bone weary. I feel as if this semester I've been broken all the way down and built only halfway back up. Everything I thought I knew has been challenged, and my deepest emotional privacy invaded. I have loved every minute! Because I'm good. I'm really good, and I know it, have always known it, but something about having all these people validate me in a studio that has turned out some of the country's greatest actors . . . it's so hard to describe. Walking the halls, touching things other people might have touched – chairs, desks, tables – Karl Malden, Marlon Brando, Anthony Quinn. How many of the people in my classes will be sharing a stage or screen with me someday? Who will go down immortally as these greats have? It gives me goose bumps.

I've chosen my name. Say goodbye to Sylvia Moore from Jackman, Maine, may she rest in peace. Say hello to Jillian Croft! The world will be hearing a lot of that name, I can tell you that.

Saving best for last – so so so many good things in my life here in New York City – I think I caught Daniel Christmas shopping at Tiffany's.

I can scarcely breathe wondering what he might have bought me.

I think it might be time soon to tell him the truth. I'm just so very afraid.

Love to Sylvia, God bless you and good riddance.

From Jillian.

Rosalind's rental car beeped its I'm-locked signal. She'd just pulled into Eve's curved driveway on Littles Point Road in Swampscott, Massachusetts, one of the more modest houses in the pretty, quiet neighborhood close to the shore. Her sister had bought the place as a present to herself after she made it through Harvard's Graduate School of Design, emerging with a Masters in Architecture, the only Braddock sister with an advance degree.

The house was a simple white colonial with black shutters, white trim and a bright red front door. Since Rosalind had last visited, probably five years earlier, not long after Eve bought the place, the landscaping had grown and changed dramatically. The scraggly pine in the front yard had been replaced with a vigorous blue spruce whose needles made a healthy showing of the faintly powder-blue color. The sprawling bed in front of the house had been neatened with holly and rhododendron, the meandering flagstone path had been restored straighter with new stones in varying shades, bordered with darker-hued cobblestones. Eve's design eye was impeccable, but Rosalind also missed the vegetal free-for-all cultivated by the previous owner.

'Hey, Rosalind! You made good time.' Eve stepped out of the house, arms open for a hug. She looked thinner even than last summer, not good on an already thin body.

'Hi, Eve.' Rosalind hugged her tightly, annoyed by the unwelcome thought that her sister was probably not related to her by blood. It didn't matter, not now, nor would it any time in the future, but the change was still hard to internalize. 'Traffic wasn't so horrible once I got through Connecticut.'

'Great. Come on in. I'm so glad you're going to see Dad. He's been sort of . . .' Eve gestured aimlessly.

'I know. Angry at me for not coming sooner.'

'Yes.' She turned back at the front door. 'But also, you need to prepare yourself. Recovery has been slow. Slower than anyone wanted, most of all him. The doctors let him move into the cottage with Lauren, as long as he has a full-time nurse, but they're not sure what's going on.'

'Okay.' Rosalind's stomach started knotting up. 'Thanks for telling me.'

'Poor Lauren is getting the worst of it. Come on, I'll take you to your room.'

'Worst of it?' She followed her sister up the plain wooden staircase, which must have been recently refinished.

'His frustration, temper, et cetera.'

'When has *that* been any different?'

'Good point. Here.' Eve turned down the hall and opened the first door on the right. As she moved, her wide-leg beige pants and striped beige and white tunic clung to her legs and torso at various points, drawing attention to her too-thin frame. 'You stayed in this room before, didn't you?'

'Yes.' When Rosalind stepped over the threshold, she was no longer sure. 'I think. You redid it?'

'We redid a lot. Like it?'

'Beautiful.' She ran her hands along the soft gray and white bedspread, accented with pillows in muted shades of green and navy that picked up the colors in the curtains and the painting hanging over the bed. 'You have such incredible taste. My apartment is stuff I like all thrown together.'

'Nothing wrong with that.' Eve opened the closet door and

pulled out a suitcase rack. 'Here you go, towels are in the bathroom across the hall. Unpack, get settled, then come on downstairs. Marx is in the kitchen, he'll be so excited to see you.'

'If he remembers me.' Marx was Eve's mixed-breed dog, who'd been instantly smitten with Rosalind on her last visit and followed her everywhere.

'He will.' She moved toward the door. 'Need anything else?'

'No, this is perfect, Eve, thanks.'

'Good.' She turned and laid a hand lightly on the jamb. 'Mike won't be home until later, so it's just you and me for dinner.'

'That sounds nice to me.' Rosalind was delighted. Mike knew how to suck the air out of a room, especially if he was in one of his moods. The darker he got, the more she was determined to counter his negativity with cheerful chatter, the end result being that his monosyllables exhausted her, and he undoubtedly thought her a brainless fool. Olivia knew how to tease him out of his silence, draw him into conversations that interested him, another trait she'd inherited – or rather copied – from their mother, but Rosalind didn't have that kind of gift, nor did she care enough to try to develop one.

She unpacked the next days' outfits into the empty cherry dresser, ornate with carvings, including the dowels support- ing its mirror, one of the few things Eve had asked for when Dad moved out of the Beverly Hills house – it had been in her childhood room – then washed her hands and came down- stairs.

Immediately Marx, a beguiling medium-sized tan mix of who-knew-what, bounded up to greet her, sniffing with his blackish pointed snout, feathered tail wagging.

'Hey, Marx.' She bent down to rub his cream-colored chest

and got a lick on her face. Not her favorite type of kiss, but it was Marx. 'Blech, I love you too.'

'Marx, keep the body fluids to yourself.' Eve appeared in the kitchen doorway in an apron, holding a wooden spoon. 'I'm having a glass of wine. Want one?'

'Sure.' Rosalind straightened and headed to the kitchen, doggy escort wriggling joyfully beside her. 'Mmm, something smells good.'

'Red lentil soup with coconut. It's really good and very easy.'

'A perfect recipe.'

'More importantly, it will sit there until we're ready to eat it.' Eve handed her a glass of red wine, took off her apron and picked up the bottle to bring with her. 'Come see the surprise.'

Rosalind followed her out toward the rear of the house, where the surprise turned out to be a gorgeously installed three-season room that expanded out into the back yard. 'Ooh! Very nice.'

'Yeah, we live out here when the weather's too cold or too hot to be in the yard, which is most of the year. Have a sit and let's talk.' Eve pointed to the room's olive-green armchair and flopped into the green and white patterned love seat opposite. 'Tell me what's been going on. I'm guessing life has been interesting lately.'

'Interesting.' Rosalind laughed uncomfortably, going over in her mind the events of the previous month. How was she supposed to fill her sister in without sounding like a Lifetime movie summary? 'I don't even know where to start.'

'You found your birth mother in Princeton, I know that much. You think she and Dad had an affair, you and I had a fight, you've been avoiding Dad, and . . . ?'

Rosalind hunched and released her shoulders. 'It was kind of a mess. You were right, I should have told them sooner who

I was. I should have been more careful about how I did certain things. In short, it started great, ended badly. Leila told me to leave Princeton and never come back. Caitlin, my half-sister, and her fiancé Emil's wedding blew up less than a month before it was supposed to happen. The only thing that didn't get screwed up was my relationship with my grandmother, Zaina, and with . . . Bryn.'

Eve brightened. 'Bryn . . . ?'

'He's a friend of the Allertons. I'm . . . we're seeing each other.' Rosalind couldn't meet her sister's eyes. 'Pretty seriously.'

'No kidding. That's really great.'

She looked up to find Eve staring curiously. 'What? Why are you looking at me like I might be a stunt double?'

'Because every time you've told me about a guy you've started seeing, it's always been this huge rush of hyperbole. *Oh, he's the most amazing, he's so hot*, et cetera. This sounds real.'

Rosalind was pretty sure her face was the color of her wine. 'I hope so.'

'I'll drink to that.' Eve was beaming, which wasn't unusual except that it made Rosalind realize how unsmiling she'd been so far. 'Way to go, Rosalind.'

'Thanks.'

'As for the rest.' Eve tipped her head side to side, the way she always did, as if she were a scale needle seeking a resting place. 'You knew there were risks. This was what you wanted to do, and you did it. Nothing wrong with that. Admirable, in fact. Neither Olivia nor I had that courage.'

'Thanks.' Rosalind patted Marx's golden head, currently resting on her lap, to hide her pleasure at her sister's compliment. 'I can't help feeling like there's more. I mean, that it isn't finished. That the Allertons will calm down, and then I'll be able to—'

'Rosalind.' Eve was shaking her head. 'You need to leave it. You tried, and it didn't work. We're your family. We're still here.'

'Yes. I know. I know. You're right.' She made her hand slow its accelerating pace on Marx's head. 'I was thinking maybe if I talked to Dad about it, carefully, he might—'

'Just. Leave. It. He's in no shape to be upset. It could be dangerous.'

'Still? He's not past that?' She wasn't going up there just to pay a daughterly social visit, tell him to keep up the good work, stiff upper lip and all that. She wanted to understand, she wanted to show him, gently, that his betrayal was not only to his wife, but to the three people who depended on him most to do only good. Then she wanted to sit back and really listen, past his typical bluster and denial and outrage, until he came up with some truth she could understand.

'No. It takes a long time for the ruptured blood vessels in his brain to heal and get strong again. Further bleeds are always possible. One theory is that he already had a smaller second stroke, but he refuses to let them do another CAT scan, so it's guesswork right now. You need to keep this away from him.'

Rosalind stared down into her glass. Marx nudged her knee, then again, looking up at her beseechingly, then leaned heavily against her thigh with a doggy sigh of resignation.

'You're right. I'd never forgive myself. Neither would anyone else. It's not worth it.'

'I'm really glad to hear you say that.'

Rosalind nodded, took a gulp of wine, not paying much attention to the taste. 'I watched one of Mom's movies the other day. *Dangerous Fall.*'

'Uh . . .' Eve's brow furrowed. 'Which one was that again?'

'James Coburn is crippled by an accident, Mom helps him recover, then dies.'

'Oh, yeah, sorta.' She still frowned, holding her chin, tapping her cheek with one finger. 'Something about a bucket?'

'Don't stop bailin' 'til your boat's plenty dry.'

'Ha!' Eve's face cleared. 'That was it. I don't remember the movie, but I do remember the family jokes about that line. We told those for years. Don't blah blah blah until blah blah blah. That was hilarious. Some of the really good times.'

Rosalind leaned forward, Marx's eyes following her movement. 'Do you ever think about the night Mom died?'

'*No.*' Eve's expression fell. 'Why on earth would I? That was a nightmare.'

Rosalind shrugged. 'I've been thinking about it. About what she said at dinner. When she was crying.'

Eve looked pained. 'Do we have to do this? I was hoping for fun sister-bonding tonight.'

'We're the only people who were there, except Dad. I can't talk about this with anyone else.'

'Okay. Okay.' She picked up her glass, cradled it to her chest. 'Go ahead.'

'I always believed what Dad told us about Mom being upset over her career. But I have been wondering if maybe she was upset about something else.'

Eve raised a perfectly shaped eyebrow. 'I'm listening.'

'Like maybe the fact that Dad cheated on her not just with Leila, but with Olivia's mother before that and your mother after, and got Mom to raise us as hers.'

Eve's other eyebrow flew up into a skeptical stare. 'Are you kidding me? You think he *forced* Mom to raise his illegitimate daughters?'

'Yes.'

335

'Come on, that wouldn't work. Can you imagine anyone forcing Mom to do anything? She had to have wanted to.'

'I've been wondering if that night she died, he told her there was yet another mistress. Or maybe he told her he was leaving her. Remember what she said? *I'm too old. I'm not enough anymore. It's all over.*'

'That's total garbage, Rosalind. After decades together, doing everything for her, he suddenly decides to walk out when she needs him most? When she was at her lowest? Mood and career in the toilet? That is the most ridiculous thing I've ever heard.' Eve jumped up and walked over to the French doors facing out on to the spacious back yard, then spun around, nearly spilling her wine. 'Mom wanted us. All of us. Why would she pretend to be pregnant, pose in *People* magazine, make this big deal about motherhood if she wasn't thrilled about adopting us?'

'She was an actress.'

'Dad would have to be a monster.'

'It's not impossible.'

'It's impossible. You left home after Mom died. I was with him and Lauren for a lot of years with both of you gone. He was a different person without her. Calmer, kinder.'

'That's my point. He got rid of—'

'*And* he talked about her all the time. Affectionately. Tenderly.'

'He was an actor, too.'

'Stop, Rosalind. Just stop.' Eve glared, causing Marx to get up from Rosalind's side and trot over to his mistress. 'You are freaking me out.'

'I know. It's ugly.'

'No, *you* are freaking me out. You are totally romanticizing our mother. She was a selfish and manipulative woman.'

'No.' Rosalind thought of the girl in the diary, so coldly neglected by her own mother, desperate to be thought of as normal, wanting so much on the one hand to shine, and on the other to fit in. 'I know her better than you do.'

'I'm sure you do. I was a kid when she died. But I remember things about her that I am able to process now, from an adult perspective, and it's . . . it's easy to see that she was an operator.'

'She was deeply unhappy.' Rosalind started weighing the pros and cons of divulging the receipt of the diary, then thought *screw it* and plowed forward. 'Someone sent me a diary Mom kept when she was a girl, from high school up until she met Dad in New York and was finally diagnosed.'

Eve walked a few steps toward her, looking alarmed. 'Who sent it?'

'I don't know. I thought maybe Lauren. Or a close friend of Mom's who wanted us to have it. The timing was weird, since it came relatively soon after we found out about her condition. Which made me think of Lauren. I'd talked to her, so she knew I knew . . .'

'Unlikely to be Lauren. She's big on staying low to the ground. I can't imagine her wanting to stir anything up. Maybe Leila had it.'

'Leila? Are you serious? Dad's *mistress*? No way.' Rosalind shook her head so emphatically she got dizzy.

'Nothing surprises me anymore.'

'You should read the diary, Eve. You get to know Mom as a girl, how terrified she was of not being normal, how badly Grandma Betty dealt with—'

'God, Rosalind.' Eve plopped back on the love seat. Marx saw her safely to sitting, then returned to Rosalind's side. 'Why do you do this to yourself?'

'Why aren't you curious?'

'Because this isn't a black-and-white factual situation. It's subjective. Human nature makes every conflict subjective. And it's so far in the past, there is no point speculating or getting ourselves upset.' Her voice gentled, little sister counseling older insane one. 'Focus on what was good about our lives together. There was a lot. You're usually so good at looking for the positive.'

Rosalind forced a smile, feeling shot down on her maiden flight. Bryn would say that as long as she knew she was right, it didn't matter what Eve said, but that was small consolation in a battle this personal, when she so wanted her sister on her side.

Outside, the breeze kicked up. A squirrel ran across the yard, making Marx tense and growl – exactly how Rosalind felt. 'Okay. Maybe you're right. Again.'

Eve leaned forward, clearly relieved, and poured herself more wine.

Rosalind bent to give Marx a good petting, needing the comfort more than he did. 'Have you talked to Lauren any more about the architecture job in Wisconsin?'

'Ah.' Eve held up the bottle to Rosalind, who shook her head. 'Funny you should mention that.'

'Why?'

'Because I can't get the idea out of my head.' She turned sideways and put her long legs up on the cushions, leaning against the armrest. 'It's totally impractical, it's a million miles away, I'm sure I could find a different project equally as rewarding somewhere locally if I wanted to take time away from work, but . . .'

'You're going to do it?'

'I can't see why I should, but honestly, as I said, I can't stop thinking about it.'

'That means you need to do it. Has Mike come around?'

Eve put down her wine, drew her knees up and hugged them to her chest. 'Not really.'

'But you're not letting him influence you, are you?' Rosalind couldn't bear the idea of her beautiful sister being kept down by Mr Leadweight.

'Probably not as much as I should. I'm feeling too young to be in a rut this deep.'

'I agree. I think you should go for it.'

'Lauren sent me pictures of the house.' Eve bounced herself off the love seat and left the room, Marx standing anxiously looking after her until she came back with her phone, swiping until she found what she wanted and handed the device to Rosalind. 'Look at this. Swipe right for more.'

'Wow.' The place was beautiful, right on Lake Michigan, white with a railed front porch the width of the house, and four dormer windows that would share the beautiful lake view with whomever was inside. The picture must have been taken in early spring, too soon for leaves on the trees, but with thick green grass on the lawn, punctuated by masses of daffodils. 'It's gorgeous.'

'Twenty acres. Faces east for spectacular sunrises. Lauren said I could stay there with her friend, the owner, a retired teacher. The house has six bedrooms, empty except for her, and she wants me to design a guest house for when her kids and grandkids visit. Obviously she's a private person, so she wouldn't be depending on me for company all day. I could really work.'

'Marx would love it too.' At the sound of his name, the dog leaned against Rosalind's thigh, earning himself a good head-scratch. 'And you'd get to design really cool stuff.'

'Yes.' Her sister's eyes were shining, face flushed. 'I am tempted.'

Tempted? Judging by her flood of excitement, Eve was sold. 'Can you get time off from your job?'

'Not sure about that. But I might go even if it means quitting. I like my job, but it's an old-boy kind of place, and they're not big on moving young people up fast. Maybe I'm just impatient – *I know* I'm just impatient – but I'd like to do more, and do it soon.'

'Fabulous. You should.'

'We'll see.' Eve took her phone back. 'You getting hungry?'

'Yes.' Rosalind put a hand to her empty stomach, glad they had the difficult conversation behind them, even if it hadn't gone quite the way she'd imagined. 'I had road food for lunch, so a real meal sounds great.'

'I'll go heat up the soup and bread.' Eve picked up the bottle of wine and started for the kitchen. 'Don't need help, but I'd love the company.'

'I can at least set the table.' Rosalind stood to follow her sister. Her phone rang. She dug it eagerly out of her pocket. Bryn?

She stopped walking. 'It's Leila.'

'Oh my God.' Eve turned in her tracks.

'Hello?'

'Rosalind. Mama is just home from the hospital. She's gone down quickly. Much faster than any of us expected. There's nothing more they can do for her. She's here with a hospice nurse.'

'Oh, Leila. I'm so sorry.' Rosalind's eyes filled with tears. 'Thank you for calling to let me—'

'She's asking for you. She'd like you to come down and be with her. And with Caitlin.' Her voice broke. 'And with me.'

Chapter 21

December 26, 1968 (Thursday)

Happy happy happy *news. I was right! Daniel asked me to marry him yesterday. He invited me to have Christmas dinner at his parents' place. His parents were very nice to me, and we all got along great. It was the most astonishing Christmas you ever saw. So much food, so fancy! Afterward, we came back to his apartment to exchange gifts. I gave him a scarf from Saks because he'd lost his. He gave me a scarf too, because mine is so old and ratty. We laughed at that. Then he pointed under the tree where there was another box, a small one, for me.*

My heart was thumping so hard I thought the apartment would shake and he'd think there was an earthquake.

I unwrapped it to find a velvet box.

I knew then, but managed not to cry until I opened it and saw the ring. Diamonds and diamonds and diamonds.

I could not say yes fast enough. It would all be an utterly perfect story except for what happened next, when it got bad, though after that it went back to amazingly wonderful.

I had thought about what I would do in this situation, so I was ready when he wanted to go into his bedroom. I told him everything first. So he would know. It was the hardest thing I've ever had to do. I was shaking with fear that he would reject me

341

for not being normal or totally a woman, and yet also hoping he could get me to a doctor who could help me.

He looked scared, but only for a second, then pulled me into bed with him and held me until my shaking stopped. We kissed and kissed and then he undressed me and him. He looked at my abnormal body, all of it, while I died a thousand deaths. Then he told me I was nothing but beautiful to him. He meant it, I could tell. I nearly burst from happiness and also relief.

But then . . . we couldn't do it. He wouldn't fit in. He tried all different angles, but all of them hurt me. It was like the doctors, all prodding and muttering, only of course Daniel didn't mutter.

He said I must have an unnaturally thick hymen, and that we'd go – thank you, God – to a doctor to have it taken care of.

I cried and cried and cried. Of course! Of course! Of course! A hymen so thick and impenetrable that my period has had nowhere to come out!

I'm normal! I'm normal! A real woman.

I'm a real woman.

Daniel has made me that way.

Rosalind pressed the doorbell of the Allertons' house on Laurel Road, shivering from the damp cold and from fear and grief. Heavy, wet snow had fallen the previous night, unusual for this early in November. Cars passed with a muted swish. Branches and bushes bent under their burdens; the occasional crack and thud of a falling limb bore witness to the weight. Rosalind shifted, transferring the pan of namoura she'd made the previous evening as a present, after searching the Internet for a Lebanese dessert that would be easy to make and not difficult to eat or digest.

Footsteps sounded inside; the handle rattled, then the door opened. Caitlin, wearing pajamas and an old blue bathrobe, her hair pulled sloppily into a ponytail, swollen eyes free of makeup. She looked young and sweet and emotionally flattened.

Rosalind's heart tugged. 'Hi, Caitlin.'

'Hi.' Caitlin glanced at the covered pan in her hands. 'Come in. She's in her old room upstairs.'

'Okay.' Rosalind followed, grateful that her half-sister was at least being civil. 'How is she doing?'

'She sleeps a lot. She says there's no pain.'

'Good. Is she eating? I made her some namoura.' She pronounced the word uncertainly, wondering if it had been another mistake to bring Lebanese food to a Lebanese house. She was only a quarter Lebanese herself, maybe not qualified.

'Namoura.' Caitlin pronounced it with rounder, more elegant vowels. 'She'll enjoy that.'

They reached the upstairs landing and headed for Zaina's door, Rosalind reminding herself to stay calm and breathe.

Inside, the bed had been pushed to one side. Next to it, a hospital bed, in which Zaina lay, her dark eyes open. Beside her sat Leila, who looked up when Rosalind walked in, her expression not changing. 'Mama, Rosalind is here.'

'Oh good.'

Rosalind moved closer so Zaina could see her without turning. 'Hello, Zaina.'

'Ah, Rosalind. *Habibti*.' She put on a disapproving face. 'But you forgot to call me Teta.'

Rosalind glanced at Leila's impassive face, then smiled warmly at Zaina. 'Sorry, I forgot. How are you feeling, Teta?'

'Like someone is sucking out my soul.' Zaina managed a faint smile. 'Hope it's the Lord and not the alternative.'

'No chance, Mama.' Leila took her mother's hand.

'I'm so glad you're here, Rosalind.' Zaina's fingers closed around Leila's. 'Now we are all together, I am content. Except for the dying part. I thought I'd get to cook for you again. For just us four.'

'I made you some namoura.' She tried to pronounce it the way Caitlin had.

'Mmm.' Zaina's eyes were drifting shut. 'Cecil could live on namoura. I will have some later. Thank you.'

'You're welcome.' She was finding this surreal. Her mother's death had been so chaotic, so traumatic, the body in the bedroom such a profound and terrible shock. This one was gradual, calm, accepted, achingly sad.

'Here.' Caitlin slid a chair behind Rosalind. 'I'm going downstairs to make some tea. Anyone else?'

'Yes, thanks, Cait,' Leila said.

'Rosalind?'

'I'd love some, thank you.' She had no idea what kind of ground she was on with either woman. 'Need help?'

Caitlin shook her head and reached for the pan in Rosalind's lap. 'I'll take the namoura down. We can bring a bit up for her when she gets hungry.'

'Yes, sure. Thank you.' Rosalind was being too polite, too formal, but until she got some sense from either woman as to where she stood, she'd remain in safe territory.

Rosalind and Leila sat for a few minutes, watching Zaina breathe.

'Thank you for coming.' Leila's eyes were still on her mother.

'You're welcome. I'm sorry this is happening so soon.'

'We thought we'd have another month at least. We hoped for more.' The space between her brows narrowed. 'The doctor said any time, today, tomorrow, the next day. We just wait.'

'It must feel endless.'

'It does.' Leila glanced over at Rosalind, her eyes tired but clear, and while not warm, neither were they cold. 'I am so grateful that she and I always talked. That everything we wanted to say to each other we said. There's nothing left unfinished or uncertain between us.'

'That's so important.' Rosalind wondered if Leila was talking only of her relationship with Zaina.

'So this is sad, but peaceful. Natural. As children, we fear this moment from the second we are old enough to realize our parents are separate from us and mortal.' Leila spoke more as if she were delivering a gentle sermon than conversing. As long as she was talking, Rosalind had hope. 'Now it's here, and it's not a terrible death, not like Dad's. That's what we all hope for, for our parents and for ourselves.'

'Yes.' Rosalind felt called upon to say something equally profound, but still felt too uncertain, a foreigner in an enemy camp. She'd let Leila lead the way.

'How is your father?'

'Slowly better.' She felt herself coloring, laced her fingers tightly together, keeping her eyes on Zaina's peaceful face. 'I was on my way to see him when I got your call.'

Somewhere not far off, there was the crack of a branch breaking. Leila and Rosalind looked toward the window.

Thud.

'Such heavy snow,' said Leila. 'Were the roads bad?'

'No, it was mostly highways. They were clear.'

'Good.'

They turned back to Zaina, whose lips moved in rhythm, as if she were a suckling infant, disturbing but also sweet, a return to birth in death.

'I'm sorry I sent you away.' Leila still gazed at her mother.

Rosalind had hoped for this moment, but hadn't dared

Muna Shehadi

expect it. 'It's all right, Leila. I needed time away, too. Coming here last month, meeting everyone was so much more . . . complicated than I thought it would be.'

'Yes.'

Caitlin came back into the room with a tray on which sat three mugs of tea, a small pot with a cup and saucer next to it, and a plate of Rosalind's namoura. 'I brought some for us, and for Teta, too, in case she wakes up and wants to try.'

'How long has she been home?' Rosalind took a mug of tea and one of her little cakes, curious what they tasted like. She'd agonized over what to bring, unable to imagine showing up empty-handed. It had been Eve who'd suggested a Lebanese dish or dessert, and Eve who came with her to the market to find the ingredients and help her bake. Rosalind had brought enough clothes to travel, so she'd packed up the namoura, gotten back in touch with the New Jersey realtor to let her know she was going to be using more of the time she'd already paid for, and driven the five hours plus to Princeton with only one stop.

'Three days,' Leila said.

'She came home Thursday.' Caitlin took a square of cake and bit into it. Her eyebrows went up. 'Good.'

'Delicious.' Leila held up her own bitten square, turning it back and forth. 'Very nice.'

'Thanks.' Rosalind tried her piece and was rewarded with a tender, crumbly cake, sweet and sticky with orange flower water syrup.

'What is this?' Zaina had woken and was watching them eat.

'Rosalind brought you namoura, remember?' Leila asked.

'That she made herself. Want a bite, Teta?'

'Oh yes, I remember now. Of course I want some.' Zaina smiled weakly at Rosalind, but her eyes were vivid and warm. 'Thank you, my dear.'

346

Rosalind nodded, cake turning sodden in her mouth, tears burning her throat.

'I'll raise your head, Mama, so you can eat.' Leila pressed some remote control down beside the bed, and the top half lifted Zaina nearly to a seated position. Leila broke off a crumb of cake and fed it to her mother.

Zaina closed her eyes and chewed blissfully. 'Mmm.'

'More?' Leila held out another tiny piece.

'Oh, yes.' She ate that one too, then another, then shook her head at the next offer. 'Water?'

'Here, Teta.' Caitlin held a cup for her.

'Thank you.' Zaina's dark eyes swept the trio. 'I will miss this. I will miss being with you all. My girls, all of you.'

'Mama, you're going to make us cry.' Leila's voice had risen half an octave.

'I'm sad to be dying. But I had such a good life. No regrets.' Zaina smiled again. 'Maybe one.'

'What's that?' Caitlin asked.

'After Cecil died . . .' Zaina's eyes sparkled, though her words were labored, 'I should have had more sex.'

Leila, Rosalind and Caitlin burst into laughter. Zaina grinned, closing her eyes. In several more seconds, her breathing slowed again into sleep.

'Let's go downstairs. I'll call Jane.' Leila saw Rosalind's confused face. 'Jane is the hospice nurse. She sits with Mama at night and when we're not in the room. She'll keep watch.'

Rosalind followed Leila and Caitlin downstairs, nervous again, unsure how to act when Zaina wasn't there, unsure also how their behavior would change. 'Can I help with anything? I thought about bringing dinner, but wasn't sure if it was needed.'

'We have plenty.' Leila opened the refrigerator. 'We raided

this fabulous market up Route 206, Lucy's Kitchen. Artichoke ravioli and a Greek salad. All we have to do is boil water.'

'Sounds perfect.' Rosalind glanced between her mother and half-sister, tempted to ask: *On a scale of one to ten, how much do you still hate me?* 'Should I set the table in the other room?'

'Let's eat in here.' Caitlin gestured to the kitchen island with the black and yellow stools. 'I don't feel like a formal dining experience. I bet none of us does.'

'You got that right.' Leila opened the liquor cabinet and pulled out a bottle of Jack Daniel's. 'I don't know about the two of you, but I need a drink.'

'Count me in,' Caitlin said.

'Three.' Rosalind wasn't much on whiskey, but with apologies to moms everywhere tonight, if Caitlin and Leila jumped off the Empire State Building, yes, she would too.

Leila poured three shots of whiskey over ice while Caitlin put a pot of water on to boil and Rosalind set the kitchen island for three. They sat side by side with their drinks, Leila between her two daughters.

'Cheers.' Leila hoisted her glass straight up in the air.

'Cheers,' Caitlin repeated. 'Here's to Zaina.'

'Here's to her.' Rosalind took a healthy sip and got it down without shuddering, remembering with her body more than her mind how Leila had come to sit next to her in the same spot her first day in this house.

So much had happened. So much was still happening. It felt good to be back here, able to be part of the sadness. She could only hope the truce with Leila and Caitlin would last.

'Thank you for inviting me here after everything. It means a lot.' The words came out confidently, as she'd planned in the car, but along with them, a burn of adrenaline fear.

'Zaina wanted you,' Caitlin said.

'You could have refused her.'

'We wouldn't have,' Leila said.

Rosalind fidgeted on her chair. That wasn't exactly the warm reaction she'd hoped for, but she refused to let it stop her.

Another sip of her whiskey and she put the glass down, clutching it with both hands.

'I never felt as if I belonged in my own family. My sisters are so tall and glamorous and self-assured, and I'm small and sturdy and scattered all over the place. My mother was . . . well, you know what my mother was. Challenging, but special, and in a way untouchable, as much as we loved her. My father was very critical, very demanding; his love always seemed conditional on knowing how to live the way he wanted you to, on being the person he wanted you to be.'

She paused, hoping either for encouragement or a clear indication that she should shut up.

Caitlin was looking at her folded hands. Leila picked up her glass and drank, ice cubes tinkling loudly in the silence.

No help.

'I came to Princeton hoping to find that other family, the one I fit into, the one I was really supposed to belong to.' She spoke louder to stop her voice trembling. 'Naïve, maybe, but I felt it could happen. It seemed at first that I had done exactly what I set out to do.'

Still nothing.

She cleared her throat, unwilling to take the next sip she was desperate for in case her hands shook. 'I just wanted to say that I made some pretty bad mistakes, for which I apologize sincerely. I hope you understand at least a little better why I came, and what I wanted here.'

'We do,' Leila said.

'Caitlin . . .' Rosalind leaned forward to see her sister, who only half turned her head. 'I messed up with you the worst. Every time I tried, I found I'd done the wrong thing.'

'It's okay.' Caitlin still didn't meet her eyes. 'Mom and I have talked about it a lot. Well, Zaina started us talking. *Insisted* we talk. To her and to each other.'

'She's the only nice person in the family,' Leila said.

Nervous laughter from all three of them.

'Emil would have bolted anyway.' Caitlin's voice thickened and lowered. 'I knew he was freaking, I just didn't realize how badly.'

'Because the jerk didn't *tell* you,' Leila said.

'He did eventually.' Caitlin ducked her head, lips pressed tightly. Then she blew out a breath. 'That wasn't your fault, Rosalind. And the whole *Surprise! Rosalind's your sister!* thing would have been easier to navigate if I'd known sooner. Like decades sooner.'

Leila raised her hand. 'There's a reason, but that's my fault.'

Rosalind raised her hand too. 'It only became an issue because I showed up.'

'It's . . . hard being an only child your whole life and then suddenly not.' Caitlin looked directly at Rosalind for the first time. 'It's also hard suddenly finding out your mother didn't give birth to you. You said so, but I wasn't hearing anything that night.'

'Of course you weren't.' Rosalind allowed herself to hope that had been a peace offering. 'You were in shock.'

'I still am.' Caitlin sniffed and wiped her eyes. 'I'm not a big fan of this month.'

'That makes three of us.' Leila rubbed her daughter's back. 'It isn't going to get easier over the next few days. But then we grieve Mama, and Emil, and get over it. That won't be fun either, but at least there's a happy ending.'

'I try to believe that. It's too soon, but I'm trying.' Caitlin took a sip of bourbon and gestured to Rosalind. 'Tell her the story, Mom. Let's get all this secrets crap over with. I want to know too.'

Rosalind shifted her gaze to Leila, skin prickling with anticipation.

'Yes. All right.' Leila lowered her head, hands cradling her drink. 'First, I need you both to understand why I didn't tell either of you earlier, even though I knew who you were right away, Rosalind. I promised not to say anything. I swore and signed my name saying that I would never tell anyone about the arrangement. If I did, the money would stop. That was Daniel's incentive.'

Rosalind gritted her teeth, remembering Lauren saying she'd been sworn to silence as well. Two women totally controlled by her darling father – make that four, since it probably included Olivia and Eve's birth moms also. 'Money for your silence after he'd finished with you.'

'And for my use, to make my life and that of my family more comfortable. Your father was generous. He understood what a big deal it was for me to carry and give up our child, and he was very supportive of my wanting to have a career on stage.'

Rosalind took a big swallow of her drink, needing something to do, because otherwise she'd probably scream in rage. 'What was the "arrangement"?'

Leila closed her eyes, smiling grimly. 'My mother is probably the only person on the planet who could convince me to break my promise.'

Caitlin laid a hand on her arm. 'Mom . . .'

Leila raised her drink to the ceiling. 'This is for you, Zaina Serhan Allerton. I hope to God you are right.'

'She is.' Rosalind nodded firmly. 'My sisters and I – our lives have been upended by decades of Dad's lies. It's time to put it right.'

'Okay.' Leila lifted her head and stared across the room. 'About a year or so before you were born, Rosalind, I went to one of your dad's book signings. I was in LA at the time; I think I told you I went to school there. I spoke to him while he signed my copy – after I dropped it twice because I was so nervous. I told him I was interested in taking one of his courses.

'He was very friendly, and I was flattered and thrilled that he was taking that much time talking to me, since the line was still really long behind me. The manager came by and coughed pointedly or whatever he did, so your dad told me to wait around, that he wanted to talk to me after the event.'

Rosalind had to work to keep her face from contorting. Hitting on a girl nearly half his age, very nice. How often had he tried this and failed? It made her want to throw up.

'When everyone else had left, we chatted for quite a while. He asked me a lot of questions. For a while I thought he was coming on to me, but then he said he and Jillian were going to have dinner and did I want to come along?'

Rosalind started, appalled at her father's cruelty. 'He invited you to a meal *with my mother*?'

'Well, yes.' Leila glanced over, obviously puzzled by Rosalind's surprise. 'I was flattered, thrilled – my God, not only this hero of mine, but Jillian Croft! Your dad and I drove to Chasen's, a big celebrity hangout back then, not far from Beverly Hills. Your mom wasn't there yet, so we ordered drinks and waited. And waited and waited.'

Rosalind nodded smugly. 'I see now.'

'Just as I was bracing myself for him to say, "Gee, my wife can't make it, let's go to a hotel", she walked in.'

Rosalind gasped. 'Mom showed up?'

'She did.' Leila sipped her drink, put the glass down carefully. 'She was so beautiful. Even more beautiful than in the pictures, because somehow you expect movie people to be beautiful on screen. But here she was, the reality equally as stunning. I was so starstruck, I could barely speak. But she could not have been more gracious, more lovely. She seemed so interested in me, how I lived, what I did, what I wanted out of life, just as your father had been.'

Rosalind's mouth opened to speak, but she was so dumbfounded, no words came out. 'We had a beautiful dinner with lovely wine. They made me feel like the star of the show. I had the time of my life.'

'I don't believe this.'

'Literally? You think I'm lying?' Leila turned to her. 'Or it's just not what you expected?'

Rosalind had to whisper. 'I didn't see this coming.'

'That makes two of us,' Caitlin said. 'Mom, I can't believe you never told me this.'

'I never told anyone, sweetheart. I couldn't.'

'Go on,' Rosalind said.

'That night, he and Jillian drove me home, said they'd had such a good time, and that they wanted to see me again, that they had a business proposition for me.'

'*They* had?' Rosalind had prepared herself, but not for this story. 'Did my mom seem unhappy? I mean, was there any sense that Dad was making her do this?'

'Your father?' Leila turned with horrified eyes. 'God, no. Jillian was all over it, incredibly excited. Your father was the reluctant one. He was doing it for her.'

'What? Wait, *what*?' Caitlin signaled 'T' for timeout. 'Doing *what* for her? You lost me.'

'Apparently Jillian was unable to conceive. She hired me to

carry Daniel Braddock's child while she pretended to the world that she was pregnant.'

Rosalind couldn't move. Her mother did this. *Her mother.*

'Are you *kidding* me?' Caitlin looked stunned. 'How did they ever make that work?'

Leila shrugged. 'No one questioned it. She wore costumes, did interviews, told everyone she was pregnant and feeling fine, that she was going to deliver at home. When I started showing, they set me up in an apartment not far from where they lived, made sure I got good care. When I got close to delivery, they gave their staff vacation time, saying they wanted to be alone while the baby was born, and snuck me into their place. I doubt even your sister Olivia knew I was there.

'When I went into labor, Jillian's sister, your aunt Christina, delivered you. Apparently she'd gotten a midwife license in order to help her sister. I recovered for a while, then they flew me back here. Mom knew I was pregnant, but not by whom, though she had a pretty good idea. When you showed up here, Rosalind, she put it together pretty quickly, though she wouldn't give away my secret.

'Back then, I let her know I'd given the baby up for adoption. That was hard on her. She must have known something was strange about the whole setup, especially when I started having more money than my career would justify. But she always respected my privacy.'

'I still can't believe that worked.' Caitlin's astounded face mirrored Rosalind's feelings. 'What about your friends? Your professional contacts? How did you keep a pregnancy from all of them?'

'I was twenty-three, I had no real career yet. I stayed away from Princeton once I started showing. It was easy to disappear. People assumed I was off somewhere auditioning or performing.'

'I can't believe you pulled this off.' Caitlin sat up straight. 'Wait, please tell me you didn't give birth to Rosalind's sisters, too.'

Leila held up her hand. 'No, not me. Those were other women. Jillian wouldn't let Daniel have more than one child with any woman.'

Rosalind let out a half-sob, half-laugh that made her sound as insane as she felt. 'She wouldn't *let* him?'

'No.' Leila turned calmly. 'She wanted this, but was insanely jealous as well. It was torture for all involved.'

Rosalind flinched. Her conception and birth. Torture.

'But how did the logistics work without people finding out?' Caitlin was clearly fascinated. 'He must have been followed everywhere. You met him in a hotel?'

'No, no. Too obvious. At the house of one of his friends. Once a month. Very clinical. It was awkward for both of us. We arrived separately, got it done and left.' She lifted her whiskey to her mouth with a hand that trembled. 'Your dad told me that if we were together any longer than your mother thought the business should take, she'd scream at him and throw things as he came in the door.'

Rosalind got to her feet, shoving back her chair. 'I can't hear any more of this. I'm sorry.'

The Allerton women stared, round-eyed, as she stood breathing too hard, feeling like a fool.

'I thought this was all my dad's doing. I thought he cheated. I thought . . . it all happened differently.'

'Why is that?' Leila asked gently.

She had no answer.

'I'm sorry.' Leila touched her shoulder. 'It's not a pretty story. But your mother wanted you all so badly. She was—'

'There was already so little of her *left*. Now you're taking the rest from me.' Rosalind covered her face with her hands. 'I don't even know what I'm saying.'

'Shh.' Leila got up and put her arms around her, stroking her back until Rosalind gave in and returned the hug, a detached portion of her brain wondering if her birth mother had ever got the chance to hold her as a newborn.

'Your mother was a brave and very strong woman who fought hard for what she wanted.' Leila spoke into her hair, her breath warm on Rosalind's scalp. 'That's what you should remember.'

Rosalind allowed herself another few seconds in Leila's protection until she felt she could cope, then released her grip and stepped back. 'Thank you for telling me. Especially in the middle of everything else you're going through.'

'You're welcome.' Leila rubbed her arms as if they'd been left cold. 'I hope it does more good than harm.'

The women went back to their seats and their drinks. Rosalind's mind whirled.

Her father hadn't betrayed her mother. Rosalind had been punishing him for nothing.

Mom had not only been in on the plot from the beginning; she had come up with it herself, convinced her husband to go along with it, then blamed him for complying.

She drained her glass, leaning miserably into Leila, who slipped her arms around both of her daughters and pulled them close.

Chapter 22

*I'm not normal. I do not have a hymen. I do not have a vagina.
I do not have ovaries, never had ovaries. I had testicles removed.
I'm a hybrid man-woman, with the reproductive capability of
neither, a freak of nature in a pretty package. I will never have
my own children to love and nurture and teach about the joys
of being human, to be every bit the mother mine wasn't.*

*The only way that I can become a real woman is to play one
in the movies.*

The memorial for Zaina was held a week after her death, at
Nassau Presbyterian, a charming church in the heart of Princeton
whose exterior looked a little like a Greek temple. Friends and
members of the congregation who had known and loved her
crowded the pews. Leila insisted Rosalind and Bryn sit with her
and Caitlin in the front, Leila in burgundy and black, Caitlin in
navy and white. Rosalind had worn a dress of purple, yellow
and green, since Zaina made her promise not to wear somber
shades to the service, but to come as her beautiful, colorful self.
Emil sent an enormous bouquet of flowers, but was unable to
attend since he was on his motorcycle somewhere in western
Pennsylvania heading for San Francisco and who knew where

357

after that. In a baby-step first show of trust, Caitlin had mentioned that he texted her regularly to let her know of his adventures and his progress, which Rosalind worried would keep her tied to him.

After the service, Leila hosted a small reception at the house with Lebanese food catered by a restaurant in nearby Skillman. She introduced Rosalind as her other-daughter-recently-come-home so many times that Caitlin said they should save time and write the phrase on a name tag. Any follow-up questions were deftly handled by Leila's bright smile and repetition of 'We're so glad she's with us!' until the questioner gave up and went away.

Doubtless there would be more fallout and questions for Leila to cope with later, but the decision had been hers, and Rosalind was thrilled to be outed in public, awkward as it was to see the shock and speculation on so many faces.

Shortly after the last guest left, when Rosalind was thinking she and Bryn ought to be heading for the airport – she was resuming her delayed trip to Maine – Leila pulled her into the living room while Caitlin and Bryn chatted in the kitchen.

'Are you going to tell your father you found me?' She spoke calmly, but one foot twisted right and left in a nervous dance step.

'No.' Rosalind had thought about this a lot over the past week. 'There's no point. It would only upset him, which at this stage of his recovery is dangerous. Apparently he's still high risk for another stroke.'

'Oh dear.' Leila clutched Rosalind's arm, clearly distressed. Over the course of their conversations this past week, Rosalind had come to agree with Zaina that Leila had been at least a little in love with her father, which made Rosalind's conception easier to think about without cringing.

'Even when he's better, I don't think I'll tell him.' Rosalind gave her birth mother's hand an affectionate squeeze. 'What matters is that I know, that I found you and Caitlin and that we ended up not hating each other. Eventually.'

Leila's grin was fleeting. She lowered her head. 'You will need to tell him to stop sending money.'

'If I tell him that, he'll know I found you. Keep the money. You earned it.'

'No.' She looked up with troubled eyes. 'It's not right. I told you and I wasn't supposed to. That was the condition for the payments to continue.'

Rosalind had opened her mouth to argue when she had one of her best ideas ever. 'Use it to help pay for Caitlin's graduate school.'

Leila looked astonished. 'Her *what*?'

'Oh God.' Rosalind went cold. 'Am I doomed to *continue* doing horrible things to Caitlin without meaning to?'

'It certainly looks that way.' Leila softened her scolding with a smile. 'Good for her. I'm sure she'll tell me when she's ready. She's probably only testing the idea and knows I won't let her back down once I hear it. She needs something to keep her from sliding back to you-know-who.'

'My dad was a teacher his whole life. He'd be glad to help.'

Leila raised an eyebrow.

Rosalind laughed. 'Who knows, maybe he would be. In any case, he has way too much money, and my sisters and I don't need any more either, so don't worry.'

'Thank you.' Leila kissed her cheek and pulled back, gazing at her fondly. 'You are a generous and lovely person, Rosalind, and I'm proud to know you.'

Rosalind misted up. The moment was sweet indeed. 'Thank you.'

'Rosalind?' Bryn appeared in the doorway. 'Sorry to inter-rupt. We need to leave or you'll miss your plane. Google shows backup hell on Route 1.'

'Ugh. What else is new?' Leila gave Rosalind a fierce hug. 'Travel safely. Come back and see us.'

'I will.' Rosalind blinked away tears threatening once again on what had been a very emotional day. Then she crossed to her exhausted-looking half-sister, who'd followed Bryn in from the kitchen. 'Bye, Caitlin.'

Caitlin returned her hug rather gingerly. 'Bye, Rosalind. Safe travels.'

'I promise I won't visit too often.'

'No, no!' Caitlin tightened her arms. 'Come whenever you like. You'll be welcome.'

'Great. I'll be back next week. Maybe we can room together.'

Caitlin dissolved into slightly hysterical giggles. 'Yeah . . . uh . . .'

More goodbyes all around, then Rosalind and Bryn drove off, Rosalind waving to the two women standing on the front walk, arms around each other, until they disappeared from view and she could turn forward again.

'Well.' She let her head drop back against the headrest.

Bryn grinned at her. 'Well.'

'It's been an experience.'

'Think you'll visit often?'

'I have no idea.' She pushed the lever to recline her seat another couple of inches. 'Maybe.'

'Think you'll come to see *me* often?'

'Hmm.' She took his hand. 'It's possible.'

He turned right on Jefferson, then left on Terhune and past the Princeton Shopping Center to Snowden Lane. 'Have you thought about what you're going to say to your dad?'

'Not really.' She cracked the window and sighed. 'He has no clue about the emotional battles I've been having, so I'll probably keep it to "Hi, how are you, sorry I haven't visited."'

'Fair enough.'

They drove on, through Princeton's wooded residential neighborhoods, Rosalind wishing she and Bryn were heading in the other direction for a week of playful relaxation at his house. Or that they were heading together to the airport for a trip to Hawaii.

Instead, another difficult conversation.

'Bryn . . .' She tried to keep her voice light. 'I'm thinking of staying in Maine for a while.'

His hand went limp in hers. 'A while.'

'It's important. Dad will need me. I need him. And so on.'

'How long is a while?'

'I'm not sure exactly. As long as I can stand it. A few weeks?'

'Oh.' He laughed nervously. 'I thought you were going to say years.'

'No, no. But it's something I have to do.'

'Okay.' He adjusted his mirror. 'Sure.'

'There's something you're not saying.'

'Yup. There is.'

'What?'

'I'll tell you at the airport.'

'Argh, I have to wait that long?'

'Yes.' He merged on to Route 1, which was flowing nicely, at least this close to town.

Rosalind settled into her seat to watch the not-very-beautiful scenery go by. She knew and trusted Bryn well enough by now that she wasn't worried about him dropping some horrible bomb right before a long goodbye, but she didn't love the delay.

The rest of the trip sped by, not because, God forbid, Google was wrong, but because in spite of herself, Rosalind drifted off, leaving Bryn to cope with the traffic.

She woke up shortly before he started maneuvering the twists, turns and ramps of Newark airport to reach the Delta terminal. They drove in companionable silence until he pulled up to the drop-off curb.

'Thanks for the ride.' Rosalind got out of the car and stood by the trunk until Bryn popped it open and she could retrieve her suitcase. 'I'll text you when I get there.'

'Okay.' He put his arms around her and held her for a long, sweet moment, then kissed her as if he was saying goodbye forever.

'I'll miss you.' Her voice came out breathless and goopy, which was fine because she *was* breathless and goopy.

'I love you.'

She could only gape at him, at his blue eyes and his cocky dimpled grin.

He'd known he'd floor her. He'd waited until this moment to rock her world.

'Bryn.' She felt the same way. She knew she did. But this wasn't her time. 'There's too much going on in my brain right now. I can't—'

'Shh.' He put a finger to her lips. 'Fly safe. Come back. We have plenty of time.'

She was the luckiest girl in the world. 'You were right when you said you're patient. I would have kicked me to the curb a long time ago.'

'I told you.'

'You did.' She kissed him again, and walked into the terminal, pausing to wave one more time, heart squeezing to be leaving him, hoping he meant what he'd said about them having plenty of time. She'd very much like to hang out with him when she wasn't being driven insane by family issues.

The flight to Bangor was nonstop and non-problematic, landing early. Rosalind texted Bryn that she'd arrived, and called Lauren to say she'd show up sooner than expected. Then she picked up her rental car and drove to Blue Hill under a darkening evening sky with a mixture of dread and impatience, Route 1A, Route 46, Route 1.

After checking into her room at the Blue Hill Inn, and picking up the box of Black Dinah Chocolatiers truffles she'd asked the concierge to buy for her chocoholic dad, she drove to Pine Ridge, following her stepmother's directions to the new cottage.

Lauren answered after the first knock. 'You're early.'

'Yes.' Rosalind leaned in to hug her, having learned the embrace would never be offered. 'I left you a voicemail.'

'I always forget to check that phone.' She looked Rosalind up and down, weaving and twisting her fingers. 'I like your hair its normal color. Big improvement.'

'Thanks.' Rosalind touched her head, pleased with her decision to keep it short. 'How's Dad?'

'You'll see in a minute.' She looked over toward the road, a flush visible on her neck. 'How was . . . New Jersey?'

'Fine. Exhausting. I'm glad I did it, but I'm not here to talk about that.'

Her stepmother relaxed visibly, taking in a couple of quick breaths as if she'd been holding the previous ones. 'Come in. He'll be glad to see you. Though he might not act like it, since you've been away.'

'Right.' Rosalind rolled her eyes. 'I have to be punished for my sin.'

To her surprise, Lauren nearly smiled. 'This way.'

The house was small, but Lauren had carefully arranged

enough of their furniture that it captured the familiar classic style her father had always surrounded himself with, about as far from their mother's insistence on following design trends as one could get. His big oak desk dominated one corner; the living room was set up nearly as it had been on Candlewood Point, minus a chair and table or two. The kitchen was visible around the corner as Rosalind stepped into the room, and across the house a breakfast nook beckoned, with large windows that looked out on to Mount Desert Narrows and Mount Desert Island rising behind it. Not too shabby. 'Where's Dad?'

'I'm here. Nice of you to show up.'

She turned, grinning widely, her smile faltering when she spotted her father, looking ten years older than last time she saw him, on his feet, struggling into the room with his walker. 'Hi, Dad.'

'Too busy to visit your father, huh.'

'Much too busy.' She crossed the room and gave him a hug, wanting to lie down and bawl on the floor over how she'd both judged and misjudged him. 'More important things to do.'

'Like what?'

'I'll never tell.'

'Hmph. I suppose you have a new boyfriend.'

'I do.' She beamed at him, searching his withered features for the virile, magnetic father she knew and, with relief, finding him. 'He's a sculptor.'

'About time one of you girls landed someone with a creative bone in his body. Though I suppose he doesn't make any money.'

'He does fine, actually.' She centered herself, kept her gaze steady. 'He's going to show his agent some of my paintings.'

Her father frowned his infamous frown, made less frightening by his weakness and more by his bushy, uncharacteristically unkempt eyebrows. 'What paintings?'

'I told you. Mentioned them anyway, didn't I?' Rosalind tried to remember and couldn't. She'd probably been sure he'd make some scathing comment that would keep her from enjoying her work.

So much fear.

'I would remember that. Unless my bray didn't hold on to—' He swore under his breath. 'Unless my *brain* didn't hold on to it.'

'Maybe I didn't tell you.'

'Why don't you come sit down, Daniel.' Lauren lifted an arm toward her husband, as if she could summon him over with its power.

'I will, I will.' He pushed the walker over to the couch, following its wheeled progress with fumbling steps. 'Thank God your hair is back to normal, Rosalind.'

She sent Lauren an amused look. 'Yeah, I've been hearing that a lot lately.'

'I'm not surprised. Now you need to stop dressing like a scarlet macaw. Help me sit.' He took her arm and tottered the last steps to the couch, where he lowered himself with a grunt. 'It's bloody awful being like this. They're teaching me how to walk. They treat me like I haven't got a brain in my bed – *head*.'

'Sounds like you don't.'

He chuckled. 'Sassy girl.'

'He still has trouble with words,' Lauren said. 'The doctor says that will gradually improve.'

'I hate gradually.'

'I can imagine.' Rosalind took his hand and held it tightly, achingly glad to see him, but with so many questions running through her mind she wasn't sure she could hold them all back.

'So you have a new boyfriend and now you're a painter. What's next? When are you going to settle down and stick with something?'

Rosalind took a calm breath, framing her answer before she spoke, something she'd promised herself that she'd try. 'What if it takes me another ten years to figure that out, Dad? What if I *never* figure it out? Would that be so awful if I'm engaged in my community, productive and happy?'

'Hmm.' His still vivid dark eyes pinned her from under those straggling brows. 'The satisfaction from doing one thing really well can't be matched by your scattershot approach.'

'Maybe that's true.' She smiled, squeezing his hand, keeping her voice gentle. 'But this is my life and I get to decide what works for me.'

'Hmph.' His glare grew darker. 'The problem with you girls is that I raised you to have minds of your own. It's damned inconvenient.'

She laughed and patted his shoulder, not bothering to mention that he raised them to have *his* mind, and it was a miracle any of them survived it. She felt surprisingly peaceful keeping arguments out of the picture. Too much energy already wasted beating her head against the Braddock brick wall. 'Yeah, sorry about that.'

The front door of the cottage opened. Rosalind gasped and shot to her feet. 'Oh my God! Both of you!'

'Surprise!' Olivia swept in, put down a shopping bag and held out her arms for a long, expensive-smelling hug. 'God, you look *fabulous*. Look at her hair, Eve.'

'Nice.' Eve grinned and kissed Rosalind. 'It's good to see the rest of her, too.'

'I can't believe you're both here! How did this happen?'

'Eve's idea,' Olivia announced. 'We haven't all been together in a long time. As it happened, I had nothing going on this weekend.'

'Eve.' Rosalind hugged her younger sister again. 'Thank you.'

'Just a fun idea.'

'How about this, Dad?' Olivia walked into the living room, her tall figure instantly the focal point of the cottage. 'All of us are together.'

'I see that.' He was trying to look cranky, but a smile was working hard to break through. 'I can still count *all* the way to five.'

'Did you find everything you needed?' Lauren asked.

'We did.' Eve picked up Olivia's abandoned shopping bag along with her own and headed for the kitchen. 'Nice selection.'

'They've organized a special dinner for us,' Lauren told Rosalind. 'It's a surprise.'

'You're cooking?' Rosalind looked at her watch. It was already well past six. Lauren and Dad ate early these days.

'God, no. Caterers arriving any minute.' Olivia brought out a foil-topped bottle from the kitchen. 'Who wants champagne?'

'Me!' Rosalind raised her hand. 'Thank you, Olivia.'

'I know Eve does. I certainly do. Lauren?'

'Sure, I'll have a little.' Lauren clasped her hands together, nodding, owl eyes blinking behind her glasses. 'But just a little.'

'Dad?'

'Do I look stupid?'

'You do not look stupid.' Olivia smiled fondly. 'You look handsome as ever.'

He waved her away. 'Always the flatterer.'

Rosalind joined her sisters in the kitchen, where Olivia was getting down stemware and Eve was unpacking what looked like enough champagne for an army, along with crackers, tins of smoked oysters, and cream cheese – all her father's favorites. 'Need help with anything?'

'Sure. I thought we'd let people make their own canapés. I bought sugar snap peas and baby carrots too. Maybe get down some bowls and plates for this stuff? The caterers are bringing everything else.'

'Should we set the table now?' Rosalind asked.

Olivia shook her chestnut head. 'No, no, they'll take care of that. They'll be here any second.'

On cue, the doorbell rang, and for the next half-hour or so, the five of them sat drinking champagne and eating smoked oyster canapés while uniformed caterers wheeled in a round table, which they set with a white cloth, platters and silverware, candles, and a low centerpiece of Lauren's favorite burgundy chrysanthemums. The chef and assistant lugged in an enormous pot and bags of supplies that disappeared behind the kitchen door. Delicious, distinctly seafoody smells began seeping into the living room, until finally the door opened to two uniformed men carrying an enormous platter heaped with scarlet lobsters, yellow corn, gray steamer clams, beige potatoes and pink links of sausage.

'Clambake!' Rosalind's cry of delight was echoed by her dad and Lauren, while Olivia and Eve beamed.

'We thought since we were together in Maine for the first time in a long while that we'd honor the old tradition.'

'Your mother loved a good clambake.' Daniel struggled to his feet, with assistance from Rosalind. Lauren had the walker ready. 'She insisted we do it every year. I'm sure you girls remember.'

Rosalind made her smile stay put. She'd promised herself she'd try to keep loving the mom she thought she had, and work on forgiving the rest.

Easier said than done.

'Of course we remember.' Olivia came back from chatting with the caterers, who'd quietly left the cottage. 'We loved it also.'

'You can get clams in winter?' Eve eyed them dubiously.

'What, you think they migrate?' Olivia brandished another bottle of champagne. 'Bring glasses to the table. We'll drink this with the meal, too.'

'Not much for your father.' Lauren put their flutes on the table. 'His medication—'

'Screw the medication. My daughters are here.' Daniel pointed to his glass. 'Fill 'er up.'

Lauren pressed her lips together disapprovingly as Olivia poured him another glass. Rosalind hovered near his elbow while he lowered his withered body into a chair.

They stuffed themselves with the delicious, perfectly cooked seafood and sides, their father insisting on a third refill of his glass, brushing aside Lauren's pleas that he be sensible, growling that he'd be sensible the next day, that one evening of excess wouldn't hurt him. Rosalind hoped he was right, even as she acknowledged, somewhat ironically, that it was great to see him with enough returned energy to be feisty again.

Finally, after they thought they'd eaten as much as they could, Olivia brought the caterers back in to clear, then serve decadent slices of fresh raspberry cream pie.

'I think my stomach might explode.' Rosalind pushed back her plate and lifted her glass. 'Thank you, Eve, for doing this.'

'Olivia helped.'

'Not much.'

'Dad, here's to your recovery.' Rosalind turned to him, desperately glad she'd been able to find out the truth before this reunion, though it had been difficult and confusing to shift gears into goodwill and forgiveness. At least it was easier and healthier than resentment and bitterness. 'Long may you reign.'

'How can I reign if you keep taking over? It's my job to give the sentimental toasts.' He tried and failed to get to his feet.

'Dad, you don't have to stand,' Olivia said. 'We can hear you fine sitting.'

'It lacks the proper touch. Help me, Rosalind.' He reached out to her.

'No.' She folded her arms. 'You've had three glasses of champagne. Sit.'

'Thank you,' Lauren said.

Rosalind caught looks passing between her sisters. 'What?'

'Since when did you grow some?' Olivia asked.

'Jeez, Olivia.' Eve shoved her sister's shoulder. 'What kind of question is that?'

'I want to hear Dad's toast.' Rosalind motioned them to be quiet, pleased they found her different. She *felt* different. Calmer. More solidly in herself. As if she belonged. 'Dad? What were you going to say?'

He lifted his glass and looked at his daughters, taking a second to connect with each of them. 'Here's to you three girls. It was so important to your mom to become a mother. Each of your births was anticipated with big, big excitement.'

Electric silence fell over the table. Rosalind snuck glances at her sisters. Eve looked back, widening her eyes briefly. Olivia stared steadfastly at their father, smile frozen on her perfectly made-up lips.

'Each of you has been such a delight to me, as you were to her.' His eyes started filling up. 'She would be so proud of the beautiful women you've become. So proud. I often think of how much of your mother is in each of you. How proud they . . . how she . . .' He broke off, looking confused.

'That was a lovely toast, dear.' Lauren rose and rounded the table, put a firm hand on his shoulder. 'Thank you.'

'Is the limo here yet?' He looked up at her, frowning. 'Don't we have to get going?'

'No, my love.' Her voice was achingly gentle. 'You're here in our home with your daughters.'

He looked around, bewildered, then grunted irritably. 'I know that, I can *see* that.'

Olivia and Eve were looking as panicked as Rosalind felt. 'Dad, do you need to lie down?'

'Of course not.' He glared around the table. 'I'm fine. Why are you all fussing?'

Water. Lauren mouthed the word at Eve, who jumped up and got a glass from the kitchen.

'Is he . . . is everything okay?' Olivia asked quietly.

'Too much wine,' Lauren whispered. She calmly removed her husband's champagne and handed him the water from Eve, which he gulped obediently. 'He still gets confused now and then, but not nearly as often anymore. He'll be fine now.'

'Really?' Olivia looked doubtful.

'I promise.'

Dad put his glass down with a flourish. 'That was excellent, *excellent*. A finer meal was never had . . .'

The girls finished the familiar line in unison. '. . . by gods nor men.'

He gazed up lovingly at Lauren. 'I used to say that every time Sylvia outdid herself in the kitchen.'

'I remember.' Lauren bent to kiss the top of his head. 'A few more minutes, then you need to turn in.'

'*Or else* . . .' Rosalind said, cracking up her sisters.

Her dad rolled his eyes. 'Like I'm a baby out past his bedtime.'

'You need to get strong again, Daniel. The girls will still be here tomorrow.'

'Yes, all right, all right.' He flung his napkin on the table. 'Help me get to the damn walker. I'm tired.'

Olivia, Eve and Rosalind kissed him goodnight, and Lauren

helped roll his walker unsteadily back into his bedroom, where his nurse waited to help him to bed.

While the caterers cleaned up the kitchen and the table, the girls headed to the breakfast nook with another bottle of champagne, and discussed plans for the next day, Eve's conflict over taking the job in Wisconsin in early spring, and Olivia's victory convincing Derek to try IVF in their continuing battle to get pregnant. Rosalind told them about her paintings, about Bryn, about her new ideas for dress designs, for the first time not feeling like the odd one out, the mismatched child, the crazy stork mistake.

When they were finally ready to leave, at an appallingly wee hour of the morning, Rosalind was the one who insisted, over Olivia's objections, that they use a car service to take them back to their hotel. Those good citizens of Blue Hill still on the roads did not deserve to encounter any of them behind the wheel.

After the most affectionate goodnights she'd shared with her sisters in years, even factoring in the love-boosting effects of alcohol, Rosalind let herself into her room and threw herself on to the bed to call Bryn. She'd had the *greatest* idea, and absolutely *had* to tell him immediately, crossing her fingers that he'd left his phone on and wouldn't hate her for waking him. 'Hi, were you asleep?'

'Am not now.' His voice was thick and groggy. 'What time's it?'

'Two? Something like that. I just had the *best* idea.'

He groaned, then sighed with heavy resignation she knew was faked. 'What?'

'No, no!' She bounced up to sitting on the bed, holding up two fingers. '*Two* best ideas.'

'Then what-what?'

'First, to tell you that . . .' Her breath caught. 'That I love you. I'm sorry I couldn't say it earlier. I had . . . emotional constipation.'

A beat of silence. 'Rosalind?'

'Yes?' She was a little worried she hadn't chosen the right words for her announcement.

'Are you drunk?'

Apparently she hadn't. 'It's very possible. But I loved you at the airport and I was sober then, just . . . scared. I'll be sober tomorrow and I'll say it again, I promise. The first one is the hardest . . .'

He was chuckling affectionately. 'All right.'

'The thing is . . . I don't love you the way I've loved anyone else, Bryn.' Her bubbly mood vanished into calm certainty. 'This is a big deal. I want you to know that.'

She heard him take a breath.

'Thank you.' His voice was so reverent and gentle she felt tears rise in her throat. 'You're a big deal for me too.'

'Oh.' Tears rose further. She could almost understand how it was possible to die from happiness.

'What's the second idea?'

'If you're not doing anything this weekend . . .'

'Nothing important.'

She got off the bed and pushed aside the curtain to stare up at the moonless sky. One tear spilled over – for her father. Another for the self she used to be. A third for her mother; there would be more of those to come.

She wiped them all away and smiled. 'Please come up to Maine. I want you to meet my family.'

Want more of the intriguing family secrets
and compelling romantic entanglements of the
Braddock family?

Look for Eve's story in *Hidden Truths* and Olivia's story
in *Honest Secrets* as the Fortune's Daughters
trilogy continues.

Private
Lies

Bonus Material

Muna reveals her favorite . . .

Book: Because I could never choose a grown-up book, I'm going with *Where the Wild Things Are*, by Maurice Sendak. I think this little story is perfect. It reads like poetry.

Film: *The Sound of Music.*

Food: Either a combination of flavours I've never encountered, or a perfect specimen of something very simple.

Drink: Champagne.

Place: The porch on my house in Maine, or down on the rocky shore.

Season: Fall.

TV Programme: I'm always too busy reading.

Song: Anything that makes me feel too much to describe.

Possession: My family-inherited Oriental rugs.

Item of Clothing: Black pants.

Colour: Hot Pink.

Flower: Alstroemeria.

Perfume: 4711.

Way to spend the day: Cooking an over-the-top-meal or exploring a new city.

If you found your mouth watering at Muna's descriptions of the Lebanese delicacies throughout *Private Lies*, why not try your hand at making some of them?

Tabouli – and a little history

What follows is an essay I wrote for a food-writing class. I never could tear myself away from novels, but when I wanted to include a recipe in this book for tabouli, the pride and joy of Lebanon's cuisine, I dug out the story as well.

From 1971 to 1973, my Lebanese grandmother, my teta, lived with my family in Princeton, New Jersey. From my girlish perspective, she was about a thousand years old, her face a mass of wrinkles, body bent, step plodding. Convinced she had an ulcer – which my father was equally convinced she didn't – Teta restricted her diet to boiled patties of ground beef, potatoes and carrots, in a soup for lunch, dry and separate on a plate for dinner. For breakfast, white bread toast with Neufchâtel cheese and jam. She might have eaten more than that, but those are my shudder-inducing memories.

Occasionally, usually on my father's exasperated urging, she allowed herself a taste of hummus or a small piece of dessert – she'd indicate the amount by pressing her thumb to the very tip of her finger. And always a bit of tabouli.

Lebanon is tabouli's country of origin, and only the Lebanese know the right way to make it. Do not try to argue this point with any native. Period. It's not the beige, parsley-flecked wheat concoction too often seen in this country. Real Lebanese tabouli is a vibrant green parsley salad, mixed judiciously with bulgur, studded with tomatoes, fragrant with mint and scallions, enlivened with salt, then drenched in olive oil and lemon.

In the era before food processors, tabouli was a special-occasion-only treat. While the finest grade of bulgur soaked, my full-blood Lebanese teta, my Scottish-Canadian-American mother and I would gather around the kitchen table to pick what seemed like eternal amounts of parsley leaves and mint (out of season we'd use dried), which we'd then wash and spread onto cotton towels.

Later, we'd gather again, this time with knives (a small one for me) and cutting boards, and we'd chop. And chop. And chop. 'Is this fine enough, Teta?' She'd consider my effort and either nod her approval or tell me to keep at it: 'A little bit more.'

After the parsley and mint, we tackled scallions, split lengthwise several times, then minced, and tomatoes, finely diced. We halved and juiced lemons and squeezed fistfuls of the softened bulgur to drain it.

Then the magical moment when my father took over and it all came together, bulgur, parsley, mint, scallions and tomatoes – Lebanese flag colors against the dark wood of the salad bowl we used only for dinner parties and this dish. Dad would move his arm around and around, pouring Lebanese olive oil over the ingredients in somber concentration. Lemon juice next – always more than you think you need – and salt, a few grinds of pepper, then mixing, tasting, mixing, tasting, until he was sure it was right.

At dinner, we'd gather around the table, gleeful in

anticipation. The adults would scoop up tabouli with pieces of romaine lettuce. My brothers and I would make 'boats', using whole leaves loaded bow to stern. The crunch was irresistible, the bright flavors addictive, the juice running down chins and elbows a necessary part of the experience.

Teta passed away in 1973, food processors came on the scene, fresh mint showed up in supermarkets all year round, and suddenly tabouli was demoted from special-occasion-only to whenever-we-felt-like-it. I was no longer part of the preparation – Dad used the magic of the Cuisinart to whirl ingredients to the proper fineness in seconds. But I still watched him pour the oil, the lemon, the salt, as always with ceremonial seriousness. Since I was older, he'd let me taste. 'Does it need anything? Lemon? Salt? Oil?' I'd consider gravely, and either nod my approval or shake my head and pick one ingredient that seemed lacking. 'A little bit more.'

I make tabouli now in my own kitchen, a thousand miles from where I grew up. Only sometimes do I manage to capture my father's skill with seasoning, but I always think back with wistful nostalgia to the days when three generations of women sat around one table wielding busy knives on their cutting boards.

At dinner, my sons, only one-quarter Lebanese, beam at me over their tabouli boats, juice running down their chins and elbows. I feel my father and my grandmother with me, nodding their approval.

My father's recipe for Tabouli:

The Lebanese call bulgur wheat *burghul*, but I have changed it to bulgur for clarity.

Ingredients
2 large bunches of parsley, washed and dried
Fresh mint, about ¼ the amount of parsley, by visual estimate, washed and dried
5 scallions
1 large tomato
¾ cup of Number 1 bulgur (Number 1 is the finest. Do not use coarse.)
½ cup extra-virgin olive oil
Juice of 1½ lemons
1 tablespoon pomegranate syrup (optional)
2–3 teaspoons sea salt, to taste
5–6 grinds of black pepper

Method
Soak the bulgur in water, covering it by an inch or two, for an hour.

Pick parsley and mint leaves. Cut scallions into one-inch segments.

In food processor, chop parsley, mint and scallions in batches, about 30 seconds per batch, until fine but not mushy. Put into large serving bowl.

Chop tomato into small dice. Add to bowl.

Squeeze bulgur by handfuls to dry it out some and add to bowl. Mix thoroughly.

Drizzle olive oil, lemon juice and pomegranate syrup (if using) over the salad, and sprinkle with the salt and pepper. Mix well.

Refrigerate to let flavors mingle, an hour or two at least. Take out one hour before serving.

Serve with romaine lettuce for scooping.

Discovering Namoura

Confession: My grandmother never made namoura. My father never made namoura. It wasn't until I visited Lebanon in 2008 and saw it as part of a fabulous buffet, that I tried it. Immediately I whirled on my father. 'Why didn't you ever make this?' I don't remember his answer, but I know he preferred cheese and fruit over sweets, and he wasn't a big cake fan. He was, however, crazy about what most people know as baklava, which in Lebanese Arabic is pronounced (as close as I can approximate) *b't-LAY-wee*. Which looks a lot funnier than it sounds when pronounced by a native. Dad loved the stuff, and his was the best I've ever tasted.

But back to namoura. When I wrote this book, ten years after that first taste, I needed something uncomplicated that Rosalind could contribute to the Allerton household as Zaina lay dying, and I chose this cake.

There are many recipes online. Some are made with all semolina flour, some include unsweetened coconut. Since I don't have a family history with this dish, I have created my own version, not too different from what's out there, but with a few touches of my own. If you'd like, you can substitute rose water or vanilla for the orange blossom water in the syrup, or combine them. You can also add or substitute other flavorings, like cardamom, cinnamon, or citrus zest. Many recipes call for greasing the pan with tahini, but though I loved the old country touch, I didn't think it added much, so if you don't have any in your pantry, don't run out and buy it for this recipe. However you usually grease your pan works fine.

Enjoy! Or as the Lebanese say, *sahtein*!

Namoura

Syrup

1 cup (200 grams) sugar

¼ cup water

¼ cup strained orange juice

1 tablespoon strained fresh lemon juice

¾ teaspoon orange flower water (more if you like it strong!)

Cake

1 tablespoon tahini for greasing the pan (or whatever you usually use)

½ cup (114 grams) yoghurt, whole milk or low fat

1 teaspoon baking soda

1½ cups (245 grams) fine semolina flour

1/3 cup (68 grams) sugar

¼ teaspoon salt

6 tablespoons (85 grams) unsalted butter, melted

16 blanched whole almonds

Method

In small saucepan heat sugar, water, orange juice and lemon juice over medium-high heat, stirring until sugar is melted. Bring just to a boil, lower heat and let simmer gently, without stirring, for five minutes. Remove from heat and stir in orange blossom water. Pour into measuring cup with pouring spout and let cool while you make the cake.

Mix yoghurt and baking soda in a small bowl and set aside to rise.

Heat oven to 375°F (190°C). Grease 8″ by 8″ pan with the tahini or whatever you're using. (Hint: the butter stick wrapper makes a great spreader.)

In a medium bowl, melt the six tablespoons butter in microwave. Add semolina flour, sugar and salt and stir until the mixture is evenly moist. Gently fold in yoghurt just until combined. Turn into prepared pan and spread, smoothing top with an offset spatula. Cut into 16 squares and decorate each by lightly pressing in a blanched almond.

Bake until golden brown, about 25 minutes. Recut the pieces and pour syrup over the cake. Let cool in pan.

The Fortune's Daughters
Trilogy

A compelling and enthralling series of family secrets, romance and self discovery . . .

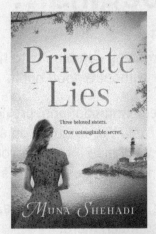

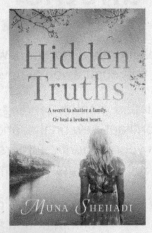

Available from

REVIEW